NIGHT
FOR DAY

NIGHT
FOR DAY

PATRICK
FLANERY

atlantic·*fiction*

First published in hardback in Great Britain in 2019 by Atlantic Books,
an imprint of Atlantic Books Ltd.

With thanks to the editors of *Film Comment* for permission to quote from the
article 'Some Visual Motifs of Film Noir' by J. A. Place and L. S. Peterson
in Vol. 10, No. 1, January–February 1974.

The quotation from *My Secret Beat: A Notebook of Prose and Poems*
by Michael Burkard, Copyright © 1990 by Michael Burkard, is used
by permission of W. W. Norton & Company, Inc.

1 2 3 4 5 6 7 8 9

A CIP catalogue record for this book is available from the British Library.

Hardback ISBN: 978 1 78239 6 055
Trade Paperback ISBN: 978 1 78239 6 062
EBook ISBN: 978 1 78239 6 079

Printed at ScandBook AB, Sweden

Atlantic Books
An imprint of Atlantic Books Ltd
Ormond House
26–27 Boswell Street
London
WC1N 3JZ

www.atlantic-books.co.uk

for
Andrew

'Above all, it is the constant opposition of areas of light and dark that characterizes film noir cinematography. Small areas of light seem on the verge of being completely overwhelmed by the darkness that threatens them from all sides. Thus faces are shot low-key, interior sets are always dark, with foreboding shadow patterns lacing the walls, and exteriors are shot "night-for-night." Night scenes previous to film noir were most often shot "day-for-night"; that is, the scene is photographed in bright daylight, but filters placed over the camera lens, combined with a restriction of the amount of light entering the camera, create the illusion of night.'

– J.A. Place and L.S. Peterson, 'Some Visual Motifs of Film Noir'

'For in some recognitions comes a refusal, and your life had become such a refusal, a conversion of day for night, night for day, and there was no beginning and no end. And there isn't, except you were not able to see that way.'

– Michael Burkard, 'The Sun'

PART ONE:
Day

1

The last time I saw you was the day my life ended. I say that it ended but you understand this is only a figure of speech. Say instead that my life up to that point came to an end but in the intervening decades my body has kept walking around in the world, although I have now reached an age when such movement occurs at what feels like a nearly geological pace. If I manage a mile in forty-five minutes I have accomplished something significant. That last day we spent together we both still had the energy of our youth, the resilience of our bodies, never imagining how quickly our energy might begin to dissipate or how long and unswerving the decline would prove. To say that I have wished to hear from you without ever expecting you to phone or write suggests I believed the onus was on you to initiate contact, as if I felt no sense of responsibility to do so myself. This was never the case. Shame has kept me silent, distant from you and Helen and all the people I used to call friends, though even to call you friends fails to admit of the strength of our bond, the way we managed for a few brief years to craft the closest thing to family I have known since leaving the home of my parents.

Over the course of the preceding night I began to formulate what I knew I must do. I can no longer recall whether this private planning – plans I did not share with you until far too late – was the spur for the argument we had, or if the argument itself prompted the decision. You would tell me now, I suspect, that even asking the question suggests a denial of guilt. Perhaps you will reply to this letter and tell me what you think, whether and how I should judge myself in the last months of my life. It was not my intention when I decided to write that I would return to grievances, because I know after all these years that you are, if not entirely innocent, at least more so than I. So this is my defense, an explanation of how I came to the decision I made that day so many years ago, and an apology for the consequences that have marked us both.

Let me start much earlier, back when we met, four years before the day we parted, on the set of a film in which you had only one line but a line I nonetheless wrote, and in seeing the boy they had cast – for then you could have been no more than twenty-two – I rewrote the line to suit the face cast to speak it. And you, performing a naïveté as intoxicating as gardenias in twilight, slouched across the soundstage and asked me the meaning of those words I had blown into your mouth. That was the first time we spoke, although we had noticed each other on the lot at various points, since your arrival fresh from military service, unscathed because you never reached a battlefield. You caught my eye, and I flatter myself to think I might have caught yours. We knew what we were before you ever spoke to me – at least I knew what you were even if you might have been unsure of me. It was not how you walked or spoke but the way your gaze lingered when it fell upon my face.

Because following the eye as it traveled could lead us into the arms of a sting if we were reckless or unlucky, it was natural to distrust our instincts, to doubt the pull of our attraction. You were young and beautiful enough that I thought it possible you were no one I should allow myself to follow. I understood that I was attracted to you and hoped you might be attracted to me, but there was no guarantee that you were conscious of any attraction you might feel, and I could not trust you knew yourself well enough to accept what you were. Dark skin and pale hair and eyes the shade of California lilacs. Who could fail to notice? We bumped into each other at the newsstand one December morning when you were buying a copy of *Life* with Ingrid Bergman dressed as Joan of Arc on the cover and I noticed how embarrassed you were to be seen holding a magazine like that, or perhaps it was because a woman was on the cover, or because that woman was dressed as a man. I remember thinking you needed someone to show you how to comb your hair differently, to move the part from the center and off to the left, and then, when I saw you again a few weeks later, catching your eye in the commissary, you had done just that. In changing your hair, you looked more yourself, self-contained without being smug. You were having lunch with Helen that day, the two of you cast in the same film, and because Helen was already my friend I drummed up the courage to ask her a few days later who you were. A kid from Montana, she said, a farm boy. A ranch boy to be precise, with two brothers. But does he have a girlfriend? I asked Helen. I remember the way she turned to me. We were sitting in my living room after a Christmas party to which only five people came. I had filled the picture window with poinsettias and bought a white-flocked tree hung with red ornaments and matching lights. Helen let her head tilt back and half closed her eyes. No, the farm boy does not have a girlfriend. Why do you ask? And then she must have seen me blush because she whispered, Oh, is that it? Well, I can't say for sure but you might have a chance.

Before we ever spoke I imagined you in denim and cowboy boots and a plaid shirt with a bandanna around your neck, a Stetson on your head and a lazy way of sitting in the saddle, one hand on the reins of your appaloosa, one gripping a copy of *Life*. That evening in December 1946 I could not have imagined how only a year later I would be in bed with you in that same house, discovering you were not the innocent you appeared, that I should have had no fear about whether you accepted yourself or not. That was the miracle. So long as the truth remained hidden you were more at ease with who you were than I have ever managed to be. It was only outside of the house that you became your public self, and that man bore as little resemblance to the one I knew as Ingrid Bergman to Joan of Arc.

In my living room that Christmastime, I was conscious of Helen's hand shaking where it lay on the back of the sofa. What's wrong, I asked. Her lips drew taut and her chin quivered. Why don't we get married, she said, it would make things so much easier for you.

I was sensitive enough not to laugh at the suggestion because I could see what it cost her. But you know that wouldn't work, Helen, I'm not suitable for marriage, not to someone like you. That's just it, she said, I'm not someone like me. I'm someone like you.

Weak for a man in uniform? I joked, and her eyes began to water. You know what I mean, Desmond. I'm as unmoved by men as you are by women. I wouldn't put it quite that way, I said, taking her hand in mine and holding it until it stopped shaking. I love you too much to risk making you hate me. Why would I ever hate you? she asked. Anyone who lives with me long enough eventually hates me. I'm sure that's not true, she said, and besides, who have you lived with apart from your parents? No one, I admitted, except the man who cleans my house and cooks my food and if you ask Max tomorrow he'll tell you he could do without me.

Helen laughed and we never spoke again of her proposal. I could not have imagined that only six months later, the night after you and Helen were married, I would be in bed with you in my own house, because the two of you did not yet have a house of your own, and we presumed it safe enough to suggest I was a friend of the couple letting them stay before they departed on their honeymoon.

The night before my last day in Los Angeles, not even four years after we first spoke to each other, we argued about the terms of our arrangement. In the months leading up to that night in April 1950 I had allowed myself to believe I was on the margins because you and Helen and Barbara were able to live together while I had to retreat to my own house. I feared this meant you did not really love me. Perhaps I was looking for a way of cracking a rift between us, seeking fodder for an argument that would allow me to escape with a conscience less burdened by guilt. When we fought, which was not very often, it felt as if my chest were wired up with electrodes, the air supercharged with electricity and the anger between us waiting for a spark. Because I had risked being too intimate in public, at the studio, on set, I can no longer remember, you found me at fault. I had been standing too close, perhaps I touched your hand or your shoulder, maybe I spoke words that betrayed an intimacy whose exposure to the scrutiny of strangers you feared, and not without cause. I accused you of being more concerned about your own reputation than mine and you said that wasn't fair and I said that didn't make it untrue and you said you were just as concerned for my wellbeing as your own and I said that's a fucking lie and you took my head in your hands and for an instant I had a vision of you head-butting me hard and knocking me out but instead you kissed me just as violently, cutting your lips into mine with an anger that made me almost afraid of you, but then you held the kiss and softened it and I let you keep gripping my head, your fingertips pressing into my scalp, consuming your rage because that was what I had learned to do since we first fell in love.

So much fury for such an angelic man.

Don't resent me for saying what you must know is true.

When we were exhausted by fighting, we went to bed, not speaking as we undressed, you snapping your slacks tight and draping them over a hanger that clattered in the closet as you put

7

it away, the door shutting too sharply, and then we were in bed, in your house with its walls of glass, a window cracked open to admit fresh air and the sound of the Pacific. You rolled over to press the length of your body against mine and I sighed with relief.

So my last day in Los Angeles began with me inside you and you inside me in the happiest hour of sadness I have ever known. I sensed the end was coming and you did not. If it were possible to do this for the rest of my life, exploring your body from within as you explored mine, I would, but then the swell started in my gut, a sensation of pleasant seasickness, that weightlessness of the stomach rising as an illusion of being borne away by tides took hold. Then the swell crested and whatever was watery turned to light. I squeezed my eyes shut and in the eclipse of that moment a measure of me rushed into you. After we finished, we lay chest against chest and you angled your head to kiss me.

That was the day my life ended.

I could hear the ocean crashing and, down the hall, Helen and Barbara talking in their own darkness. You nuzzled my neck and whispered, I trust you completely.

I could never forget the words because they broke my heart. You too, kid, I said, and you scowled. Don't call me that, Desmond. Maybe I smiled, let's say I did, or perhaps I apologized and kissed you again, gripping you tighter, and told you I had to work. How could I sleep knowing it was the last time I would make love to the man who might have been my husband in another world and time? My ear pressed against your body, I listened as your heart stepped down to a slower dance, felt you relaxing, legs twitching as you began to drop into sleep.

Don't leave, you mumbled.

Now, too late, I know that I should have stayed.

I have to work, I said.

You're so diligent.

Who else will put words in your mouth?

I love you, Desmond.

I love you, too, I hope I said. I hope I told you that as often as I felt it. Even in the wake of a fight I was no less in love with you than in the long stretches of days when no disagreements flared between us.

Four hours later, four in the morning, fourteen days into the fourth month of the fiftieth year of the twentieth century and the last day of my life in Los Angeles, I was sitting at the library table in your Pacific Palisades living room trying to type as quietly as possible on my portable Remington, rewriting scenes you were meant to perform later that day.

Because I knew what was coming, I had been meditating for several weeks on beginnings and endings, knowing already that I was approaching the point where I would have to take flight or face whatever our government might inflict. At that moment I had told no one because I could not risk telling anyone before you. In the living room, looking out on the swimming pool and the dark bank of sky above water, staring at my own scarecrow reflection, I knew the time when I should have told you had passed several weeks earlier.

When that house was built, I remember Helen thought it a magnificent joke, a home more glass than wall, nothing but windows facing west, open to anyone who might scale the fence around the property to look at our queer band apart. And now, instead of writing the scene I had to revise, I was thinking about how I would tell you what I could no longer conceal. With one hand I was drinking cold coffee while pecking the keys with the other, trying to figure out what to say to you at the same time I was censoring myself, struggling to make the story of underworld Los Angeles we were all trying to finish appear less worldly to the censors. Beneath the scene heading INT. LOS ANGELES – DAY I had typed a screed of rambling thoughts about the primacy of language. I no longer have the draft but I remember the gist.

In the beginning was the word. True for creation, true for cinema. Once sound entered the pictures, the word came before images, and even in the days before sound, words were the foundation of pictures since the people making the images first had to think what to shoot, how to point and focus a camera, whether to cut a shot here or there, place it in sequence before this one or that one, and all that thinking about images necessarily happened through language, thoughts spoken or articulated silently but no less verbally in the mind. That great queer Wittgenstein said something like this, how the *limit* of our ability to express thought must be described through *language*, and beyond that limit there is only *nonsense*: *The limits of my language*, he wrote, *mean the limits of my world*.

I ripped the page of nonsense from my typewriter, wadded it up, and threw it in the wastepaper basket. Once more I typed the location at the top of a blank page, rewriting what I had already written countless times over the past months. Night became day, exterior interior, sex a less thrilling connection. None of these last-minute revisions were my idea. You may remember that ever since the start of production Porter had been haranguing us, claiming that without the changes he and the censors were demanding the project would fall afoul of every moral guardian and legion of decency self-elected to police what ordinary Americans consume when they close themselves together in a dark public place. I never felt you understood what such pressure did to me, or perhaps you understood in logical terms but could not appreciate how traumatizing it was to work under the force of the censor's gaze. It had a deranging effect, making me see titillation in the most innocuous lines, or driving me to encode double-entendres in language so arcane I hoped none of the puritans in the Production Code Administration would ever figure it out. Lately, I had started to believe that the only safe creative territory was one populated solely by books, in whose pages more daring material could still be recorded in ways history has suggested may yet have greater durability than the reams of celluloid that bought us both such comfortable, dishonest lives. I say that not to rebuke either you or me for the choices we made, since no better choice seemed possible. The choice was to lie or to live in the wilderness.

On that morning in April 1950 I had realized the lies were taking too much from me, that pretending we were nothing but friendly professional acquaintances to all but the tiniest circle of intimates was not only exhausting but also dementing. In feigning that we were nothing to each other, part of my brain began to believe this was true, so that the suspicion you did not love me as much as I loved you infected all of my thinking about you.

In the end, the political threat in combination with the personal one was enough to make me conclude I had no better choice than exile. Americans do not like to believe that their own would ever feel compelled to flee. Most cannot conceive that law-abiding citizens might find themselves in a moment when logic seems to have twisted inside out and everything we think we know about our country appears no longer true. Overnight, a nation so recently an ally had become our enemy. The ideology it followed would become a crime in a country that claimed freedom of religion and freedom of speech as its highest principles. We had smashed through the mirror and into the darkest wonderland we could collectively imagine.

I caught myself staring again at my reflection in your wall of glass. A man not yet middle-aged, still with a slender body and a full head of sandy-red hair, sat naked except for your silk dressing gown, which I had swiped from the chair where it lay in your bedroom. The irony was not lost on me: although sleeping with one of the studio's leading men I was rewriting his lines in the middle of the night because the Head of Production said it was too risqué to suggest an ex-serviceman might want to go to bed with his wife's sister. I had written the part especially for you, hoping it would give us a thicker layer of insulation, that the performance of Orph Patterson's virility would convince any who might have cause to doubt – gossip columnists in particular – that you were no less interested in women than one assumed men like Gregory Peck or Kirk Douglas might be.

Beneath the scene heading the new page was blank, glaring white under the lamp. I reread the previous one. On paper the dialogue you would speak flowed, the progression of scenes made sense given the changes Porter had forced me to make, the narrative logic was intact. The shit was fine. The shit would do. Most days it scarcely mattered what quality of shit I put on the page because the director, or actors, or Porter or Leo Krug would rewrite at will without touching a typewriter, cutting and adding as if they knew my business better than me. Sometimes you did so yourself, and I never let you see how much the liberties you took lacerated my pride. John Marsh, although my friend and collaborator, was among the worst offenders. He would stand on set and tell you not to say the line I had written because it now struck him as unnatural, and rather than asking me to come up with an alternative, offered one himself, a phrase either hackneyed or homespun. In the case of the film we were then trying to finish, John had already claimed half-credit for the script without writing one line. Ideas were enough. Conversations about plot and setting. Half-drunken arguments about the structure of a character's arc. What a certain kind of man calls 'spitballing', throwing ideas in the air and seeing what sticks to the ceiling. That was John's idea of writing. When I came to Hollywood from New York I quickly learned that this was the way: words attributed to me in a film's credits were never entirely mine. The name *Desmond Frank* hid the labor of a dozen women and men typing furiously in the Writers' Building, and most of the time they were never, any of them, making up original stories, just adapting the ideas of people too principled to sell out and migrate West.

Days come upon me now when I wish I had never made that journey, when I think I would have been better off staying in New York, that if I had done so I might never have been forced to leave America. Then I look up at my library here in Florence and see one of the photographs of you in your youth, one of the dozens of reproductions of your face that decorate my walls, you in all your multiple selves, archiving the faces of your own ancestry (even, I like to think, archiving the history of our love for each other), and the regret bends into a feeling more complex, less polarized. Light and shade. Day and night.

I have never stopped loving you, Myles, even as I have been forced by the choices I made a lifetime ago to seek out the love of other men, not one of whom has burned as furiously through my heart as you did. What you do not know, what I never had the heart to tell you, is that you were not my first love, nor my greatest. By the time you and I met, that love was long dead.

In the years before I moved to Los Angeles, having returned from Ithaca to Manhattan, back to my childhood bedroom on the Upper East Side because no one expected I would actually look for a job, I passed most afternoons escaping to the baths to find some relief from my sadness, and in the mornings wrote *The Argosy*, the novel that made my name. In writing about two college rowers from opposite sides of the tracks who fall in platonic love only for their friendship to end in the histrionics of tragedy, I was trying to tame the grief I felt. I took the problem of our both being men and turned it into a story of friendship thwarted by class, even as the characters were undisguisedly me and the boy I had loved, the feelings and affection between them legible as romantic for anyone with the sense to look for such things. When the studio paid me a small fortune for the film rights, that windfall propelled me westward from my parents' home and ultimately to you, Myles, the second greatest love of my life.

On that morning after we had fought, as I sat looking out at your swimming pool in the dark, I was certain *The Argosy* would never be a movie. It had been years in development and, as you may remember, no one could conceive of how to make the story play on screen without adding a female love interest. *Faggots*, was what Krug said the last time I had spoken to him about it. *Without a dame, everyone will think it's a flick about faggots*. It went without saying that such a thing was impossible. I had tried several times to write the script myself until Krug had decided I was not up to the job and took me off my own project. *I don't believe you're man enough, Mr. Frank*, Krug said, and ordered me to get the hell out of his office.

The dismissal struck me as ironic. Although I knew that I was male, I have always struggled to think of myself as a man. That is not to say I have ever been effeminate, or would prefer to be a woman – by accident rather than design I have tended to present myself to the world in a way that is not obviously queer. What I mean is that when I walked down the street in 1950 people may have seen a man but inside I felt no different than I had at eighteen, even sixteen, as though still trying to find my place in the world, brokenhearted and terrified of the risk you and I took every time we were together. Even now, at this great age, the disjunction between the face I see in the mirror and the self that I actually experience whiplashes my mind.

That morning in your house, however, I understood that I had reached a moment when I could no longer allow myself to think as a boy, in other words with all the idealism and hopefulness and optimism we tend to ascribe to the young. To make such a change required accepting my time in America had reached its end. If I did not leave, I was certain to face summons for doing no more than my birthright, thinking and associating freely, trying to imagine a better world. The only solution was to escape somewhere I could become anonymous, recommitting myself to books and turning my back on the movies forever. That is what I had decided while you were asleep upstairs, ignorant of all that I planned. But as soon as I thought of leaving you behind, parting seemed as impossible as staying, and the struggle between these two impulses tore at my heart until it was nearly dawn and my fingers collapsed on the Remington's keyboard. The last work I would do for the studio was finished and my hands began to shake as I stacked the new pages together. I knew what I was thinking without wishing to own the thought.

In the face of two impossible choices that each seem destined to present a future too painful or dangerous to bear, there always remains one solution. The idea kept coming, bubbling up, almost physically present, like a hemorrhage or cardiac event, even when

I resisted holding it in my consciousness, and the force of that idea, the strength of the intention, sent me to the sliding door. I opened it and crossed the terrace, slipped out of your dressing gown, stepped into the water at the shallow end, waded across the pool and allowed my head to drop beneath the surface until I reached the deep end where I sat, fingers typing across the concrete as angels circled above me screeching, beaks plucking insects from the water, all those synchronized swimmers, Esther Williams and her rubber-capped cadres splashing around before finding themselves in mid-air and dangling from the talons of Republic XF-12 Rainbows dispatched to return them to some central processing unit of military intelligence where their costumes would be searched for red understitching on a blue suit, *what subversive costuming, male stunt doubles in pink frills and headpiece!*

The temptation to open my mouth and breathe the water into my lungs came upon me.

Because of the burden of secrecy and obfuscation, the toll of living publicly a version of the self that lacked so much of the greater self, which had to remain hidden, I had been imagining what it might be like to kill myself for more than a decade. And because for me the disparities between the public and private self were not only about desire but also about belief, in the years since Congress grilled the Hollywood Ten, all friends of mine, I had been thinking about killing myself more frequently. In the days since the Supreme Court had dismissed the appeals of the Ten and doomed them to time in federal prison I did it almost hourly. I had these thoughts when I was inside you and you were inside me. I fantasized about killing myself even when I felt happiest.

Under the water, my chest began to ache. A stream of air escaped. A few seconds more and it would all be over, but then the thought of you or Helen or Barbara finding me face-down in your pool stopped me. It would be impossible to cover up a scandal like that. Gossip columnists would suggest a love nest and ambiguous couplings and the last thing I wanted was to complicate your already complicated lives. If someone was going to suffer or sacrifice, it should be me alone, and alone meant doing whatever I must away from here.

You see how I thought. I worried about your secret. I thought always of protecting your reputation. It did not occur to me that finding my body would be anything other than a problem to be managed because it was too dangerous to believe you might truly love me. If I believed that, I could never have left.

I pushed myself back to the surface and gasped. It was the closest I had come. Closer than almost swerving off Mulholland two nights earlier or nicking my wrist with a paring knife in the kitchen three days previously. Closer than taking twice my usual dose of sleeping pills over Easter weekend. I watched as a light came on in your room. My head bobbing in the water, arms and legs churning to stay afloat, I told myself I should go get into bed with you, let you open me up, make love one last time before our story was over. Instead I climbed out of the pool, stood wet in the morning air, put on your dressing gown, and went back inside to look over the pages I had rewritten. Light skimming over the mountains struck through eucalyptus boughs, casting a red sheen across the waves to the west that developed into a faint ruby glow on the living room walls. *Interior — A house on a cliff. Pacific Palisades. Dawn.* In the distance, a horizon of water caressing sky, two dark bodies approaching without ever meeting.

When I looked up from the pages you were standing next to me in khaki slacks and a white T-shirt that grazed your torso like gauze across stone. I wanted to put my hands all over that dark open brow, cover your hunted eyes, lock you in a room, never let you out. You're all wet, you said. Do you remember how I stood and parted your lips with my own, or the way you pulled away after a moment, as if you already knew? Maybe I recited a line of poetry, *Frühling, Geliebter!… Unendliche Schöne!* Maybe you asked me what it meant and I said it was just a poet you wouldn't know, my infinite beauty. If that's what I said, forgive me. I withheld knowledge not because I doubted your intelligence but out of a selfish desire to preserve your innocence. Now you should know, it was Goethe on Ganymede, the loveliest of mortal men, abducted by Zeus to preserve his beauty among the gods. You relaxed as I held you. Through the dressing gown I felt the dampness on my skin penetrate your cotton shirt, and wished, despite myself, that one of us could be reborn, bury ourselves in solid ground, one body pass through another and emerge anew, a woman, so that the world would leave us alone. But there was no consolation in fantasy. I pushed my body against yours but you said we were out of time, and I wondered how you knew.

At breakfast in the corner of your kitchen you and Helen were brushed and sleek, two human tigers reading the trades as if industry news could tell us anything of substance about our standing in the world. What's your call? Helen asked and you said it was eight. Men always get it easier, Barbara complained, biting into a corner of toast. Did you know Porter's wife just left him? Helen asked. It won't be easy to find another woman who hates herself enough to play Mrs. Cherry. He wasn't always a monster, I said, and the three of you looked at me as if wondering what I knew.

It seemed so natural, the four of us coupled off and eating breakfast together. We imagined ourselves free inside the glass walls of your house, but what kind of liberty is such cloistered isolation? When I asked you this question the night before you shouted, *Don't play that card*, and that was when things got heated. I had been trying to imagine a world in which one man might call himself the husband of another. It was neither semantically nor theoretically impossible. The original meaning of *husband* was the head of a household, so why could there not be two husbands of a single house, two heads being always better than one? But such a household was impossible when one of those hypothetical husbands was a man recognized on every street corner in a country that did not believe two men should share a house unless they were father and son, or two brothers, and even two brothers set up alone might attract the suspicion of such crusaders as believe the best job of a red-blooded American man is to marry and provide for a *wife*, from the Old English *wif*, for *strong*, once meaning only *woman* (and so, for the sake of Helen and Barbara, why not a household of two strong women and no head?). *Husband* became the name of a man wed to a *wife* hundreds of years after a *wife* had become a woman wed to a man.

You're confusing me, you'd said. Randolph Scott and Cary Grant lived together once.

That's in the past. No one believes in bachelor roommates these days.

Anyway, a word means what it means, doesn't it?

I shook my head. A word often means more than one thing. Meaning was more malleable before codification and definition and setting down on the page. As long as language remained in the head, on the lips, it was more fluid, mercurial, ambiguous. Film recaptures some of that ambiguity, particularly when meaning has to be conveyed through suggestion and elision, when even the reminder of the origin of every man and woman on the planet, the

19

simple navel, cannot be shown in American movies because it's too like orifices lower on the body, never mind that anyone can wander down to Muscle Beach and stare at all the male navels they could hope to see. But not in the movies, and that is Joseph Breen's doing, I said, Breen who thinks a navel too like a cunt or an asshole, who cannot abide the idea that men might have penetrable orifices as well as women, who wants us to imagine we were all delivered by storks to the cabbage field, every one of us a virgin vegetal birth, already saved because never touched by sin.

You screwed up your face in confusion. Forgive me. I never meant to lecture you.

At least you did not hold it against me. Even though Helen and Barbara were still there in the kitchen that morning you turned, put your lips against mine, pulled me into you, and said, Maybe we should go back to bed again.

No, better not. You and Helen have calls, and I have appointments. John wants to see the rewritten pages first thing.

What if this is your last day on earth? you whispered into my ear, and I truly wondered whether you knew, if I might have been talking in my sleep earlier that week. Or had you been watching me at the bottom of the pool, counting the seconds and calculating how long I had before my time was up? Your heart fluttered against mine. That was the moment I should have told you, the three of you, all of us together.

Instead I said only, It's not my last day on earth, Myles, but it might be my last on the lot.

You laughed and sun broke through the window, gilding your hair so you reminded me of an altarpiece saint. You never had any idea how beautiful you were. *Fountain of that stream…named Desire, overflows.* If I'd said it you would have asked me who the poet was

20

and I would have had to tell you it wasn't poetry, at least not the kind you imagined, but philosophy. You looked at my empty cup.

Would you like another? you asked, rising from the table and slipping across the room.

Square your hips, Helen said, your gait's too sultry for a down-on-his-luck veteran wronged by the fates.

But wasn't that also the idea? In casting you as Orph Patterson, we were transfusing the ordinary with a dose of the divine so that men and women in movie theaters across the country would imagine for the space of ninety minutes that your character was a man just like their brothers and husbands and sons, a man come back from the war having seen and done unspeakable things that must nonetheless be suggested clearly enough to send a shiver down the backs of all those necks as you stared just off to the left of the camera's gaze, as if probing the deepest fathoms of Orph's imagined consciousness. What did you think in those moments when the camera recorded your expression? Did you silently recite the following line? Did you try to inhabit the life of the character I invented for you? Or were you always yourself, marking time until the next cue?

I assume that you must have sent Helen to talk to me before I left that morning because you could not bear to ask me what I was planning. She found me in the carport, my hair still damp from the pool.

How many times have I told you it's not nice to leave without saying goodbye, Desmond? Helen had that way of raising her left eyebrow and pursing her mouth, which made her as ghoulish as Norma Desmond ready for a close-up. If you're planning something, don't keep Myles in the dark. He doesn't deserve that from you.

When she said this I was certain all of you must have guessed

21

and been discussing it among yourselves in my absence. I told her I had to go, indicating the pages for the rewritten scenes and glancing up the drive at the gate, hoping there weren't photographers lurking. One night earlier that week I had dreamed of sealing the whole house in black cloth, to keep all that Pacific light from exposing our lives.

Find a way to tell him whatever you've got to say.

How do I tell him I have to leave and don't know when I'll see him again?

Helen trembled at the words and I realized she'd only been fishing. What the hell does that mean? she asked, clinging to my sideview mirror.

It means I've concluded I can't risk sticking around.

That sounds a little extreme.

I told her it was not a decision I'd made overnight, although in a way I had.

You sound so flippant, Desmond. You should remember that even if he isn't yours, you are definitely my husband's first love. If you're not careful you'll break his heart. He didn't even know what he was until he met you.

That isn't true, Helen.

You always seemed more confident than I was, so joyful when we were alone together, but Helen insisted I had given you permission to be yourself.

When you're not around, Myles sits by the pool reading and rereading your books. He said to me once, I know if I read them enough times I'll understand him one day. You're a mystery to him.

Is it true, Myles? I never thought you'd read my books, but when I told Helen this she laughed and said you'd already worn out one copy of *The Argosy* and knew it backwards.

Dammit, Desmond, stop crying.

The two of us stood in the shade of the carport, blushing in the breeze that whipped off the ocean.

I wish it were easier.

Don't we all? At least give Myles fair warning. He'll need a week or two to prepare. A month if you've got it.

I couldn't bring myself to tell her we were long past any such notice period. Time was up.

If only one of us could turn into a woman.

Helen snorted and wiped her cheeks. All these categories. I don't see why categories matter so much. Why don't you just marry Barbara and the four of us can build houses next to each other and dig a tunnel between them? Wouldn't that solve everything?

But to me that sounded just as fantastic as being reborn in the body of the opposite sex. All such miracles are the stuff of fantasy, and ours was a desperately real life. It was a truth you reminded me of in your own way, telling me once when we were in bed, not long after we first declared ourselves to each other, that you could never disappear entirely into a character.

That's not what audiences want, Desmond. They want to see me every time I appear on screen, just different versions of me. It's what people expect of a star.

2

Are you alone now, Myles? I mean not only are you alone when you read this but are you alone despite your marriage to Helen? I see that you two are still together. I remember that Barbara died many years ago. I know almost nothing beyond that. The little I can gather from magazines and newspapers suggests you and Helen still live in the same house in Pacific Palisades after all these years, always such creatures of habit, and she has written to me with that return address I could never forget. *It would be nice to hear from you*, she says, *after your silence all these years.* Forgive me for asking, is it only she who wishes to hear from me and not you as well? I tear open her letters and find such scant lines, revealing nothing about her or you or the life you've made in my absence, while imploring me to tell her about myself. Why must the responsibility of communication and narration, the telling of a life, be entirely mine?

In the press I have seen references to your family ranch, inherited after the death of your parents. One profile describes it as a refuge to which you retreat from your life in Los Angeles. Between the lines I infer this is where you have sequestered your real life, or your real love, whoever he may be, hidden in that Montana cabin. When you are there I hope you are not alone, as I myself am not alone.

I now have a companion I hesitate to call a lover, although he would be hurt to know this. While I love Alessio, because he is much younger, I am never certain his love for me is genuine. He is an artist but without the temperament I might have expected from one who closes himself in a room each day and comes out in the evening paint-scarred and sweating, presenting me with canvases so brutal in their imagery I sometimes go to sleep wondering if I will wake the next morning. And yet the physical trace of his work, the exhaustion in his arms as he prepares dinner for us, is the only sign of drama. In all other ways he is a presence of calm and nurture, caring for me as if I were an infant, stroking my hair into order and washing me when I cannot manage it myself. I trust him with the greatest and most shameful of intimacies. Perhaps you will say he is after my money. I wonder this myself but try to silence such doubts before they have a chance to ruin what is otherwise a relationship of balance and care. No passion left, or at least not the physical kind. I am grateful for a kiss, an embrace, grateful that he does not flinch when I reach for him, that he is not miserly with his body and lets me look and caress as I wish, as it seems to please him. Does he have a father complex, I wonder, or even a grandfather complex? I asked him as much and he laughed, charming in his amusement. But don't be so ridiculous, Desmond, I love you because you are loveable not because I am seeking the love of my fathers and grandfathers. They were all loving men. I mean not men-loving-men, he clarified. No, I understand, I said, they loved you. But completely, he said, and they were always affectionate. So don't imagine I am seeking in you something they failed to give me. I love you for you. *Not for my money? Not even a little?*, I think to myself, despite myself. At least I have the sense never to say it aloud.

Alessio shook his head when I started writing this letter to you a few days ago. What do you always say, Desmond? *Sleeping dogs.* If you have not heard from Myles in all these years then why should you bother him now? Because, Alessio, I will be dead sooner than later and I would like to say what I must while the chance remains, and in any case, Helen has opened the door, she has said it would be nice to hear from me, and although she does not say whether Myles wishes that as well, it is what I choose to infer. You must promise me, Alessio said, fingers embedded with pigment stroking my face as if I were young and beautiful, one of the angelic artists who flock around him rather than an old prophet, wrinkled and stumbling, you must promise me if it becomes too much, if you start not sleeping again, or if I find you weeping at your desk over these pages, then you will stop and talk no more of it ever. I smiled at him, one of those conciliatory smiles that flash and fade quickly and so betray the falseness of their feeling. I cannot promise, but I will try, I said, and he leaned over to kiss me on the mouth. You have *me*, he said, and I am not going anywhere, not ever.

So you see, I am not alone, and I hope you are not alone, that Helen and your children are not the only people who care for you, as Alessio cares for me.

In beginning to write this letter to you, I went looking through my files and discovered a manila folder from the 1950s that had escaped my memory. When I opened it, relishing the particular odor of paper from the last century, American paper that smells to my nose different to any other, I was astonished by the series of fragments I found. Some would call them stories but I am not sure that is what they are. Inventions, speculations, assaults. Each one has a date at the end. A few I remember writing once I have read them, others still come to me with a shock – not only because I cannot recall them but because I no longer recognize the state of mind I must have been suffering at the time. Perhaps I thought they would become a novel or collection of stories, but I also sense that in writing them I might have been trying to settle scores as much as to understand, and so I describe people we knew in ways that would have been unpublishable during their lifetimes without disguising identities, but I also write about people I did not know, with whom I had only scant encounters, or people only related to others I *did* know or met only once. In each of these cases I can see myself trying to understand what had happened to me, to you, to all of us. They were written following my departure, some in spring and early summer of 1950, others a few years later, typed up on my portable Remington and put away to rot. How quickly the worlds we invent can disappear from view. I wonder if you feel this about parts you played, if you look at yourself in a film from those years and have no memory of the person you must have been on the day when a camera captured you riding pell-mell on horseback across a river, or the morning you were climbing from a bomber with your face artfully grease-smeared, or the evening when you closed your hands around the neck of a man so much like yourself he might have been your twin. Do you always know what you were thinking in those moments captured on film, or is the person you were then unreachable now? Do you recall the date and place of each performance, seeing those moments whole in an instant that you can stretch and reinhabit at will?

To remember that day when I last stood by your side and kissed you, I have to step out of the present, forget Alessio upstairs in his studio with its view over the city, and slip into a state of mind closer to trance. It is only through letting consciousness fall away that I begin to see clearly what happened, but just as I grasp your image, the way you looked that morning, you threaten to turn fugitive and escape my mind. If only I could live that day again, not only to do everything differently, but to remember you more clearly, in your ungraspable singularity. The closest I can come to repeating those hours is to submit myself to the dangerous will to dream, here, fingers on my keyboard, summoning you back to my mind. Why did I not work harder to learn you by heart in the years you were mine, that I might now play you more convincingly for my own if for no one else's consolation, play you as automatically and instinctively as I make a pot of coffee or brush my teeth? That would be impossible, of course, and I know that even dreaming you now, trying to dream in order to recapture who you were when I saw you last, you exceed my capacity to know, to understand. I cannot reduce you to a trope, to Myles Haywood as he appears in the photographs covering my walls or Myles Haywood as he moves, framed and edited, chopped apart and reassembled with varying degrees of continuity and fragmentation on my television screen. So I project the details of my memory onto you now, hoping I will capture, by chance, even a few of the same images you may recall when you remember that day.

And I know you must remember it.

The sun was in my eyes as I pulled out of your driveway and turned from Chautauqua onto Sunset. In half an hour I should have been at John Marsh's house, in time for me to discuss the rewritten scenes with him in the car and still arrive at the studio by seven-thirty, grab something more substantial than toast and black coffee in the commissary and sit through the morning on set before the lunch during which I was certain the studio heads were going to tell me that unless I could satisfy the right people, and only if I was willing to betray my own beliefs, I could find a different line of work. My agent Stan had already made it clear that no other studio was going to hire me: every one of them would condemn me for being Red, even though by that time I was no longer a member of any party, and if that failed to stick then I was certain someone would eventually discover our secret and find a way to condemn me for being a man who loved men.

Did the studio know the truth about you from the beginning, Myles, from the moment they decided you were going to be more than a body in the background? Did they know before your engagement to Helen was announced? Was your marriage their idea or yours – or even Helen's? I asked Helen this at the engagement party after watching her gulp three martinis so fast I felt drunk myself. She narrowed her eyes and kissed me on the cheek. That was not an answer, or perhaps it was the clearest answer I could have hoped for. At the time I wondered if it was her way of telling me I could have been her husband myself if only I'd had the sense. Now I suspect she was just as sad and confused by it all as I was, as I suppose you must have been too.

Driving east on Sunset that morning I had to squint against the glare. Even with the visor down, the angle of the sun turned the windshield's layer of dust into a scrim of diamond. At the switchback beneath the polo grounds an eagle flew up from the side of the road, veering towards the car, and at the last instant I swerved into the oncoming lane to miss it. In turning I thought of that moment on Mulholland earlier in the week when I was coming back from John's, imagining you and Helen and Barbara already at home, how it would feel to ring the bell at your gate and steer down the long drive, take my berth in the carport, and find you in the living room watching television, relaxed with each other in a way I could never be since there was always the prospect of my next departure, the fear of photographers catching me as I was coming or going and having to explain myself if the pictures ever slipped into the hands of Hedda Hopper or Louella Parsons. When I left John's that evening I intended, perhaps not quite with full consciousness, to drive off the road. I went up to Mulholland thinking it was a sensible way out, an exit that would cause you the least distress because it could be explained as an accident. If I left behind no suicide note you might allow yourself to believe I'd had one too many bourbons with John and perhaps chose that route – so out of the way if I was just going home – to see the view and take the air, as if I ever cared about views or airs. But as my wheel went off the road onto the gravel that night, I braked hard, anxious that you would blame yourself for what I had done, and that was something I could not risk.

To avoid colliding with the eagle on Sunset I did end up driving off the road, pumping the brakes just before hitting the trunk of an old eucalyptus. A strip of bark sailed down onto the hood as the left front tire collapsed, while up in the tree the eagle ripped the guts from a snake.

Since I had no spare tire, I started walking towards home. Twenty minutes later, not halfway there, a car pulled to the side of the road and a gentleman in the front passenger seat rolled down the window. He was wearing a homburg and little round glasses and a brushy moustache. The driver, whom I had at first mistaken for another man, was the gentleman's daughter. I recognized them both from parties we had all attended. These were not parties you would have enjoyed, Myles, but ones where all the artistic and intellectual misfits who fled Europe before the war gravitated for sympathy and moral support.

Can we offer you a lift? the man asked. I told them I lived in Brentwood but actually needed to get to Beverly Hills and they offered to take me all the way.

We so like driving, the daughter said. My father woke early and fancied an outing. He said he could not sleep and could not work and American roads are made for such a state.

I explained about the eagle and the flat tire, telling them it gave me a look as though it had achieved something significant.

The man mumbled to himself, *Jupiter's bird*. A winged lion. If you had not been walking, we should never have stopped, and then we would not have had this nice…he paused, searching for the right word…*chat*. So perhaps your eagle did achieve something. Worse things can come from the sky. You were lucky it was not a flying saucer! Again, the man and his daughter laughed. This United States government of yours does not want us to believe in flying saucers or objects in the sky that cannot be explained, even things they might have put there themselves, unless they can blame it on Russia. But anyway, we also live in Brentwood, so we are neighbors who did not know they are neighbors and nowadays, sympathetic neighbors we need even more, especially in this – you will forgive me if you do not agree – this country of *gangsters*. I do not mean to be so critical, but these men with their witch hunts are no better than criminals.

Sounds as though you have the measure of the place, I laughed, and the man and his daughter said yes, after all, they had been in the country more than a decade, escaping fascism. You outran it for a while, I told them, but it's back on the march.

Only now I am an American citizen, the man sighed, so where would I go? I fled insanity and danger for what must have seemed like security, I cannot now remember. Hope and reason, purity, even maybe innocence. But I did not know you Americans only pretend at innocence, while in fact you are always play-acting, and the reality, what is beneath the masquerade, is so, so dark. Anti-Semitism everywhere.

What about returning to Germany, I asked, but the man mumbled, No, I do not think I can go back.

France?

No, nor England. Too depressing their weather, and the English do not like a foreigner unless he wears a sign around him saying *Just Visiting* and even then… No, Switzerland, maybe we go there. Neutrality is the last refuge, but I think it is a boring place.

The man's daughter turned onto Summit Drive and glanced at me in the rearview mirror, raising her eyebrows to ask where she should stop.

Up on the right, I said, the one with the tall hedge.

The man wondered if he recognized me from the movies but I told him I was just a writer and reminded him of several parties we had both attended. At this his face brightened. A brother writer as well as a neighbor! Perhaps I will come to see you sometime, and we can talk about birds and accidents and...beauty. Presently I go to Scandinavia so it will have to wait. But you must come visit. I live at the corner of San Remo, just by Monaco. These European names give a nice idea to people who have never been to such places, thinking they belong to a culture older than this young city. It is very pretty, my house, an enchanted garden for an old man. Tell me, your eagle, was he beautiful?

I had no time to reflect on the bird's beauty, but it was as attractive as any other I've seen.

The old man chuckled as his daughter idled their car outside John's house. Another car, a dark coupe, was parked across the street. Not every bird is beautiful, the man sighed, glancing at the coupe. Vultures. Buzzards.

When I leaned over to thank them the man gripped my arm. If you need another lift, now you know where I live, and he winked in a way that surprised me less once I had bothered to read his books with all their aging male characters besotted by the beauty of young men and boys.

Even though the age difference between us was not nearly so great, is that how it felt, Myles, to be desired by an older man, to suffer that leering gaze, the hungry possessiveness which presses against the skin as tangibly as a hand? It was flattering but also unnerving to find myself the object of such scrutiny again, as I had on several occasions in my adolescence, to feel that my admirer had not just peeled off my clothes with his eyes but flayed my body so my heart was exposed to his longing.

On the walk to John's gate I felt a sense of disquiet at thinking how you might have felt the first time I stared at you, the way I'm sure I failed to control the fire in my eyes as we spoke, how I must have been unable to keep myself from studying your face and letting my gaze dart across your shoulders, down your arms, devouring the angles of your torso, the symmetries of your chest, the neat waist and muscular legs, how my eyes would have held your own even when you tried to look away in embarrassment, those lilac eyes that could burn cobalt or coppery blue in different lights, a blue so transparent it seemed as if one were looking not just at the surface of the eye but into and through it, deep to the opposite side, only to realize that in those depths were only further depths, bluer and more remote.

John and Mary's housekeeper, Nathalie, opened the front gate. In the past she always did this from inside the house, pushing a button that made it swing open. That morning, however, she took the trouble to come out in person and I wondered if the remote-control mechanism had failed, or if something else were afoot. Oh, it's just you, Mr. Frank, she said, sounding relieved, and turned the latch to let me in.

In an upstairs window I could see Mary moving across a room, her hair catching the morning sun. A cameraman once joked that if they shot her without a filter she overexposed every frame. She paused in the upstairs window and stared out, frowning, not at me but the dark coupe on the street. The two men in the car – men exactly like those I had seen frequently in recent weeks, often blond and bronzed, always in dark suits and snap-brim hats – looked at me the way you and I might glance at and hold the gaze of strangers, wondering whether the object of our gaze will be receptive or hostile, if the man we regard desires in the same way that we desire.

John was on the phone in his study when I knocked and he motioned me to come in and close the door. Forgive me, but you don't sound like any friend of mine, he grumbled into the receiver. I handed him the rewritten scenes and he shook his head. You're not alarming me, buddy, he said. Then whatever the person on the other end replied made John wince as if he had stepped on a shard of glass. Sweat beaded his brow and he loosened his tie. I think you've got the wrong idea, he said, swiveling the chair so his back was to me. What kind of trouble are you trying to make? If you phone again I'll call the police. Then he spun the chair back around, picked up his watch from where it lay on the desk, wound it, and glanced out the window towards the terrace and the topiary hedges bordering the lawn. I could hear the dial tone throbbing as he held the receiver at arm's length, staring at it, before dropping it back on its cradle.

Damnedest thing, Desmond. I was having a dream this morning, just before the alarm went off. It was three parts *She Turned Away* and one part I don't know what. He glanced again at the squat black phone. I was in a cellar, three or four floors below ground, and I was a killer, I mean in the dream I knew I was a murderer and probably on my way to the gas chamber if I got caught, and all my victims were lying around me. I was using a broken shovel to dig into the concrete floor, trying to bury the bodies, and some of them weren't even dead yet, they were groaning and turning over in their death throes, and I was hitting the blade of the shovel against the concrete so that sparks flew and it vibrated like a tuning fork and the vibrations went straight up my arms and made a ringing in my head, and then I realized the ringing wasn't in my head – it was police drilling through the walls, trying to get to me, and every time I looked around there were more and more bodies, like they were multiplying, filling up the room to the ceiling and threatening to suffocate me. Then the alarm went off, or it must have been going off already. The ringing, I mean...

Who was that on the phone?

Damnedest thing, John said again. At first I couldn't tell if it was a man or a woman, maybe even a child. Iris can shred her voice into a pack of barking dogs and mimic men three times her age, so there's no telling, but the more the fellow talked the more I think he might have been like you.

Like me, John?

You know, he said, like *you*...

You mean a pansy.

John blushed. I wouldn't have put it like that. He was young, sort of breathy and adenoidal. Peter Lorre with a Southern accent.

And what did your Southern pansy want?

John grimaced and I could tell he didn't like me using that word. He stood up, tiptoed to the door, and flung it open as if expecting to find someone on the other side. When there was no one there, he almost seemed disappointed, but then closed it again and turned the lock. The guy on the phone said that tomorrow Mary's going to give a statement about her past. Probably about my past, too. And what she knows. Do you understand what I'm saying?

What he meant, of course, was that the anonymous caller was suggesting Mary had volunteered to give the FBI names of people she either knew to be or merely suspected of being Communists.

Jesus, John, I said, pretending to be stunned, but the fact is I was not in the least surprised, or perhaps only insofar as it had taken Mary that long to turn informer. While I knew she had once been party to progressive causes I understood that such activism was well in her past. I remember how I used to complain to you, Myles, that on his own John had a sense of determination to do good in the world and champion the poor because he himself came from such humble beginnings, but every time his ideas grew a little too radical Mary killed them in the cradle. Although I had never confessed this to John because you don't tell a friend that his wife makes your skin crawl, from the moment I met her I knew Mary was not on the side of the gods.

I can't imagine it's true, John said. It must be someone trying to make trouble. What do you think of Nick Charles for instance?

I think he'd put a knife in his own grandmother's back.

John nodded. Every day Nick shows up on set smiling more broadly and Mary won't even meet my gaze. He picked up the rewritten scenes I'd placed on his desk. How are the pages?

Given the constraints, I told him, they could be worse. The truth is that having rewritten those scenes in the middle of the night, on the back of our fight, preoccupied with the secret I was keeping from you, I feared I might have inadvertently shown my hand, allowing a character to speak in a way that, properly decoded, could have revealed what I was, or even what you were, Myles. Not that I was trying to hide from John. Perhaps I never told you that when he was deciding to cast you he took me aside and asked whether our relationship was going to complicate the production and I said quite the opposite, it would make everything run more smoothly because your happiness and safety were always my chief concern. I suspect you won't believe that but try to imagine me balancing the anxieties of my own situation with an absolute love for you, even if it was not my first or the greatest, whatever 'greatest' might mean to me now. A great love might simply be one that is comfortable and sustaining and has a sense of longevity – even just the assumption of permanence. We never had the chance to discover if we loved each other enough to last decades, but I still choose to believe that we did.

John rubbed his eyes and put down the page he was reading. I thought of telling him I was intending to leave the following day, but didn't know whether I could trust him not to tell you. That was the moment I knew the secret I was keeping from you was a betrayal as grave as if I had gone to bed with another man.

I haven't had any coffee, Desmond, I can't see straight.

Even now, at this moment late in my life, living south of the Arno with a young Italian who makes me quietly happy, there are days when I imagine sending you a plane ticket and pleading with you to come live with me, so that we can reclaim whatever time remains to us both. Like so much else – including this reconstruction of a single day in our past that is the object of my letter to you – I know this is fantasy.

In the kitchen John's daughter Iris was in the breakfast nook reading the trades and drinking a glass of orange juice. John ruffled her hair and kissed her brow.

Go back to bed, viper.

Iris stood up from the table taking *Variety* with her but John reached out and plucked the magazine from her hand. 'H'wood Pix in Virtual Blackout Behind Iron Curtain', one of the headlines shouted.

Iris hesitated at the door. Why is that car outside?

What car?

The one across the street.

Autograph hounds.

Why don't they come to the door like all the others?

Different breed. How long have they been there?

I heard the car stop before midnight. It hasn't moved since then.

Good girl. Now back to bed.

We watched as Iris walked down the hall towards the front door and turned up the stairs. John squared the pages and pushed them across the table to me.

You don't think it's possible Mary might make a statement behind my back, is it?

Given the chance I would have told John I thought it was entirely possible, but this was not a question I could answer because a moment later Mary arrived in the doorway of the kitchen wearing a scarlet gown with a platinum mink over one arm and a clear acrylic purse dangling from the other. Oh, you're here, Desmond. What's the call, Marsh?

Seven-thirty, John said, as if he had reminded her half a dozen times already.

Bergman isn't on set before nine.

You're not Bergman.

I could get you fired, Marsh.

In the past I had seen them argue on set, but never at home, and never with such rancor. Whenever you and I fought I always felt we were conscious of the stakes, aware of how awful it would be to lose what we had found in each other. Between John and Mary, I sensed little remained but anger and suspicion. He asked her if she had any plans for the weekend and her whole expression altered, eyes widening. What's that? she asked, in a voice full of bubblegum and soda pop. Plans?

Since it's your birthday tomorrow, I thought you might have plans, John said.

Still in the same voice Mary asked why on earth she should have any plans. I couldn't tell if this was coyness, hoping John might reveal a birthday surprise, or actual dissembling. The party that night had been planned long before we knew shooting was going to overrun and it was too late to cancel because Mary had sent invitations months earlier, hired a band, arranged catering from Chasen's, ordered flowers and fireworks.

I thought we might go to Malibu, Mary.

Malibu? No, Jesus, I'd rather stay in town.

Where's Nathalie?

Ironing tablecloths.

And the boys?

Is this a census? They're not my children.

Have you said goodbye to Iris?

If she's awake at this hour you should have spanked her.

She's too old for that.

A girl's never too old for a spanking.

Is that an invitation, Mary?

Cool off, Marsh. I have to go places. She turned towards the door, taking the mink and acrylic purse with her. I'll meet you at the car.

Whatever venom the anonymous caller had poured in John's ear was beginning to seep. He tilted his head at the sound of Mary moving around upstairs, listening for the flush of a toilet and water in the pipes, but there was only the sound of a door opening and closing again and Mary's heels clicking back along the hall.

She's up to something, he said.

*

In the garage we found Mary standing next to her white Coupe de Ville, waiting for John to open the door. She had slipped into the mink and still had the purse hanging off her arm. Do you have the scene, Desmond?

I handed her the pages and she began to read as John backed out of the garage, idled for a moment while Nathalie opened the remote-controlled gate, and then pulled onto Summit where the dark coupe with the two men in hats was still parked. When the other car turned to follow Mary glanced over her shoulder, pulling the mink tighter around her body. You drive too fast, Marsh. Slow down.

It was only seven but the streets were crowded with shades of baby blue, canary yellow, ruby red, hunter green, black and navy. Sunlight caught a curve of chrome and must have dazzled John because he ran a red light and nearly hit a turning truck. Mary shut her eyes, mouthed a line, then spoke it aloud.

Not exactly riches you sent me. Not exactly riches you sent me. *It's not like you sent me riches* – that would be better. People don't talk like you make them talk, Desmond.

John frowned and kept his eyes on the road. What's the line on the page?

Mary and I spoke it at the same time. Not exactly riches you sent me.

Then *Not exactly riches you sent me* is what you say, Mary.

She turned back to the pages, saying the line in a number of different ways: angry, perturbed, put-upon, resentful, self-pitying. What does Ursula feel in this moment? she asked.

Defensive. She has to convince Orph she isn't a criminal.

When Mary heard this, her eyebrows pinched together.

Wouldn't it be riches you *send* me?

She's talking about the past. Her husband has returned. Riches you *sent* me.

Stop trying to think, Mary, John snapped. Do as you're told and we'll all go home happy.

Do as you're told, she mocked. You should learn to treat me better, Marsh, or I might throw you over for someone less economical.

Now who sounds like one of Desmond's characters?

At the studio gate the wash of morning light made the columns and porticos look like marble instead of the stucco and concrete used twenty years earlier when the whole place was rebuilt from its more modest beginnings. Beyond that phalanx of ersatz Grecian temples, the soundstages loomed like airplane hangars, and down one of the long studio streets I could see the open-air sets of the backlot, its shifting jumble of European villages and castles, Wild West ghost towns and New England main streets, as if the essence of every place and culture could co-exist while remaining mutable, capable of being built and torn down and reimagined as some other space and time all in the course of a day. The longer I spent there the more I came to believe it was the atmosphere of unreality and impermanence that conditioned the way those of us who made our lives within it imagined the world. I don't mean that as a criticism of you or anyone else, Myles, but as a proposition that we all struggled to see truth even when it stood right before us. We wanted the illusion because it thrilled or terrified or seduced us into believing in the possibility that beauty could be conjured from the ordinary. Reality was too alienating, its contours and colors too prone to numb or bewilder.

John parked the car in Mary's spot and jumped out to open the door for her.

Beyond the arches of the studio gate the dark coupe that had followed us all the way from Summit Drive pulled to a stop. I knew

John and Mary both saw it but they acted as if they had not. Then, without saying anything, Mary handed me the rewritten pages and slipped into the backseat of the car that was waiting to take her to her dressing room suite.

I have visions sometimes, John said as we watched the car driving Mary slowly down Main Street, I can see myself racing to catch up to her, flinging open the car door, slugging the driver, pulling her from the seat and shaking her until she confesses. I don't know what to call them, Desmond, but these fantasies have become more frequent in the past few weeks. Do you think I'm a violent man? Mary says I hate women and just can't admit it. I don't know where the anger comes from sometimes. I open my mouth and it's my father speaking and when I shout at her Mary becomes my mother and all of it gets jumbled in my head until I'm convinced I'm replaying one of the fights my parents had when I was a boy and my mother wanted nothing more than for Dad to show her a little kindness. In those moments the roles are dizzyingly reversed, so I can see myself as my mother and Mary as my father.

I suppose that's often the way, John. I knew I sounded impatient but I wanted to be free of him and see if you were already in your dressing room, except your car was not in its spot. It made me wonder whether you had been delayed in leaving home or if something had happened en route. Without having a way to contact you I imagined an accident, fearing you had figured out what I was planning and became so wracked with grief you succeeded in doing what I nearly did earlier that week and drove the car off a cliff or – as I nearly had that morning – waded into the pool and inhaled until water displaced all the air in your lungs.

*

At the Executive Building John and I parted and I stood trying to calm myself, then dropped off the new pages at the Writers' Building and walked up Main past the commissary toward the soundstages. It was the last day I would ever make that short journey, the final time I would look at the sun on those streets or wave hello to people I recognized but never really knew. I turned onto Third Avenue and walked past Stages 3 and 4, my heart beating faster again because I was anxious to find you.

The day the studio gave you one of the Star Suites I remember you seemed as excited that your room had a view of Joan Crawford's as you were to be getting a suite of your own. That innocent enthusiasm, the star-struck exuberance you kept even when you were a star in your own right, never failed to charm me. How could you be so innocent of your talent, or of your beauty?

I was about to knock on the door of your suite when you came up the stairs behind me. Before I'd turned around I knew it was you because I could hear your ankles clicking as you climbed and I've never met anyone else in the world whose body makes that sound.

Checking up on me? you asked, a smile in your voice. It's true I usually avoided coming to the suite, always trying to keep my distance in public so no one would chance to suspect us. When we were both inside you locked the door and then your arms were on my shoulders and your body against mine and you were kissing me so warmly and gently – your lips soft and moist where they had been sharp and cold the night before – that I nearly burst into tears. How could I leave this? How could I be so rash to think I would ever find your equal, or that finding an equal would compensate for the loss of someone I had learned to trust absolutely and who seemed to trust me as well? I inhaled the scent of your body, your breath, the Italian cologne I had brought back from Florence for your twenty-fifth birthday, the scent of ambergris and laundry starch and hair oil, all those odors visible in your eyes, which had gone turquoise in the grid of light slicing through the blinds. Your head twitched to be sure the slats were closed tightly enough that no one would have been able to distinguish our forms, but then your focus was back on me, your tongue moving against mine, the fine brush of chin abrading my jaw.

How long do you have? I asked and you said not long enough. You had to go to wardrobe and makeup.

But stay, Desmond, and if I'm not back in half an hour I'll see you on set.

Just as quickly as you'd appeared on the stairs you unlocked the door, tossed me the keys, and left. The nonchalance of that action told me you had not begun to suspect my plans, that Helen had kept my secret.

Alone in your suite, I felt I was trespassing on your subconscious, although I had helped you decorate the room, choosing to put in bookshelves and hang nautical prints to make it look like a London club. I've never been to London, you told me, and I said it didn't matter, it was about the image such furnishings convey: the smart young man who might have come from nothing but still has a sense of culture. The contents of the shelves and prints of schooners had somehow acquired a patina from being in your presence, so it seemed as if the ships could have been ones you captained in an earlier life, or the books contained all the stories through which you had come to understand who you were.

I noticed you had bought a new bottle of bourbon, the second already that month, and I wondered if you were drinking too much. Because you trusted me to stay there alone, to leave me the key to your suite, I had no reason to snoop and yet I was tempted to see what I might find. Letters from fans were piled on the desk, people from all over the country writing to ask for your autograph or tell you how much they had adored you in your last picture, many of them assuming an intimacy that made me jealous despite myself. Once I asked if you enjoyed reading fan mail and you said, Of course, it's flattering, and I asked whether flattery was satisfying and you said No, but that doesn't mean I can't enjoy it once in a while, like a joint or a drink. Maybe you wish I flattered you more, I said, and you blushed. I don't need flattery from you, Desmond, I'm just grateful you stick around. What does that mean? Nothing, you said, forget it. I've always wondered why you should have thought I might be doing you a favor by falling in love with you.

When the half hour was up and you had not returned I locked your suite and headed downstairs. In the courtyard between the men's and women's buildings I ran into Mary. She was holding a letter, swatting it against her gloved hand.

Angry creditors? I asked, smirking.

Letter from a friend, she scowled, but you wouldn't know from the tone of the thing that we haven't seen each other in more than a decade. I usually respond to every single letter I receive, but not this one, and then she dropped it in the trashcan by the curb, her eyes narrowing as if she had momentarily lost control of her face.

As soon as I was certain no one was watching I plucked the letter from the trash and read it. Perhaps this will strike you as strange, even indefensible, but because of what John had told me that morning my usual sense of wariness about Mary had turned into more active suspicion. I thought the letter might give me some hint of her plans, or what was driving her.

There was a sadness to the stationery, its edges uniformly yellowed. Although excellent quality, it carried the smell of mothballs and looked as though it had been purchased twenty years earlier. The handwriting started off with precision but by the middle of the first page loosened up and became more difficult to decipher, although these qualities were incidental to the hints of a life behind the words. Perhaps it should not have surprised me that Mary had such connections, but surprise me it did. Even if it did not function for me as an excuse for the actions John's anonymous caller warned him Mary was about to take – in other words turning over the names of friends and colleagues she believed to be Communists to federal agents or whoever she might have arranged to meet the next day – it did offer a certain context for her actions, suggesting a network of relations remote from the image Mary presented to the world, and one whose potential exposure to public scrutiny might have struck her as no less perilous than the threat of being called to testify before Congress herself.

Kay

She stared at the boy sitting at the dining table in the living room.
There was simply too much furniture what with the buffet and
the blue-and-white-striped couch and the two armchairs in green
upholstery and the matching coffee table and end table, both
decorated with inlaid floral patterns. The furniture had been made
to look expensive but she knew it was cheap, not like the solid
pieces in her parents' house. The boy was eating a piece of dry
toast and drinking a glass of milk. He was wearing his khaki slacks
but she could see the bottoms of his blue pajamas sticking out from
under the cuffs.

Roll down your pants, she said.

The boy looked at her and went on chewing and he had this
preoccupied squint and sneer that she had started seeing in the
last few years. It was the same expression she knew as her own,
also her mother's. The boy did not move but a vein pulsed in his
neck and his knuckles were white. As if he thought she would not
notice. The spit of his father.

Roll down your pants or people will think we're Communists,
she whispered, only she could tell from the way the boy flinched
that when the sound came out of her mouth it had arrived with
the force of a scream. The boy dropped his toast on the plate and
leaned to roll down the cuffs so his pajama bottoms were no longer
visible and then he finished the toast in two bites but she could see
he was shaking, like as though frightened, or angry. Possibly both.
There had been a fight the night before.

You're holding a grudge, she said, don't you dare hold a grudge,

48

it's unchristian. He stood up from the table and took the plate into the bathroom and she could hear running water in the bathroom sink and him washing the plate. He came back through the living room carrying the plate, which was dripping, water drops hanging in the air and then plip-plop-plip as they landed.

You're dripping all over the floor! she said, shouting the first two words and then, realizing she was shouting, dropping her voice to a whisper because their landlords, the Smiths, who lived in the bungalow next door and kept both their cars in the garage under the apartment, would think they were Communists if she went on shouting like that. Her hand flew to her mouth and she rested her chin on the heel of the palm, then cupped her hand so the tips of her fingers were tucked between her lips. She had seen her mother do this and as a girl had started doing it herself. Some of her brothers and sisters did it, Ruth did it, and now the boy did as well, she had seen him, when he was fretting. Fretting was a family word. As was dithering. And frugal. She would say, don't fret like that, you remind me of someone, and slap his hand away from his face.

Who? he would say, giving her that crazed look and crumpling his chin into a bright red pincushion.

Never you mind, she would say, and slap his cheek for good measure.

When she shouted that he was dripping all over the floor he did not even slow down, just kept heading into the kitchen, and she could hear the dishcloth rippling off the handle on the oven and the squeak as the worn white cotton swept across the ceramic plate and then the door of the cupboard crying open, the plate rattling hard on the stack of other plates, the door closing, and the dishcloth being put back in its place with the swish of cloth on enamel.

You forgot to clear your glass, she called in a stage whisper, because of shouting and people thinking them Communists and not wanting to risk that someone might hear.

The boy stood in the doorway to the living room and glared. Insolence. The face of his father. That awful under-bite, just like his father. Upper lip cupped and beaklike. She could see what he would be as an old man, the near-toothless worrying of a piece of bread beneath that cupped upper lip, the fretting fingers tucked between his lips, tapping his teeth. Oral fixation. She had heard about oral fixations. The boy swiped the glass from the table and walked to the bathroom. Kay could hear him washing the glass in the sink and she thought about the waste of water because of two washing-up sessions and then he came back through, dripping again, and she nearly said something but he gave her this look that drained the life out of her, as if a twelve-year-old were capable of murder. He had nearly killed his dog seven years ago, when they were living in the Motor Lodge, and there was the business again of the dishcloth, and a higher-pitched whine of cotton on glass and the cupboard doors, slamming this time, no doubt about it, and the murmur of cotton falling against the enamel. People will think we're Communists slamming doors like that, she stage-whispered. From where she was sitting on the couch she could see a circle of milk on the table, which would leave a ring, and it was only a cheap table. It looked expensive when it was new, mahogany veneer, walnut maybe, but the legs were not even solid pieces of wood, they were machine-made of separate parts that kept falling off in the heat and had to be re-glued. It had all come with the apartment, cheap furnishings for a cheap place, never in her life did she think she would live above a garage, and now the whole town probably thought they were Communists and her husband an adulterer and embezzler and all of it such a sudden and perilous fall. She caught a whiff of her underarm. Onions. She hadn't eaten onions in months but the smell persisted.

She had not seen Hank properly for two weeks – at least not during the day – and could not answer the boy when he asked where his father was. When he demanded to know last night, she slapped his cheek and told him to lean over the chair and he did and she pulled down his pajamas and whipped him with one of his father's belts until she raised welts and then said he was to go to bed, but not unless he had done a B.M. Have you? she asked him and he said that he had not and she said, well then, and he said, no not again, we're not doing that, and she said, then you sit until it comes, and she had closed him in the bathroom and put a chair against the door and it had taken an hour and a half, was nearly midnight, but she finally heard the sounds and she knew it had happened and let him out again and given him the broom handle on his calves for good measure, as her mother had done to her. If he would not do it the easy way, he would have to wait and let nature and so on. Now he was standing there, this stick of a boy who ran to the window looking for his father every evening, was disappointed, ate alone with his mother, watched TV with her afterward even though neither could pay attention to the shows, always wondering where Hank might be, Hank with a hundred different jobs and a hundred different names, a hundred different women and for all she knew a hundred different sons in a hundred different towns. Traveling salesman. Farmer. Rancher. Whatever he called himself now.

At night, she could hear the boy sitting up on the couch where he slept, turning on the light, checking the clock. She had taken to telling him that his father was unwell, that he had to go to hospitals, although this was a lie. She had no idea where Hank might be and during the day she spent hours gazing out the cloudy window hoping her husband might appear in his red pickup truck, hoping he would come home and rant about the evils of labor unions because at least that would mean he was present.

The boy was out the door without saying goodbye and she ran after him, chasing him down the stairs and hitting his back with her fist on every step, so that by the time he reached the bottom he lost his balance and fell, splayed in the dirt.

Don't let me see you until dinnertime, she said, and the boy got up and sneered and squinted, and then he ran as the municipal truck came down the street, spraying DDT. The boy ran faster, following the truck until he disappeared into the fog. Kay heard the back door of the house open and she looked around and there was her landlady, Mrs. Smith, and she said Good morning, Mrs. Smith, and the woman said Good morning to *you*, but said it in that snide way, as if Kay had caused an affront by greeting her, and then she was sure Mrs. Smith thought they were Communists and it was just a matter of time before the eviction. Kay ducked her head and walked back up the stairs to the apartment above the garage and carefully shut the door behind her. The room was warm and she could see dust hanging in the air in the sun that came through the dirty windows and on the floor the place where the plate had dripped as the boy was carrying it from the bathroom to the kitchen. It would dry as a spot and then there'd be hell from Hank because of mess and damage and losing the deposit and not managing the boy as she should and that was her responsibility. And then she would get the belt as well as the boy.

There was nothing in the icebox save milk and that almost sour and two eggs and those rotten most like. In the cupboard a tin of peas and another of cling peaches. The bread was gone. No

meat. Not enough for a growing boy. She looked at herself in the
bathroom mirror and could see her own death's head beneath the
skin. Always thin, the only one in her family, and still her little
brother had teased, you better not eat too much, else you'll get
fat like brother George. Back when there was always enough, too
much. Sister Flora's lime Jell-O salads with gherkins and canned
pineapple at Christmas. Fried okra. Beef every night. Fresh rolls.
She wished she had never met Hank. She wished she had stayed
in Oklahoma and gone on being a teacher even though useless,
always late, flapping out of the house and running headlong to get
to school before the first bell, wished she had gone on coaching
the girls' basketball squad because at least she had been good at
that, wished she had finished the stories about her family she had
started writing but gave up when Hank said it was not the business
of a wife to make up stories because how could a husband trust a
woman who lied so convincingly?

From the desk in the corner of the living room she drew the
letter she had been writing.

Dear Rosa (am I still allowed to call you that?),

I had your address from my mother who had it from your
brother so I hope you will not mind that I write to you. No,
do not worry, I am not asking for money. If I needed money
I would ask mother or Vernon, who in fact now holds the
purse strings tighter than anyone else in the family ever
did, but I suppose you know that from your brother. Do you
know also that Vernon converted to Roman Catholicism
when he came back from Italy after the war? I cannot
imagine. We have always been Lutherans. I hope your
brother is well and that Vernon gives him fair terms. My

brother drives such a bargain I expect it cannot be easy, but I am in no position of influence so expect there is little I might do to improve the situation.

I wished to congratulate you on your success and to be back in touch since we used once to be such pals. I think you and I were best friends as girls. Do you remember it that way? I do not know if your brother has kept you up to date with my family news. I am living now in the San Joaquin Valley with my husband, Hank, and our son, after some years in Kansas on our own. (Again, do not worry, I am not proposing to bother you in Los Angeles, nor would I turn up to a 'premiere' and cause embarrassment. I imagine the last person you would want standing by that red carpet is your old country chum!)

Hank was a farmer at first, though I do not think you would have known his family, Missourians in any case, so never part of the social set back home – Irish, too, but Protestants like us. Our boy, now twelve, is almost more trouble than he is worth. I see that you have a daughter, just younger than my boy, and from the magazines she looks a pretty child. How lucky you have been. Not that luck comes into it. You were always so talented – the most talented of anyone in town, I always said.

That was where Kay left off in the middle of the previous night, satisfied the boy had gone to sleep on the couch, making sounds so troubling she almost woke him, because of sin and the body and what he must have been dreaming, but instead had gone to bed herself, hoping not to hear any more of it. She had woken in the night with Hank taking what he judged his to take, and she was about to scream until he put a hand over her mouth and then he was finished and gone again as if she had dreamed it, but leaving in the bedclothes scents of beer and whiskey and cigarettes, the perfumes of other women, all that stale reek of a man in decline. He would be dead in a decade, she thought, his stomach exploded from wickedness. She took up her pen with the dirty light on the page and continued.

As I say, I am not writing to ask for money or help for myself. My motives are selfless. I am writing because I am concerned about what is happening in this country and I see from my humble place in the world how it affects you. I hope you will not think I presume too much in saying this, but we once were the closest of friends. So much you once confessed to me – I remember, still, all that you used to confide. Do not think that is a threat on my part. No, please do not think that. I remind you of those confidences to demonstrate how much I care for you and how much you once trusted me. I am writing to you now

With what difficulty the words came, how slowly and grudgingly, catching on the tip of the pen rather than flowing as they had in the night.

because I have begun to read things about your husband and the people close to him. I mean not you or your daughter but the men and women who are his closest business associates, people with whom he collaborates, the causes to which he has given contributions, the many risky things that he has said. These are not American attitudes. I would say they are foreign but I do not possess knowledge of what foreign attitudes might entail, except that normal folk might see them as giving

comfort to our enemies. No, do not be offended. Remember I
say this as your oldest friend. What I mean is, because of your
stature, and to secure the safety of your daughter, and also
of my son (if you should care to think of him as well), and so
many other boys and girls, then I believe you have a duty to
speak. Do not think I say this lightly. I know what difficulty
there is in a marriage. I understand how a wife wants to be
loyal even when her husband is a rogue. But there is more at
stake now. The nation is under threat. Our world is in crisis.
If people like you do not speak, what hope those of us who live
closer to the ground, who must mix with agitators because
we have no choice but to walk among them? I ask for the sake
of the little people, Rosa, that you raise your voice and say all
that you know to be true, as I trust that you do.

Yours always and affectionately,

Kay

She read through the letter and folded it in thirds before slotting
it into an envelope and writing the address of the studio, and then
instead of Rosa Schumacher she made it out to Mary Dawn. In the
upper left corner she wrote her own name, including her maiden
name as she would not usually have done so that Rosa would know
it was a personal letter rather than one from a fan, assuming, that
is, that Rosa even opened her own mail. Presumably there was an
assistant who took care of the bags of fan mail but that assistant
must know when opening a letter and finding it written to Rosa
not Mary that it must be unusual, that it would warrant reading
by Mary – that is Rosa – herself, and not just a form reply and a
signed photograph, is what Kay hoped.

Once she had put on her face she would walk to the post office
and then to the grocer. In her purse she had two dollars, which
was all that was left from the last time Hank gave her money.
Whatever she bought would have to last. She found an old envelope
and a pencil and began doing sums. Milk at 18 cents a quart.
Succotash for 17 cents a pound. Pot roast for 49 cents a pound.
Butter for 66 cents a pound. A 15-ounce loaf of bread for 12 cents.
At $1.44/pound she would have to skip coffee unless there was
a sale. Perhaps she should be thinking about taking in washing
or ironing, and there was rent coming due to the Smiths at the
end of the month and no telling whether Hank would be back by
then and have the money to pay them or they'd be out looking for
somewhere else. When she had come west with Hank her mother
said no, she could not take the Limoges or Bavarian china they
had received as wedding gifts from the whole family, nor the silver
service nor the crystal with its gold-leaf embellishments. All of
that remained in Mother's house in Oklahoma and Kay thought
now, well, perhaps Mother was right, because if I had it here, this
morning, I would take that silver to the pawn shop to eat.

Mrs. Smith, who was a lady of culture, Kay suspected,
subscribed to the *Los Angeles Times*, which meant it was possible
to fish discarded issues out of the trash at night and so keep up
with matters and expand her vocabulary. The issue from Monday
announced that lightning had hit a house in the Wilshire district
of Los Angeles and a boy in Amarillo, Texas, claimed he had
touched a flying saucer that released a spray before flying off into
the sky and this had left his face and one arm scalded. The United
States Air Force denied the existence of flying saucers. Russians
most likely. There had been seven traffic fatalities in Los Angeles
County last Sunday and 172 since the beginning of the year, all

because some fools didn't know better than to swerve across lanes or collide with trams. Here was better news: there were Easter services at the Hollywood Bowl with Celeste Holm and Colleen Townsend and Mary Dawn. People, all those good Christian people, had started arriving in the middle of the night just to get a seat. That was heartening. But Groucho Marx was divorcing his wife. With a man of that kind it was no surprise.

Kay checked the sums on the envelope and searched again in her purse. She would buy ground beef instead of pot roast. They could live without butter.

May 23, 1950

Mr. Joseph I. Breen, Director
Production Code Administration
5504 Hollywood Boulevard
Hollywood 28, California

Dear Mr. Breen:

I enclose for your attention and authorization one copy of:

SHE TURNED AWAY - Eighth Draft, dated April 10, 1950.

As you will remember there have been a great number of
problems with this particular project, which is already
well into production owing to budget and casting pressures.
I appreciate that you have had concerns about some aspects
of the story that sail close to the wind in matters of
morality and depiction of violence but it is our studio's
strong feeling that SHE TURNED AWAY represents a new kind
of picture, of the sort we have been seeing since the end
of the war, a picture that tries to tell the true stories
of ordinary American people and reflect something of their
own difficult realities, however far removed they may seem
from the concerns of men like you and me. I also want to
remind you that in the lead roles we have cast two of this
studio's most prominent stars, Mary Dawn and Myles Haywood.
You will know of their impeccable characters and reputa-
tions. Mary Dawn was one of the featured players in the
Hollywood Bowl's Easter Service this weekend and Mr. Haywood and his wife Helen Fairdale are among our industry's
most upstanding young couples.

Please note changes dated 4/5/50 on pages as follows: 9,
14, 23-2, 35-39, 51-56, 70-74, 77-88, 90. Also changes
dated 4/9/50 - pages 1-10, 25-55, 61, 65, 93. The
screenwriters trust that these alterations will address
your concerns as outlined in previous correspondence.

Cordially yours,

Porter Cherry

PC/sc
Enc./1

<u>SHE TURNED AWAY</u>

Screenplay By
Desmond Frank and John Marsh
Based on a story by Desmond Frank

PART ONE

INT. TRAIN - DAY

A Southern Pacific train slices through the bleached-
out flatlands of the San Fernando Valley. Distant
peaks jag the horizon as light shimmers over a
treeless landscape passing outside the windows.

It's just past dawn, six in the morning, and CORPORAL
ORPH PATTERSON, a lean, dark young man, slouches in
his Army uniform. A caduceus in the insignia daggered
through his jacket identifies him as a member of the
medical corps.

Orph gazes out the window, strumming a guitar, the
look in his eyes as haunted as the notes he plays.
This is the face of a kid who turned into a young man
before he knew it was happening.

An OLD LADY in a flowery dress sits knitting on the
other side of the aisle. With each chord Orph plays
she sucks her teeth and squints.

                    OLD LADY
     Young man! I say, young man.

Orph turns to glare at her. Without speaking, he
continues to strum the strings.

                    OLD LADY (CONT'D)
     Won't you stop that noise?

                    ORPH

What's the matter, don't you like it?

                  OLD LADY

I most certainly do not.

Bundling her knitting into a large carpetbag the
woman stands and bustles out of the carriage.

At the other end of the car a door opens and a
middle-aged SALESMAN - a little fat, a little bald -
comes limping down the aisle and sits directly across
from Orph. The Salesman fans himself with a newspaper
and puts his leather case on the neighboring seat.

                  SALESMAN

Good morning, good morning! Heavens to Betsy!
Am I glad to see someone else up this early!
Go West, young man, isn't that what they say,
but they never warn you how gosh darn hot West
is gonna be. Isn't that right, Corporal?

                    ORPH

     (shrugging)

I'm used to the heat.

The Salesman scratches his bare head. He seems
surprised to find it as bald as it is, and laughs.
He's a congenial fellow and looks as though he wishes
the young Corporal were a little friendlier.

                      63

SALESMAN

I bet you saw some things, didn't you, kid?
France? Germany?

ORPH

Far East. Saw more than I care to remember, if
it's all the same to you. Next time they go to
war they can recruit someone else.

SALESMAN

Course, some of us had to do our part from
here. Keep the home fires burning, as they
say.

Orph glares at the Salesman, seeing a man with a
paunch and a face that knows nothing of nightmare.

Strumming a series of pronounced, descending minor
chords, as if the music itself were a commentary on
the man, Orph raises an eyebrow.

SALESMAN (CONT'D)

Yes, sir, some of us weren't so lucky.

ORPH

You think going to war is lucky?

SALESMAN

Now listen here, friend, I only meant...

                    ORPH

What part did you play, friend? Selling Bibles
to old ladies? Faking a limp for the Draft
Board?

                    SALESMAN

Hey now, kid, there's no call for that. I'm no
shirker.

                    ORPH

And I ain't no kid.

The Salesman lifts the cuff of his trouser and reveals
a polished wooden leg. Embarrassed, Orph sits up a
little straighter, pushing the hat back on his head.

                ORPH (CONT'D)
Sorry, mister, I didn't realize.

                    SALESMAN

No harm done, Corporal. Truth is, I'm my own
best customer.

The Salesman flicks open the latches on his suitcase
to reveal an array of prosthetic arms and legs from
the Jenkins Artificial Limb Company.

                    ORPH

Dog bite you? Or was it a dame?

SALESMAN

Train accident. Almost twenty years ago. I
was only a kid, not much younger than you.
Turned me inside out. Though I'm sure that was
nothing to what you saw.

ORPH

Like I said, I saw plenty.

Orph stares out the window at the passing valley
floor, the scrub flats and tom-tom sun punctuated
by the rhythm of the train on its tracks. He keeps
strumming minor chords, stringing them together
without hitting a tune. The CONDUCTOR comes through
the car, shouting.

CONDUCTOR

Glendale, next stop Glendale. Last stop Los
Angeles Union Station in half an hour.

SALESMAN

This is where we part. Good luck to you, young
man.

The Salesman gathers his things and moves to go but
then pauses, steps back, and puts a brotherly hand on
Orph's shoulder.

SALESMAN (CONT'D)

A word of advice, if you'll indulge me. Try
to forget what you've seen, son. Look forward
to the future. Why, I bet you've got a pretty
little girl waiting for you right now. She'll

help you forget what you've seen. Trust her to
do that.

Orph gives him a half-ironic salute and pulls the cap
low over his eyes, gazing out the window as the train
slows into Glendale Station.

                    ORPH (V.O.)
I tell ya I coulda punched the guy. I'd seen
things I was never gonna forget, not if I had
to ride to hell and back. How can a man forget
dragging what's left of his best friend out of
a jungle only to lose him in a river? How can
a fellow forget holding the broken head of a
Virginia farm boy who talked every night to his
mother's photograph as if she was there in the
tent or the foxhole or wherever else we had to
put up to keep dry and away from the hot end
of a Japanese Arisaka. After all that death
and misery, the only thing I wanted was to come
home to my wife and a quiet life in the City of
Angels. Little did I know there was nothing quiet
about it. What a chump I was, what a sucker.

The train starts moving again as Orph's fingers thumb
the strings of his guitar.

INT. LOS ANGELES UNION STATION - DAY

A TALL BLONDE in a knockout suit and sunglasses that
cover the top half of her face stands waiting for a
train. She draws the eye of every man who crosses her
path, and makes other women ask their husbands why
they never get diamonds on birthdays.

As the train pulls into the station she checks her makeup in a compact. In a CLOSE UP on the mirror she sees the reflection of a THUG wearing a cheap dark suit and snap-brim hat standing behind her.

The blonde looks at the man's image in the mirror but snaps the compact shut just as a NEWSPAPER BOY lopes past. She taps the boy on the shoulder, buys a paper, and reads the headline:

DOZENS CUFFED IN MIDNIGHT RAIDS:
VICE SQUAD BUSTS GAMBLING DEN

Her eyes linger on the byline: NOAH ROY. Folding the paper under her arm, she glances up and waves as Orph drops from the train, kit bag slung over his shoulder. He looks ground down, spat out the wrong end of life.

When she sees him the blonde's hand drops to her side, fingers curling into a fist, nails digging into the flesh of her palm. As Orph walks towards her she relaxes again, waving at him. He sees her and starts running across the platform.

In her arms all the misery disappears from Orph's face. But the blonde stiffens when he raises a hand to stroke her hair.

WOMAN
I'm not a cat, Orph.

ORPH
Hey, what's the matter, sweetheart?

68

                    WOMAN

Why, nothing, darling, it's just that it's
been such a long time. I have to get used to
you again.

He pushes himself away, examines her flawless hair,
the line of her suit, and the gold watch on her
wrist.

                    ORPH

Hoo-wee, Ursula. You look -

But then he hesitates, shaking his head as he takes
in the full picture. Who is this woman? It isn't the
girl he remembers, not the one who kept him going
all though the war. Time and a life on her own have
turned URSULA PATTERSON into someone else.

                    URSULA

Flatter a girl why don't you?

                    ORPH

Of course you look beautiful. But if you
hadn't waved I might have passed you by.

                    URSULA

Don't let me stop you.

                    ORPH

You've been stopping me since I first laid
eyes on you, baby.

                              URSULA

Maybe you need a new engine.

                               ORPH

Maybe I don't wanna go.

                              URSULA

Maybe you don't know what's good for you.

                               ORPH

Maybe I like what's bad for me.

                              URSULA

Keep moving or die, I always say.

        (a pause)

Like a shark.

                               ORPH

Why the cold fish routine?

                              URSULA

A girl gets used to being on her own, swimming
in circles.

        (realizing she's gone too far)

I'm sorry, darling. You know it's good to have
you home.

Ursula embraces her husband but she's watching as another train pulls from the station. The reflection of the thug in the cheap dark suit is there once again, this time in the windows of the last car. He's shaking his head and wagging his finger at Ursula, as if chiding a naughty child.

                    ORPH (V.O.)

    Sure I was glad to see Ursula, but from
    the moment I put my arms around her I knew
    something had changed, and whatever she said
    it wasn't the truth. If I'd had any sense I
    should have caught the fastest train to the
    other side of the country. But not me. I just
    had to have the girl with the golden hair who
    twisted me through her braids like a moth in a
    web.

Slipping out of the vaulted station lobby under the bright blade of morning, they pass FIVE BLIND SINGERS harmonizing that old Gospel, 'I'll Never Turn Back No More'.

INT. URSULA'S APARTMENT - DAY

Ursula opens the door to an apartment high in a building overlooking Wilshire Boulevard and the Hollywood Hills. The living room is covered in plush brocade fabrics. It's a poor girl's idea of taste, which makes it look both expensive and cheap, like a high-class bordello or opium den but without the red lights or silk scarves draped over lamps.

                    ORPH (V.O.) (CONT'D)

It was only when I saw the place she'd rented
that I knew for sure something wasn't on the
level.

Ursula flicks open the curtains to give Orph a better
view of the room. He pushes the army cap back from
his head.

                         ORPH

Jeez, Ursula, how much <u>is</u> this joint?

                        URSULA

I'm the one worries about money these days.

                         ORPH

I don't get it, baby. First the clothes and
gold watch and now this flash-house. Explain
it to me because it ain't making sense.

                        URSULA

The truth is, Orph, I had to find work. Not
exactly riches you sent me.

                         ORPH

Now let's get one thing straight. I don't like
the idea of my girl working. We don't gotta
live like this. We're <u>simple</u> folks. We just
need a little place, no fancy stuff, no big
car, no diamonds, no nothing, just each other.
Come on, why don't you look at me like you
used to?

                          72

Ursula slides a cigarette from an engraved silver case, flares the end with a lighter, and stands smoking in the shafts of sunlight grating through the window. The line of her leg cuts in and out of shadow. Everything about her is combustible.

> URSULA
>
> Take it off the fire, Orph. It's all in the family. Jack gave me a job at Malavita.

> ORPH
>
> (teasing)
>
> Malavita? Sounds a little shady even for the Great Shade.

> URSULA
>
> Jack says it's Italian for the social set. High society.

> ORPH
>
> I know some Italian. That ain't what it means.

> URSULA
>
> Words mean a lot of things.

> ORPH
>
> In Italy it means the kind of business you wouldn't want to know about.

                    URSULA

Your brother does all kinds of business these
days. Some at the club, some not. Faye works
there, too... And if it's good enough for
Jack's wife, it must be good enough for yours.

                    ORPH

Twin waitresses. Customers must love that.

                    URSULA

I'm no waitress. Jack's letting me sing.

                    ORPH

Doesn't the husband get a say?

                    URSULA

You've been away, Orph. Times change.

                    ORPH

You sure ain't the Ursula I remember. What
gives, baby?

Ursula turns to stare out the window, fingering the
curtain as if she thinks someone might be watching.
Smoke twists above her head. Orph stares at the back
of her neck, at a small birthmark in the shape of an
oak leaf. He reaches out to touch her but she moves
closer to the window.

Outside, the same thug in the dark suit and snap-
brim hat who was at the station is leaning against a
lamppost. When he sees Ursula at the window he raises

                      74

his hand to wave. All of a sudden, she turns around
and rushes to Orph.

                    URSULA

Why don't we go away, get out of town for a
couple days, start over, begin like we've
never been apart all these years? I have
money, so if it's the cost you're thinking
about - well, don't. Consider it covered. Your
wife's worked <u>hard</u>, Orph.

                    ORPH

I didn't think I married a workingwoman.

                    URSULA

Don't be so <u>proud</u>! Now that you're back I'll
stop. You can get a job, a real job, and we'll
start a family. A boy and a girl. We'll find
a little place in Santa Monica with a view of
the ocean. I can bake cakes on the side, just
to keep myself in dresses. What do you say?

Orph holds her again, like he's beginning to feel
the woman he remembers come back to life. When he
grips her bare arms a little too hard she winces,
struggles, and he grips her harder. Her eyes flash
and she slaps him in the face.

                    ORPH

That's more like it. That's the Ursula I
remember. My beautiful little bear.

URSULA

I hate it when you call me that. Why you wanna
call me that? Just say we'll go away. I can't
tell you how I want to get out of here!

ORPH

So let's leave now! Anywhere you like!

Ursula fixes her eyes on his. He might be holding
her but there's no question that she's the one in
control.

URSULA

We can go up to the lake like we did when
we were kids. Rent one of those cabins, you
remember, cook on an open fire...

EXT. MOUNTAIN CAMPGROUND - DAY

A cabin in the Sierra Nevada Mountains, shingles and
eaves and gables bathed in sunrays cast through the
boughs of tall sugar pines.

Ursula and Orph are both in casual country clothes,
although Ursula looks as though her thoughts are
still pacing city sidewalks.

ORPH (V.O.)

It was okay at first, almost like old times,
the two of us laughing and cooking, singing
round the campfire. And then on the second
day, everything changed.

Leaning in the open door of the cabin, Orph strums
his guitar while Ursula, hair tied in a handkerchief,
makes up a picnic basket. There is wind in the trees,
breezes moving boughs so it sounds like a distant
waterfall. Ursula whistles along to the dark melody
Orph plays, a cowboy riff on 'I'll Never Turn Back No
More'.

                    ORPH

   See baby, we can still make music together,
   just like we always could.

Ursula stops whistling, looks at her husband, and
deliberately leaves one of the two sandwiches behind
on the counter.

EXT. MOUNTAIN LAKE - DAY

Orph and Ursula sit in a row boat in the middle of a
wide, clear lake, the shore dense with pine trees and
manzanita bushes. No one else is around, not on the
water, not on the shore.

The sun nakering against the water, Ursula fans
herself with a magazine. A woodpecker hammers
somewhere in the distance. Orph puts down the oars,
strips off his jacket, and rolls up his shirtsleeves
to reveal arms scarred by battle.

                    URSULA

   This'll do.

ORPH

Not too sunny?

URSULA

There are clouds over the valley.

Ursula begins to unpack the basket, handing Orph his
sandwich. He opens a couple bottles of beer.

ORPH

Ain't this nice?

URSULA

(flatly)

Just like a fairy tale. Only hotter.

ORPH

Come on, sweetheart, it was your idea to come
up here. Can't we be happy?

URSULA

How do you expect a girl to be happy when
everything's so second rate?

ORPH

I thought this was what you wanted. Why pick a
fight already?

                    URSULA

That's the problem with you: too much thinking
and not enough action.

Ursula takes off her blouse to reveal a white
sharkskin bathing suit. She tightens the handkerchief
holding her hair in place.

                     ORPH

Maybe you married the wrong guy.

                    URSULA

Not like I had much choice.

                     ORPH

There's nothing holding us now.

                    URSULA

Mother warned me about men like you.

                     ORPH

I've heard that one before.

                    URSULA

Maybe you don't want a woman after all.

                     ORPH

I just wanna be happy, baby. I've seen too
much death to stare it in the eyes every time
I look into yours.

Pretending to be shocked by his words, Ursula starts
to cry, turning her face away and gazing down into
the water.

CLOSE UP on the dark waters of the lake and Ursula's
reflection, hard and composed, staring at herself
with no trace of tears.

                    URSULA
    You'd be better off with someone else, a girl
    who knows how to make you happy. I'm cursed,
    Orph, snake-bitten.

Ursula raises her head and catches sight of something
behind her, in the line of Orph's vision.

                    ORPH
    What kind of crazy talk is that?

                    URSULA
    Turn the boat. I wanna go back.

Orph rows the boat around, and as he does, a MAN
begins shouting from the shore behind Orph's back.
It's too far for Orph to get a good view of the guy.

When Orph turns back to Ursula she only shrugs. He
puts down the oars and pivots all the way round in
the boat to look at the man.

                    ORPH
        (shouting)

    What? I can't hear you! Say again?

The man's cries become more panicked and urgent, but
his words remain unintelligible.

                  ORPH (CONT'D)
        (still shouting)

    Slow down. I can't hear you!

Stomping up and down at the shore, the man waves his
arms, shouting and pleading.

Orph turns around to pick up the oars, but when he
does, Ursula has vanished. He's alone in the boat.
Where is she? How could she just disappear? She must
be under the seat. No, she must be in the water...

He scans the surface of the lake but there's no sign
of her anywhere. The water is as still and unbroken
as a pane of glass.

                  ORPH (CONT'D)

    Ursula? Ursula! Where are you? Forgive me!
    URSULA!

Orph turns again and shouts to the man on the shore,
who starts to run into the woods.

                      81

ORPH (CONT'D)

Mister! Hey, mister! Call the police! Call an
ambulance! Help!

As the man disappears into the trees, Orph thinks
he sees the flash of another person. He squints but
can't be sure. It's too far away. The sun shimmering
off the lake is too bright, the forest too dark.

In a panic, Orph begins rowing back to shore, looking
across the water and searching for Ursula.

ORPH (V.O.)

A guy with any sense would have got the
message, rowed home, and started a new life
after whatever statutory period had to pass in
the state of California. Any other dope would
have found an average-looking girl with average
tastes and no interest in the high life. He'd
have taken her somewhere quiet and simple away
from this paradise hell. But not me. No sir, I
was just too dumb to read the smoke signals.

EXT. MOUNTAIN LAKE - LATER

As the afternoon wanes, Orph stands near the
lakeshore with the SHERIFF and his DEPUTIES. Behind
them, DIVERS slip into the water.

SHERIFF

Mean to tell me she just vanished when your
back was turned and you didn't hear a thing,
Corporal?

                    ORPH

I wouldn't lie to you, Sheriff. The man was
shouting -

                    SHERIFF

And who was this fellow?

                    ORPH

That's just the thing, I don't know - he was
so far away I couldn't see.

                    SHERIFF

And you say he just ran off into the forest?

                    ORPH

Like he was trying to get away from something.

                    SHERIFF

And by that time your wife was gone, into thin
air.

                    ORPH

Into clear water more like. I turned around
and she had vanished.

EXT. MOUNTAIN LAKE - NIGHT

Floodlights have been rolled in to illuminate the
dark lake. The Sheriff and Orph look on as the divers
come out of the water, dripping with fatigue.

                    SHERIFF

No sign of her?

                    DIVER

Not a trace, Sheriff. We've been all over the
bottom and there's nothing but fish.

                    ORPH

She's gotta be there!

The Sheriff wipes his brow.

                    SHERIFF

Listen, Corporal. Any chance you've made up
this fairy tale?

                    ORPH

No! It's just like I said! My wife –

                    SHERIFF

Here's what I suggest, kid. Put yourself in
your wife's car and drive back to Los Angeles.
We'll dredge the lake again after daybreak,
but if my boys say there's nothing there, then
there's nothing there. I reckon your wife swam
to shore and ran off with some fellow who's a
little less highly strung.

EXT. FREEWAY - NIGHT

Orph drives the winding expressway through the Tejon
Pass, his face screwed up with confusion.

                        84

ORPH (V.O.)

I didn't know what to do at first and kept
thinking of how quiet it was when she
vanished, except for that man shouting on
the shore, and my own voice like gunfire, but
otherwise silent - no breeze, no birds, no
sound of water or wind or the world turning
fast in its infernal orbit. And then I started
thinking how Ursula wasn't the first person
I'd lost, how there was my best friend, and
that farm boy from Virginia, all of them gone
because of something I'd done. Sure I was
dumb, I was dumb in love with a girl who'd
tried to tell me she was poison but I just
wouldn't listen. The simple truth was, I got
the bad sister and my brother got the good.

EXT. MALAVITA CLUB - DAY

Orph parks Ursula's white convertible coupe in the
lot behind the Malavita Club on Sunset Boulevard.
It's mid-morning and the sun is a white-hot poker
that has melted and spread itself across the sky so
even the streets seem to be sweating.

ORPH (V.O.) (CONT'D)

Next morning, I went looking for the only
family I had left in the world. Jack and I
had the same mother but different fathers.
His old man did a runner and left our mother
broke in a seedy little town south of Santa
Cruz. She found my father just in time to pick
her up and dry her off. Nine months later I
showed up. Then my old man did a runner, too,

85

and Jack's been looking after me ever since,
making sure I don't fall down the same wet
hole our mother was in.

INT. MALAVITA CLUB - DAY

Malavita is a playground of drink and decadence where
dinners cost fifty bucks a head and men upstairs lose
more in a night of poker and blackjack than most
people make in five years of hard graft.

Orph weaves through the club's back rooms. He finds
his way to the stage and peeks out from the wings as
the FURY GIRLS rehearse 'I Hate to Lose You' with the
BAND. The piano player, MODEST JONES, keeps hitting
bum notes.

JACK 'SHADE' PLUTONE and FAYE PLUTONE, Ursula's twin
sister, sit in a deep booth at the edge of the dance
floor.

                    SHADE

   No, no, no! You're late again, Jones!

                    MODEST

   They sing too fast, boss!

The three Fury Girls protest.

                    SHADE

   Get off the gin, Jones! Start again at the
   second verse.

From his place in the wings Orph catches sight of
Faye, glowing next to Shade. She's a dead ringer for
Ursula and Orph has to look twice.

When the song is over, Orph slips onto the stage,
crosses the dance floor, and joins Jack and Faye at
their booth.

> SHADE

Look who it is! My kid brother, back from the
dead!

> ORPH

Just call me Little Lazarus.

> SHADE

Take a break, Modest, and learn to count!

Modest Jones slumps against the piano keys while the
Fury Girls retire to the wings.

As Faye puts out her cigarette and lights another,
she eyes Orph suspiciously.

> FAYE
> (chilly)

Where you been keeping my sister?

> ORPH

Thought maybe you could tell me.

FAYE

I'm sure I don't follow.

ORPH

We went up to the mountains and... I don't
know how to put it. She disappeared. I thought
I might find her here.

SHADE

Disappeared how, kid?

ORPH

We were out on the lake, and the next thing I
know, she's not in the boat.

Faye looks alarmed, stiffening her back and putting a
hand to her mouth.

FAYE

What've you done to her?

ORPH

Now hold on a minute, sister!

Orph sits, shoving in beside Faye so she's trapped
between the two men, one side of her face deep in
shadow, the other caught by the hard glare of a
spotlight.

FAYE

Turn that darn thing off me!

The spotlight swerves away and dims, leaving the trio
gazing at one another in the dim glow of the table
lamp.

                    ORPH

     I didn't do nothing to Ursula. There was a man
     on the shore and I like that she ran off with
     him.

                    SHADE

     And you thought us two might know something?

                    ORPH

     If you don't know then I can't guess who
     would. The police say there's no - I'm sorry,
     Faye, but there isn't a body, so there can't
     be a crime. I just know something's not right.

Faye turns away from Orph, pulling a handkerchief
from her pocket and raising it to her mouth. She does
a pantomime of mopping invisible tears. It smells
like bad acting.

                    SHADE

     She'll turn up. Bound to be here somewhere.
     How you fixed for work, Orph?

                    ORPH

     Truth is, I'm not.

                    SHADE

But you're still the little brother who could
play birds from the trees, ain't you? Don't
tell me a few years overseas rusted them
fingers solid?

                    ORPH

If you're asking can I still play piano the
answer is yes.

                    SHADE

Modest!

                    MODEST

Boss?

                    SHADE

You're fired.

Modest Jones slams down the piano lid and storms off
through the wings, bumping into the Fury Girls.

                    ORPH

Thanks, Jack, but I didn't mean -

                    SHADE

You know me, I like to keep things in the
family.

                    ORPH

What about Ursula?

SHADE

Maybe Faye can help out. What do you say,
doll?

FAYE

What could I possibly do?

SHADE

Show our boy around. You know where Ursula
lurks.

FAYE

But, Jack, I just don't see –

SHADE

If I say show him around then show him around.

ORPH

Thanks, Jack. I promise –

SHADE

Didn't I swear when we were kids I'd always
look after you? I swore it again the day the
four of us got married. I swore it when your
pops disappeared and I swore it when our
mother died. We're in this together, kid,
until one of us checks out, and you can bet
that if I go first I'll be looking after you
from the great beyond, whether it's above or
below, and if you go first I'll be praying
every day for your eternal salvation and
giving money to the church to intervene on

behalf of your immortal soul. So go find your
wife. I didn't want to say it, but Faye can
tell you, Ursula was mixed up in some things.
Nothing serious, but we'll shake down a few
people and see how the cards lay when they
fall. Now get up there and play.

Orph slides from the booth to take his place at the
piano. When his fingers start hitting the keys it
sounds like the job he was born to do. With every
note we see a different Orph coming into focus:
confident, serious, and happy.

                    ORPH (V.O.)

It was good to be in front of a piano again,
even better to see my brother, the big man,
looking bigger than ever. I wanted to stay in
his pocket for as long as I could. But I was
sure Faye knew exactly where her sister was
and it was only a matter of time before she
let slip that the deck was stacked and I was
the chump being taken for the last cent he
had.

INT. MALAVITA CLUB - NIGHT

An evening performance at Malavita is in full swing,
the Fury Girls singing 'I Hate to Lose You' as
Orph, in a dark suit, plays piano. At the end of the
number, the Fury Girls exit backstage and Orph begins
playing 'Crazy He Calls Me'. Faye, in a shimmering
black gown, appears from behind a screen at the rear
of the stage.

She sings as though she's making love to the
audience. Then, towards the end of the number, she
turns her attention to Orph, addressing the last
lines of the song to him rather than all those well-
dressed people clustered at tables in the dark.

The notes are a silk stocking unrolled down a perfect
leg, the curve of hips under a satin negligee, the
taste of lips like ripe apricots. Orph is under her
spell, swooning as he plays.

Shade, near the back of the room, seems to notice. He
leans over to whisper to one of his bouncers, EDDIE
MAJESTIC.

CLOSE UP on Eddie, nodding and staring at Orph. We
recognize him as the thug who was lingering at the
train station when Orph arrived back in town. We
might even recognize him as the man from the lake,
but it's too early to be sure.

As Faye and Orph reach the end of the number she keeps
her eyes locked on his, turning him over in the music.

                    ORPH (V.O.) (CONT'D)
    When Faye sang that night it was better than
    any music Ursula and I ever made together. It
    was poetry, love under moonlight, enough to
    make me feel like I didn't care whether I ever
    found Ursula again if I could only have Faye,
    the twin I'd loved from the very beginning. I
    knew she was working me, and part of me liked
    it. I couldn't help myself, not anymore, and
    with Ursula out of the way...

                        93

INT. URSULA'S APARTMENT - NIGHT

Orph, exhausted, opens the door of Ursula's Wilshire
apartment. He pours himself two fingers of bourbon
and knocks it back like it's lemonade - a little bee
sting in the throat but not enough to slow him down.

He pours another, then opens the curtains and pulls
up the venetian blinds to look out on the lights of
the city against its black patent sky.

                    ORPH (V.O.) (CONT'D)
     Even still, I couldn't help wondering where
     Ursula was, if she was at the bottom of that
     lake or here, lost in these streets. There was
     nothing I could do that night but hope she was
     alive, and if she wasn't, hope that wherever
     she might be it wasn't too hot.

INT. URSULA'S APARTMENT - NEXT MORNING

Orph wakes on the couch, the bottle of bourbon more
than half empty on the floor. He reaches for the phone.

                    ORPH
     Operator? Get me the Fresno County Sheriff's
     department. ... Hello, Sheriff? It's Corporal
     Patterson, I...

                    SHERIFF (O.S.)
     I'm sorry, Corporal, but there's no trace of
     your wife.

                    ORPH

But did you - ?

                    SHERIFF (O.S.)

Yes, we dredged the lake again.

                    ORPH

And in the woods? No sign of her anywhere?

                    SHERIFF (O.S.)

If you still want to file a missing person's
report then I'll go ahead and do it, but
frankly, it's not the first time I've seen
this. Fella comes back from the war and the
wife's moved on. It's a tough steak but chew
on this: she's got another beau. Either find
her and fight for the dame or quit while you
can.

Orph slams down the phone, catches up a framed
photograph of Ursula, and smashes it against the
corner of the table. The glass shatters, but the
photo remains intact, unblemished.

A knock at the door pulls Orph out of himself. He
places the portrait with its broken glass back on the
table and goes to answer. Faye is standing in the
hallway, as glamorous in her hat and suit as Ursula
was in the photo.

                    FAYE

You look like you've been to the bottom of the
river and forgot to hold your breath.

                    95

ORPH

Want a drink?

FAYE

It's a little early, Corporal, even for me,
but I can make you something that'll put the
dog back in its kennel. Where's the kitchen?

ORPH

Haven't you been here before?

FAYE

Ursula only just - I mean she wasn't here very
long. I didn't have a chance to see it.

ORPH

Through there.

He points to a hallway off the living room and his
eyes follow her, checking what he's just seen against
the photograph on the end table. Carbon copies of
each other, so uncanny he has to shake his head.

ORPH (CONT'D)

Not sure you'll find much. Ursula seemed to
live on air and I haven't had a minute to get
in anything else but booze.

FAYE (O.S.)

(brightly)

We've got eggs, bread, tomato juice, and if you
bring the vodka and Worcester sauce I'll set you
upright so the two of us can hit the streets.

INT. URSULA'S KITCHEN - DAY

Orph sits at the table eating a plate of eggs and
toast and drinking an extra-large Bloody Mary swirled
with a celery stick.

FAYE

Ursula and I weren't speaking much in the last
few weeks. I don't know what was going on. Some
problem she wouldn't tell me about. She knew she
could come to me but it was like we were strangers
for the first time in our lives. I really felt she
was keeping something from me, Orph.

ORPH

Was she in trouble?

FAYE

(hesitating)

I wish I knew. She'd become so mysterious.
Every time I asked what was wrong she'd almost
bite my head off. She wasn't the Ursula I
knew. It was as though she'd been replaced by
somebody else.

~

Internal Memo

April 4, 1950

To: John Marsh and Desmond Frank
CC: Leo Krug

From: Porter Cherry

Gentlemen, have you seen yesterday's <u>Times</u>? I refer
to the case of the gentleman who disappeared from his
boat off Catalina, and who, as you may remember, was
convicted of treason, had his American citizenship
revoked, and was sentenced to prison for aiding a
Nazi fugitive.

I do not suggest that there is any serious similarity
between the boat disappearance in SHE TURNED AWAY
and this recent affair, but I do think that, given
the circumstances and the importance of German
markets (you will remember that the apparent suicide
was a German national) we consider eliminating
any unintentional suggestion that the film is a
commentary on such disappearances that might be
misinterpreted as supporting the vigilante or
extrajudicial punishment of America's former enemies,
or of appearing to take undue pleasure in their
demise. I would appreciate your consideration of this
matter.

Also, it has come to my attention that you have not
yet corrected two points in particular that Mr.
Breen has identified as potentially standing in the
way of approval. I must insist that you eliminate
any and all suggestion, however arcane, that Ursula
Patterson is a prostitute, or that her Wilshire
Boulevard apartment is somehow connected to the
taking or distribution of narcotics. A great many

people no doubt will see nothing sinister in your underworld slang, but those who do recognize it will, as Mr. Breen has rightly noted, find nothing but encouragement and glamorization of that particularly odious lifestyle.

Yours truly,
Porter Cherry

Internal Memo

April 5, 1950

To: Porter Cherry
CC: Leo Krug

From: John Marsh and Desmond Frank

Porter -

We have taken into consideration your concerns. We
find them unwarranted and are not minded to make any
further alteration to a script that has already had
more than its share of amendment, emendation, and
modification, at the expense of narrative coherence
and character plausibility, which we are still,
in this very late stage, trying to correct while
already in the middle of production. Only if Breen
himself insists on a change in relation to the boat
disappearance - which as you no doubt remember has
already been filmed on location at considerable
expense - are we prepared to consider further
adaptation. As for the language about whores and
junk, that can always be fixed in the rerecording
process once shooting has finished.

Sincerely,
John and Desmond

3

From my bed I can look across the piazza to the church of Santa Maria del Carmine, its modest façade such an unlikely mask for the splendors of the Brancacci Chapel. In the fresco depicting the payment of the tribute money, Masaccio's portrait of the Apostle John with his bronze skin, soft curls of golden hair, and penetrating whiteness of the eyes, reminds me of you in your youth, Myles. A trembling old man, I go there often to stare at that image, remembering the way you used to gaze at me with a reverence and adoration I hope I deserved. In looking at that portrait, I imagine the possibility that you are aware of me looking now, that the painting opens a portal through which we can regard each other as we were when still young.

Outside, a group of schoolboys is shouting as they cross the piazza on their way to the Liceo Niccolò Machiavelli a few streets away. I cannot help being amused by the idea of children studying in a shrine to the prophet of state scheming and duplicitousness, mastering the arts of intrigue and expediency. In this season of crisis in Italy, with no government and no pope, one feels that all the fathers have abandoned us by our own volition. I find graffiti that broadcasts the anarchic will of the people, or is it rather the symptom of panicked despair? *Contro lo stato dei padroni,* they scrawl, or *Un giorno senza papa, senza governo, senza capo della polizia* slashed in black marker on Renaissance walls. And yet those boys, my Machiavellian acolytes (I imagine they must be the authors of such proclamations, they or their older siblings, mothers or fathers), with the sound of their carefree shouting and laughter, their slouching slenderness and casual affection with one another, their facility with the easy platonic touch, make me think how you and I never managed to live in the world with a comparable sense of freedom. We were too conscious of letting the truth become visible, fearing how the legibility of that truth would imperil us. For the whole of my American life after I began to understand what I was, who I desired, since our country chose to make that desire the sign of my entire identity although I would have preferred to think it only one facet, I never shouted for fear my voice would betray me, become histrionic and feminine, as if either of those qualities were bad, as if either were the mark of attraction to a body as male as my own. We never even risked traveling in those early circles of liberation, the Communists who became Mattachines before the Mattachines decided associations with Communism might imperil the struggle for gay liberation. Letting ourselves be known as ourselves outside our most intimate friendships seemed unduly reckless, a risk not worth taking, even as others dared to be more open. In public you and I made ourselves as little like women as we could in hopes of convincing everyone – men and women alike – that women were the sole focus of our desires. Be unfeminine to suggest exclusive adoration of the feminine. Be masculine to suggest total erotic and affective abhorrence of the masculine. The same for Helen, for Barbara: an exaggerated femininity as denial of attraction to the same, they refused every trope of the masculine lesbian, dared not even wear a violet or an item of clothing with a pattern of violets because Barbara had once heard that flower was an unmistakable sign. It is perverse, this logic of opposed dualities, grotesque how it made us disfigure the ways we inhabited ourselves. Think what we might have been had we lived in a place and time that allowed us freedom to be a man and sound womanly, to proclaim and ring histrionic, to be male and female and both all at once.

At the moment I try to recall the hours of that day when I last stood in your presence I find the memories evaporating, the effort of recollection forcing memory beyond the reaches of consciousness, and so I have to wait at my window, allowing my mind to refocus on those roving adolescents framed by the piazza and blind to their place in history, thinking their discovery of anarchy, or for some their espousal of fascism, an entirely new historical occurrence. So I sit hoping that the ghostly flash of memory will explode out of darkness and return you to me, the memory of you a specter even if you and I are not yet specters ourselves. Nothing but fear prevents me from asking Alessio to book a flight, drive me to the airport, accompany me across the Atlantic, traverse the continent of North America, a ghost pursuing a ghost. When memories of you – of that day, of the day I am trying to reconstruct – happen to flash out of the dark room of my unconscious, I recognize them as mere fragments of the experiences they encode, which can never be made whole again, never lived fleshly, never bringing me and you together as we once were, and too often they are interrupted by involuntary memories triggered by the chance encounter with a texture, an object, a flavor, or odor. The juice of blood oranges pooling on a white china plate recalls from obscurity a moment I was shaving at the sink in your bathroom and nicked my chin, a drop of blood streaking the porcelain, you lying naked, visible in the mirror, a script propped on your abdomen, the static of some disagreement scorching the air between us, and the memory of feeling I was justified, that you were wrong and failing to see a point I believed to be logical. I do not search for these involuntary memories of discord and still they develop in all their painful granularity, sometimes more distinctly than those happier ones I wish to recall, but which seem always to evade me.

You know what is required to stitch together the fragments of memory that explode between the closing and opening of the mind's shutter. You know what acts of imagination and inference. So if I err, if your fragments of that day are not synchronous with or duplicates of mine, I can only beg forgiveness and forbearance. Everything I say here is an attempt to remember you in your fullness, in the moments before you were shattered irrevocably in your own person, shattered irremediably into shards of my own vanishing memory.

Before I went to meet you at the soundstage, I picked up the duplicated pages of the rewritten scenes and glanced over the stack of correspondence John and I had recently exchanged with Porter. I ought to have left then, without saying goodbye. There was nothing keeping me at the studio except the desire to see finished what I had started, and the hope that the lunch to which I had been summoned might result in a reprieve which would allow me to prolong my life with you. That hope, however misplaced, kept me from telling you sooner. If there was to be no bad news to hear, Myles, better to keep it to myself. You will say again, rightly, that I was withholding knowledge from you, but I feared even on our last day together that the innocence you wore with such lightness might darken and vanish at the first sign of trouble. I wanted to preserve who you were, to keep you young and unblemished.

If I had been less selfish in my desires, perhaps that day would not have ended as it did.

From the Writers' Building I went to the soundstage, determined to spend every minute I could in your presence, watching you even if we could not touch or talk, but when I arrived you were not there and the stage was in chaos. Mary stood in the doorway of her dressing room shouting, demanding to know if anyone had seen her assistant, Mozelle. People froze at the sound of her voice. The electricians and grips, the special effects men, the makeup artists and wardrobe staff and stage guard, the sound boys and camera crew, all stopped what they were doing and looked at her. Then, just as quickly, they turned away again. To be caught in the beam of Mary's gaze was to risk becoming the object of her anger.

Someone get that girl on the phone and tell her if she's not here in five minutes she's fired, Mary shouted, slamming the door so hard the whole dressing room shook. People looked at one another but no one moved until John stood up from his chair and strode across the stage, opened Mary's door, walked in, and swung it closed behind him. It was a sad performance of authority. The gaffer and best boy went back to adjusting the lights for the first set-up while the director of photography chewed orders to the camera operator. I was trying to look nonchalant, as if my attention was actually focussed on the pages in my hands, but I must have been doing a poor job because Nick Charles came up behind me and sneered, You look like you got left at the altar, Mr. Frank. Have you seen Mr. Haywood? He's keeping us waiting.

The remark was so pointed it made me wonder if Nick knew about us. Perhaps he only recognized my fixation on you and nothing else, but his words brought me out in a sweat. I was about to claim ignorance when Mary's dressing room door opened again and she stormed out with the latest issue of *Vogue* in one hand and her ugly acrylic purse in the other. She veered to walk right past me, offering the same sidelong look of suspicion worn by the *Vogue* cover model, glowering through a black mesh veil. A light swung around, shining in my face, and when I looked away towards the door I noticed Nick at the telephone, cupping his hand around the

105

receiver as if trying to keep from being overheard. After a moment he noticed I was watching and hung up, shooting me a look before following Mary out the stage door.

Because you still had not arrived I began to panic, imagining you might be in the arms of some other man, younger and more beautiful than me. Even though I claim to have trusted you completely, I ran back to the Star Suites where I had to stand in the hallway collecting myself before I knocked. You answered with such an expression of relief that I hugged you and kissed you while I was still only halfway through the door. You'll get me in trouble, you said, kicking it closed. I kissed you, sucking your bottom lip between my teeth as you pushed your hips against mine. If I had tried to speak I would have cried with relief, knowing that I could trust you even as I was betraying your trust.

The phone rang and when you reached to pick it up I pulled your hand away.

Mr. Marsh will be furious.

He's just plain old John to you. Let it ring.

You protested that he was older and deserved your respect.

Walk with the weight of your stature, I said.

What does that mean, you asked, reaching to pull the cord that would close the blinds more tightly than they already were.

No one can see, not even shapes, not without X-ray vision, I said, and you're the only superman I know.

The phone had stopped ringing. I was on the verge of admitting I had already bought a ticket to New York but when I looked into your eyes they were a barricade to confession, your body both detour and destination, and I could not find my way past your chest and arms back to my first intention. I held onto you in hopes that the feeling between us would erase all the pain that was pending.

When the knock came we both jumped. Whoever it was knocked again but after a few seconds gave up and went back downstairs just as the phone rang once more. You reached for it and I slapped your hand. Then there was another knock, lighter than the first, and Helen whispering *Myles, Myles,* from the other side. I stood and opened the door. It wasn't locked. What a risk we had taken. Helen looked at me, looked at you, and smirked. You boys better get straight, there's a hunt on.

The image of your body – the image that *was* your body, your body that was also, I admit, only ever an image to me, lingering in my mind whenever I left you, the image in the flesh – was fixed in my mind as Helen and I walked downstairs while you finished getting ready. I held your image as I suspect others held you, still hold you now, and not just those who knew the feeling of your skin, its perfumes, the touch of your tongue against their own. Your gaze changed me, as mine changes everything I look upon. You changed me each time you looked at me, Myles, as I hope I changed you.

On the street outside we ran into John, who looked more frantic than I had ever seen him, his face pale and fixed. After Helen parted from us, he took me by the arm and asked if I knew where you were. I nodded towards the window of your suite.

I've been phoning Myles for the better part of an hour. Is he having another neurotic attack?

I lied and told him your phone hadn't rung all morning. Then I lied again and said everything was fine, nothing was amiss, you'd just been delayed at makeup. Have you spoken to Mary yet?

John shook his head and looked past me, towards the window of Mary's own suite.

You act as though you're afraid of her, John.

Maybe I am, he said, squinting into the sun.

In that case there's no better solution than to speak with her directly, without delay. I'll come with you, I offered, even though I suspected my presence would do nothing to change Mary's mind.

When John tried the door to Mary's suite he found it unlocked. The room was as neat as if no one had been there for days, the beige carpet unmarked, pink cushions on the couch fresh and plump, the Cecil Beaton portrait of Mary in a pastel blue gown staring imperiously at us from the opposite wall. John picked up the telephone receiver and shook his head.

Still warm. We must have just missed her.

I could imagine Mary on the chair by the telephone, speaking to men in snap-brim hats. I had started thinking of them as Agents Leopold and Loeb, boys from good families who destroyed innocent lives for sport. Like those murderous lovers, the agents who had been trailing me were always well dressed, rather epicene, their movements marked by the same furtiveness I recognized in men of our kind. Perhaps it had more to do with Hitchcock's *Rope* than anything else. I remember thinking it had either been very clever or very cruel to cast a couple of closeted actors in a film about closeted lovers.

There was no sign of Mary's acrylic purse or platinum mink, no impression of an earlier note torn from the phone jotter, which John held up to the light, tilting it this way and that as if he were a detective. We were about to leave when a sound came from the bathroom. Mary? Is that you? John called.

It's only me, Mr. Marsh, and then Mary's assistant, Mozelle, appeared in the black-and-white maid's uniform Mary insisted she wear, as if she were perpetually playing Lottie in *Mildred Pierce*. Your wife left a while ago, she said, standing in the door of the bathroom. John asked if she knew where Mary was but Mozelle shook her head. Mrs. Marsh doesn't tell me anything she thinks I don't need to know. Never mind she expects me to prophesy her heart's desire before she knows it herself. But I expect I don't have to tell you that, Mr. Marsh. You least of all.

You shouldn't talk about Mary in such a tone.

Would you fire me for speaking the truth?

What's your game, Mozelle?

No game. I'm a friend. Then Mozelle lifted a scarf from the back of a chair, drew it across her mouth, dropped her voice, changed its sex, race, and age, so that when she next spoke she sounded uncannily like me. *A very good friend of yours, Mr. Marsh. I would have told you sooner if I'd known.*

John crossed his arms over his chest. One of his hands was shaking. It was you on the phone. I never took you for a troublemaker.

I'd have to be pretty senseless to make trouble, she said, dropping the scarf and letting her voice return to its natural register.

What proof do you have?

I walked in yesterday and heard it all myself. You'll just have to believe me. Sorry, I didn't have my Dictaphone.

I find it hard to believe Mary would do this behind my back.

Your wife is not a well woman, Mr. Marsh. You have to understand, she thinks her whole life is a motion picture. Some days she's in a romance, other days it's historical drama. This week, it's spies.

What are you saying?

She'll say anything to those men tomorrow, no matter if it's true or not, because it'll come into her mind as dialogue for the role she thinks she's playing. Spies. Fifth columnists. 'Red fascists.' She has it all on her tongue, ready to convince those men she's whiter than white.

Sickness of the times, I said, pulling apart the blinds to look out onto the street. John glanced at me as if he had forgotten I was in the room.

Especially in this town, Mr. Frank. It's a terminal case.

You should be in New York, Mozelle. Better opportunities for someone like you.

Someone like *me*, Mr. Marsh?

A smart colored girl—

Is that all you see?

John blushed. What I mean is, I don't understand why you thought Los Angeles would be better than wherever you started out.

Mozelle sat down, slapping her legs. I came to be in the pictures! Like every other fool in this town who ends up washing cars or waiting tables.

Could it be you just gave up too soon?

Gave up? I didn't give up. But I can't sing, I can't dance, and I'm not funny. I thought I'd be a real actress, but do you think there are serious parts for *someone like me*, as you put it? Not a chance. I'd leave this town today if I knew I'd find something better, but it's a risk I can't afford.

Maybe you didn't talk to the right people.

So give me a part in your picture, Mr. Marsh. Put me in the background. Make a black woman the goddess from the machine. I read that script of yours, Mr. Frank, and the plot makes no sense. You need a solution. Let me provide it. It would be easy to do. Even people like me go to nightclubs. I could be the gangster's moll who tips off the cops.

No, John said, I know what Mary would say.

And shouldn't that tell you something about your wife, Mr. Marsh?

You look as if you pity me, Mozelle.

That's because I don't believe there's anything wrong in having a different idea about how this country might be run.

I'm no Communist, John said.

I never said you were, Mr. Marsh, but there's no law against being one, is there? I didn't mean to offend you.

The three of us sat there for a moment in silence, the sounds of studio life reaching us muted, at a distance, and I thought how different this conversation might have been if we could have had it in a version of America where John and Mozelle and I could sit as equals at the same table. I would like to believe such an America remains possible, somewhere, but it certainly was not in the studio, not on that day in 1950, not with a man like John who could never overcome the bias imprinted on his thinking. I don't mean to suggest he was a bad man, you understand, but one who could not escape the conditioning of the place where he had come from or the family who raised him.

I'm sorry I can't do more for you, Mozelle, he said.

I was surprised to hear John sound so genuinely sorry, as if he were repenting not only for his missteps over the past few minutes, but for anything he might have done wrong in all the time he had known Mozelle, even for everything Mary had ever done, for what his ancestors had done and what Mary's own people might have done, what all the white people of America had done, for all that we were still doing and would keep on doing.

Today, though, I wonder whether those layers of regret and intent were only in my head.

Thank you, Mr. Marsh. May I say one last thing?

I expect you can say whatever you like.

Your wife's just a decoy. She's flushing you out so the hunters can get a clean shot.

As we walked back to your suite, I could see how unsettled John was, and how eager he remained to dismiss Mozelle's warning as troublemaking, but I told him I thought she was telling the truth. Given what's at stake it would be foolish to doubt her, I said. She's trusting you to understand the gravity of the situation and not do what ordinary circumstances might demand.

Everyone's turning on me, John grumbled.

That's right. Even me, I said, hearing my impatience with him, and then I admitted that I had been with you, told John how we had ignored the ringing phone. I could see how my confession affected him: triple-x *Kopfkino*, double feature, banned in every country on earth and nothing like the truth of that sweet quarter hour you and I spent alone. But I could not yet tell John why it would have been unbearable to let the ringing phone derail our lovemaking, I could not yet tell him I was counting down the hours left to me in your presence just as I could not yet tell you.

When we first met, Desmond, I never would have guessed about you.

That's because I'm no different from anyone else, I said. Though of course I was different, as you were, Myles, but because we policed every aspect of our behavior, never letting our laughter get out of control, never crossing our legs at the knee, never holding our hands palms outward to examine our nails, never dressing with too much extravagance, most people would not have guessed what we were. We knew how to hide in plain sight. I'm no different from you, John.

The suggestion seemed to disturb him and he staggered as you opened the door. I was struck by your strength, how you helped him down onto the sofa where you and I had so recently been entwined. I knew John had tolerated knowing what I was, what you were, only because he did not have to imagine precisely what this meant. So long as what we did failed to impress itself on John's imagination and he did not have to envision the way his own body might perform the same acts we enjoyed, he could tolerate us, tolerance being but a distant cousin of acceptance.

Perhaps if you had not poured John that glass of water and dropped in a couple of bromide tablets or doubled the dose when John twitched his finger to ask for more, the day would not have unfolded as it did. Perhaps if John had not chased the bromide with a double bourbon from your bar cart, a solution would have presented itself and you and I could have gone on living our secret life until secrecy was no longer required of men like us.

But that is all speculation. Nothing you or I did that day would have changed the next decade of American politics, and that I cannot allow myself to forget. In the absence of the personal, there was always the political.

John whimpered, wiping his brow. I think I ate something last night. We went to Don the Beachcomber and Mary insisted on a table in the Cannibal Room. I had too many Zombies on top of the mandarin duck. It was gruesome.

John swallowed the bourbon in one and you poured him another, which he drank so quickly he almost choked. Some days the world has too much clarity and it's easier not to see everything in such sharp focus. Get a filter, smear petroleum jelly on the lens, bring in the smoke machine and dim the lights. Betrayal looks better with atmosphere. John stared meaningfully at the bourbon and you poured him a third. He was drinking like he could already see himself testifying before Congress, walking a tightrope between spilling his guts and betraying his friends, or, if he took the moral high ground, condemning himself to prison.

I told him he had nothing to worry about. You're as political as paste, John.

If Mary talks, I don't think it matters that I only went to meetings and signed a few letters. She'll blab about us all and then the pink slips will come and they'll haul us before the House Committee and ask the same questions they asked Trumbo and the others and we'll feel just as cornered and angry and stubborn as they did.

Although one could invoke the Fifth Amendment, it was my contention that this just made a person look guilty. The only conscionable choice was to plead the First, to insist that being a member of the Communist Party was the very definition of freedom of speech. Perhaps I said as much then. How easy to claim bravery when one's bags are packed. In my mind I was already on the plane, it had already touched down in Shannon and then again in London, I was already crossing the Channel, already in the pied-à-terre in Paris, already at home in my mother's family villa outside of Florence or their apartment in Rome. How little I had to fear given the comforts my parents could provide.

Even if you get summoned, John, and even if you refuse to name names, as you certainly should, and even if they find you in contempt of Congress as they have the others, and there's no guarantee that they will if scores of us are resisting, then you can still drag it through the courts. You can always appeal.

In truth, I knew that I could never manage to sustain such a battle myself. The fight would kill me. I would never be able to write again without imagining philistines in bad suits reading my words and seeing political intent where there might be nothing of the kind, or seeing the politics only and failing to see everything else.

It's all gone to hell, John said. He poured himself a glass of water and took another two bromide tablets.

Go easy, buddy.

It only works for me in high doses. I've got a bitter taste in my mouth. It's been there all morning. My wife – John sniffed the air and swayed where he sat. I'm getting the vapors. He squinted at me as if trying to pull my profile into focus. Please help me, Desmond, you're my best friend.

You too, John.

While it is true that for several years I had thought of John as one of my closest friends and colleagues, the only straight man I could trust with my secrets, I had never quite thought of him as my best friend because I loved you and Helen too much to consider anyone else could be closer. It was surprising to hear John describe me in this way, and yet what could I do but agree? When I said that, I wonder if you felt I betrayed you, or that I was suggesting love and friendship were mutually exclusive orders of sentiment, that you could be my lover but not my friend. I propose this might have been the case because of what you did next, something that struck me as so incredible at the time I wondered if I was hallucinating. You leaned over from the chair where you were sitting and opened my mouth with your lips, slipped the tip of your tongue inside, and flickered it against mine as John watched, red-faced. He looked away but when we kept kissing his gaze returned to us. We were conscious of him watching but continued, open-mouthed and gentle. I wondered if John had ever kissed Mary in that way. He always struck me as a prude, but then he shifted on the couch and adjusted the flaps of his blazer the way a man will when he finds himself aroused in public. We parted and he began laughing. It was not a laugh of derision – this is how I remember it – so I started laughing as well, as if the three of us had been drawn into an alliance through realizing the force of their connection. I am not suggesting John was secretly queer, only perhaps that he understood how his own attractions were neither as fixed nor as polarized as he might once have believed.

I pulled you close again, kissing you once more because the taste of your mouth made me hungry and no matter how much of it I had I always wanted more. John began giggling again. Somewhere a bell was ringing but no one was down, no fat man counting. Then you picked up the phone and the bell stopped and you spoke a few words in your soft western drawl before putting the phone back on its cradle and rolling your eyes.

It was Nick Charles.

Our studio's own Sammy Glick.

That kid's a skunk but he knows his job.

He says Mary's on set and wants to know where I am and whether I've seen you, Mr. Marsh.

When John tried to stand he lurched forward and raised his arms to balance himself. Halfway to the door he stopped, glanced over his shoulder, and leaned against the wall. His words came at us fast and angry.

Knock it off! I don't want to hear dirty talk like that.

Neither you nor I had spoken.

The bromide, you whispered, on top of the booze.

Outside in the glare, swerving through costumed bodies, panels of medieval scenery, a trolley of extras, I noticed a stout man in a panama hat catch my eye. The newsstand pulsed with actors coming and going, and then it was just the three of us again and the ex-carnie who sold papers and traded in daily gossip. There was no chatter that morning so I started reading the front pages of the *Los Angeles Times* and *New York Times* and *San Francisco Chronicle*. Every headline made me laugh because the news was so absurd. American airmen lost over Latvia were nothing but spies who had to be taught a lesson by Russia, according to the Russians. Bookies had paid off the law to the tune of $108,400 and the law had been only too happy to play racketeer. The City of Los Angeles was close to broke but jobs in the region were on the rise. Some California boy married the sister of the Shah of Iran. Korean ships being rebuilt in Long Beach were the suspected targets of recent alien submarine sightings off the coast. President Truman had credited himself with America's successes at home and abroad. The whole spirit of the time made me feel out of place, as though I was no longer at home.

By the time we arrived on set, Mary had stepped out again. We'll start anyway, John said, we can shoot around her. I have to get this picture in the can before they kick me off the lot. He turned to Nick Charles and asked him to bring a cup of coffee, and when it came the director of photography offered John a slug of bourbon from his flask. How many drinks was that? How much bromide had he taken in your suite? How could he be lucid enough to do his job? It seems impossible that he could still have functioned, but this is what I remember, the steady drip of booze and drugs all morning, most mornings, just to keep John going until lunch.

Without Mary, John had to shoot the club scene instead of the one in Ursula's apartment, so they got you changed into a dinner suit and everyone assembled on Stage 4, extras slouching at tables while chorus girls leaned against planks that let them rest without ruining the press of their gowns. The cameraman measured the distance to you, the lighting was adjusted, and everyone fell silent. It was a short take, you playing the piano as the Arran Sisters sang 'I Hate to Lose You'. Nick called for *quiet on the set* and *roll it* and the camera operator said *rolling* and *speed* and someone shouted the scene number and *take one* and then John shouted *action*. In the background the song was playing and you began striking the piano keys in time to the recording, fingers dancing while the Arran Sisters yelped their lyrics and it was all over in less than five minutes. People waited for John to call *cut*, which he did nearly a minute after the action had finished. This had been happening all week, his distraction growing, as if he had known for days that Mary was up to something and the call from Mozelle merely confirmed what he already suspected.

How's it look? John asked, his words starting to slur. The director of photography nodded and the operators checked the gate and someone said looks good and John said one more for safety so you did it all again and as the work progressed I felt myself coming into focus. Every time Meg Arran sang a high note against the recording of herself singing it in another room on another day it struck me as so artificial I began to wheeze and the deep laughter rising inside me brought clarity. Meg noticed my spluttering and looked so furious John called *cut* and you had to do the take again and each time it went a little faster, six takes in the end, gate checked, and then John yelled, print that last one, it was the angriest piece of singing I've seen in forty-five years.

When he turned around Mary was standing behind him. Where have you been? John spoke in a whisper loud enough for the whole stage to hear.

In my suite, Marsh. Waiting for you.

I've been to your suite. You weren't there.

Mary stood still so her makeup and hair could be fixed. I went for a cup of coffee and then Krug wanted to see me.

John tried to force Mary to make eye contact with him but she kept turning her head. Okay, John shouted to the room, we do it from the top but with Faye's entrance and number. Master shot and then close-ups.

Everything started again. You were playing, the Arran Sisters singing, and when the number was finished Mary appeared from behind a curtain at the back of the set and mumbled through 'Crazy He Calls Me'. After a dozen takes John was still unsatisfied but there was no time for perfection. Half an hour later, between one set-up and another, the stage consumed by the chaos of lights being adjusted and the camera rig moved, Mary disappeared again. As usual, Nick Charles had an explanation. She needed to speak privately on the phone with your housekeeper, Mr. Marsh, about arrangements for the party. They were interrupted earlier because someone showed up at the house. A couple of men.

John glanced at me. I knew what he was thinking, that it was probably the same men who had been sitting outside the house that morning, and if not them then their colleagues. A different breed of autograph hound. John called for a break and I looked across the set to where you were reading a newspaper. The lights drained the life from your complexion, and in an awful flash I imagined how you might look in death. Later, I wondered if it might have been a moment of foresight, but perhaps it was only coincidence, as such occasions must be.

John turned to me with a sudden expression of panic, no doubt brought on by all the bourbon and bromide sloshing through his system. Will you help me? he asked. In that moment I pitied him, this man who called me his best friend, and because when I glanced at you there was no invitation for me to approach, no glimmer in your eye that said, please, Desmond, find an excuse to come stand beside me and speak for half an hour while we wait, I went with John.

Of course, I said, let's go.

Not long after I left Los Angeles, I received that letter you wrote, unsigned but unmistakably in your hand, your voice, castigating me, expressing incomprehension at the way I had drawn out the deception and failed to tell you what I was planning until my plans were already complete. Now I think that I had to disappoint you, to make you hate me, because if I had not, if I continued to believe you still loved me, I would never have been able to leave you.

Although I still dream that we might have gone on living in happiness despite the pressures of government and society and the industry that employed us, I know this is fantasy. I had to leave to save us both from misery and my unfolding disaster. I had to remove myself from America so that all temptation to see you again, a temptation that has dogged me for decades, would be impossible to satisfy. In every instant of desiring to see you again, I have been faced with the insuperable barrier of travel. At first this was genuine, material, because I could not return to America without risking that legal action might be taken against me. Once that threat had passed, the obstacle became psychological, me saying to myself, *But how can you go back? You are no longer of that place. Even a brief visit would reopen the wounds of exile. You would see that you no longer belong, that you have adapted not just to another kind of life, but to another culture entirely. America would refuse you and you would find no place for yourself there.*

Henry James once wrote that 'Americans, rightly or wrongly, are commended for the ease with which they adapt themselves to foreign conditions', and yet adaptation takes time, while acculturation – or its cousin assimilation – may require a lifetime to achieve. On my walk this morning through the Piazza della Signoria, pausing to stare at the statue of Hercules and Cacus, I noticed a young man, tall and bronzed and muscular, unmistakably American, unmistakably also a soldier, wearing mirrored sunglasses and hoisting a camouflage rucksack, glancing wildly around him as if a backfiring truck in the Via Calimala were an IED. He made himself a target, as so many Americans abroad seem unwittingly to do, and I felt sorry for him even as the militarism of his bearing, the unapologetic Americanness of his attire and attitude, the ways in which he seemed unconscious of how his appearance might affect the locals in this place, in any place not his by birthright, profoundly irritated me. I wanted to help him as much as I longed to shout at him to get rid of the damn rucksack and take off the mirrored aviator glasses and wear something other than jeans and running shoes. Try to blend in, adapt by changing yourself, not only by assuming you can go on living as if you were at home in your own land. Adaptation means change. Adapt or die.

Instead, I nodded at him, tipped my hat, and he looked at first as if he could not imagine I might be addressing him. I nodded again, offering an Aschenbachian flourish, a camp flick of the wrist, me in my pale linen suit and matching panama, my cane, my hungry eye, and this time the soldier understood. What am I doing, I asked myself, for this young man is precisely the type who might take offense and fly at me in fury, ending my long life before I have yet accomplished all that I wish.

But he did not. He blushed beneath his bronzed skin, grinning almost despite himself. He took off his glasses, nodded back at me, and I noticed his hand twitch, as if he were governing an impulse to salute. Poor boy, poor fool. I should have liked to talk to him, to find out what he had seen, whether he had just arrived from Afghanistan or elsewhere, why he had pitched up in Florence on a cold spring morning.

As he walked away I decided to follow, tapping my cane on the uneven streets so that he knew I was not trying to conceal my pursuit. He could not help stopping to ogle the displays at Rivoire as I ogled him, the store's windows already stocked with extravagant Easter eggs, and as he did so he noticed me once more. I removed my hat and touched my hair, almost involuntarily, because it occurred to me that this young man shared your coloring, Myles, the olive complexion, hair the same blond as your own, pale blue eyes precisely the shade of my suit. But this time I saw impatience, a response less flattered than anxious, and so I nodded once more and turned away from the soldier, back towards the Palazzo Vecchio. It would have been foolish to follow one of your doppelgängers, a phantom who resembles you only in the most obvious ways but lacks the clarity of your gaze or the vulnerability of your bearing as you used to walk through my world.

You see, though, how I continue to chase you even now, to allow myself these moments of derangement and fantasy as consolation for the agonies of loss.

Nathalie

The doorbell rang at the Marsh residence on Summit Drive and
Nathalie Gebhart, just returned from taking her sons and the
Marshes' daughter Iris to school in Mr. Marsh's dark sedan,
straightened her apron and spoke into the intercom.

Yes, may I ask who is this?

Is that Mrs. Nathalie Gebhart?

Speaking.

Could we have a word, Mrs. Gebhart?

But who might you be? I don't just open this gate to anyone. You
could be crazy people for all I know. Or autograph hounds. We are
not interested in that. Crazy people especially. Explain yourself.

We're agents of the Federal Bureau of Investigation. We'd like to
have a word.

Nathalie sucked a breath and checked her hair in the hall
mirror, smoothed the cloche of artillery-helmet curls, opened the
front door, clopped across the brick-paved drive, and stepped up to
the gate where a black coupe was idling with two men in the front,
both in dark suits, wearing snap-brim hats. One man was swarthy,
the other pale.

Do you gentlemen have some identification or something like
this? You may say you are agents and suchlike but without badges
I am not so stupid as to let you inside this property. You could be
rapists or murderers. Some sex stranglers even.

The agents eyed each other, one passing the other a wallet.
The pale one, who had spoken into the intercom, held up his own
and the other man's identification badges. I'm Agent Lawrence

Leopold. This is my partner, Stygius Loeb.

Stygius?

His father was a professor of Classics at Harvard. Disgraced.

But Stygius is a terrible name for a boy.

They called me Gus at school. You can call me Agent Loeb, said the swarthy man in the passenger's seat.

Might we come inside?

But do you have some kind of warrant? Is that not necessary in this situation?

Agent Leopold looked at Agent Loeb and then they both looked at Nathalie Gebhart.

We don't want to make this unpleasant, do we, Mrs. Gebhart?

No, of course we do not, said Nathalie, opening the gate and standing to one side while Agent Leopold drove the car onto the property and parked it in front of the garage.

The two men stepped out, closed their respective car doors with ginger force, and followed, unsmiling, as Nathalie led them into the house and through the front hall to the living room. The three of them stood on the plush pink carpet waiting for something to happen. The clock in the hall chimed.

Always this clock is so slow. I must get her fixed. Perhaps you gentlemen would like to sit?

The men nodded and sat next to each other on a pink davenport facing the window that looked onto the drive and the gate and their car parked in the sun. As the cushions collapsed under their weight the men slid towards each other so their knees were touching until Agent Loeb edged away from his partner.

I'm afraid Mr. and Mrs. Marsh are both at the studio. I have just got off the phone with Mrs. Marsh because of you ringing the bell at the gate. At this moment now it is just me here in the house. The children, they are all of them at school. I have much work to do. My employers are hosting a so huge party tonight. Some people will be arriving later, quite soon now, to set up the tables and such.

That's why we've come at this hour, Mrs. Gebhart, said Agent Leopold. We know the plans.

We know that caterers—

Not just caterers, but Chasen's.

Indeed, Chasen's, as well as decorators and technicians from the studio are coming.

We have been conducting enquiries.

We have very reliable sources.

We know the day's schedule.

You see, we wished to speak with you privately, Mrs. Gebhart, said Agent Loeb, which is why we have chosen the hour of our calling down to the minute.

To speak with you.

Without being interrupted.

What, to speak with *me*? Nathalie drew her knees together, crossed her ankles, and tucked them under the slipper chair where she was sitting. Cocked her head to one side. Clutched pearls she was not wearing. Perfect coquette pose. Masterful in its execution.

That's what we said, ma'am, to speak with you.

To speak with you alone, ma'am.

But, gentlemen, do you not want some coffee? Only I have just made a pot to see me through the morning, and there is plenty should you wish. Cream and sugar? Maybe also some cookies that only just now I bake?

Agents Loeb and Leopold frowned at each other.

No, ma'am, no coffee.

Thank you, ma'am, no, ma'am. We won't be needing any cookies.

No? said Nathalie, the word drawn unnaturally out and tumbling down through a pregnant decrescendo.

No, the men said in unison.

So how might it be that I can help you this morning? Bright again. Quick recovery. Super instincts.

We have been attending to your movements since you entered the country in 1946 with your ex-husband. That is, your American ex-husband, Mr. Archibald Anderson.

Not your first and now late husband Wilhelm Gebhart.

Just to be clear.

We want no confusion on this point, ma'am.

No, indeed, as Agent Loeb says, not Wilhelm Gebhart but Mr. Archibald Anderson.

Nathalie shook her head as if she had smelled something rotten. Archie was not such a nice man. Cruel to my boys. But what do you mean you have been attending to my movements? This sounds very strange. Nathalie lowered her chin, cocking her head to the opposite side.

The government has been waiting for the right moment to capitalize on your obvious talents.

They should be put to good use, ma'am.

And now is the time. Agent Leopold had dark green eyes and long, slightly red lashes which fluttered whenever he came to the end of a sentence. Also coquettish, in a more menacing way. Also masterful.

My talents? Nathalie laughed. It was a professional-grade performance. You must be mistaken, dear agents, I have no talents. Polishing silver. And my cherry pancakes, made with yeast and a dusting of confectioner's sugar. That is a talent maybe you

could say. Also a nice onion cake recipe I learnt from my mother.
I once played the violin with some skill, but not many years now.
Schubert. But any fool can play Schubert. Nothing I would call
talent. I came to this country after the war with Archie to find a
better way of life. I always admire you Americans your directness.

Don't be so modest, Frau Gebhart. We know about your talents.

No, it is *true*, you have to believe me, I am only just a
housekeeper these days.

What was your job in Germany, before you came to America?

In Germany I was only ever a housewife. My late husband,
Wilhelm, he was—

Your late husband was an officer in the Abwehr and executed
by the Gestapo following his involvement in the Solf Tea Party. You
also worked for the Abwehr but were already in Britain at the time
of said Tea Party, having entered the country with your sons posing
as refugees. A nice little family of spies. The British eventually
captured you and turned you pretty quick from what we hear.

Threat of execution of the youngest Gebhart son, is what our
intelligence says.

And you became one of their most effective double-cross agents,
codenamed The Baker. In London, you met your American husband,
that is Archibald Anderson, who was stationed in England. You
married and returned with him to Detroit, Michigan, in 1946. In
1947, you divorced Anderson and moved to Los Angeles where
you immediately entered the employ of Mr. and Mrs. John Marsh.
Excuse me, ma'am, is this *too* direct an approach?

Nathalie's feet came forward and she planted her dark brown
shoes on the floor, pushed herself back in the chair, and slumped
a little. Her neck straightened. Her head was square on her
shoulders. The clock ticked in the hall but the ticking seemed to

slow and all the movements of the woman and two men to thicken and sag. Agent Loeb was smiling. He had good straight teeth but breath so foul Nathalie could smell it from across the room.

No, if I were to be honest with you, dear agents, this is something of a relief.

No charades.

Fine, gentlemen, no charades.

Drop the strudel-English shtick.

Fine, if that's what you prefer, she said. Her voice dipped an octave and flipped to BBC English. After nearly four years in this country and having shared the bed of one – more than one in fact, if we're showing all our cards – I've come to the depressing conclusion that you Americans are, at base, immutably the same. You are a nation of bullies.

Agents Loeb and Leopold glanced at each other peripherally before returning their focus to Nathalie Gebhart.

You are quite fluent in English, after all, said Agent Leopold.

More so than our intelligence—

What my colleague means is, you are better trained than we had been led to believe.

My husband and I were both very rigorously prepared during our time in the Abwehr, but let me assure you, since I have little doubt you are wondering, that we were neither of us committed Nazis. In fact, we were trying to work *against* the party, as I assume you must know.

The intelligence on your husband was clear, said Agent Leopold.

On you, not so much.

But that's no longer of interest to us. Any ideological sympathies you might have harbored for the Nazis we are willing to excuse as, let us say, a temporary—

A moral lapse, Agent Loeb interrupted.

That chapter of history is closed as far as we are concerned –
by which I mean, as far as Agent Loeb and myself are concerned.

And as far as the men to whom we report are concerned.

Agent Loeb means the Director of the FBI.

Do you mean to say that J. Edgar Hoover himself knows about
me? By name? Nathalie asked, blue eyes sparkling.

That is not something we can confirm.

Neither confirm nor deny, ma'am.

So what can I do for you gentlemen and your illustrious
Director now that we've cleared the air about my unfortunate past,
which, you must understand, was entirely a matter of historical
circumstance?

We're here because you know how to handle yourself in covert
operations.

That's the assumption on which the Bureau is working.

Nathalie reached for an enamel box on the side table nearest
her chair, withdrew a cigarette, lit the end with a ceramic lighter
in the shape of a pug dog whose squashed snout exhaled a flame,
inhaled, held the smoke in her chest for longer than seemed
physically possible, and blew it directly in the faces of the two
agents. Agent Loeb paddled the air with one hand. Nathalie noticed
that his nails had been professionally manicured.

You gentlemen are trying to recruit me.

Not recruit in so many words.

Ham-fisted way of doing it.

We would like you to provide us with information.

On the Marshes, to be specific.

Specificity is important, to be sure.

To be sure.

Nathalie drew on the cigarette, held it, again sprayed the men with smoke, and smiled. No, I cannot do what you so kindly request. Not possibly.

Can't?

Listen, gentlemen, the Marshes are my employers. One has a sense of loyalty and duty to the people who allow one to put food in the mouths of one's children, children who have, you must remember, experienced the trauma of losing their father and their fatherland. One is beholden to keep the secrets of one's lady's boudoir and one's master's study.

Gentle, slightly mocking ripple of laughter from the agents.

Quite apart from such abstractions, Mrs. Marsh is a distant cousin of mine, although you would not guess as much the way she treats me and my boys. Never mind I have a proper education and she is nothing but a farm girl who failed to finish high school because she had to come to Hollywood to be in the pictures. Schwab's Pharmacy. Casting couch shenanigans. Chorus girl promoted to starlet overnight. Don't think, gentlemen, it had anything to do with talent.

Agent Leopold nudged Agent Loeb's knee with his own. Agent Loeb blinked at Agent Leopold and then turned back to Nathalie.

You are an educated woman, Mrs. Gebhart.

After a fashion, yes. The daughter of a general is often more worldly than other women. I had the benefit of my father's library and his conversation at the dinner table.

Why choose to work as a maid?

When you could, one might think, find much more—

When you could find more gainful employment, said Agent Leopold. Appropriate to your station.

Unless you were trying—

Unless you wanted a comfortable life but also wished—

Unless you hoped to keep a low profile.

I think you underestimate the difficulty of being an immigrant single mother in America, said Nathalie.

But you could call yourself Nathalie Anderson and talk as you talk now and pursue just about any job a woman might wish to do. You yourself could be in front of the camera, if you did something a little different with your hair.

Unless you wanted—

Unless it was imperative that you keep a low profile.

Go on, Nathalie said, convince me.

Agent Loeb leaned across to Agent Leopold and cupped his hand around his partner's ear. Agent Leopold turned his head, positioning his lips against Agent Loeb's ear. Cupping of hand. Whispering that was inaudible from a distance greater than one foot. The two men looked at each other, locking eyes, then parted, moving to opposite ends of the davenport.

Before joining the Abwehr you were *Chef Oberaufseherin* at Ravensbrück, said Agent Leopold.

And your name was not Nathalie, said Agent Loeb.

It was Charlotte Becker. When you immigrated to America you neglected to mention your birth name or your senior position—

Neglected even to mention that you had spent time at Ravensbrück.

Which gives us grounds to deport you.

Fiction, Nathalie said, her voice low. I was never in my life at Ravensbrück.

We have witnesses who say otherwise. Witnesses who have hair-raising, I mean truly spine-chilling things to report about the behavior and activities of *Chef Oberaufseherin* Charlotte Becker, who is wanted, who somehow managed to escape after the end of the war. Would you like us to turn you over to the West German authorities?

Or perhaps to the state of Israel, Mrs. Gebhart?

Israel is too busy with Arabs to care about someone like me.

Are you in the mood to test the Israelis' degree of interest?

I hear our Israeli friends are extremely interested in anyone who might have been a camp officer and has thus far managed by deception and dissimulation to avoid capture and trial.

That's what I hear, too.

They are interested in anyone who might be of even the remotest significance. Especially when there are eye witnesses.

Eye witnesses who can pick someone's photograph out of a book and say with certainty—

More than one eye witness, I should like to mention—

More than a dozen eye witnesses, in point of fact—

I heard two score eye witnesses and then some, Agent Leopold, and all of them providing a positive identification and corroborating testimony of the most detailed variety.

Would you like to risk the interest of Israel on those terms, Mrs. Gebhart?

Or do you in fact prefer 'Frau Becker'?

Nathalie interlaced her fingers and rested her hands in her lap.

What information do you want?

Agent Loeb smiled. Thin lips. Fine jaw. Adam's apple smooth and brown and ovoid as an unshelled pecan bobbing in a vat of caramel.

We want to know whether the Marshes are Reds. About the husband, John Horatio Marsh, we have a pretty fair idea. It's the wife who remains opaque.

Carefully covered tracks. A little like you, Mrs. Gebhart.

Nathalie finished her cigarette and ground the butt in a cut-glass ashtray.

Call it a family trait, she said, and stood to show them out.

June 6, 1950

4

Despite accepting John as a friend, I knew little of his domestic life beyond the rumors that Mary made every decision, or that before their marriage, which predated my arrival in Los Angeles, John was a happier, wilder man with less compromised politics. We had spent significant time in each other's company, making half a dozen films together during my time at the studio, and yet John remained essentially mysterious to me. Even before you and I met, Myles, I was rarely invited to his house and always assumed this was because Mary did not like me and John was afraid to oppose her. I mention this because when I set out with John that morning, leaving the soundstage once again to help him look for Mary, I was mindful of the limits of our friendship. Other than revealing the nature of my relationship with you, I had rarely shared intimacies with John. Perhaps he guessed the kind of family I came from, the privileged childhood I had spent in Manhattan, the circles in which I moved at Cornell, but I was never conscious of speaking about myself in that way. The substance of our exchanges was primarily cinematic and narrative. We lived our friendship as an ongoing rumination on the films we liked, the films we would ourselves have wished to make, and those that we dismissed or despised. Over the course of a conversation we could speak entirely cinematically, using *Un Chien Andalou* or *Man with a Movie Camera* as shorthand for a certain style, commending the comic genius of *His Girl Friday* or *The Philadelphia Story* while feeling impatient with the romantic melodrama of *Casablanca*, admiring the visual artistry and narrative framing of *Double Indemnity* while decrying the bowdlerization of *The Lost Weekend* or comparing the histrionics of Joan Crawford's performance in *Mildred Pierce* with the histrionics of Edward G.

Robinson's performance in *Scarlet Street*, wishing that we had a film industry in America that would allow us to make work as naturalistic as *Bicycle Thieves* or dreaming that every extant print of *Mr. Blandings Builds His Dream House* might be burned. Because we could fill hours talking this way it became possible never to speak about ourselves *except* in this way. For me it was neither intellectually nor emotionally nourishing, even though much could be expressed in a coded, submerged way: for me to tell John I admired an experimental film called *Fireworks* was to admit of my access to a side of Los Angeles life I assumed remained foreign to him, to admit of the pleasures I took in that film's celebration of the male body, to admit that my taste would always be less conventional than his, but also to admit of the dueling forces of fear and hope accompanying my desire, fear that my desiring gaze would be met with physical violence, hope that my desiring gaze would be reciprocated and that in a moment of union with some other man the two of us might become, together, content with each other. I doubt that John understood half of this. For him, to reveal that his greatest professional aspiration was to make a film as strange and beautiful as Hitchcock's *Spellbound* suggested more about him than such personal information as he finally shared with me that morning in 1950.

While walking alongside him (perhaps you will say I was following, that I was no longer in command of my own decisions, deranged by anxiety over telling you what I was still keeping secret, even avoiding you in order to forestall that moment of catastrophic confession), I felt as though the disguise John had been wearing for so many years began to slip away and at last the real man was standing beside me.

Until then he had never told me he'd had an older brother who died young, or a sister shut up in an institution, or parents who had never been to see even one of his films, or that his and Mary's housekeeper was a shirt-tale cousin who fled Germany after the war, or that Mary's brother sent a telegram every month asking for money to keep the family farm in Oklahoma out of the hands of the banks. A life's worth of information came spluttering out of John in the space of a few hours and by the end of the day I was certain I would never speak to him again.

We returned to Mary's suite and once again found Mozelle by herself, this time reading a book on the sofa, still stiff and uncomfortable in that lacy white cap, cuffs and collar, the prim leather ankle boots and white apron. For months I had allowed myself to believe she was an actress playing a succession of bit parts: comical, indomitable, mute and put-upon, back-talking, but forever in the same costume. All that time I had failed to see her or understand that she was forced to wear the demeaning outfit in order to serve Mary's notion of Mozelle's position, or perhaps her own.

It's still just me, Mr. Marsh. You've missed her again.

Do you know where she went this time?

Mozelle put her book face down on the sofa. Said she was going for a walk to clear her head.

I know what that means. She's gone out to the jungle. Mary always goes to the backlot when she needs to cool off. We'll find her there, he said, turning to me with a look in his eye that made me want to run back to you, Myles.

But the backlot is huge, I said, picturing the fake country roads crisscrossing the studio's eucalyptus forest, paths meandering around artificial bodies of water, the old world and new world and imagined worlds jostling cheek-by-jowl and reinvented over the course of a single day, one morning's Siberian train station becoming a small-town Connecticut railway platform by mid-afternoon. As a place to disappear it was second to none. We should just get back to the set. Can't you shoot around Mary until she returns?

John crossed his arms over his chest. His face was turning red again. She's in every set-up, Desmond. I can't stand around waiting for her to come back. And then he turned and pointed angrily at Mozelle. You might have phoned to let me know she'd left. His voice was so inflated with rage that both Mozelle and I jumped, and then, as if realizing he had been too abrupt, John opened the door, walked out into the hall, and tramped down the stairs.

Although he liked to think of himself as progressive, I had often seen John act highhanded with black waiters or push past black extras on the lot in ways I was sure he would not have done if those people had been white. I knew I had my own failings, too. Even in reflecting on John's behavior, I could only summon waiters and maids and extras, bellhops and laborers and fry cooks. I could not say how he would have acted towards Langston Hughes or Zora Neale Hurston or Paul Robeson, or for that matter Cab Calloway or Lena Horne or Dorothy Dandridge, nor can I say why I feel unsettled by the hope that he would have treated them as equals. Perhaps because I know that he would not have, or that he would have performed a belief in their equality that he did not actually hold. And although the experiences are distinct and not directly comparable, I also feared that when he treated me as an equal that was no more than performance of a belief he could discard when it became too burdensome. A man of no conviction, or a man who wanted to please, never to appear foe to anyone, such a person cannot be trusted, I finally understand. There is evil in the world and when faced with it we must say no, I cannot allow this to pass, but too often John Marsh failed to do that.

I'm sorry, I said, turning to Mozelle as she picked up her book. It's an awful mess.

She looked over the top of the page she was reading but did not raise her head. I could see the title, *Annie Allen*, but did not know what it was about.

Good book?

Not for someone like you.

I would have thought a book could be for anyone with the patience and interest to read it.

Mozelle clapped the book shut and sighed. I've seen your pictures, Mr. Frank. When you bother to put black people in your stories they always wear a uniform. Part of the problem is that you see us as an undifferentiated mass. Nothing but a parade of repetitions with no individual who might stand out from the crowd and be her own person.

I'm sorry if that's true.

Don't doubt it.

Okay, I won't. You'd think we might do better in America, but I guess not.

Mozelle threw back her head and laughed. You still believe in American exceptionalism, Mr. Frank? I gave you too much credit. America is just another outpost of European empire. No more exceptional than the others that have brought people from across the world into their borders and then torn themselves apart, dancing and drinking through the decades of their fall. We are in the first hours of the next age of decadence, another Weimar, and after the decadence, fascism.

That's a grim view for a free country.

A truly free country would have been a land in which all were free and equal from the first heartbeat of its foundation, Mr. Frank.

In that we don't disagree.

This country's founders couldn't see true freedom when it smacked them in the face. Instead they trampled all over a land with history that was illegible to the likes of them because it did not build palaces and temples and cathedrals out of stone or paint its art on the woven fabric of plant fibers sealed with glue rendered from rabbit gut. Nothing but a nation of the unequal led by people who think they are prophets, that's what this country has always been. Most white people in America want everyone, black and white alike, to think black people are no more than day players in the motion picture of this nation's unremarkable history. And you, even you, when you write your stories, you only think a black person is good for menace or service. Write me and I'll end up the same, the woman in service who menaces you.

So what's the solution?

For you? I don't know. For myself, I believe black people must seize their liberty. Demand to sit at the same tables, use the same benches and water fountains. And if you won't give us equality when we ask nicely, then maybe the time will come to fight. Don't look so surprised. There are many others who think as I do. It will be rebellion in the name of equality. A second civil war to create the nation of liberty and justice for all that white people already claim exists. I suppose you think I'm being uppity.

I wouldn't have said so.

No? That surprises me. You should pay more attention to your politics.

They are never far from my mind, believe me.

I guess that's something at least.

Desmond! John shouted from downstairs.

You better get going. See if you can't track down his second-rate

Veronica Lake. And then Mozelle raised a hand, shooing me out of
the room with a single twitch of her fingers.

As I settled next to John on the trolley that ran between the
soundstages and the backlot, I failed to call him on his rudeness
to Mozelle, just as I failed on other occasions to mention slights I
had witnessed, remaining silent for the sake of friendship (what a
mistake in John's case), or simply because I lacked the courage in a
particular moment to stand up for what I knew to be right.

That morning I was too preoccupied by my own concerns
even to challenge him when he gave me a look of wild impatience
and barked, I'll show them I'm loyal, goddammit! It was unclear
whether he was speaking to me or himself, or even to some phantom
interlocutor. When the trolley braked at a stop sign John raised his
hands, shouting, Stop the Reds!

A young woman passing on foot cheered while two older men
on the trolley glanced anxiously over their shoulders.

Stop it, John, you're scaring the Trotskyists.

I thought you were a Trot.

I'm far too inclined to dissent.

You're too inclined to a lot of things.

If you mean my own sex, I don't see that's a weakness.

Which is not a popular position, or a legal one.

True enough. There was a story in the paper recently. I
committed the headline to memory: 'Congress Hears 5000 Perverts
Infest Capital'. Think about the language: *Perverts Infest Capital*. By
perverts the headline writer could only mean homosexuals. If you
read the story, you would discover that this tasty bit of information
came in testimony from an officer of the vice squad, who went so
far as to claim that three-quarters of these perverts actually work for

the government. By my reckoning that makes 3,750 homosexuals employed by the United States Government in Washington, D.C. *alone*. Now if that is actually the case, then why isn't this a much happier and more enlightened country? Just how many government employees can there be? What proportion do those notional 3,750 constitute? Anyway, that's beside the point. The officer of the vice squad was testifying before a Senate Appropriations Subcommittee bent on eliminating homosexuals from the ranks of government employment, and no doubt from any employment anywhere if most of them had their way. According to those senators, we – homosexuals that is – are security risks. Don't they know that we're better at keeping secrets than anyone? Our whole lives are secret. The State Department has already fired ninety-one homosexuals, which the article elects to describe as 'sex perverts'.

As if there are other kinds.

Oh but there are, John! Religious perverts, for instance. Apostates! It was the Victorians who perverted 'pervert' into a sexual category. The point is, these senators and vice squad officers believe homosexuals are all potentially disloyal. They think that because we have turned away from the opposite sex we can be made to turn our political loyalty – as if finding that you love the same sex were in fact a turn and not just the way a person is born. If they can't hound us out of our jobs and into hiding for our politics, they'll crucify us because we love the wrong sex. Have you seen the treatment that's been circulating? John shook his head. It wouldn't have come across your desk. An underground project, a fable, the sort of film that even if it were made would never be processed because the lab technicians would burn it for obscenity. An experimental message picture based on Gogol's *The Nose* and set in Washington, D.C.

Always a winner with audiences, a patriotic story. Tell me about it.

We begin with a man, a humble young barber, who looks after the beards and thinning top thatch of the most important men in our nation's government.

Man of the people. Jimmy Stewart type.

Not quite, John. Because he's respected as a fellow who never opens his mouth, reliably discreet in all matters, politicians confide in him, and have on occasion let slip information that is classified and whose public revelation might compromise national security.

Excellent. Has promise as a B-thriller. Plight of the everyman lashed by a brutal system. Atomic-era update on *Mr. Smith Goes to Washington*.

This is a different kind of picture than any you've seen, I assure you, and it is unlikely ever to be made, except as an obscure animated short for the right class of audience.

Wouldn't get it past Joe Breen, then?

Nor the studio censors. Cocteau might take a stab at it. It is not a story for the great masses of American moviegoers who have grown accustomed to the obfuscation of sex as the endpoint of intimacy between man and woman, not to mention the genesis of all higher life on the planet. Or perhaps because of that very disavowal of sex it's a story meant *precisely* for the edification and enlightenment of ordinary women and men who desire nothing more than to live vicariously through the fantasy exploits of people just as ordinary as they. And if you have any doubt about its legality – obscenity aside, and the most graphic elements can all be done through suggestion off screen – then remember this is satire, protected under law.

The trolley stopped and while actors and crewmembers boarded and disembarked I muscled John to the back of the car where we could speak without being overheard. As we continued out towards the backlot, I handed him a mimeographed copy of the treatment I'd been carrying folded up in the breast pocket of my blazer. I don't know what I thought I was doing showing it to him. Perhaps it was a way of indicating I had already given up, that my sense of alienation and estrangement from the dominant mood of the country was such that I had no choice but exile. John began reading, his face shifting between puzzlement and shock.

The trolley stopped again, letting off two young men in overalls and picking up a handful of women dressed as antebellum debutantes. One of the men in overalls I recognized as a carpenter I had slept with half a dozen times before you and I were introduced, Myles. I knew when I went to bed with him that he had a wife and three kids and a great deal of confusion in his heart, because he loved his wife and found her beautiful and she was pregnant with a fourth child, and yet he had looked at me with a strength of desire I could not ignore. If he remembered our encounters he gave no sign that morning, and I had made a point of forgetting his name. John noticed me staring and nudged me in the ribs.

You should watch yourself, Desmond.

That is the problem. I've been watching myself all my life, and I'm tired of it. I want to go somewhere I don't have to watch myself anymore. I never belonged in the country of my birth, not really. My parents saw to that.

We turned a corner and on the hills in the distance oil derricks were rhythmically pumping, an industrial backdrop to the fantasies we concocted that was always hidden with optical mattes, each of us daily ignoring what was before our eyes because we knew that the ugliness of reality could be made to disappear. John reached inside his jacket to retrieve a flask and took a long sucking pull as the trolley continued deeper into the backlot, passing corridors of scaffolding. I watched while he flipped the pages of that underground treatment, leaning over the side at one point to heave, although nothing came up. When we had reached the oldest part of the backlot, passing the walls of what was usually a hacienda but on that particular day had been dressed as a Chinese village, we slowed for a moment and I thought I saw the same stout man in the panama hat I had noticed earlier outside the newsstand.

After John had finished reading, he loosened his tie and wiped his brow. I worry about you, Desmond. It might be by Anonymous but you can't fool me. It's trademark Frank. You should burn it before it falls into the wrong hands.

Who's to say I wrote it? It's a copy of a copy of a copy of a copy with no original. Even the material is a copy, and I suppose Gogol copied from somewhere else, too.

Then, as if we were traveling backwards and forwards in time, we came out of the old and into the new, the parts of the studio lot only recently developed, land acquired in the previous decade, where morning heat radiated from the snow-covered roofs of a mock Siberian village along whose streets a horse-drawn sledge careered on hidden wheels, the actors struggling to appear frozen as they sweated in their furs, while the world beyond the set shimmered in greens and golden browns. As the trolley finally came to a stop at the far eastern limit of the lot, John stepped to the ground and I followed him, blindly, dazzled by the day.

THE COCK

BY 'ANONYMOUS'

FREELY ADAPTED FROM NIKOLAI GOGOL'S 'THE NOSE'

STORY TREATMENT
March 30, 1950

IRVING JAKOBSON, a barber in Washington, D.C., runs
his own shop not far from the Capitol Building.
There being few places where such pleasures can be
procured, Irving also acts as masseur to a select
number of influential clients who phone to make
appointments for a tonic rub in his backroom, where,
relieved of their clothes, the men of the law give
their bodies over to another man who is, unlike them,
a youth of mild beauty who came to Washington seeking
neither fortune nor power nor the responsibilities of
public service, but the stability of continuous work
that would earn no more than a comfortable living. He
has been in the city a little under ten years, and
after starting as another man's apprentice, saved
enough money to open his own establishment a few
years ago, when he expanded his services to include
these tonic rubs.

Irving rubs down the politicians with his own blend
of fragrant oils, despite the fact that many of
these powerful men fail to practice adequate personal
hygiene, so that Irving often finds himself holding
his nose. When it becomes clear that the politicians
might be receptive to more intimate manipulation –
the message is often unambiguous – he removes the
towel covering their most personal areas and provides
the relief they seek, perhaps even relief they were
unaware of wanting until that moment when, alone in
a room with an angelic younger man and clothed only
in a white slip of a towel too small to wrap all the
way round their ample mid-sections, they could not
control that part of the body whose behavior is often

beyond the governance of the conscious mind.

Irving has given tonic rubs to Senators and
Congressmen, to members of the President's Cabinet,
a Supreme Court Justice, Generals, and even the
Director of the FBI, J. Edgar Hoover. But Irving's
most loyal client is that oiliest of recent arrivals
in our nation's capital, the JUNIOR SENATOR from
Wisconsin, who, as soon as the door to the backroom
is closed, dispenses entirely with the fig leaf
of towel and allows his fleshy body to be worked
without any concession to modesty, complaining only
that Irving's hands are sometimes too rough and that
his breath stinks. 'You smell like garlic,' the
Senator complains, and Irving will apologize, suck
a peppermint, and spray the air with cheap eau de
cologne.

One morning, Irving arrives at his shop on Capitol
Hill, unlocks the door, and discovers, sunk in the
bottom of one of his jars of fragrant oil, a well-
preserved penis and pair of testicles. No signs of
cutting or trauma or blood, and very little indication
of use. Irving looks in horror at these jewels, not
because they are gruesome, although they are, but
because he instantly recognizes them. The coarse
quality of the hair on the testicles, rising more than
halfway up the shaft of the stubby little cock, its
oily slackness and atrophied veins, as well as the
small but unmistakable birthmark in the shape of a
hammer on the glans, means that it could only be the
cock and balls of the Junior Senator from Wisconsin.

149

[Remember: satire. Protected by law.]

Irving pulls down the shade on the front door and
carries the jar of fragrant oil to the backroom where
he extracts the penis and testicles he knows so well.
The cock wriggles like a fish out of water, as if it
has a life of its own, and even seems to turn and
look at him, gasping through its tiny mouth.

Irving quickly wraps up his discovery in the pages of
yesterday's newspaper. He posts a sign on the door
announcing he will only open at noon and walks out
onto the streets of Washington, intending to drop
the parcel into a trashcan, or perhaps even to buy
a box and return it to the Senator himself so that
the organ might be reattached, although he fears that
he, Irving Jakobson, might have cut off the cock and
balls and simply repressed an act the Senator can be
expected to remember.

Who knows, Irving thinks aloud, perhaps the Senator
is already plotting revenge, having identified Irving
as the ringleader of America's Communist spies, a Red
horde intent on emasculating the whole of American
manhood!

Irving glances over his shoulder, worried he's being
followed and that the police or Feds are just biding
their time until they can get him alone in a dark
alley and bundle him off in a paddy wagon. As soon
as he thinks he's found a suitable place to dispose
of the incriminating parcel, Irving is accosted by a

FRIEND who wants to know why he's running late and doesn't he have any early appointments this morning, since, after all, Congress is in session and the leaders of the land prefer to handle such business before the flashbulbs of the press can catch them. The friend winks as if he knows about Irving's secret other business in the backroom and asks him what's in the bundle of oily newspaper. 'Just some sausages,' Irving mumbles. 'My cat's not feeling well, so I'm taking him these sausages.'

'But they're moving,' his friend says, eyes bulging in horror.

'A fish, too. I bought a fish for him. It's still alive, I guess,' Irving says, and bashes the writhing package against a lamppost until it stops moving altogether.

He and his friend part ways and Irving hurries along, the streets filling up with morning traffic. Every corner Irving turns it seems less likely he'll be able to rid himself of the package, which has started wriggling again in his grip.

At last he catches a bus to Arlington Bridge where he walks to the middle of the span, pretends to be staring into the swamp of the Potomac, perhaps we see his anguished reflection in the waters below, and then he drops the Senator's cock in its bundle of newspaper down into the water, watching as it wriggles free and begins to swim upstream, jumping

151

like a salmon, leaping and diving and twirling ecstatically in mid-air.

As Irving walks back towards the Lincoln Memorial, a car pulls over, stops, and out steps another of his clients, the CHIEF JUSTICE of the Supreme Court.

'Here now, Irving Jakobson, what on earth do you imagine you're doing?'

'I don't know what you mean, your honor. I was just going for a stroll on this beautiful morning.'

'But tell me, boy, what did you drop in the water? You shouldn't litter, you know, it's a criminal offense.'

Irving smirks at the Chief Justice, whose cock he also knows well, and raises an eyebrow.

'Really, your honor, I'm sure you wouldn't want to test the discretion of a barber privy to all of his clients' secrets.'

The Chief Justice blushes, scrambles back in the car, and shouts at the driver to step on it, and how. As the car rounds the Lincoln Memorial, it accelerates just at the moment another car, traveling in the opposite direction, crosses into their lane, colliding at high speed. In the midst of the crash the door of the Chief Justice's car swings open and his honor falls out onto the road, blood flowing everywhere – blood of a surprisingly red hue for a man of such patriotic fervor.

Fearing that someone might have witnessed his brief confrontation with the Chief Justice, Irving catches the nearest bus and returns to his shop, where he goes to work on heads and hair and stiffened muscles.

MEANWHILE

On the other side of town, the Junior Senator from Wisconsin wakes from a deep but troubled sleep. As he has every morning of his adult life, he shouts, 'REDS! REDS! REDS!' and then makes a rumbling rat-a-tat-tat sound, aiming an imaginary machine gun as he mows down his spectral enemies. 'REDS! Reds everywhere! Reds crawling down the walls! Stop the Reds!'

He pulls a bottle of bourbon from his side table, fills a tumbler, and drinks it down in a single draft. He's been dreaming of ways to derail the Communist Plot, and his latest brainwave is to ban the letters K, G, and B, since these are obviously subversive, and then he remembers that there are other undesirable letters as well, such as N, K, V, and D, and he thinks these should be placed on a watch list. When it comes down to it, there are so many suspicious letters it might be better to ban language altogether and rely entirely on images for communication, since these can be controlled so much more easily! The purchase of cameras and writing

utensils could require a license and all image-
making rendered subject to prior review, which is
not such a difficult thing to manage, since image-
making and its reproduction so often requires the
cooperation of multiple individuals, technicians
and the like. Writing, on the other hand, is far
more dangerous. Writing can be done so privately
that no one ever knows where words may spring up or
what they might hazard to say. Writing, the Senator
feels certain, is the worst abomination since the
birth of language because it can never be trusted
to mean what it says. So much better if language
could be expressed only by men and women speaking
to a camera, held accountable for what they say,
words always attached to their persons without the
ambiguity and reproducibility, not to mention the
dangerous anonymity, of the page.

Although past forty, the Junior Senator from
Wisconsin has never married and rumors about him are
beginning to spread. As a man content in the armed
services, and happy in the halls of Congress, he has
never sought or desired the company of women. After
finishing the glass of breakfast bourbon, he asks his
houseboy, BILLY (20s), to give him a rub down. When
he takes off his pajamas he is astonished to discover
he has lost his cock and balls. In their place,
the Senator finds a smooth, hairless cleft, like a
freshly baked fan-tan dinner roll.

The Senator runs to the bathroom, bathes his eyes
with seltzer, and examines himself in the full-length

154

mirror. He spreads his legs, crouches down, reaches deep inside the cavity, and digs around, his panic growing.

'Billy!' he shouts to the houseboy. 'Fetch a flashlight!'

Billy arrives a moment later with the light and shines it inside his employer's shiny new orifice.

'Feel around in there and see if you can find it. It must have gone spelunking.'

Billy reaches inside the Senator, feels around, the Senator shrieks with surprise and not a little delight, slaps Billy on the ass, and then Billy removes his hand, which is slightly damp but entirely empty, sans cock.

And so, the Senator dismisses Billy, showers and shaves, has his first double bourbon of the day, all the while continuing to examine the cleft between his legs, fascinated but also repulsed (he's a misogynist, of course), and still convinced the cock must be hiding somewhere deep inside his abdomen. 'Call the doctor!' the Senator shouts to Billy. 'He should cancel all his morning appointments!'

No sooner has the Senator stepped onto the street than a limousine pulls up, a DRIVER opens the back door, and there, in the billowing black robes of a Supreme Court Justice, is the Senator's very own

COCK, shuffling on its protuberant balls, now shod
in a pair of smart brown brogues. Instead of the
diminutive creature it was only hours earlier, the
Cock has engorged itself to the height of a man. It
glares at the Senator, coughs once, and wrinkles its
face (if face it can be called), before slithering
back into the car. In a deep, congested voice, it
burbles to the Driver, 'Take me to the Court!'

The Senator feels a fever coming on and his legs
buckle, but darling Billy is there to catch him
just before his fall. 'Get the car, Billy. We have
to go after it.' And for the first time, we hear
the Senator's voice crack, as if puberty might be,
well...reversing itself.

By the time they arrive at the Supreme Court, the
Cock has been appointed the new Chief Justice,
already replacing the recently deceased former Chief
Justice on the logic that since the Court is mostly
a bunch of dicks and the Cock's the biggest dick
in the land, it should be cock of the Court. Our
poor Senator wonders how he can possibly approach
his dismembered member since he, the Senator (he
wonders if he should still call himself 'he') has no
particular standing in the Court. At last, he's so
desperate that during a lull in the proceedings he
pushes forward to the bench.

'Excuse me, your honor!' he shrieks. 'Your honor,
please, I'm sorry to interrupt you, but I wondered if
I might have a word?'

A GUARD tries to restrain him until the Senator threatens to have him blacklisted.

The Cock squints down at the Senator and speaks from the same orifice it uses for seeing, eating, and excreting. 'What do you want?' it bellows in a loud but strangely thin, strangled voice.

'It's just, if you'll excuse me, I wonder what you think you're doing up there on the bench? I mean you <u>know</u> where you're really supposed to be, your honor.'

'I don't have the foggiest idea what you mean,' says the Cock, wheezing between each word. 'Are you accusing me of something, you little pervert? What do you think this is, a freak show? This is the Supreme Court of the United States of America. This is the greatest court that ever was courted in the history of the world's courts!'

The Senator shuffles, conscious of a draft drifting between his legs, a heaviness in his chest, hair tickling his usually clean-shaved nape. 'But I'm a Senator! I need you in your proper place! Without you, I'm no better than a congresswoman, don't you see? A congresswoman can do very well without a cock but I certainly can't! This is a matter of the most profound honor and dignity and precedent. There are no women senators!'

'Does anyone know what this putz is talking about?' the Cock splutters to his fellow Justices. 'I don't

have a clue what you mean. You're wasting our time.
If you have something important to say, say it
plainly,' the Cock spits, sounding impatient.

'Your honor, please, I beg of you, I don't know
how to make it plainer,' the Senator wails. He
looks around the chamber for support from the other
Justices, lawyers, members of the public, but
everyone turns away from him, ashamed on his behalf.
Dropping his voice to a whisper, the Senator pleads,
'Don't you see, your honor, that you are my cock?'

Disgusted by the suggestion, the Cock glares at the
Senator. 'I've never heard something so perverted!
What an impertinence!' it roars, gurgle-gurgle. 'I am
me! I am myself! And anyway, I'm a Justice and you're
nothing more than a senator. I got appointed for
life. You just serve your piddling term of office. I
outlast you. You're wasting the Court's time. I deny
certiorari to your case. I find you in contempt! Get
the hell out of here! Guards, escort this sex fiend
from the Court!'

The Guards approach but the Senator brushes them off
and runs from the building. As he descends the steps
towards the Capitol, he is aware of his right hand
rising at his side, wrist bent, fingers extended, arm
sashaying. Billy is waiting for him in the car.

'Billy, baby, I don't know what to do! That fucking
dick refuses to come! How can I be a senator without
a propagator?'

It's a bright floral day, cherry trees in bloom, bunnies bouncing on lawns, birds doing the dirty dance of spring, but the Senator's world is ashen. The heaviness in his chest grows, his breasts swelling, straining the buttons of his shirt. His usually short hair is now hanging in his eyes and when he speaks again, his voice is higher than it has been since boyhood.

'Billy, quick, take me to the FBI!' When he hears the pitch of his voice and sees the threads of stubble that have already grown since his morning shave raining in a fine dust across his lap, the Junior Senator from Wisconsin shrieks in horror.

They arrive at FBI headquarters and the Senator rushes in to the office of the Director. 'Is J. Edgar in?' the Senator asks, breathless.

Hoover's SECRETARY squints, as though the boy thinks he recognizes the Senator but can't be sure. None of the parts seem to fit.

'Let me check whether he can see you,' the Secretary drawls. He picks up the phone, cups his hand over the receiver, and whispers into it.

'I'm no pervert,' the Senator protests, 'don't you know who I am? I'm the Junior Senator from Wisconsin.'

'The lady...' says the Secretary, 'claims to be the Junior Senator from Wisconsin. Yes. Yes. No, I wouldn't say so. She doesn't... Okay, I'll send her in.' The Secretary puts down the phone and stares suspiciously at the Senator. 'The Director will see you now, madam.'

As the Senator steps through the door, Hoover falls out of his chair. 'Mac?' he cries.

'Speedy, you gotta help me.'

'But Mac, is it really you?'

'I don't know anymore. I've lost my cock. It's been appointed Chief Justice of the Supreme Court. It's become the Cock Court! That tool's going around as if it doesn't know me. It has to be a Communist plot!'

'You better let me see,' the Director leers, licking his lips. 'Drop those pants.'

The Senator unbuckles his belt, unbuttons and unzips his trousers, lets them fall to the floor, and steps out of his shorts. The Director stares in disbelief and then kneels before the Senator. He looks up between the legs, spits on his fingers, reaches inside the cavity, and rummages around. The Senator lets out a whimper, bracing against the desk as the Director's hand sinks in up to the wrist making a squelching noise, like someone stirring a bowl of warm macaroni.

'By gosh, your whang's really gone, isn't it?' The
Director exclaims, retracting his hand. He grimaces,
seems about to be sick, and fastidiously wipes
his fingers on a handkerchief. 'And you say your
whizzbang is now Chief Justice?'

'I've just been at the Court! I've seen it with my
own eyes.'

'I'll have to inform the CIA and Joint Chiefs of
Staff. A prong as small as yours will never be up to
the job!'

'What about the President?'

'Truman's the goddamn problem! This has gotta be his
doing - a recess appointment! I've long suspected the
old haberdasher of being a Russian agent but this
proves it. Don't worry, Mac, we'll get your little
pecker sniveling back in place before the day is out.'

LATER

It's the end of the day, and nothing has happened
to reunite the Senator with his missing part, so he
goes home, examines himself in the mirror, and tries
to accommodate himself to his new body, the ovoid
pertness of his breasts, the hips still growing wider
by the hour, the lustrous hair spilling across his
shoulders. Billy looks at him in astonishment. 'It's
going to take some getting used to,' Billy mumbles
dejectedly.

The next morning, no one will take the Senator's
calls. Word has spread that he's a pervert given
to dressing in women's clothes and wearing a wig.
Over the course of the week, the transfiguration
continues until the Senator no longer recognizes the
person he used to be. Shunned in the halls of the
Capitol, he finds himself removed from committees
and when he appears on the floor of the Senate,
colleagues call him 'Congresswoman'. There are
threats of an investigation, removal from office,
institutionalization, and even imprisonment.

MEANWHILE

Chief Justice Cock has been busy transforming the
Supreme Court, fulminating from the bench against
the Red Menace and expanding the powers of our
nation's highest court to handle matters of national
security. A series of televised trials begins, each
one condemning the accused Communists and homosexuals
in government and civil society to life in prison.
Six senators are tried and found guilty, forty-seven
congressmen and congresswomen, one of the Joint
Chiefs of Staff, several dozen members of the FBI,
CIA, and local law enforcement. Even the President
himself is called to trial, cross-examined by Chief
Justice Cock (who, when excited, begins to foam at
the mouth), found guilty of being a Russian spy, and
sentenced to life in federal prison. Chief Justice
Cock appoints himself President-Chief Justice and
moves into the vacated White House. The trials
continue until the Junior Senator from Wisconsin is

also arrested, charged, and delivered one morning to
the Supreme Court to face trial.

Since the Senator was last there, the Court has
been redecorated in fascist style, little parallel
lightning-bolt cocks adopted as the symbol of the new
order, black silk bunting flowing from the rafters.
The WARDEN OF THE COURT calls for the public to rise
as the Chief Justice and his fellow Justices, now
looking like a group of cowed, terrified men relieved
only by the fact they themselves have not been tried
and sent to prison, enter and sit behind the bench.
The Senator is called to the witness stand and,
wearing a demure wool suit in pale blue tweed with
a matching pillbox hat, swears to tell the truth.
Trials are brief, with only the Chief Justice asking
questions, ignoring the answers of the accused, never
hearing other testimony, and passing judgment after
a brief recess. Condemnation is swift and absolute
because there is no court of appeal.

The President-Chief Justice is more erect than usual,
head red and throbbing, a thin white stream dribbling
from his mouth, but since his apotheosis the capacity
to speak sense has declined appreciably. 'The
defendant's accused of compromising national security
by making outrageous, I mean totally unfounded,
ridiculous... the defendant is a fantasist, made
these claims against the President-Chief Justice,
that is myself, and also compromised, you know, by
perverting his own body to that of a female while
still, STILL, holding public office, so in the

opinion of the court, this is, you know, a huge
Communist plot and undoubtedly, I mean, it's clearly,
any dick can see, a contravention of the morals
clause, the man is a pervert, disgusting, sad to see
the state of the country, this is a national crisis,
the clause in his contract with all you good - you
American - people. How does the pervert plead?'

'Not guilty, your honor,' the Junior Senator says in
a voice ringing with confidence.

The Cock purses its mouth and smirks, looking to the
other Justices who, in turn, titter nervously. 'What
do you say in your defense? I mean, we shouldn't
even give you the chance, you've wasted our time,
you've put the American, all those good Americans,
the people of our country, they're in grave danger,
mortal, I mean moral, but I guess we have to do it by
the, we'll let you say what you have to say because
we are the highest, due process and all that, I
mean this is a great democratic, the institution is
everything. What do you say?'

The Senator shimmies at the lectern, looks to the
Press and then to the Cock, and speaks:

'You are in fact my <u>own</u> cock, and by some magic you
removed yourself from my body and in that removal,
my body, through no fault of its own, turned into
a woman. I don't want to be a woman, but I will be
since I have no other choice. The real perversion
would be if I continued to dress as a man while

clearly now being a woman. I don't know what you
would wish me to do. You refused to reattach yourself
to me, and yet you condemn me for being a woman.
Would you have me steal another man's cock? That
would amount to theft and assault and a perversion
all its own. There seems no possibility of me
answering you to your satisfaction.'

'The Court finds the defendant guilty,' yells the
President-Chief Justice, banging his gavel.

'But you haven't even conferred with your fellow
Justices,' the Senator protests.

'Quiet! <u>You</u> shut up! You've had your say!' the
Cock sputters, a white stream shooting across the
chamber and blinding the Press corps. 'The guilt of
the defendant is, you know, it's obvious. Any fool
can see, you've made, how you've just made the same
claims against the President-Chief Justice you're
charged with yourself, and you, right here, you said
it, I heard you say, you admitted to being a woman.
Nothing could be plainer. I'd say "Off with her head"
and maybe I should, but for nostalgia, because I
remember and whatnot, I won't. I sentence you to life
in a secure psychiatric facility along with all the
other Communist agents. It's sad, really, the state
of this country. Huge mess. You caused it, people
like you. Disloyal. Sex perverts. Thinking you can
change your sex just like that, overnight, like it's
a choice. You should be ashamed of yourself. The
Court is recessed.'

A couple of Supreme Court thugs muscle the Senator
into a straitjacket for the journey to a federal
asylum in Virginia. En route, the Senator rants about
the plotting of Red Fascists.

WEEKS LATER

One morning, the former Junior Senator from Wisconsin
wakes from a sound sleep to find his cock back in
its place, his chest as flat as it once was, ample
hips almost as narrow as they once were. Just as
astonishing, the doors of the asylum are open and
when the Senator returns to Washington he discovers
the President-Chief Justice has disappeared, the real
President returned to office, and life carrying on as
it had only a short time earlier. Because his hair is
long, he goes immediately to see his barber, Irving
Jakobson, who greets him with a look of surprise and
not a little fear.

Irving cuts the Senator's hair, gives him a
shave, and offers a tonic rub, which the Senator,
repossessed of his cock and eager to see if it
works, happily accepts. As he lies on the massage
table in the backroom, enjoying the capable hands
of the barber, he thinks about all that his cock so
quickly accomplished. Before the day is out, he vows
to subpoena everyone he suspects of being Communists
and sex perverts, many of whom were locked up with
him in the asylum. Like his cock before him, he will
bring them to trial and condemn them for subversion,
perversion, and plots against the state. He has to

166

admit, privately of course, that the other great Joe of the moment, the Uncle Nemesis on the other side of the globe, got something right in his purges and show trials. Create fear and chaos, and you can do whatever the hell you want.

5

Tonight, my neighbor is holding a party, a book launch for an Austrian writer whose new novel has just been published in Italian. The young writer, who is dressed as I imagine Hans Castorp might have been, with an Alpine crispness, also reminds me of you, Myles. At first, spotting him from behind, across the salon with its modernist furniture beneath a ceiling of grotesques, waiters passing trays of canapés and glasses of prosecco to Marchesas and Contessas and Baronessas, to the mayor and heads of local cultural organizations, I think for an instant that this blond young man *is* you, that I am seeing you as you were in 1950. While I know this cannot be true, the fantasy is so bewitching it makes my heart beat faster.

During the speeches – one from our host, one from the publisher, one from the Austrian novelist himself – a Spanish novelist I know is holding my arm, whispering to me about the Austrian's book, which reviewers in Germany have savaged as racist. When the Austrian eventually turns so that I can see his face, I realize he is not particularly young, perhaps already in his fifties, and he looks nothing like you except for being blond, his skin bronzed, his height more or less your height. But his face is plump where yours has always been lean (even in the most recent pictures I can find, from ten years ago, how angular you remain), his skin pocked and uneven. At last seeing him for who he is, the fantasy shatters and my heart collapses in on itself. I lean against my Spanish novelist friend for support, but he is on fire, trashing this Austrian in my ear because he does what the Spaniard regards as being in unthinkably bad taste in contemporary literature: he writes about dreams, employs the weather as a signifier of narrative and characterological affect, overtly references myth: the new novel, set in the Caribbean, uses

Homer's *Iliad* as a structuring device. None of this is possible, not anymore, says my friend. Modernism killed all of that, but *all of it*. Now we must only write about the real. Satire is dead. Symbolism is dead. Even comedy, it has no place anymore, not in serious writing.

I touch his hand, the long beautiful fingers of a caballero, fingers I suspect may recently have been running through the hair of my companion Alessio, have perhaps done even more than that. I stare into his blue eyes and tell him I think we have a different notion of literary rules and timelines and what may or may not be possible. Nothing is dead, Néstor, nothing verboten, anything remains possible, I tell him. Otherwise, why even try? He smiles beneath his moustache, a smile that disarms and devastates me. A different tradition, perhaps, he says, and offers to fetch me a drink.

Alone in my corner, gazing at this salon full of people in beautiful clothes each in their different way trying to ignore the crisis of this moment, when Italy is leaderless and it feels as though anything might happen, I am struck by what has changed. Our host, my neighbor, is queer, the Austrian writer is queer, my Spanish novelist friend and myself and Alessio and more than a dozen other men and women in the room are queer, and we no longer apologize, at least not in a gathering such as this. We no longer suggest we are anything other than ourselves when the Marchesas and Contessas and Baronessas (who claim in many cases to be Communists) ask us how we have been. They know the names of our partners. They know Alessio is not a 'friend' or 'assistant' or 'roommate' but my lover, however much younger he is, however increasingly emotional rather than physical our love becomes. They invite us for dinner, treat us as friends, and I have no sense of myself as an ornament or pet, no suspicion that when the door is closed and they are speaking with one another or their husbands or children that they gnash their teeth and make disparaging remarks about us because of who we are, by nature, destined to love. Was it always this way in a certain milieu? I am sure it was not so among the people you and I once knew professionally. We could never be certain of safety without prior knowledge. We were always on our guard and wondering if we might be betrayed. And we would never have been so flagrant as the two men I watch now across the room, arms and legs draped over each other, paging through the Austrian's impossible book.

You may wonder whether I regretted my decision to accompany John that morning in April long ago. The truth is I doubted nearly everything I did that day and the intervening years have done little to reassure me the decisions I made were the right ones. I should have told you sooner of my plans. In not telling you I should at least have remained in your presence. Or, in leaving your side, I should have done something to fight for my place, even if that meant going to war with my own conscience.

The trolley had already rattled back towards the soundstages and John and I were left alone on the shores of an artificial lake. A bridge led us into the African Jungle, which was neither of the things its name proclaimed. It had done service as Africa and Asia and South America, even as North America and Europe, but was nothing more exotic than a stand of eucalyptus trees interplanted with a thicket of tropical ferns, palms and cycads garlanded with artificial vines of varying tensile strengths from which Tarzan could swing. The air was heavy with the astringent scent of gumtrees, the ground dry, and the day was already hot.

Of course I regretted my decision.

John swept his hand across his brow and stared at me with a wild eye, as if he suspected me of betrayal as much as he did Mary. I had the impulse to run after the trolley, recognizing that in following John I was allowing myself to be led, and certain that even if we did find Mary, we would fail to convince her to do anything other than what she intended. Mary did not take direction, she *was* direction, all force and speed and bearing. Believing you might convince her to do anything other than what she wished was like sneezing into a passing freight train in hopes you might derail it.

I knew I was junking my time on a fool's errand that was worse than quixotic. It was the folly of cowards believing they could change the mind of a bully. I followed John because I was cowardly – not for the decision I had made to leave America but because I lacked the courage to tell you what I planned. That was my most egregious cowardice. Perhaps you will say that my refusal to sit before our elected representatives was the greater weakness, but the older I get the more I believe there is nothing cowardly in fleeing certain defeat. I recognize how self-justifying that may seem to those who have never been faced with such a critical moment of danger. I was afraid of what would happen if I stayed, afraid even of what I might do to compromise myself in order to preserve my liberty. You see even here, decades distant, how easily I regret my principled stance, how quickly I start to think that a less ethical response would have been a price worth paying if it meant staying with you.

You were the first man since college whom I had loved for more than a month at a stretch, and the anticipation of your heartbreak, the twin expectation of my own anguish, knowing I could not possibly leave without speaking to you and giving you the chance to come with me, was enough to hold me in John's thrall for a time. Distraction, nothing more. Maybe I still hoped that the outcome of my meeting with Krug and Cherry would save me from exile, that those two brutes would offer a solution, but confusion and fear muddled my thinking. The argument with you the night before had not helped, nor the late-night coffee that fueled my revision of scenes which would never arrive unaltered on screen, nor the sense that my capacity to speak an honest word had diminished so precipitously that everything dribbling from my mouth was more than half fiction. It is not that I lied to you, never intentionally, only that I withheld great volumes of truth, afraid at what you would say if you knew.

John walked quickly, arms pumping at his sides, head bobbing left and right, his lips moving as if he were talking to himself. A few yards into the trees a sign left over from the jungle's service as an enchanted forest warned us: TURN BACK NOW WHILE YOU STILL HAVE A CHANCE.

Thick-crowded with ghosts.

You know I don't read poetry, Desmond.

Just a line from an old picture.

In the heat, trying to function on so little sleep, I began to feel unsure of the boundaries of my body so that objects were both farther and closer than they appeared, as one feels when succumbing to fever or experiencing the vertiginous effects of a dolly zoom. It would not have been the first time my body produced illness to avoid a crisis. I had already been in a car accident that morning, never mind that I blamed it on a bird, and I knew that worse might happen if I did not keep a close watch on every movement I made. Trip over a vine and break a bone, walk into a low-hanging branch and suffer concussion. My subconscious was trying to manufacture ways of making me stay.

The path was uneven and John stumbled, catching himself on a vine. I called out to see if he was okay but he was so oblivious to my presence I began to feel no more than a shadow at his side. Within a few more paces the path branched and branched again and when I looked around I could no longer see the way back to the lake.

Which way? John shouted. Don't you have a compass?

The Boy Scouts wouldn't have me. My sense of direction has always been terrible, but I think we should turn left.

You always think that.

Better than turning right.

John squinted back at me. He set his lips, narrowed his eyes. Are you suggesting that's what I've done?

You said it, not me.

I never had much in the way of political conviction, Desmond. My father and mother both come from old southern Democrat families and they're as racist as Brownshirts. Even as a boy I knew that neither of them stood for anything that made sense to me. I couldn't hate anyone for being a different color or having an accent or speaking another language or believing in some other god or even not believing in a god, but I could also never imagine being a Republican. Most people I know would say that makes me a nutcase.

No, I think it makes you independent-minded. That's a quality I've often admired in you. That and your willingness not to condemn me for what I am. There are plenty of people who can say what you've just said but when it comes to people like Myles and me, all that independence of mind goes out the window and they follow what everyone around them believes.

I suppose you think that's what Mary does.

I don't really know what Mary thinks. We've never had a conversation long enough for me to have any notion of her beliefs apart from what I've read in the papers, and that does not persuade me she has much time for people like me. I'm only grateful you're not like that.

John unbuttoned the cuffs of his shirt and rolled up the sleeves. My brother Lionel was like you. He died back in twenty-eight. Killed by the father of his – what would you call him? The man who was to him as Myles is to you.

His lover?

John blushed. Yes, I suppose. His lover's father killed him when he found out about the two of them. That's how I understood it.

What does Mary think of that?

She thinks Lionel was killed in a bar fight. It was Prohibition, he was a bandleader who worked speakeasies. A bar fight was a natural conclusion even if it wasn't the truth. It's what the police report said. He was killed in a bar but it wasn't a fight. The man's father came in and shot him three times in the back. As John spoke his voice cracked. He shuffled and came to a stop, leaned against a tree, wiped his face, then started walking again, faster, as if he wanted to outpace the memory.

I'm sorry, John. I wish I'd known.

That was twenty-two years ago. It makes me crazy to think I'm more than a decade older than he was when he died. I never thought I'd make it past thirty myself. When Lionel was killed I said to myself: You'll end up that way, too. It was foolish but somehow it made it easier to take the loss.

And you've never thought to tell Mary the truth?

What good would it do? She never knew Lionel. She'd say he deserved it. John seemed to realize what he had said and chewed his lip like a little boy caught writing obscenities on a chalkboard. You have to understand, Desmond, when I met Mary I had started feeling old, even though I wasn't yet your age now. I'd been working in this business since I was twenty-one years old. My career was up and down so many times that when Mary came along I thought she might keep me from drifting into obscurity. That doesn't mean I didn't love her, but I always admitted to myself how my pursuit had a purpose, to borrow some luster as my own was fading. And now she's fading too, and trying to fight it in her own way. She must know that in time she'll disappear like all the other stars people couldn't live without for as long as they were young and beautiful. She's just trying to slow down the inevitable. That's what this is. I don't think she believes one way or another about anything except herself. She's her own politics and religion and pantheon.

John was panting, out of breath. In the years I'd known him he had gone from tall and lean to heavy in the legs and barrel-chested. His back arched forward, brow grew thicker and angrier, upper lip tightening and pushing out, eyes sinking into his skull, his whole person beginning to curl in on itself so that he became monstrous in a way I had never seen him in the past. Perhaps it was all the chemicals in his system, or the catastrophe of waking one morning to the news that his wife was about to betray him.

For another half hour we wandered in circles until we found ourselves at the castle the studio had used for *Frankenstein* and *Dracula* and a dozen other tales of the European night. Revamped with a coat of ivory paint and colorful flags it was, for the span of a few days, the home of an enchanted princess unlucky in love. We found a couple of horses tied up behind the façade and while the director was yelling at his actors John and I galloped off before anyone noticed.

We rode in silence but I could guess what John might be thinking, that finding Mary was the least of his problems. He must have known that if he did not name names himself he could, at best, look forward to a life begging for handouts or scrounging for work abroad. At worst, it would probably mean a stint in prison. Was it harder for him to imagine losing everything than it was for me? Did the prospect of abandoning the life he had made for himself terrify him more than the prospect of losing my freedom terrified me?

I struggled to focus the camera of my mind on the years I had spent as John's friend and collaborator, trying to capture and develop a few good memories that might redeem him, but the moment they appeared I watched them flash in my vision and disperse into air, combining with the smog that caught in my chest and on bad days made me pant when I mounted a flight of stairs. Imagination is not the same as memory. As I rode alongside him I could certainly imagine moments between us that might reassure me of his loyalty, but I could not recall any that I was certain were genuine.

I knew I had to go. I could not risk waiting to see what John would decide.

Alessio enters, removing his tie, sweeping a hand through his dark hair, and his sudden appearance grabs me, this living, breathing man calling me to bed, suggesting that perhaps this weekend he will try out his mother's recipe for *torta pasqualina* in anticipation of the Easter party we will host in a few weeks' time. I let myself be coaxed from my chair. The past has no power except as a storehouse of guilt and bad feeling, an archive of regret, and yet one that has still not exhausted me. Its exploration feels urgent for as long as the question of us, of you and me and the way that we parted, Myles, hangs pendant in my mind. Alessio waits at the door as I stand, push back my chair, walk haphazardly through a grove of books piled like the trunks of so many trees cut off in their prime, past the photographs of you captured in your youth, others that I have clipped from magazines in subsequent years, images of you as I no longer know you staring from the forest of my mind like phantoms, each of them calling, asking me why.

Come, Desmond, you will hurt your eyes in this light.

My eyes are nearly gone already, Alessio, and he lets out a puff of air, out of patience with me. I ask why he did not go home with Néstor, our Spanish novelist friend with such strict aesthetic ideas. Alessio blanches, looks at me as if I have really lost it at last. But this is my home, is it not? And anyway, Néstor is just a friend, and really not my type, too macho, too much of a top, and that is all beside the point anyway, because you are my partner and it is you who I love, even if you are still in love with that boy from the past, who is now an old man. You imagine Myles young but look at him now, he is not like me anymore, he is like *you*. Would you love him so much if he were standing here now?

I pause in my transit to the door, glance back at my desk, at the light from the corridor falling on your face, Myles, your face as it was in 1949 or early 1950. Poor Alessio, he deserves better than me.

Of course I would love you as much now, Myles. As much as ever, more than ever before.

SHE TURNED AWAY

Part Two

INT. FAYE'S CAR - DAY

Ten in the morning and the City of Angels looks like
it's waking from a long night in the bar and two
hours' rough sleep.

Orph and Faye sit tight in her car. She drives like
she sings, as though the road and the note are always
in the heart of her range.

Orph's gaze strays to Faye's hands on the steering
wheel, the little gold charm bracelet around her
wrist, the neat manicure and every other detail that
tells him she's the wife of his half-brother.

                    ORPH (V.O.)

    Faye said she'd take me round to see Ursula's
    haunts. The car was hot and the perfume coming
    off Faye's neck was the same one Ursula wore,
    a flower that was sweet till it turned rank
    and started smelling of corpses. It was hard
    not to think my brother got the better deal,
    the solid sister who didn't have a screw
    loose. Sure, I was in love with Faye. I always
    had been.

An oncoming car honks and Faye swerves, smiling as
though she enjoys the near miss. In the rearview
mirror's reflection, a dark coupe trails half a block
behind her, its bulldog front end snarling in the eye
of the mid-morning sun.

Faye runs her tongue over her lips and glances at
Orph before turning her eyes back to the road, whites

180

glinting through dark glasses. What she does with the car is less like driving than sorcery, hands sliding off the steering wheel as if testing how far she can go.

                    FAYE

     Who'd you kill to earn those stripes, soldier?

                    ORPH

     You know I didn't kill anyone. I was in the
     medical corps.

                    FAYE

     That mean you're a doctor now?

Faye swerves hard into the right lane as they careen through one of the tunnels of the Arroyo Seco Parkway and Orph has to brace himself against the door. The shift is threatening and purposeful, as if Faye were daring the door to fly open and let Orph fall to his death.

Faye checks Orph's reaction and lets the car drift back into the left lane. A truck honks its horn and Faye swerves right, tossing her blonde curls as if each near miss is part of the fun.

                    ORPH

     Just means I can tie a bandage and hold a
     man's hand when he's dying without he gets the
     idea he's on his way out.

                    FAYE

So you're more like the grim reaper? What are
they called? Ferrymen.

                    ORPH

Been working the crosswords, huh?

                    FAYE

Try to expand my vocabulary when I can.

She checks the mirror again and the dark coupe is
closer this time. As they arrive in downtown Pasadena
Faye accelerates through a yellow light and the coupe
gets caught at the red. A smile skews her mouth
deadly and she stretches her fingers, wrapping them
tighter around the wheel.

                    ORPH

Not all of them died. I applied pressure to
stop the gushing, doused wounds in sulfa, kept
airways open. I swabbed cuts and held a man's
head together in my hands. I wrapped fellows
in dressings and bandages when there wasn't
much left to bandage.

Faye makes a little shiver but if anything, she likes
the idea of violence.

                    FAYE

So you _have_ touched death.

ORPH

What is it with you? I was trying to save
lives, sister. I was looking after my buddies
and helping put 'em back together after the
Japs got done with them. Some of the fellas
in my platoon weren't so lucky. Not enough
tape and glue and medicine to save them in a
hundred years. Death's no nursery rhyme.

When she comes to a stop at an intersection Faye
turns to look at Orph, catching a drape of blonde
hair with two fingers and pushing it behind one ear.
Her lips keep drying out. She rolls them in on each
other, wets them, checks the mirror. The coupe has
caught up with her.

FAYE

If you're not a doctor does that mean you're a
nurse?

ORPH

You've got funny ideas.

FAYE

Just that I've never heard of a male nurse
before, except in a mental hospital.

ORPH

I wasn't a nurse. I don't know what I was. A
medic I guess. They called me an aid-man. I
served my country.

                    FAYE

But you didn't kill anyone.

                    ORPH

What is it with you and killing?

                    FAYE

Girl likes to know what the man next to her
might have done... Or be capable of doing. Do
you have a gun?

                    ORPH

Sure I've got a gun, locked safe in a drawer
where I don't have to think about it.

                    FAYE

But you'd know how to use it. You've used it
before. You must have...

                    ORPH

I didn't kill anyone, you hear? I saved lives
and I was good at what I did. I came back and
now I want to get on with my own.

The light changes and Faye doesn't move until the
coupe honks its horn. She makes a face, thumps the
car into gear, and veers to the left, racing the
turn.

                    FAYE

Didn't mean to suggest anything, Corporal.

                    184

                    ORPH

Cut it out with the Corporal stuff.

                    FAYE

Cut out too much and you've got nothing left.
First rule of seamstressing. Every housewife
should know.

                    ORPH

Cut out too little and the suit won't fit.

                    FAYE

Didn't know you were here for a fitting.

                    ORPH

Maybe I'm in the market for a new look.

                    FAYE

Trust me, Corporal, you could never afford <u>my</u>
tailor.

Faye smirks as she pulls the car to a stop outside a
bungalow in the Craftsman style. A stubby ten-year-
old Dodge sits in the driveway.

               FAYE (CONT'D)

First stop. No bleeding to staunch, Corporal.

                    ORPH

Whose is it?

                         FAYE

     Friend of Ursula's called Rose Zapatero. Used
     to dance at Malavita until - well, until she
     had an accident when her husband was on shore
     leave. Now he's dead and she's stuck with the
     kid and an inadequate Navy widow's pension.
     Tough little character, but she might point
     us down the right road. I have a hunch Ursula
     confided in her but I don't like Rose myself.
     I think she's cheap. You'll see what I mean.

EXT. ZAPATERO BUNGALOW - DAY

Faye rings the doorbell and a second later ROSE, a
tired young woman with a LITTLE GIRL propped on her
waist opens the door.

                         ROSE

     Ursula! Sweetheart, I'm so -

                         FAYE

     It's Faye, Rose. I'd like to introduce you to
     Ursula's husband, Corporal Orph Patterson.

                         ROSE

          (simpering)

     Oh! Oh, a pleasure I'm sure. Won't you come
     in?

As the three of them enter the house the little dark
coupe pulls to a stop down the street and we see the
driver for the first time. It's Shade's fat right

                         186

hand, Eddie Majestic. He pulls down the brim of his
hat to block the sun and slumps in the seat to keep
watch.

INT. ZAPATERO LIVING ROOM - DAY

Rose Zapatero's living room is full of shabby
furniture and black wrought-iron fixtures. Rose is
twenty-five if she's a day but she's already seen
twice as much life.

Orph and Faye stand under an arch in the threshold of
the room, Faye in her neat white suit and Orph in his
dark one. Next to each other, they look like bride
and groom.

Rose clears away newspapers and magazines before
showing Orph to a chair, then seating Faye on the
davenport. All the while the kid on her waist squawks
demands.

                    ROSE (CONT'D)
    If I'd known you was coming I'd have cleaned
    up a little. But where's Ursula? There's
    nothing wrong – but – oh my goodness there
    must be something wrong, just look at your
    faces! Oh my stars!

Rose's hand flies to her mouth as she glances back
and forth between Faye and Orph. The child screams.

                    ROSE (CONT'D)
    I swear, Maggie, one day I'll kill you.

Realizing what she's said Rose looks embarrassed,
puts her hand to the child's head, smooths down the
golden curls and kisses her on the brow.

                    ROSE (CONT'D)
          (to Orph and Faye)

     Don't think I'm a bad mother. It ain't been
     easy since Lawrence died.

                    FAYE

     I'm sorry, Rose. It must be difficult.

                    ORPH

     Thing is, my wife, Ursula that is, she
     disappeared a couple days ago.

                    ORPH (V.O.)

     Then I told Mrs. Zapatero what had happened,
     how strange Ursula had seemed, and how she'd
     vanished up in the Sierras.

As Orph tells his story, Rose looks more and more
concerned, her eyes locked on his, as if his voice is
casting a spell. She's mesmerized.

                    ROSE

     You say there was a man at the lake? Didn't
     you get a good look at him?

ORPH

It was too far away to be clear. But he was taller than me I'd guess, and built like the sharp end of a V-2.

ROSE

Course I don't want to point you in the wrong direction, but I wonder –

FAYE

What is it, Rose?

ORPH

If you know anything, you gotta tell us.

ROSE

Just that Ursula mentioned some trouble with a fella who'd loaned her money. Now I don't say I know what the money was for or nothing, but his name was Woody Montez and he helped out a few of the girls at Malavita, you know, when they couldn't make it to payday.

ORPH

You don't mean a loan shark?

FAYE

I have to say, Rose, that doesn't sound like my sister.

                    ROSE

All I know is Ursula mentioned having to go
see Woody. I coulda used a hand every now and
again myself but I was worried, see, about
what such a racket might lead to. I mean a
girl's gotta be careful when it's just her
and a kid – shut up now Maggie or I swear I'll
belt you one – and you don't know what a fella
like Woody Montez might do if you missed a
payment.

                    ORPH

You know how to find him?

                    ROSE

Ursula always met him at Café Casino, that
burlesque joint on South Main. Pretty pungent
stuff. Woody's across the street most days in
his car, 'doing business'. I bet you'll find
him there all right.

EXT. ZAPATERO HOUSE - DAY

As Faye and Orph leave the house Faye glances over
her shoulder at Rose, pauses, and slips a couple
twenties to her. Rose nods and gives Faye a wink.
Orph is already halfway to the car.

                ROSE (CONT'D)

Will you shut up, Maggie? I swear one day I'm
gonna <u>kill</u> you!

INT. FAYE'S CAR - DAY

Faye pulls away from Rose's house, checking the
rearview mirror and watching as Eddie Majestic's dark
coupe begins to follow.

                    ORPH

     Help me out, Faye, because this doesn't make
     sense. Ursula said she was on good money at
     the club and I was sending home most of what I
     earned. Why would she need a loan shark?

                    FAYE

     I admit it sounds strange, but people have
     secrets, Orph - Ursula especially. She was
     always mysterious, even with me. Maybe you
     never understood that about her.

                    ORPH

     Mysterious how?

                    FAYE

     Oh, just little things at first, when we were
     girls. If someone invited her to a party and
     didn't ask me along she'd say she was going
     to the library to study, and I'd have to hear
     about it from somebody else.

                    ORPH

     Maybe she didn't want to upset you.

Faye shakes her head and smiles, as if pained by the
memory. In the mirror, Eddie Majestic's coupe is a
couple cars behind them.

                    FAYE
     You're sweet, Orph - too sweet for my sister,
     if you'll forgive me saying so. I always
     knew I was the unpopular one. We might have
     looked the same but we couldn't have been less
     alike. I was the studious girl. I was the one
     with my head in the books and my heart on my
     sleeve. I knew when Ursula said she was going
     to the library it had to be a lie. I learned
     fast not to ask for the truth. It was that
     way all through school. The only time we were
     ever together was during choir practice, and
     she was the one who shined, you know, the
     girl with all the solos, belting out her Ave
     Marias. Then, in the year after I graduated,
     I met Jack, and everything changed. I'm just
     lucky Ursula didn't meet him first.

FLASHBACK TO:

INT. DINER - DAY

A much younger-looking Faye reads a newspaper dated
June 1, 1941. She's drinking a milkshake, more like a
kid than a young woman, perched at the counter.

The door opens and a fresh-faced Jack 'Shade' Plutone
rolls in, except his roll is punctuated by a limp and
a cane that he handles as if it were an affectation
instead of a necessity, swinging and pointing it

to draw attention to its polished wooden shaft and
intricate silver handle. It's the first time we've
seen him walking.

Hanging on a stool at the other end of the counter,
Jack can't keep his eyes off Faye. She notices him
watching and turns, swiveling on her stool. He picks
up his cup of coffee and moves to the opposite end of
the counter, closer to Faye, so he's directly in her
line of sight.

Aware of his gaze, Faye sucks the straw and turns
away from Jack once more. He moves again, returning
to the side where he started, but a little closer
this time. She turns, he moves, she turns again, and
on the final move Jack sits right next to her. It's
chess by soda counter, and nothing but a queen and
king left on the board.

                    JACK

   You should watch out. You might get dizzy and
   fall down.

Faye blushes and looks away from him.

                    FAYE

   I've never fallen in my life.

                    JACK

   What if someone was there to catch you?

                    FAYE

   A fireman, maybe?

                    JACK

    Oh no, firemen, you don't want nothing to do
    with them. They've got hot hands.

Jack holds up his palms, puts them together and draws
them quickly apart, as though singed by flames. He
shakes the right hand, blowing on it. Faye smiles.

                    FAYE

    Maybe I'm chilly. A little warmth might do me
    good.

                    JACK

    Where I'm sitting it's about 500 degrees.
    Maybe you do need a fireman. Lemme give you a
    lift to the station.

                    FAYE

    I imagine a girl who takes lifts from you
    needs rescuing. Whoever you are.

                    JACK

    I'm Jack.

                    FAYE

    Couldn't you be more original? You might at
    least call yourself Walter or Monte or Wally.

Jack produces a wallet and shows her his driver's
license. CLOSE UP on the license, and his face, which
is a little too cocksure, menacing but seductive, and
the name JACK PLUTONE in clear black letters. Faye

                    194

smiles when she sees he isn't lying and she finishes
her milkshake.

                    JACK

   I'm original in other ways. Let me show you.

Faye hesitates, then notices Jack's car key and the
convertible in the parking lot.

FLASHBACK MONTAGE

The scene dissolves to a montage of the couple
together, driving fast in Jack's car along the coast,
eating romantic dinners, going to horse races,
playing blackjack at a casino, Jack always acting
like the perfect gentleman, helping Faye out of his
car and waiting while she takes his arm.

                    FAYE (V.O.)

   I'd hardly attracted the attention of any
   boy in all my school years and I didn't want
   Ursula to know about Jack. I guess I was just
   as secretive with her as she was with me, but
   I was so afraid that if she met Jack she'd
   want him for herself, and I'd be back where
   I always was, with my head in a book. Life
   started <u>fast</u> with Jack. Everything about him
   was fast. It was thrilling and I wanted to
   keep it all to myself for as long as I could.

EXT. CIRO'S - EVENING

Jack and Faye arrive at Ciro's in his convertible and
he leads her up the shallow steps to the entrance.

His limp and cane look more than ever like the props
of a man trying to make a mark.

                    FAYE

    But isn't this where all the movie stars come?

                    JACK

    We're not here for two-bit stars. There's a
    horn player I want you to know.

INT. CIRO'S - EVENING

Ciro's opulence is a little too sophisticated for
Faye. She checks her dress against the gowns around
the room.

                    FAYE

    Do I look all right, Jack?

                    JACK

    Mrs. Asterbilt in the flesh.

On stage Orph is playing lead trumpet in a
performance of 'Song of the Volga Boatmen'. As Jack
and Faye take a table at the edge of the dance floor
the two brothers wave to each other. When the number
is finished, Orph runs over to join them.

                    ORPH

    Jackie! Shoulda told me you were coming!

                         JACK

What, and give you the chance to back out on
me?

Orph notices Faye.

                         ORPH

Wowza! Looks like you hit a gusher. Aren't you
going to introduce me?

                         JACK

Hey, wise guy, be polite around the lady. This
is Faye, the girl keeping me up nights for the
last month, and

     (to Faye)

this is my oldest and dearest burden, I mean
brother, Orph Patterson. Hippest horn south of
San Francisco. Not bad on the keys, either. In
fact, he can play just about anything.

                         FAYE

Pleased to meet you, Orph. But Jack, you never
told me you had a brother.

                         JACK

     (teasing)

Believe me, I try to forget it.

                    FAYE

But I don't understand, why the different last
names?

                    JACK

Let's just say our mother was unlucky in love
the first time. My old man croaked before I
knew him but I got stuck with the name.

                    ORPH

Listen, kids, I have to get back up there,
but stick around afterwards and we'll have a
drink.

                    JACK

You hear this? Kids he calls us! Why I
oughta...

INT. CIRO'S - CONTINUOUS

The scene dissolves through a brief interlude of Orph
playing, although as the evening continues he can't
keep his eyes off Faye and more than once he almost
misses his entrance until the BANDLEADER raps him on
the head with his baton. Orph shakes himself out of
the trance and struggles to focus on the music but
remains spellbound by Faye.

                   FAYE (V.O.)

When I met you I knew I couldn't keep Ursula
a secret from Jack, or Jack a secret from
Ursula, and that scared me more than anything,
Orph.

                     198

INT. CIRO'S - LATER

Faye looks preoccupied, glancing between the two
brothers. Jack may be in love with Faye but Orph has
seen a vision of something he doesn't know how to
live without, and Faye seems to sense it.

                    FAYE (V.O.) (CONT'D)

     So I decided I had to tell Ursula before she
     found out on her own.

INT. FAYE AND URSULA'S BEDROOM - DAY

Looking at each other's reflections in their
respective mirrors, the twin sisters sit at matching
vanity tables on opposite sides of the bedroom.

                    FAYE (V.O.) (CONT'D)

     Both of us were living at home, you remember,
     as if we hadn't stopped being children. I
     guess in a way we hadn't.

Faye's hands shake as she puts down her lipstick and
turns to Ursula. As beautiful as Faye is, she doesn't
have the same gifts of style and poise as Ursula.

                    URSULA

     What is it, dear? You look like you're about
     to boil over.

                    FAYE

Can you keep a secret?

                    URSULA

You're running away at last!

                    FAYE

No! Well, not quite. Oh, Ursula, I've met a
boy.

Ursula drops her lipstick and turns to face Faye.

                    URSULA

Just what <u>kind</u> of boy?

                    FAYE

His name's Jack and he's very handsome and I
think I'm in love with him.

                    FAYE (V.O.)

Then I told her all about him, and everywhere
he'd taken me, and meeting you, Orph, and
then, all at once, I felt that fear again...

                    FAYE

I'm warning you, Ursula, if you ever try to
take Jack away from me I'll, I'll... why I'll
<u>kill</u> you, I swear I will.

Faye realizes what she's said and looks shocked, but
not as much as Ursula.

                    URSULA

Cool off, little sister, I won't go near your
sugar daddy.

                    FAYE

    He's not a sugar daddy! It's nothing like
    that! This is why I was afraid to tell you. Oh
    but I wanted you to know, because I just can't
    tell you how happy I am!

                    URSULA

    You say he has a brother?

Faye looks surprised, but then her face settles, as
if a path out of trouble has presented itself.

                    FAYE

    Yes, as a matter of fact.

                    URSULA

    That's fine then. One for you... And one for me.

INT. RESTAURANT - NIGHT

The two couples are out to dinner, Faye and Ursula in
the middle of a crescent-shaped booth, Jack and Orph
on the outside. Ursula, who seems to know she got the
handsomer of the two brothers, looks as though she's
won a prize.

BACK TO PRESENT:

INT. FAYE'S CAR - DAY

On the Arroyo Seco Parkway, Faye and Orph glide over
the hill toward downtown Los Angeles, throwing their
faces into shadow.

                    FAYE

It was like fate had written the story before
we knew we were part of it. I have to admit
I was relieved Jack had a brother. It meant
Ursula could have what I did, or something
like it, but when she started seeing you, a
part of me still worried. You must have begun
to realize she didn't really care about me at
all...

                    ORPH

But Faye, what do you mean?

                    FAYE

She knew when Jack and I were getting married
and she went ahead and set your wedding for
the same day, so it would have to be a double
wedding, because she couldn't stand for me
to have my own moment. She had to prove to
everyone that she was the most beautiful, and
of course she was. She wouldn't even tell me
what her dress looked like until I saw it on
the morning of the wedding, and I knew when
I saw the train and veil that she'd done
everything she could to make me look like
the little sister who chose second best, the
husband who walked with a limp. With a name
like Plutone we were never going to be on the
social register.

The car slices into the shadowy city streets until
they pull to a stop outside Café Casino. Across the
road a dark sedan sulks, but there's no one inside.

                    202

                    ORPH

What now?

                    FAYE

Let's check inside the club. Someone's bound
to know where we can find Montez.

INT. CAFÉ CASINO - DAY

The club is mostly deserted, chairs upside down on
the tables and a JANITOR punching time.

Orph watches as Faye approaches and talks to the man,
but she's far enough away that he can't hear what
passes between them. She comes back shaking her head.

                 FAYE (CONT'D)

Says he knows Woody Montez but that's not his
car. Thinks we might find him in Palm Springs.
He gave me an address.

                    ORPH

Kinda hot for the desert.

                    FAYE

You wanna find him or don't you? I'll take you
there but I should phone Jack first to let him
know.

                    ORPH

Sure, sure. I'll wait here.

INT. CAFÉ CASINO BUSINESS OFFICE - DAY

Faye picks up a phone in the cramped office. Turning
over files and closing doors, she moves like she
knows the place a little too well.

                    FAYE
          (into the receiver)

    No, darling, he doesn't expect a thing. I
    promise, this'll be the end of it. If Woody
    can't make him stop, I'll end it myself.

Internal Memo

April 7, 1950

To: John Marsh and Desmond Frank

CC: Leo Krug, Nick Charles

From: Porter Cherry

Gentlemen –

Further to Mr. Breen's review of the most recent
draft of <u>She Turned Away</u>, I have been asked to
communicate the following points:

1. Under no circumstances may there be any suggestion that the Rose Zapatero character is an
   unwed mother. It must be perfectly clear that
   she is a widow.

2. Mr. Breen urges you to eliminate any criticism
   of the military widow pension plan. This plan
   is entirely adequate in the vast majority of
   cases.

3. Mr. Breen requests that Mrs. Zapatero not
   threaten her young child with death. Undue
   crudeness in women and threats of violence
   against children are unacceptable and
   unnecessary in a picture of this kind, where
   they serve only to make a seedy atmosphere
   more distasteful. He trusts that you will
   address these concerns so that the portrayal
   of the Zapatero woman is firmly in the bounds
   of good taste.

4. As is expected, Mr. Breen has cautioned us
   that we must review all costuming decisions
   for our actresses, and the way our women are
   being lit and photographed. Breasts, I need
   not remind you, must be entirely covered

throughout the picture. Failure to clothe our
actresses as modesty demands will result in
the picture's failure to secure approval for
release.

Nick Charles has been directed to review these
concerns on the studio's behalf.

Yours truly,

Porter Cherry

Internal Memo

April 7, 1950

To: Porter Cherry
CC: Leo Krug

From: John Marsh and Desmond Frank

Porter, you great flaming ass –

Rose Zapatero is a fiction within the world of
the film. She is later shown to be nothing but an
invention, and therefore everything she says is
false, that is to say a fiction within the fiction,
so what does it matter whether she criticizes
the military widows' pension plan since she is a
character of the underworld who cannot be trusted
and is inherently immoral (thus not someone with
whom the audience would naturally sympathize)? Her
threats of violence against the child are intended
to demonstrate her unsavory character, nothing more,
and it's perfectly clear from the reactions of the
two other characters in the scene how despicable they
find her. Moreover, we later discover that the woman
presenting herself as Rose is nothing but an actress,
and therefore no real threat could have been made, if
you see what we mean (though we don't trust, sadly,
that you see anything about this picture clearly).
Besides, you should trust that Helen Fairdale will
play the part with her usual nuance and care, so that
these meanings are understood by the audience.

As for issues of modesty, we can only assert that
all costumes are, as ever, well within the bounds
of taste – achingly within them as a matter of
fact, to the point that no virile man could ever
hope to be aroused to action or perversion or even

mild onanistic pleasure by anything he sees in our castrated little picture. It will be the erotic equivalent of watching Harry Truman speak, which is to say a most powerful discourager to acts sexual.

Yours with only the greatest respect, admiration, and consternation,

Marsh and Frank

6

Sunk in fatigue from last night's party, in the haze of another cold morning, I ask Alessio to bring me a glass of blood orange juice, a strong coffee, a piece of pear cake, a breakfast that should stop my ancient heart, but I eat and drink as if I have consumed nothing for days. He offers to sit and read to me, but I remind him I am not yet blind nor too tired to read on my own, and to prove it I pick up a book from my library table and open to a random page. So often it happens that such openings present felicitous passages, sentences that speak uncannily out of the past to a present conundrum. So it was this morning.

In the sixth of his theses *On the Concept of History*, Walter Benjamin writes that trying to describe 'the past historically' is not the same as 'recognizing it "the way it really was"', which would, of course, be impossible. Instead, Benjamin says, 'it means appropriating a memory as it flashes up *in a moment of danger*'. What is a *moment of danger*? Does he mean simply a moment in the present when we are trying to recount the past while also feeling ourselves imperiled by the conditions through which we are living in the midst of such retrospection? Benjamin knew what real physical danger was: he wrote this thesis while trying to escape the Nazis, and months later, certain he would not escape, committed suicide. Danger for him appeared inescapable. Is this a *moment of danger* for me now, living through an uncertain leaderless spring in Italy when a comedian presents himself from the sideshow of media as a populist voice of the people and a mass of those people in their foolishness decide that an entertainer rather than a technocrat pulling the strings of the economy is precisely what they need? Is that what it means, a *moment of danger*?

Not quite, I don't think.

For Benjamin, the *moment of danger* is that instant in which we risk
– as we are struggling to describe the past – 'becoming a tool of the
ruling classes', turning ourselves into instruments of the oppressors.
We risk presenting the past as an unbroken narrative of reality, a
recoverable time of greatness and glory, to which the oppressors
of the present can point as their regressive goal, so often couched,
ironically, in terms of progress: *Italy used to be great like this*, say for
instance in the 1930s when the trains ran on time, *and that is how
we should be again*, or *America was great like this*, say in the 1950s when
everyone 'knew their place', *and that should be the image of the country
to which we aspire*. This is what the oppressor would say, never mind
that those images of the glorious past are always partial, or that
there are other images of other pasts, counter-histories recounting a
different story, one that the oppressors never want to see recovered,
never even want to admit existed.

My own flashes of memory I recognize as sporadic, fragmentary.
They emerge from darkness only half developed, out of focus,
eccentrically framed. I order copies of every film John Marsh and
I worked on, every film you and Helen appeared in together, and
put them on the television, playing in the background as I write
this to you, hoping the passing images will act as prostheses, that
some detail, a cigarette tapped on the back of a chased silver case
by a gloved hand or a line of hardboiled dialogue or a polka dot
scarf flying out the side of a convertible might trigger a flash that
would bring forth an image more complete, detailed, than what I
seem able to summon on my own. The desk in this apartment of
mine, though different from my desk in Los Angeles, made out of a
different wood, crafted in a different shape, according to a separate
tradition of design, nonetheless recalls to my mind that other desk

I had to leave behind when I fled my house in Brentwood never to return, abandoning all but that which was most essential, and my perception of this desk before me is thick with a thousand memories of sitting at that other desk, but also at the table in your living room in Pacific Palisades, at any number of desks and tables where I have worked in countless offices and bedrooms and classrooms spread across the long span of my life, and the recollections of those earlier desks bounce up from the surface of this desk, hovering in my perception, a parade of memory mirages that sparkle in my vision only so long as I do not try to reach out and grasp them, for in the instant I do, to hold fast to those memories as they appear, they inevitably disintegrate, dissolving into silvery ether.

Below, in the piazza, two carabinieri in their black uniforms, broad red stripes on their trousers, billowing black capes, their immaculate costume recalling to me a terrible past I was fortunate not to have lived through myself because I was, then, a boy in America, secure in my privilege, trot on horseback, their white horses snorting, ears back, as if the animals sense the proximity of their own moment of danger. How long has it been since I was on horseback, since I felt the flanks of an animal between my legs, since I even touched a horse's back or fed it a lump of sugar? Surely it has not been as long as I think it must have been. Surely it cannot have been since that April morning so many decades past. And yet, watching those horses in their black leather tack, I can locate no other moment in all the intervening years when I have touched a horse, and this realization comes at me with such force that my eyes fill with tears and I ask Alessio, quickly, shouting to him in the kitchen where he is helping the young woman who comes each day to cook and clean, if he could not help me downstairs to see the horses before they pass the door of our building. When he sees that it will take us too long, that my progress will be too stately down the flights of stairs, he in turn shouts out the open window, cordially, in a register of Italian that suggests deference but also authority – even, I think, superiority over those carabinieri. *My employer*, he says, although I am nothing of the kind, I pay him no salary, I give him whatever he needs, *my employer, the grand old man of the district, wishes to say hello to the horses*. I hobble to the window, raise my hand, wave as the Queen of England might wave, fingers erect, wrist rotating. The carabinieri look at each other, say something we cannot hear, and one of them calls up to Alessio to bring me down. Would I care so much to touch a horse if I did not feel certain I was nearing the end of my life? Would it matter if I felt decades were still before me when I might encounter any number of white horses on any number of bright spring mornings?

The carabinieri wait outside and when I approach them the horses stand still, breath expanding their nostrils. Whatever might have been alarming them has receded from perception and they appear calm, docile. They and their riders allow me to touch their heads, the flat planes of nose, to coo to them insensibly, as if they could understand me. One of them bats its eyes, almost coquettishly, and that is enough. I have had my fill. Time is short. I must return to my greater endeavor.

Even that morning more than half a century ago I felt the urgency of time. On my stolen horse, I gripped the reins tightly, anxious that the animal might bolt and send me flying backwards to my death. I was not like John Marsh, who rode almost carelessly. An experienced horseman, he claimed to have ridden before he could walk, so assured in a saddle that after dropping out of college he performed in an equestrian show that toured the state, which led to him finding work as a trick rider at MGM. Intoxicated though he was that morning, he sat with a lightness in the saddle that suggested a man half his weight and age, and for a moment I let myself believe he might be leading us to some momentary success if not actual victory – even that we would find Mary and manage, by the combined force of our persuasive arguments, to convince her the costs of cooperating with this national witch hunt were too great. We rode hard with our backs to the sun, trotting through alleys of scaffolding on the other side of which shootouts echoed around the timber façades of an Old West town. A barrage of rifle shots would be followed by silence, another volley, more silence, over and over, as if outlaw and sheriff were trapped in a standoff without end, a purgatory of repetition and waiting, making incremental progress that would only be apparent in retrospect. But as our surroundings shifted and the dust rose, collecting on our suits and dirtying our shoes, the realization that I was wasting my hours on a man who had already drifted off into his own story and appeared scarcely conscious of my presence struck me again.

We're chasing shadows, I called after him. We should go back to the set.

John shouted a reply over his shoulder but his words were lost in a barrage of cannon fire that announced our arrival at the edge of an open field where armies of extras in blue and gray were attacking each other. It was a poorly choreographed battle, done so cheaply that no sooner had a man dropped dead he was up again, shunting his rifle and jogging in place to give the illusion of forward movement. In the distance the director shouted through a megaphone over the thunder of those blank-firing cannons whose smoke drifted up to join a soup of pollution shadowing the sky all the way to the Santa Monica Mountains.

An explosion close at hand spooked our horses, who broke into a gallop, rushing around the back of the Union Army before turning sharply at the sound of another blast so that we soon found ourselves on the front lines of the battle. John leaned forward in his saddle as he reached out to seize a saber from one of the extras in blue. Blade slicing the air, he charged at the vanguard of Confederate soldiers who looked up at him in his dusty wool suit as if faced with the devil himself.

That's not in the script! one of the extras howled.

Get out of there, John, I shouted, but a shimmer of blonde hair in the open window of a stagecoach had caught his eye and he spurred his horse to ride in its direction, saber flying above his head. I turned my horse to follow but another blast startled the animal and it carried me past John towards a riverboat docked at a pier on the far side of the field. That's not Mary, I called to him, but John had already pulled the reins of his horse so that it circled around. At the sight of John, the team of horses pulling the stagecoach reared back on their hind legs, batting the air with their hooves, before coming to a sudden lurching halt.

What the hell do you think you're doing? the stuntman driving the coach yelled. We have to get to the river in the next thirty seconds or the shot's ruined.

John charged up to the driver's box and pulled the man from his seat, throwing him to the ground. The actress inside was shouting in a deep voice, Help! Some psycho's attacking us!

In the distance behind us the director yelled *cut* and *goddammit* but John was lost in his own story. He dismounted and ran forward, thrusting the tip of his saber into the gut of the fallen man. The blade went in slow and jagged and then stopped all at once as feathers spilled out and littered the ground.

You could have killed me! the stuntman screamed. You're lucky that's only a prop!

The actress stepped from the carriage and her blonde wig caught on the door, exposing the shaved head of a man.

You're not Mary! John flinched.

Sure as hell not, buddy.

John, I called out to him again, let's go.

I had already dismounted and John ran towards me, scrambling to board the paddleboat just as it was pulling away from the pier. Another production – or perhaps only a different unit of the same one – was being filmed on the boat, its cast assembled on the upper deck while most of the crew, dressed in waders, stood in the shallow river around the vessel. Somewhere beneath us the paddlewheel was powered by an engine chugging away, pushing the boat along steel tracks that gleamed in the concrete riverbed while a dinghy carrying the director and camera crew, huddled around the glinting black eye of a camera, swept alongside.

The director called *action* and musicians on the deck above us began playing a dirge.

I think we should stay out of sight, I said, pulling John to the floor between two benches.

Out of sight out of mind. I don't feel so well, Desmond. Everyone's out to get me. What's society but a great conspiracy to destroy the individual? Sometimes I wonder if you haven't been orchestrating everything that's happened from the moment I woke this morning.

Jesus, John, you're delirious.

Where are my friends? Who's left?

Maybe friends are only enemies in disguise, I said, scheming to use all you've ever said against you, so at the hour of reckoning your innocent words will be brought forth, perverted, and enlisted to condemn you.

Tell me the truth, Desmond. Are you working for them? The way you're sticking to me I have to wonder. Maybe you're the tail I've been wagging all these months.

Believe me, I work for no one but myself. The FBI would never have me. I'm not sufficiently crippled by self-loathing.

John glowered at me. I know how they turn your kind. You make it easy for them. Blackmail. Leverage. They find out things about you and then use that knowledge. *I* know things and I'm just a chump.

Goddamn this country. All it takes is a little panic and friends who have been friends for years wonder if they can trust each other. You know what the real problem is?

John shook his head.

Property. We're both rich and don't want to stop being rich and that's why we're being so cowardly about this whole situation.

I'm not a coward! They wouldn't let me serve!

I'm not talking about the war. If we weren't cowards we would hold our ground and when they come calling refuse to attend their unconstitutional hearings. And if they force us to attend we should refuse to speak, and if they throw us in jail we should be uncooperative. We should shout out the Bill of Rights and shit on the floors and throw their food back in their faces and go naked in the streets and tell everyone who will listen that we really do believe capitalism cannot be the only way, that there might be other, better ways, even if we haven't found them yet. Just because the alternatives we have at our disposal are imperfect doesn't mean we shouldn't strive to achieve a better government of the people. We're fighting against the forces of ossification and repression! The whole motion picture industry should be a model of resistance and look what we do! Hollywood is leading this country straight into a civil war! That's the end point of this kind of witch hunt! The ranging of two sides against each other that will never be able to unite again in common purpose because each will be convinced the other is composed of demons and perverts or fascists and fanatics. Who knows, maybe you and I *are* nothing but demons and perverts, but I'd rather be a demon and pervert than a fascist or fanatic. Before the religious nuts got hold of the idea a demon was halfway between a mortal and a god, a hero who becomes godlike in death, a spirit of genius. *Thy Dæmon, that thy spirit which keeps thee, is Noble, Courageous, high unmatchable!*

Scripture?

Better than that! Shakespeare! So call me demon and pervert but let me decide what those words mean. *Demon* for trying to transcend, *pervert* for refusing to be what they'd make me. It's all the fault of property in the end. Without property no defenses, no protection or offense to claim more than we have for all would be held in the common good. Without property or defenses no war. Without war eternal peace and what our enemies say they want most: a kingdom of God upon the earth. In fact, they don't want a godly kingdom because in a kingdom of God no one gets rich! It's right there in the Bible! *No one claimed that any of their possessions was their own, but they shared everything they had.* Jesus, my dear friend, was a Marxist of the first order. He might not have been a Communist, but a Marxist he most assuredly was. You only have to read the accounts of what he was supposed to have said. You don't even have to believe he was divine. You hardly have to believe he was an historical man. He can exist as a brilliant fiction created by a cult of lefty scribes. One of the most convincing protagonists in the history of the human race! Do you realize how like a movie the Bible is? It had too many writers on the script and the story doesn't make sense in the end and everyone who worked hardest gets no credit! Those scribes must have been as Red as the Revolution and probably most of them as queer as me because they were so patently in love with that carpenter philosopher! The entire edifice of western civilization is founded on a Red queer, John!

Sweat poured from my temples. My throat was sore and I nearly burst into tears. John put a hand against my brow. You have a Christ complex, Desmond.

I told you to stop seeing your analyst.

Dr. Werth is very sensible. He could help a man like you.

I've told you time and time again that psychoanalysis is counterrevolutionary. The real problems are class and economics – the horrendous flaming tomb of a base burning up the whole superstructure. We're all of us burning but we're too packed in ice cream and air conditioning to feel it!

The music grew louder and we turned to see the band descending from the top to the lower deck until the feet of the musicians were all around us. A coffin was placed on top of the two benches between which we had hidden ourselves and Trudie Page started speaking in her unmistakable high-pitched voice as a clarinet comically sulked.

Oh Lord, woe of woes, my darling son is lost and we must make this final passage across the tortuous, the troublous, the terrible swamp of my sorrow to deposit my boy on the far gray shore where he will be reunited at last with his father! I will never see either of my beloved men ever more, until my own last day, if God should choose to spare my soul…

Cut! the director shouted from the dinghy alongside the boat. It's supposed to be funny, Trudie, not so solemn!

Listen, Billy, I have the highest IQ on this lot and you make me act like I couldn't think without a man winding me up to play the tune. I don't see why this has to be a comedy. The words aren't funny. The Civil War isn't funny! The only thing funny is the way you're making me play it. This is about a woman grieving the death of her husband and son and you want schtick like I'm still at the Concord pitching for cheap yucks!

Do the scene the way I say and shut up already, the director yelled. If you break contract, I'll make sure you never work again. Not here, not at the Concord, not even in a graveyard. Okay, let's try it again.

Trudie and the other actors returned grumbling to the upper deck as the boat rattled back along the tracks to the pier. John peeked out to see what was happening as the music started again from the beginning.

Strange funeral.

We need to get you some coffee, John.

After Trudie had repeated the funeral oration five times, the boat pulled to a stop at another pier and the director finally called *cut* and *print*. The musicians trudged down the gangway and after they were gone John and I got up on our knees and looked out from between the benches. Trudie was still there and leaned over to help us stand. I've been wondering when you two would come out, she said. This picture is from hunger. They told me it was a drama but they've changed it on account of Billy has an idea a Civil War comedy is hep. I'm going to the commissary. You coming?

We followed Trudie's black ruffled skirts off the boat and around the edge of the lake to the New England town square. What were you fellows doing in the boat anyway?

Trying to get back to Stage 3.

Strange way of going. They send a car for me if I ask but I always take the trolley. I don't like all that star hooey.

We're looking for Mary.

Trudie frowned. Of course I don't know anything about it, John, but I'm pretty sure I saw her headed for the East Gate a couple hours ago.

You must be mistaken. She wouldn't leave the lot. We're supposed to be shooting.

Trudie squinted at us. Then why aren't you shooting?

Because I'm looking for Mary.

You're not making much sense. Maybe you should see a doctor, John. You look a little green.

Across the town square smoke billowed above the roofs of the buildings and after turning a corner we arrived all at once in the middle of the night, on the edge of a prison riot. John stepped back and forth between daylight and darkness, looking skyward as if he failed to understand what was happening.

Far gone, isn't he? Trudie whispered to me. What's he on?

He thinks Mary's turning snitch to the Feds.

Wouldn't surprise me. She once put a yellow star on my dressing room door. Of course she claimed it wasn't her but no one else was around. When I confronted her she said, *but Trudie, darling, why be upset? It's a star, and you're a star. It seems perfectly silly to make a fuss.* You know how she is.

We watched as John ran back and forth between morning and midnight, his eyes wild with bewilderment.

Poor fool thinks the duvetyn is real night, Trudie laughed, and then she was caught up in the mêlée and borne away by the crowd of extras. Sorry, Desmond, see you later! she shouted as the rioting men floated her body on their hands and put her down gently on the far side of the set.

The prison was on fire and those hundreds of men dressed as convicts were shouting for it to burn. Everyone looked a little panicked, as if the fire or the riot were getting out of control, flaming beyond artifice and into reality.

You guys a part of this scene or not? one of the convicts asked me.

Before I could answer another one seized John and yelled, It's the warden! He's the one we want! We're supposed to throw him in the fire!

Pig!

Fat cat!

Enemy of the people!

I watched horrified as three men tore John's jacket from his back and began beating their fists against his shoulders. He bent double to protect himself but the men forced him upright again and one of them punched him square in the face, splitting his lip open. I had never been in a fight, not once in my life, but I tried to intervene, placing myself between John and the men as the mob propelled us closer towards the prison gate where the flames were most intense. At the moment it seemed we might be pushed straight into the fire, I saw there was a gap in the flames and seized John's hand, pulling him through the blaze and around to a quiet corner behind the gate, just out of sight of the mob.

We were both out of breath, scorched but not burned, John's shirt filthy and his face covered in blood.

I lost my jacket.

You'll get another.

I seem to be bleeding.

We'll get you patched up, John.

How do we get past them?

It was a reasonable question. The gap in the flames had closed so that we were stuck between the prison set and the backlot's high perimeter fence. By chance, I noticed a manhole cover and remembered a conversation I'd had with that carpenter I once slept with which made me think it might offer an escape.

Help me with this, I said.

Together, John and I lifted the cover and pushed it aside. I climbed down first, finding my way by touch until I dropped into darkness. John followed, balancing on the narrow ladder so that he could pull the cover back into place before climbing down to join me at the bottom. In the dark he felt for my hand.

It took a moment for my eyes to adjust but sunlight was coming in from grates farther along the tunnel and that was enough to guide us. Time seemed to thicken, the planet dragging in its rotation, flattening us both. John breathed in a lungful of sewer air and doubled over, retching. I held his shoulders as he heaved, vomiting like he was bringing up organs. When he was finished he coughed a few times and wiped his face.

Any better?

Turned inside out. Where are we, Desmond?

This tunnel runs back to Main Street. There should be an exit near Stage 5. It's a half-hour walk from here. Back in the twenties they were going to build an underground train to link the soundstages to the backlot, to make more efficient use of studio land, but then they ran out of money and repurposed it as a sewer. You can't say the studio doesn't know how to reuse what it has. All the fundamental principles are already in place, you know?

I don't follow.

I mean politically speaking. Films are of necessity *communal* works, made by a community of people sharing in the labor, doing the jobs for which they are most suited by their natural talent or ability. *Jeder nach seinen Fähigkeiten, jedem nach seinen Bedürfnissen!*

You shouldn't speak German, Desmond. It makes you sound suspicious.

I ignored him and continued. The difference is most of the people on this particular assembly line don't get paid what they deserve or what they need, and the problem comes from the top, with Leo Krug and the New York executives who see this not as a great communal endeavor for the creation of art and mutual cultural benefit but as a factory producing units to sell to a populace bewitched by the screen stories and transformed by those illusions into zombies of false consciousness, believing they too might overcome the daily tribulations of life in this nation just as their favorite stars do, trusting they too might strike it rich and employ maids and own country houses in Connecticut. But you and I, John, we know better. Such dreams are only for the lucky – people like you who won the game through hard work and innate talent, and people like me born with every advantage and nurtured by parents and teachers to keep them and their offspring always advancing higher. It's a system stacked against people like you, John. You managed to beat it but you're the exception—

John had increased his pace and was walking ahead of me. I knew he had stopped listening because this was not a version of the American story he wanted to hear. No matter how much money he had, how large a house or how many cars, he would never stop being a boy from gold-rush country who had panned in streams, climbed apple trees, and stolen into vineyards to eat grapes from the vine. He would always be hungry for more, guarding his plate with both hands, and he would always want to believe that the myth of America was anything but. With a wife he had discovered he could not trust, there were only a handful of friends who might stand by his side. His parents still lived on the same land where his father had been born, and where his mother insisted she would go on keeping house although John had offered to build them a larger one, pay for a housekeeper, and give them a new car every year. When he once asked if they would consider moving to Los Angeles, his mother, raised a Presbyterian but converted to the Foursquare Gospel of Sister Aimee Semple McPherson's radio ministry, said they could not conceive of it given what they had heard about the doings of the Hollywood community. Sodom and Gomorrah. He had invited them to each of his premieres but they had never condescended to attend. *It would make your father uncomfortable*, his mother claimed. *He prefers I should read him the Bible, and that is my pleasure and duty.*

To fill the silence between us I kept talking, my voice echoing along the tunnel, arms and hands gesticulating, but John was now several paces ahead and seemed oblivious. I wondered whether he would notice if I stopped and turned back, but I hurried up to catch him so that soon we were again walking two abreast, quickening our speed as I went on narrating my screed against the studio, the system, the way America had turned against itself and turned its own people against one another, until the two of us broke into a steady run, and although we did not say why we were running haste seemed paramount: we had to find Mary, to finish shooting that film while we still had time, because time was running beside us, flowing in the filthy red water at our feet, water so red with iron it looked like blood, splashing up against our legs and reminding us that this might be our last day on the lot.

After a quarter hour of running John stumbled to a stop ahead of me, climbed a ladder, heaved a manhole cover clear, and disappeared into the light. I stood there a moment alone, the light from above catching my face. In the strange silence that settled around me, I was sure I heard another pair of feet in the tunnel, and the low murmur of a man trying to quiet his breath.

7

In my youth, I was never one to tabulate my accomplishments. I hardly kept track of what I completed, working along steadily, trying to keep myself occupied and using writing as a means of preserving my sanity. But now, as the end approaches, I feel moved to catalogue the products of my mind. In the absence of children who might outlive me, there are only these works, the films and books and stories I wrote, which may have given pleasure or solace to strangers as well as to friends, and which may, if they have any value, outlast my own presence on this earth. Is that not what everyone wishes, to be certain that something of us remains even when we are gone, that someone somewhere will remember we were present for a microsecond of history? *She Turned Away* was not my greatest work, but I feel affection for it nonetheless, perhaps because of your place in it, Myles, your role in bringing it to life, although I know that if it is remembered now or in the future it will be not because of me, not really, but because of you and Mary and John, who animated my words with such vividness.

This evening Alessio helps me begin the project of cataloguing. Copies are missing – editions of some books, particularly from the series of Orph Patterson novels that followed the film, because I was too generous in giving away what stock I had, and copies of some films, because they were made before video and DVDs and such technologies were ever invented. So we set about ordering what is missing to fill in the blanks in my own collection of myself. I describe these books and films as *myself* because what else are they, even the films, even when produced and populated and made possible by the participation and performance of so many others, but an aspect of my own mind and person? It is a narcissistic project, but no different in a way to what other elderly people do, making albums of their children and grandchildren, sending an annual holiday letter to friends and family recounting all the successes and minor dramas of their offspring. The larger archive – haphazardly maintained over the years – of correspondence and contracts and drafts of the books and scripts, is already boxed up in this study, where Alessio knows to find it after my death. Who will care about such papers when I'm gone, or about my library? I thought of leaving it to you, or to your own children, Myles, those children I have never met and yet about whom I feel a strange sense of relation, as if I had made them possible, even though I was not the one responsible for bringing you and Helen together. But perhaps I *was* responsible for ensuring that you remained together. Perhaps my departure facilitated the longevity of your union and the children you acquired.

Forgive that note of bitterness. I know that had I remained there would have been no children for me unless I entered into my own lavender marriage, and I do not mean to suggest I disapprove of your family, or resent the fact that you were able to have one. The choice was there for me to make, and I refused it. Do your children help mitigate the melancholy of old age? Do you look at them and feel a sense of consolation that your spirit will continue beyond your physical presence, that you have made some lasting mark upon them that they will in turn pass along to their own children, or do you feel just as uncertain as I that you have done anything to ensure you are remembered after all who have known you are themselves dead and gone?

Alessio tells me I think too much about such things, and instead suggests it is the fate of the queer artist without children to leave behind nothing apart from his works. Easy for you to say, I tell him, you might fall into bed tomorrow with some young woman who would produce an heir for you. But this is disgusting, Desmond. What, the idea you might love a woman? I don't see that's disgusting. Of course not, no, he says, but all this talk of heirs and inheritance. This is not a need that I feel. I am here, I live, I love you, when you are gone I will love others, and I will try to be a good person and leave behind some decent work, the best work I can produce, and if that is not enough, then at least I have tried to be kind to those who know me, even to strangers who just encounter me. It sounds very cozy, I say, and he grimaces. You are in a bad mood. This raking over the past, it makes you sour. You should live for now, or get on the phone and call Myles and tell him for goodness sake the silence has gone on long enough, you're sorry, can you please come see him, or whatever you imagine might happen. I wouldn't resent it, I would totally understand. Anyway, it's time for bed, almost midnight.

He is right, of course, but the fact is I cannot bring myself to do it, to pick up the phone, or even to apologize to you without also holding you to account for your own decisions that day more than sixty years ago.

As John and I emerged from the sewer twelve tones rang bronze and equal through the air, reminding me there was only an hour until my lunch with Krug and Cherry. A reek of vomit was coming from John so I led us to the Men's Wardrobe building and asked them to loan us a couple of suits. In a corner stuffed with armor John and I undressed, bundling our dirty clothes into paper bags. I had escaped most of the blows at the prison shoot but John's body was blooming with yellow and purple splotches. The cut on his lip had stopped bleeding and one of the wardrobe boys brought us cotton swabs and a bowl of warm water.

I can do it, John said, splashing on the floor.

No, let me, your hand's trembling, I imagine I said, and he gave me a pitiful smile of defeat. We had never been as close as this, standing in our briefs with clothes piled around us and suits of Roman armor clattering above our heads. While I dabbed at the dried blood on his face it struck me that the scene had been dressed for a different variety of encounter, one that neither of us would have wanted, and yet John put a hand tenderly, almost intimately, on my bare shoulder, as if he was imagining a future in which he would open himself to the full spectrum of desire. Nothing happened of course. Neither of us wished for anything of the kind, or at least I did not. I realize I cannot speak for John, who may have had more complex feelings than I assume.

Once I had finished with John's wound we dressed in fresh white shirts, navy suits, silk ties, and slipped back into our own socks and shoes, which one of the wardrobe boys had polished.

I want to say sorry, Desmond. I know you're not against me. I wasn't in my right mind.

Don't apologize. In this time and place you would have to be naïve not to wonder if everyone around you isn't engaged in an elaborate deception. When I lie next to Myles I ask myself whether what he tells me is true. How can you trust a genius of artifice, whose job is to sell the most convincing lies? Writers, too, we're no different, it's just that we don't have to perform our lies in the flesh. And you, John, in a way you're the master deceiver because you have to orchestrate word and flesh and make the lies convincing at one remove from reality, to make my lies and Myles's lies and the lies of the scenery and locations marry in a semblance of truth. How do I know I can trust you? How do you know you can trust me? We're caught in this rotten system of professional deception and what have we left but blind trust? I trust you because of the length of our friendship and the fact that you've always been fair with me. I trust you because you know about Myles and me and say nothing to no one. I trust blindly and wildly that Myles doesn't go to bed with his wife or, God forbid, take himself down to that gas station on Hollywood Boulevard to sleep with some man other than me. And I trust him because he assures me he doesn't. If I didn't trust him I would be alone, miserable and paranoid, until the day I died. You're right to wonder who you can trust. In the end, it's a gamble. We think the hand we hold is stronger than the hand of the man or woman across the table and so we put down our chips and take off our gold watches and lay down the deeds to our properties, strip off our clothes, and sit here naked, betting *everything* in our possession because we think we know the truth about the people in whom we've invested our trust in this hazardously blind way. And in the end, you know, it's mostly the fault of this capitalist system. If we didn't have property to lose we'd all be much happier and more trusting.

Do you know the term *idée fixe*?

Don't be facetious, John. Your tie is crooked.

I straightened John's knot and John straightened mine and we stared at each other, separated by age, desire, and background. In the end the separations mattered not a little and yet genres remained fluid. I did not desire John but I loved him in a way and so, feeling almost weightless with affection, I took him in my arms and held him, trying, though I was so much younger, to convey a sense of avuncular reassurance. I *trust* you, John. And you can always trust me. So I want you to know that I've decided to leave the country.

There you see, Myles, that I did not just deceive you, but I told others before telling you who deserved to be the first to know. Often it has proved easier to tell the hardest truths to those about whom I care less – not the least, but less than those who occupy all the rooms of my heart, as you did, as you continue even now to do.

I did not count on the effect my news would have. For me it seemed almost self-evident that this was a choice I might make, but John rocked back on his heels in shock. When, Desmond?

Probably tomorrow, depending on what happens at lunch today. I can't get out of bed another morning wondering if I'm going to have to dodge a summons or worry what will happen if I don't duck it and end up in front of the House Committee. I want to believe I'd have the courage to tell them to go fuck themselves but the idea of prison nearly undoes me. And then I could not help neutralizing the tension of the situation by talking to fill the space of emotion I had opened between us for fear that John might try to argue me out of it, or begin to cry, or hug me as I had just hugged him.

Have you seen *Brute Force*?

John nodded.

Okay, so let's assume they were playing fast and loose with the facts and it's not quite so bad, it's not stoolies getting smashed in mechanical presses and it's not crypto-fascist queer heads of security, but what if it's even a little bit true? And by the way, shame on Hume and Jules. They come to my house, they act like friends, and then they make Captain Munsey a sadist because he's a repressed homosexual, although I can see how Burt Lancaster would drive any man nuts. And you know Jules, cute as he is, he must have swum to the near side of the river a few times himself. Anyway, my point is, I love men but apart from you and a few others, I don't much *like* men. I prefer the company of women and a world without women to temper the collective brutality of men, whoever they want to fuck when the lights go out, would be death for me. I would die in prison, if not by another man's hand then probably by my own. Look at what just happened to us! Even a group of men *pretending* to be a mob of prisoners turns itself into the functional equivalent! They *were* a mob! They saw *us* as the enemy! They weren't pretending to attack! In the frenzy, they truly *were* attacking! And if that happens in a movie studio in the richest country in the world, imagine what happens inside an honest-to-god bars-and-beefcake prison! I'd never survive it! I *know* this about myself, which means that if I turned up in Washington and had no choice but to appear before that kangaroo court I might sing out a list of names. I can't face that possibility, so I have to leave. My own country is forcing me to flee it.

John gaped at me.

Do you want to come with me? We could make pictures in France, ones where we do whatever we want. Not the disembodied cocks but serious stuff, and *fun* stuff.

Are you saying you're a Communist, Desmond?

No, not anymore. I can't stomach Stalin. Any idiot can see he's a bully and a thug. I hate the show trials and frankly I've never been able to befriend a Russian – not even the émigrés. Am I a Marxist? Absolutely. A Socialist? Yes, although I don't mind riding in limousines or drinking champagne. But the fact is, why should it matter if I was ever a Communist or a Socialist or a Marxist or a Buddhist for that matter, or even if I still might be? It shouldn't make one bit of difference in a country founded on the idea of freedom of expression and association and religion. This whole witch hunt is as un-American as Stalinism itself and if we're not careful the country will end up just as oppressive as Russia! If a man can't believe what he wants in America and hold unpopular ideas then I despair for the whole future of the human race. So do you want to come with me or not?

John hesitated, giving me a look that told me I had just made a terrible mistake. I'll have to think about it, Desmond. We should get back to the set.

When we stepped inside Stage 3 Mary was leaning against a resting plank reading du Maurier's *The Parasites*. At the sight of her John looked ready to kill but she didn't even glance up from the book.

Where have you been, Marsh?

Searching for you.

We've shot two scenes while you were away. Nick's been doing your job.

Nick bounced up from the chair that had John's name printed on it and shuffled to the corner of the stage where I was lurking.

Miss Dawn told me to do it, Mr. Frank. Said she'd get me fired if I didn't and she'd direct it herself. *I know more about making pictures than all the men in this room put together*, that's what she said. Can you believe it?

I don't like her but she's right. You want to learn something about directing, watch Mary and forget everyone else, John included.

On the other side of the stage John and Mary's argument had turned into a public performance the entire crew was watching.

I've been searching the whole lot for you, Mary.

Well that was silly. I had to go to wardrobe, and then I picked up the trades, and when I came back here… She dropped her book to the floor and Mozelle was there to pick it up, catching my eye with a wry look. …You'd disappeared. I'm tired of all this fuss. No wonder we're behind schedule.

Without looking down Mary walked through a jumble of cables and hit her mark. Under the lights she expanded, grew taller, her blonde hair becoming more voluminous. It was beautiful and terrifying. As the set whirred into focus around her you stepped from your dressing room, took your place, and gazed into the lights. Either you failed to see me or were pretending not to. However we might have argued about it the night before I never wanted to do anything to put you at risk, but that did not stop me from wishing I could step out of the shadows, walk across the set, take you in my arms and tell you to play the scene as if you were acting with me instead of Mary. People would see us and that would be the end of our secret and perhaps it would be worth it for an hour. In my heart I believed there must be a place in the world where such an act was possible, but I knew it was not America. *In my heart* – People are always talking about what is *in their hearts*. I could never confine my desires to such a small organ. My heart was my whole body and you burned like wildfire through all of me, Myles.

Do you remember how you invented reasons to speak with me in public? *I wanted to ask you about that line you changed, Mr. Frank*, you might say. *The one where Orph tells Faye...* And then we would discuss a speech you understood perfectly well because you had been sitting in the room when I wrote it, trying it out on your tongue to judge whether it was speakable. Deceit of this kind was a way to talk between takes, approximating a closeness whose truth we could only enjoy in private. That day, however, the tone was different. You did not come over to ask me anything but stood unmoving in the spotlight, waiting for your cue with a coldness that made me wonder what had happened in my absence, if someone had said something to you or if you were just preoccupied – or if, as I could not help myself imagining, you had been meeting some other man, a twenty-dollar date arranged by a pimp in tight pants. There were enough of them around, plenty of younger and better-looking men than me who would not miss a chance to go to bed with Myles Haywood. Several times in previous months I had noticed a similar flash-freeze remoteness which you always dismissed as preoccupation with a part. *I'm just thinking*, you would huff, *you want me to talk all the time but sometimes I need to think*. To that I had no rejoinder. I could be aloof myself, lost in one of the stories or characters I imagined you might one day incarnate. When we fought, which was rare, ice was always your weapon of choice.

It would be another two hours before I knew what had happened, who had spoken to you, the ultimatum you had been given. Forgive me for thinking you could have been unfaithful. Forgive me for thinking you were being willfully cold. I could not have imagined what I came to discover. Had it already happened by then, or would it only occur later? This is another detail that troubles me. I do not know the sequence of events, and can still only guess. Perhaps when you seemed cold and aloof it had nothing to do with me or what I came so soon to discover. If you feel moved to reply to this, then I wish you might tell me, because if in that moment you already knew what had happened, then a decision I made shortly thereafter has no significance at all. But if you did not know, if your expression was just a look of preoccupation, of trying to focus on your character's motivation or thinking about how to deliver a line or walk across the set from one mark to another, then the decision I made shifts everything, in some way, if only by a fraction: it makes me responsible, even though I might want to place ultimate blame on the studio or the government or all the spectral powers united against men like you and me.

You began shooting the dream sequence in the nightclub after Orph has been drugged. I was still unhappy with the scene. It needed genuine danger, a hint of betrayal from inside the family, but it was already too late to make changes on that scale.

Mary was wearing a sequined black evening gown, and because both her characters, Faye and Ursula, appeared in the shot, there was a double in the same costume, but John had also put the three Arran Sisters in blonde wigs and copies of the gown so that with mirrors and double exposures he could create the illusion of dozens of the same woman. Victor Grace, so like Plutone it was hardly a performance, lurked in the shadows behind the camera rig. John told me, maybe you know, that Grace started off as a personal enforcer for one of L.A.'s biggest mobsters, then escaped the underworld when a casting agent noticed him outside of Earl Carroll's on Sunset and decided he had an appealing malevolence.

Grace once locked me in a wardrobe, Nick whispered to me. I was there half a day before anyone found me.

Why'd he do that?

He said I was a Red. Me, a Red!

Well aren't you?

Nick blushed and I guessed that somewhere in his past the accusation might find purchase. It made me feel for him in a way that left a sour taste because he was otherwise so repulsive. I don't mind if you're a Red, Nick. All the same to me.

And that's the problem, isn't it, Mr. Frank?

Someone called *silence* and *speed* and the slate cracked and John shouted *action*. As you performed a swooning confusion, spinning left and right, the Arran Sisters closed tighter around you, laughing in voices so chilling they made me queasy. There was no pleasure in being afraid for the person I loved. John called for a second take and then they checked the gate and everyone was happy so they reset for a close-up. He was shooting with speed and concentration, as if he really did believe this might be the last day he was allowed to work on the lot.

The next set-up was the nightmare landscape of sand dunes and trees dripping black leaves and thorn-covered vines flanking a stagnant river. The Arran Sisters were hustled into new wardrobe and makeup, transformed into monstrous versions of the parts they played in the film's waking reality while you changed into your corporal's uniform. The wind machines were switched on and I watched as you ran through the trees, chased by the women in their black-feathered gowns. I added the scene after discovering the Arran Sisters had written to Senator McCarthy offering to organize anti-Red rallies all over the country. You flailed around the set, breaking off twigs and limbs, exposing the faces of actors hidden in the manufactured trunks, their features contorted with pain as they cried out to you. John pushed you through three takes before moving on to the scene with the dogs, a dozen black greyhounds who chased your stunt double across the set and down to the artificial river where his body was replaced with a liver-smeared dummy the dogs tore to shreds.

When it was time for lunch you came over to speak with me and Nick. Maybe I was imagining it but the two of you seemed nervous together. There was a similarity when Nick stood next to you that disconcerted me. Both of you were lean and hungry looking. Actors are insecure narcissists, you once confessed, and what does a queer narcissist want more than another boy who looks like him?

Great scene, Myles, Nick gushed.

Thanks, Nick. Think I did okay, Mr. Frank?

Sure, Myles. I was petrified for you.

Hope I got that line right.

You knew you had the line just fine. We had rehearsed it at home and you were always word-perfect. Like Mary, you knew not only your own lines but those of every other character in the film. I tried to measure the angle of orientation between you and Nick. There was nothing there. How could there be? You hated him as much as I did. I told myself to turn off the skeptic in my head and go on trusting you for the few remaining hours I would be able to call you mine. No longer caring what he might think, I turned to Nick and said, Can you give us a moment alone? I have something to discuss with Myles.

Nick bowed, as if making a great indulgence. When he was on the other side of the stage I leaned over to you, so close that you took a step away from me.

Come find me when you're finished. I need to talk with you about something.

You're scaring me, Desmond.

No, nothing like that, I lied, knowing it would have been easier if I did not love you so desperately. If I'm not in my office there'll be a reason and you're to phone me at home. And then I whispered, I love you.

You twitched. I remember it clearly. No one was close enough to hear or see the shapes my lips made as I formed the words. Everyone was packing for lunch.

Don't be so reckless, you said.

I love you, I whispered again. Now you say it.

You know I do.

Three men from the accounting department arrived and huddled together with Nick in a corner. In a year on the lot he had gained a reputation as the assistant director most likely to keep a production on schedule, on budget, and bled of any word or image that could possibly offend. No one liked a moralizing wunderkind and no one liked Nick. Then another man appeared at the stage door, and this time I was sure: it was the stout fellow in a cheap suit and panama hat I had seen earlier. Nick looked at him like he didn't want to get too close. The man tapped his watch and Nick shook his head. Funny business, I thought, only not so funny.

Say it, Myles. Say it right here.

Your jaw seized up and the muscles were pulsing in your cheeks. I love you, you whispered, barely moving your lips. Your eyes were watering. It was cruel of me to make you say it but I wanted to know how far I could push. If I could push you farther than I had before then there might still be hope that I could persuade you to come with me. Perhaps you could be convinced to turn your back on America and the family in Montana and all the glitter of Hollywood to live a shabbier life where freedom might come cheaper. There was no reason to doubt your loyalty to me. You were all-American innocence and the fear in your eyes was enough to make me want to wrap you in cotton and lock you up for safe keeping.

You're a demon, I said, putting a hand on your shoulder. It was all I could do in the moment, all you would let me do. I felt the pace of your pulse through my fingertips and hated myself for testing you.

Do you remember when we first met, on the set of *Fanshawe*, and you genuinely needed help understanding the lines I had written? You were the one who suggested a glass of something to loosen up, and then you came and sat next to me on the davenport in my office. Did you touch my hand accidently, or was it only meant to seem that way? Whatever the impulse, accident or intention masked as accident, in the dry air, our wool trousers connecting with wool upholstery and wool carpet, there was a literal spark, bright and silver and visible to us both. We laughed and then touched the tips of our fingers together, no accident this time, no pretense, and another spark exploded. In your eyes I saw an expression I knew, longing and understanding, recognition that I was like you and you like me. Perhaps that is why there was no hesitation when we leaned towards each other and kissed.

You'll have to coach me, you said. I'm shy.

But your shyness *was* pretense. You had strong physical instincts even though they were hurried and brutal. What I had to teach you were the pleasures of breathing and slowness. The only time I ever rebuked you, I think, was after we had committed to sleeping with no one else and you said it was like we were married.

No it isn't, I said. Don't pretend it's the same.

You looked so crestfallen I regretted my words as soon as I spoke them and took your head in my hands. What I mean is it's precisely that to me, but never let yourself believe anyone else will see it that way.

Perhaps I made the point badly, perhaps I did not make clear to you that I saw what we had as a marriage and that was why you felt free to marry Helen. At the wedding I sat on the bride's side, because everyone knew Helen was my friend, and Barbara sat next to me, both of us trying not to weep. We were just lucky that Helen was as romantically uninterested in you as you were in her. Other such marriages were not so compatible.

Next to each other in that dusty soundstage, I could see how badly you wanted to get away from me. It was the first time I had ever sensed that from you.

I should be done by four, Desmond. I'll find you then.

Did you expect me to wait for you to leave? It seemed to be implicit, so I stood there alone on set, watching you walk into the sun. Before you disappeared from view, Nick Charles stopped you. Whatever he said startled you, and I wanted to shout at him to leave you alone but knew, of course, how cavalier such an intervention would be. With Nick at your side you turned in the opposite direction from the commissary, where I assumed you would be meeting Helen for lunch, the two of you always performing the dutiful husband and wife. I was about to leave the stage myself, thinking I might follow to see where you were going, when the stout man in the panama hat appeared from behind Mary's dressing room.

A moment, Mr. Frank?

I was so startled by his approach my first instinct was to deny my own identity. With his sunburned bulldog face and greasy shirt he was too sloppy to be a federal agent, but his bearing was menacing in its own way.

And you are?

He removed his hat and wiped his forehead before replacing it, cocked at an angle that made him look like a boy playing dress-up from his father's closet. That's not the question, Mr. Frank.

If I'm going to speak with a man I like to know his name.

He spat tobacco juice out of the corner of his mouth. You can call me Hank.

Just Hank. Nothing else?

Hank will do.

Can I help you in some particular way? The man squinted at me as if struggling to make sense of my words. Do you work for the studio?

In a manner of speaking. They hired me to follow you.

That must be boring, I said, surprised by how unsurprised I was at the revelation. He had not yet made eye contact with me, was in fact scrupulously avoiding looking me in the eye.

Maybe not so boring. I have some photographs that might interest you. Photographs people I know would pay a lot to see.

I tried to imagine what he could possibly have captured, certain it must be a bluff.

If the studio is paying you I'm sure you'll get what you deserve.

Thought I'd give you a chance first. You can buy them. Prints and negatives. I'll hand them over now if you give me twice what they've promised.

And what are they going to pay?

Five thousand dollars.

I laughed. I knew it was a lie. The studio might have him on a weekly retainer but that would cover whatever he gave them. So you want ten from me.

That's right.

I think I'll let the studio pay what it's promised.

Might want to think about that. Maybe I'll raise my price. Maybe I'll sell them to someone else, someone who'll let the whole country see them.

So show me. What have you got?

But there I had him, or he had me. They're still being processed, he said, fingering the brim of his hat. You pay me now and I'll turn them over as soon as I have them.

You think I walk around with so much cash?

Man like you, I bet you could get it easy. I'd do you the favor, wait until the end of the day. You could pay me tonight.

And why should you want to do me a favor, as you call it?

The man stared at his shuffling feet. We all got our problems.

A wife and a houseful of kids you can't feed? Rent you can't pay?

One kid. And a wife. She's not well. Kid neither.

How sad for you.

No call to be mean about it.

I thought for a moment but it would have been nearly impossible to raise ten-thousand dollars by the end of the day and Hank gave me no reason to believe him. I'm sorry, I have my own problems.

You'll have bigger ones now, Mr. Frank. As he tipped his hat and scuttled off through the door of the soundstage, trailing an odor of sewer gas, he nearly knocked over Helen.

Who was that?

A blackmailer, but I think it was a con.

What did he say?

Nothing we should take seriously. It was just intimidation.

I hope that's all it was. Have you seen Myles?

He left a while ago.

That's funny. He was supposed to meet me outside the commissary at a quarter to one but he still hasn't shown. It's not like him to be late. She took my hand and squeezed. Have you told him?

I haven't figured out what to say, or how to say it, and I'm still hoping I won't have to.

Helen and I started walking toward the commissary, trying to separate ourselves off from the crowds of other people. With the sun overhead it was hot between the soundstages and when I looked up I felt a sudden vertigo. It was the same feeling I'd had in the jungle with John, of distance and proximity in flux, the sky as close as the end of my nose, the soundstages around me remote as the cosmos.

Are you okay, Desmond? You don't look so well.

Maybe I just need to eat.

We turned a corner and when we were alone Helen stopped me, taking my arm. This morning in the car Myles asked me whether I thought you might be seeing someone else and I said no, that was impossible. I wanted to tell him what you'd said but I think you'd better do it yourself. Please don't torture him.

I'm not trying to, Helen.

You know he's sensitive. It's so exhausting sometimes.

Until then I had always assumed that the two of you were happy when I was not around, despite the subterfuge and performance required to support the lie. That note of weariness made me feel as though there might be an opening I could leverage, perhaps even one that would allow me to maneuver you and Helen so that I could get what I most wanted: for you to leave her and follow me wherever I might go.

Do you ever regret all of this?

Marrying Myles? Of course not, Desmond, don't be stupid. We're suited to each other in every way but the one the world assumes. Perhaps that's a perfect marriage. The studio will expect children at some point and neither of us has figured out how that might happen. I don't really want them but Myles does.

This also surprised me. You'd never said anything of the kind to me as far as I remember, perhaps because you knew I had no interest in having children myself, at least not then, not when I was still young.

Myles likes the idea of being a father. I don't have the urge to be a mother. Something about the way I was mothered, I guess that's what an analyst would say. Maybe I'm still too young. Although I feel I've aged a hundred years since this morning. I can't really imagine our lives without you here, Desmond. Myles moons around the house the second you leave. It's like he doesn't know how to be himself without you there to watch.

I don't believe that.

It's true. He likes me well enough but you're the reason he gets up in the morning and smiles and goes to work, as corny as it sounds. Without you, I worry what will happen. I can imagine him just winding down and falling over. I don't know that I'll have the means to bring him back to life each day.

Helen's eyes had turned red and she fished a handkerchief from her bag to blot them. We both looked around to be sure we were still alone.

Dammit. First you and now me.

It's okay. No one's watching.

You were my first friend here, Desmond. I would have been on a train back to Denver if it hadn't been for you turning to John and saying let's give that one a line. *That one*. Just another bit player in the background. What made you notice me?

I saw you talk back to a guy at the newsstand who whistled at you. I liked the sharpness of your tongue.

Funny, I don't remember that. I probably didn't know what else to do.

Self-defense is a good instinct. I suspected it might take you places.

Did you know then – I mean, did you guess?

Maybe in a way. But I didn't look at you and think, Oh, there's one of my tribe, I'd better recruit her, if that's what you're asking. You just looked like you needed someone to give a damn about you before the studio spat you out the wrong end.

That Christmas when you first asked me about Myles, and I said you should marry me, and then sobbed all over you when you said it wouldn't suit you

That was the worst party I've ever thrown but I don't remember you sobbing.

I did. I want to apologize for that.

Why should you apologize?

I didn't know if I'd meet anyone as sympathetic as you. I hardly knew Myles then, so I couldn't have imagined it would work out with him. I thought you might be my only chance to find someone I could live with who the rest of the world would look at and say, *What a lovely couple*, and it wouldn't be painful living through it. I feared the studio trying to match me up with someone who would expect to do whatever he liked to me and that was enough to make me contemplate going back to Denver a second time. I'd mapped it in my head. I knew the train timetables and had started looking into real estate up in the mountains. I was going to buy a cabin in the middle of nowhere only I couldn't figure out how I'd support myself. I don't know how to do anything except sing and dance and land a joke and there aren't many places where those skills make a life.

Poor kid.

Don't pity me, Desmond. That's not one of your nicer qualities.

Sorry, I didn't mean it like that.

I just want you to understand how much you've meant to me.

You would have done fine on your own.

Maybe. I could have learned to hunt and fish and gone to work in a diner in Estes Park if I had to. But you've made this particular life livable in a way it might not have been otherwise. Myles has too of course. We've been lucky with one another, the three of us.

And Barbara.

Barbara, too, yes.

You should dry your eyes again.

Helen scrunched up the handkerchief and checked her face in a compact. Lord, they'll have to start from scratch after lunch, she laughed, dropping the mirror back in her purse.

Tell Myles to find me later.

Aren't you coming to lunch? Oh no, I forgot. Good luck, she said, kissing me on the cheek.

It would have been hell if it had been anyone but you.

Yes, Desmond, I know. For me, too.

8

This morning Alessio comes to me ecstatic. He has sold a painting. Although I give him whatever he needs, I understand how this must feel, the sense of independence, and I accept when he offers to take me to lunch at a little restaurant I like just south of the Ponte Alla Carraia, a place quite undiscovered by tourists, except those with local knowledge, who tend to be more sympathetic and do not threaten to ruin the atmosphere.

As we are taking our seats, we look up and discover that Néstor, our Spanish novelist friend, has just sat down across the room. He glides over to speak with us. Always so fashionable, his black hair has been recently cut and brushed into an elegant quiff, a style that hurls me back into the 1950s. I watch to judge the energy between Alessio and Néstor, seeing the way they embrace, the kisses on cheeks, the hypermasculinity of them both, and try not to feel jealous. I can tell that Néstor is attracted to my Alessio. Unmistakably so. I want to wag my finger and say, You will have to wait until I am dead, perhaps it will not be so long, but you may not have him yet – and anyway, you are too much a top for Alessio, both of you too manly ever to be compatible with each other. I grasp Alessio's hand and he holds it, almost petting it, that clear smooth skin clutching mine, withered and spotted, and I know that he senses my jealousy, my need to be reassured that he has not already betrayed me with this Castilian princeling.

Néstor is with a young American, another writer who is teaching for the spring semester at one of the countless American universities that have acquired villas and even great estates in and around the city. When I look at him more closely I realize it's the young man I saw near the Palazzo Vecchio the other day and mistook for a

249

soldier with his mirrored sunglasses and camouflage rucksack, the one who reminded me so much of you, Myles. Why don't you two join us, Néstor says. There is plenty of room at our table. Alessio and I are too polite to decline, too generous to say that this is a private party and we want no one else to complicate it. With Néstor and his American joining us, or us joining them, there will be the bill to consider. It would be too much to expect Alessio to pay for all four, and as we move across the room, these two beautiful young men attending to me as if I were a dotard unable to walk, about to fall on my face, I worry that the encounter will ruin our little celebration.

The American, Paul, is from New York, or at least he lives in New York, but I sense that he is from elsewhere, perhaps Illinois or Iowa. He lacks a certain polish, his face is open and innocent, he speaks with a youthful intensity that makes me feel sorry for him. I remember Helen's criticism, that pity is one of my least attractive qualities. But how earnest Paul is, how desperate to please us, how assiduous in showing his deference to me, careful to pay attention to each of us in turn, to acknowledge his innocence, even his naïveté. He is like someone out of the past, not a man of this new millennium. You belong in 1950, I tell him, and he asks what I mean. So fresh, I say, so unguarded. Like an angel. George Cukor would have devoured you, made you a star and then eaten you alive. He blushes as if enjoying my flattery.

Paul, I sense, is like the rest of us at the table, a man who loves men, and while he is masculine in his affect, unlike Néstor and Alessio he has a certain softness about him that also reminds me of you, Myles. I can see at once that Alessio has caught his eye, Paul keeps staring at him, trying to engage him in conversation, rolling out a few phrases in Italian until it becomes apparent that he is far from fluent and we all switch to English for his benefit. He wants to know what to order, we consult the waiter about the specials, and choose for him. *Ribollita* for each of us to start, then *carrè di agnello* for Néstor, *triglie marinate* for me, *quaglia confit* for Alessio and *crudità di stagione* for Paul, who turns out to be a vegetarian, to Néstor's amused horror. How can you be in Italy and not eat meat? Néstor asks. You would never survive in Spain, but never.

After the soup arrives, Alessio and Néstor lapse into Italian and Paul cannot follow. He smiles, pretends to understand, but I can see he does not. Although I would rather monitor the conversation between Néstor and Alessio I throw the young American a lifeline. What is he teaching? Modernism and one Creative Writing workshop, he tells me. And your students are good? They're a mix, he tells me, one of the students was looking at a photograph of a young woman in the villa library and asked me whether that was Somerset Maugham, who had a connection with the previous owners. What did you tell her? I ask. I said, no, that is definitely not Somerset Maugham, and left it at that. It's her first trip outside of America. She's never been anywhere. I thought it would be cruel to tell her the truth.

Cruel, perhaps, but at least then she would know, instead of carrying on in her misunderstanding. You could have done it gently, while the next person might not, might instead be very cruel.

Paul looks at his soup. He seems puzzled by it. Are the croutons supposed to be so soft? he asks. And this time it is my turn not to be cruel.

It's bread soup, I laugh, a Tuscan specialty. Here, you must pour some olive oil on it, it is best that way.

And this bread? he asks, tearing at a piece from the basket in the center of the table. I think they forgot to put salt in the dough.

No, believe me, it's meant to be that way. Traditional Tuscan bread has no salt.

Have you always lived in Florence? he asks. Your English is so good.

No, I tell him, smiling, I have not always lived here.

When the bill comes, I recognize in Paul's face an anxiety that provokes my pity once more, a nervousness that wonders how much the meal has come to, whether he will have to pay a share for the two bottles of wine despite only drinking water, whether the vin santo and cantucci were additional or included, how to calculate it all in a way that will not make him lose face. To his credit he reaches for his wallet, but I am overwhelmed with pity, and want also to protect Alessio from feeling he should have to pay. I say to him, quietly, in Italian, you can buy me lunch tomorrow, and he concedes as I pay for the table. Paul is relieved but also grateful and surprised, he expected no such generosity, he offers to leave the tip, and I tell him no, don't be silly, it's hospitality from one American to another. I have confused him, he does not begin to understand, even with the information laid before him. He wrinkles his brow but does not ask me to explain, too innocent or insecure to reveal yet another thing he has failed to understand.

As we leave, I can see that he wishes to embrace Alessio as Néstor does, longs for Alessio's lips against his cheeks, wants to put his hands on Alessio's shoulders, that he desires so much more from Alessio than I would ever allow him to receive. Do not touch him, I want to scream, yet I do not know whether I would say this to Alessio or Paul or to both of them. Is this how I am destined to end my days, jealous of the last man to occupy my heart?

If you and I had remained together all these decades, would I have worried in the same way, or would our mutual antiquity have prevented me from imagining you slipping into the arms of another man and finding there a home more attractive than the one I might provide? If I had managed to stop you before Nick Charles did that morning, leaving the soundstage, if I had accompanied you to the commissary and handed you off to Helen's trustworthy hands, would we all be together still?

After leaving Helen at the commissary, I continued to the Executive Building, my feverish sense of vertigo returning. As I stepped inside the green marble lobby, one of the elevators was closing and I was certain I saw you and Nick Charles inside.

The three receptionists looked at me in unison. Lucille, the head receptionist, scowled.

I'm sorry, Mr. Frank, but Mr. Krug asked me to reschedule you for two o'clock in his office.

The other two smirked as if they were all in on a joke.

Was that Myles Haywood going up in the elevator?

I couldn't possibly say, Mr. Frank.

Guess I'm not eating in the Executive Dining Room today then, am I?

That seems like a sound conclusion, Mr. Frank, unless you know something that I do not.

See you later, then, Lucille.

Two o'clock, Mr. Frank. I wouldn't be late if I were you.

Outside, streams of people were rushing back and forth to the commissary, from soundstages and dressing rooms, workshops, costume and property departments, saucer tank, transportation department and garages, film vaults and processing laboratories, studio zoo, airplane hangar, plant nursery and sod farm, billing and accounting offices, research department and library, on-site power plant and filling station. It was tempting to say it was a city within a city or a microcosm of the nation only it was neither of those things. The studio was a factory, but instead of airplanes or refrigerators or atomic bombs it produced two-dimensional stories that created an illusion of depth and movement through time. A disproportionate percentage of studio laborers were beautiful and most of them, even the unattractive ones, believed they were doing a job more significant and meaningful than putting together the products that moved people across continents, kept food cold, or threatened to annihilate every beating heart on the planet.

By the time I arrived, the commissary's chrome-paneled dining room was heaving with five hundred people. It would be better to go on the run empty and light, but I ordered the chicken broth with matzo balls, grilled sea bass steak with sauce meunière, coconut cream pie, and a cup of coffee. There was so much commotion in the room the waitress struggled to hear my order.

As usual I sat at the writers' table, although this was a misleading name, since it was a table only for the studio's top writers, not the badly paid hacks who thought they had come west to get rich only to find themselves working on scripts that were never produced, or which were turned over to senior writers like me who received sole credit for doing nothing more than a final polish. It was only partly to do with talent. All of the top writers had been to college back east. Each of us had either published a book or written a play that had been produced in New York. Most of the junior writers at adjacent tables had only ever written for the screen, and would go on doing so as long as the studios employed them, ending their days alcoholic and embittered in Oildale bungalows pumping tall tales of stars they claimed once to have screwed.

Across the room John and Mary were hunched over a table with

Helen but you were nowhere to be seen. I usually felt the cruelty of not being able to sit with you and do a thing as simple as eating in your company, but that day I was sick at your absence, concerned about what it might mean, and disappointed that even though I now had this chance to watch over you for another hour you had disappeared. You and I had only eaten together in the commissary a handful of times, always with Helen or your co-stars, but those were never happy occasions for me because in the presence of other actors you all became so *actorly*, so performative, switching from accent to accent and character to character, living out your anxieties and neuroses and desires through the personalities of countless invented people, not a few of whom I had created myself, and in which I could recognize the operation of my own preoccupations, distorted through the performances you and your colleagues paraded for your mutual pleasure. Was it pleasure, though, or self-protection, self-defense, even an effortful campaign against the exposure of your own vulnerabilities?

By observing such gatherings, whether in the commissary or at parties or premieres, I had decided some time earlier that acting was toxic. The imaginary registered too close to the boundaries of the real. How could body or soul tell the difference between actions of falsity and ones of truth? Performance became habit, and too frequently I had noticed the voices of past characters intruding into your speech. Fanshawe, piping and Victorian, would arrive unannounced at dinner, or a tough but tender-hearted kid trying to turn straight after a criminal childhood might snarl into my ear as we lay naked together, *I ain't afraid of you.* There was no reason you should be afraid of me. *Trying to corrupt me, ain't ya, trying to make a man outta me, but I'm all the man I need to be, jocker. I'm nobody's punk.* In moments like that I worried that artifice might one day overtake us, that you would slip into some other character, remote from who you really were, and never find your way back to the self that I loved. There were other times when I wondered if the Myles I adored was himself a performance, one so convincing that I could not conceive of there being some other, genuine person hidden beneath the man who illuminated my days.

Because I was late arriving, the only free seat was between Margaret Brookes and Stuart Carmichael.

Wandering on the desert, Frank? Margaret asked.

Harrowing hell.

Conversation is a balm for misery.

How do you know I'm miserable?

From the way you're staring across the room I'd take odds on lovesick or lovelorn. Who's the girl?

You'd *never* guess.

Bet I would. She wears an anklet, and she's married.

Right as rain.

I can pick them every time. Come on, tell Auntie Mags who she is.

And read about it in the morning papers?

If you weren't a man I'd call you a bitch.

If the coat fits…

Lord, have you always been such a honey? I bet you were born with a whole chest of silver in your mouth. You know people whisper that your mother is Italian nobility?

Does it make me easier to hate?

It's not so tough already, Frank.

I love you, too, Maggie.

Final reel, Desmond. Only in the final reel.

Of the senior writers, Margaret and I were the youngest and

she was my closest contemporary, just past thirty. Everyone else was over forty-five and some had been on the lot since the silent days. Apart from Margaret they were all married, a few on their second or third marriages, all hard drinking, chain smoking. If there was another man who loved men or a woman who loved women at the table I didn't know who it might be. It was not a circle that put me at ease, and as I began eating my chicken broth and matzo balls I wondered how much I would actually miss it. Across the room a well-dressed man glanced in my direction and frowned. It took me a moment to recognize my own reflection.

The politics of the men and women at our table ran the spectrum from McCarthyite to several Trots left of Lenin, and the only thing uniting us was the craft we claimed to practice and a belief that the writer was the least appreciated gear in the whole cinematic machine. Some days that was enough to keep a bantering peace but that day in April 1950 was not one of them. Jason d'Estes was across from me and never a slimier fascist have I met. Behind his back we called him the Monologist for his long, unfilmable speeches. Like his characters he was given to pontificating.

I was looking at my nephew running around my sister-in-law's house last weekend, d'Estes said, and here's this little kid, plump and healthy as Shirley Temple in her apple-blossom years, and I thought, Goddammit boy, you were born to rule. There is an innate aristocracy that arises from the comingling of the right families and when they reproduce they generate natural leaders. You all know I'm a bastard—

And *how*, Margaret jeered.

—I wasn't lucky enough to be the child of wedlock, but my mother, however fallen she might have been, could trace her ancestry back to the Pilgrim Fathers. Can't buy that kind of pedigree. My mother was a maid and my father president of a bank. On his deathbed, with no other sons to carry his name, he adopted me and I got everything in his will. My half-sister inherited nothing, but I didn't care. You know how goddamn rich I was? Could have bought this studio if I'd had the sense. Only then came the crash, and me, a kid, I was as poor as I'd been at birth, with nothing but this tony name around my neck.

That name's a fake and we all know it.

It's as legitimate as my paternity, Stuart.

And what about that girl you left? Margaret asked. What about *her* kid? You call that legitimate? She's still scrounging Poverty Row trying to find a job. Like father like son I guess.

From across the table, Alice Lane, who was rumored to have had an affair with Jason, piped up, Don't be so mean, Maggie. Jason doesn't know how to stop himself loving someone. He has a heart of gold, that's all.

Fool's gold.

He fixed up that girl with a nice little settlement, didn't you, Jason?

She got more than she deserved.

And how much does a person deserve, d'Estes? How do you reckon what deserving is? What about the kid? Will you adopt him on your deathbed when there's no one to carry on your so-called tony name? Your mother was a maid, so maybe *you* got more than you deserved.

But there you're wrong, Brookes. My mother might have been a maid but as my father was the president of a bank I got exactly what I deserved when he left everything to me, only the Reds took it when they swindled the market.

Oh boy, here we go. It's always the Reds with you, d'Estes. You see chaos and collapse and it's the goddamn Reds.

Tell me it isn't! Prove to me the Reds had nothing to do with every disaster for the last hundred years. It was Reds behind the Civil War, Red Indians behind the Indian Wars, that imperialist Red Spaniard Sagasta behind the Spanish-American War, Communist rebels behind the Philippine Wars. Reds in South America trying to undermine American interests were behind the Banana Wars, Mohammedan Reds were behind the Moro Rebellion, Mexican Reds backed the Border War, Balkan Reds fomented World War One, home-grown Reds triggered the crash of twenty-nine and the Great Depression, Soviet Reds forced Hitler to defend his country and drag us into an artificial war against our natural ally, and now look, the Soviets have the bomb, and they're fighting to infiltrate this country with fifth columnists and nuclear spies and sleeper agents to start a second Civil War! If we don't track them down – and I'm not saying any one of you is among them, oh no, of course not, but I do think if you're a liberal who calls yourself anti-fascist you have a duty to clear your name and say *what* you know and *who* you know – then we might as well turn the country over to the Reds and give up on the whole idea of America because America was founded as the first and last bastion of capital economy and freedom...

When d'Estes was not around, Margaret and Stuart joked that the Monologist had never met a historical fact he could not falsify. In writing a picture about the *Mayflower* he had the Pilgrims fleeing early English socialism rather than religious persecution, and thriving in the New World because they saw how to impose a market economy on the American Indians. The studio didn't care if the history was accurate so long as the picture made money, which it did.

I feel like I learn so much from you, Jason, every time you open your mouth, Alice said, simpering.

The only thing a person learns from Jason d'Estes is how to crap through the teeth.

Come now, Carmichael, there are ladies at the table.

I'm with Stu, said Margaret.

I never said you were a lady, d'Estes smirked. It's Alice's ears I'm trying to protect.

Walter Simon, one of the most senior of our group, snuffled his soup and cleared his throat. We are all ignoring the issue at hand, he said. We are refusing to discuss the matter of greatest concern to each of us, with the exception of those of you – here he looked at Jason and Alice, the only known Republicans at the table – who have happily danced with the devils of fascism and failed even in the hour of international crisis to see what was apparent. If you'd had it your way America never would have entered World War Two and would eventually have formed an alliance with Hitler and Hirohito. As far as I can see it, you are the real enemies at this table, not us, although the tide of history is already forgetting which moon draws it to shore. Since the Supreme Court has failed to support the cause of our friends and colleagues we must each acknowledge that our own day of reckoning is very likely at hand, because we will be the easiest to target and smear. You understand what I am saying. They will not go after the stars, at least not the big ones, only those who demonstrate their own vulnerability and in the whole dark process who is more vulnerable than the second-tier star, the message-picture director, the writer who has tried to live as a person of conscience, supporting the democratic causes and principles without which his or her life and career would be a mockery of inconsistency and hypocrisy.

Jason d'Estes threw his napkin on the table and rose, taking his plate of beef kidneys with him. I'm not listening to any more of this Communistic propaganda. The unfriendly, untalented Ten are getting exactly what they deserve in going to prison. If anyone asks me whether I know the names of Communists on this lot, yours will be the first out of my mouth, Simon, he said, and strutted off to find an empty seat at a neighboring table.

Alice Lane glanced at the other writers and after hesitating for a second took her ham omelet and went to join d'Estes.

Walter pushed back his chair. Good riddance to them. Spread out a little. Let's make room.

But what are you proposing, Walter? What can we do but wait and see what happens?

We have to be more aggressive, Walter said. Offensive rather than defensive. We need to buy our way out of it.

How do you propose we do that? You can't buy the Feds.

No, but you can most certainly buy the studio, in a manner of speaking. It's a question of saying to Krug, 'Listen, I'll work for free for a year, give you whatever you want, and you tell the Feds to get lost.'

They'll never do it, Stuart said, finishing his bean soup. A drop of liquid dangled from his left nostril and I had to stifle the urge to wipe his nose for him as he sat slumped over the table, chin extended, a red carbuncle weeping from the lower lid of his right eye. They don't care about us. They'll just hire other people, or promote the kids who've been doing our work for us.

And even if Krug could be bought I wouldn't want to be part of it. It would be demeaning and – here Margaret lowered her voice – it would be a betrayal of what I think most of us at this table actually *believe*. Can't you see that, Walter?

I can see that I don't want to die a poor man or a man shut out of the only business he's ever known. I have bills, I have debts, you all know I have a wife who drinks and needs time away in expensive places. There are personal matters that might force us to think about the whole situation not just in political terms but also as one demanding private sacrifice, and if that sacrifice comes at the expense of our principles, then maybe it's worth the price. And anyhow, let me ask you this, all you wise and principled people: Why does this movement in which we supposedly believe insist on secrecy? Why should its members wish to conceal themselves? If it was a truly democratic movement, why isn't it out in the open?

It was in the open, Walter, Margaret whispered, until the U.S. government started prosecuting its members. Communism is fundamentally American – it existed long before the Soviet version! The capitalists have been trying to call us foreign agents since the Tories tried to tar and feather Jefferson. Jefferson who said, *God forbid we should ever be twenty years without a rebellion!* Does a secret organization publish pamphlets telling the country what its policies are? Of course not!

Then we should be fighting in the courts.

What do you think has been going on in New York for the last several years?

That's not what I mean.

Forgive me, Walter, but I don't think you know what you mean.

At that, Walter rose and left the table, abandoning his stuffed bell pepper. Walter, come back! Don't be so sensitive! Margaret called after him.

Let him go, he's a dinosaur, said Stuart.

Bert Scully, who had been twisted around chatting to one of the junior writers at the adjacent table, turned his head to join our conversation without shifting his body so that he had the uncanny appearance of his head being on sideways. Though he was only in his late forties his hands shook with a palsy most of us believed was the result of a bottle-a-day gin habit. You can't buy your way out of this, he said. Believe me, this whole sorry business hasn't even started. The nineteen subpoenas in forty-seven, that was only the first course in their poisonous feast. They were just getting warmed up. Although, really, they were setting the table back in the thirties, we all know this, and they'd been planning the menu since 1919. So let's say forty-seven was the fish course, but they haven't even cleared the plates and we've still got a very long main course to come and then dessert. Now that they've won the Hiss conviction they know they can do whatever they want. We'll see other high-profile arrests before the year is out, every one of the Ten will go to prison, mark my words. Plus all those originally subpoenaed who weren't called to testify will get subpoenaed again next year, and scores of others will follow. They'll find a way to start another war that will make the masses go along with whatever purges they insist are necessary, and even if the studios don't call it a blacklist, we all know there already is one. Any of us who have been implicated and refuse to cooperate will find ourselves unemployable. Even if we comply with whatever demands they make, I don't think that'll change anything. All we can do is hunker down, write while we can, find ways around the system, go into another line of work, or leave the country. That's as plain as it gets. I have seen the future, my friends, and you would be wise to heed my warning. As for myself, I don't have a passport and I imagine they'd find a way to refuse me one if I applied. I've never done anything in my life that could be called real work, so I will probably end up a bum or a suicide.

You should become a fortune-teller, Scully, or an astrologer.

You have to be half-magician to do that, Margaret, and I've always been a realist. When Disney called to ask if I'd work on *Snow*

White I said I was only interested if we could make it a picture about a young heiress who comes to the aid of struggling miners in West Virginia. He said no. Then he phoned a few years ago asking me to rewrite Aldous Huxley's script of *Alice in Wonderland*. I said I'd do it if I could turn it into a message picture about junkies in the urban jungle. He hung up on me.

Without warning all the lights went out and the commissary fell quiet before someone trumpeted a fart and people began laughing and the laughter soon turned to accusations of bad manners in polite company and what about the presence of children and how could such an outrage be tolerated! The vulgarity! The grossness! The tastelessness! Waitresses opened the curtains wider to let in the light and the manager of the commissary came rushing in from the lobby to apologize. Jason d'Estes was on his feet pointing a finger at Walter Simon, shouting, You're a filthy…

Go ahead, Jason. Simon's voice was deep, resonant with dignity. We all know what you want to call me. It wouldn't be the first time.

You're a dirty… *RED*, d'Estes shouted, hurling himself at Walter and carrying both their bodies into the fountain in the center of the room. Those of us still sitting at the writers' table stood to get a better view. D'Estes was one of the fanatics who went riding and shooting out in the foothills every weekend, preparing for the Red invasion; he was built like a linebacker and it took half a dozen studio cops to claw the two men apart.

The frog and the mouse, Margaret groaned, fighting it out as the hawks snag them both.

As I watched my fellow writers struggling in the arms of studio enforcers I had a vision of myself handcuffed and transported to federal prison, jostled and jeered by cops and convicts, a whole legion of men more easily man than me, recognizing vulnerability in my face and knowing they could do whatever they wished to me. I felt the nape of my neck prickle, hairs twisting with fear. If I stayed in America, I knew that one day when I opened the door the Feds would be there, and I would have to admit to being myself.

Across the room I caught Helen's eye as the lights came back on. There was such an expression of disquiet on her face that I wanted to scoop her up and go find you, carry you both to safety, start a new life on another continent. Perhaps Europe was not the answer, or only for a while, and then we would have to find somewhere even farther away to start all over once more. A nomadic life unrolled in my mind and I could see the span of my remaining decades as I sometimes glimpsed a book or a script just at the beginning of the work, perceived the whole thing in a flash, all the detail suggested in streaks of color, snatches of dialogue, a perfect shape imagined, and then, when I tried to look closer, the details blurred and the work of creation revealed itself. Life and the future might be the same: a general trajectory observed in a passing instant, the hard details left to be carved through labor and time.

Raymond Cann, a twerp with wine-barrel stomach and natural tonsure, skin waxed and buffed to a roadster shine, raised his head. The day was only half finished and he already looked defeated in his silver suit and kidney tie. What hair remained hung over his eyes, which watered with allergies and cast a glitter of tears across his cheeks. Every time he spoke he squirmed, arms and legs twisting as if his mid-section had been nailed to the chair.

I speak only for myself, of course, but I would never do anything to betray my country, Cann said. I might have been a…well, as some of you may recall, I used to be involved in certain ways…

You were a seasoned member of the Party when I first met you, Margaret said under her breath. You recruited me.

That's as may be, Maggie, but since then I have seen the light, I have re-embraced my faith, and as a man of the left and a good American I cannot now understand how any of you can continue to truck with Communists working for the destruction of this nation.

With his mincing voice, it occurred to me that if there was another male lover of men at the table it might in fact be Cann, and the thought so disturbed me I choked on a mouthful of fish. Margaret rapped me on the back and after a few soft blows the knock of her fist turned flat and soothing, rubbing the space between my shoulder blades. Maybe our barbed exchanges were always more amicable than I had assumed.

As Walter said, Cann continued, a truly democratic movement would come out in the open and declare itself. Stop taking orders from Moscow. Can any of you honestly say you think Joseph Stalin is anything other than the embodiment of evil, perhaps even the face of Satan upon the earth? I am no Republican and no conservative, but we have a duty as good Americans to expose those trying to overthrow our democratically elected government.

Margaret slapped the edge of the table and all the cutlery clattered. How can you be so brainwashed? They'll still come and get you, and you'll still have to testify, and from the sound of it you won't have any qualms about telling those hoodlums in Congress the names of everyone you ever knew to be a Communist or a Communist sympathizer. Is that about the shape of it, Cann?

I'll do what my conscience and my faith dictates. I have access to all the membership logs from 1930 to 1945. Thousands of people, my dears, and I feel it is my duty to turn them over if no one else will.

Margaret's face flushed and she pointed furiously towards the door. Leave this table, Raymond. You don't belong here. Go join d'Estes and Lane and make a bed for yourself with the Feds.

Cann smirked but continued eating his tuna salad. I have every right to stay where I am.

Take your lunch and go, Margaret said, her voice straining with anger. I don't want you here.

And just like Stalin you'll purge whoever disagrees with you, is that the way it is? I'm not going anywhere, Margaret. This is still a democracy and a free country and I am an American citizen, a taxpayer, a man of faith, and a contracted employee of this motion picture studio.

You're a hypocrite! If you insist on staying then at least keep your mouth shut. I don't want any Red-baiting bullshit at my table.

I'm not Red-baiting, I'm calling a spade—

Shut up already, Cann. Stuart Carmichael wrapped his arms around the back of his own chair, plump chest straining against his striped shirt, armpits damp. You paint yourself so white but that hasn't stopped you stealing credit from me half a dozen times. *My* scripts with your name on them!

I felt myself blush. I was guilty of this, too. It had never been my choice to take credit from Carmichael but I nonetheless allowed it to happen on several occasions.

Now, now, Stuart, you know how these things work. We were both on the same project, and it just happened that they liked my version better.

Your dialogue, maybe, but it was my plot, my story, my characters. You're a thief! And you've been thieving from me since I arrived on this lot fifteen years ago.

If there's an issue you should take it up with the Guild.

Cann placed a slice of avocado on his tongue. I knew that Carmichael himself had done exactly what he accused Raymond of doing to several junior writers at the adjacent tables, using their ideas and putting no more than a final gloss of dialogue on the stories they believed to be their own. It was, as Raymond said, the way the system worked: a team of writers and only one got the credit, so not quite like the Bible in the end, where at least the apostles and evangelists who managed to get their chapters in the book still received billing, although there's no telling how many others might have been standing in the shadow of Matthew, Mark, Luke and John, all trying to tell that particular bildungsroman in as heart-stopping a way as possible, and never mind all the other believers whose versions were pushed out at the final cut, thrown aside as mere fictions, as if the whole story was a document of absolute truth and not the textual equivalent of a well-staged docu-fiction, *Nail-driver of Nazareth* instead of *Nanook of the North*. People had been stealing stories since stories first passed human lips and no one seemed to mind until someone realized audiences would pay for them. *Money, money, money*, always at the bottom of every problem! Stuart would not be so mad about his credit if the credit did not matter. The pictures he had written which had Raymond's name on them were all smashes at the box office, but it was Raymond's fee that increased, not Stuart's.

The Writers' Guild is gutless and useless and gave up what little power it had to the studios when it agreed never to strike except in the middle of negotiations, Carmichael said.

Never satisfied with the systems we have, are you, Stu? You always have to foment revolution.

At the far end of the table, Ulysses A. Fox, who claimed to be a direct descendant of General Grant, sat up straighter in his chair. He had seen active service in the Pacific, come out a major, and wrote nothing but war pictures, modern and historical.

If any of you chumps had any sense whatsoever you'd be on the phone right now to the FBI, Fox said.

Margaret gasped. It took more than ordinary outrage to make her speechless but she sat there gaping in silence because Fox had always presented himself as a fellow traveler if not a full member of the Party.

Make a clean breast of it. Turn yourselves over to the Feds. That's what I've done. Two nice young fellows came and sat down in my living room and we talked for half an hour yesterday. That's all it took. I haven't felt this light since my wrestling days. You tell them you were mistaken, misled by the witchcraft of Stalinism, that you failed to see clearly, and you regret everything you might have done, intentionally or not, to work against the Constitution of these United States. Tell them you were beguiled by that sorcerer witch, that he made pigs of us all, turned us into swine who could not tell the difference between the nourishment of democracy and the excrement of totalitarianism. Tell them Moscow has been directing us to work against this government, to struggle for its overthrow and ouster.

But it isn't true, Fox! Margaret hit the table again and this time as the cutlery rattled the room fell silent. Everyone was staring at us.

Be quiet, Brookes. You must be contrite. Apologize for what you have said. Apologize for how you have allowed your names to be used by organizations that are fundamentally anti-democratic. You must show that you regret all you have done against America.

Margaret slapped her cheeks so hard she made herself wince. How can you repent of something you're still doing and have every intention of doing for the rest of your life? I'm not working *against* this country. I'm working for it! I'm trying to make it a better place, and people like you, Fox, and you, Cann, and people like Walter, you're making our position untenable. If the Left fractures, we'll be out of the game for generations. It means ceding all our authority to the Right, just like the Writers' Guild. It's like saying, 'No, we were entirely wrong, for the whole history of the progressive movement,' and then this country will fall straight into the hands of the fascists! If the Left vilifies and dissociates itself from socialism and labor organization and progressive reform, there won't be any Left remaining! Is that what you want? You let Joe McCarthy pretend a vast conspiracy that simply doesn't exist and then go along with the charade to placate him and all the other idiots who are motivated not by noble principles of freedom and democracy but by greed! They want to enrich themselves and their supporters, they want to make this a nation where the robber barons control everything at the expense of the ordinary person on the street, and if you tell them you were wrong, that, *Oh my dear, I made such a mistake, I was a tool of the Soviets, I was a patsy and pawn and oh so deceived*, then you give them license to shit all over this democracy and turn it into something else!

Fox shook his head, rose from the table, and left. Cann glowered, shifting his gaze from me to Bert Scully, to Margaret and Stuart Carmichael. Ninos Johns, who sat at the opposite end, had said nothing so far. Cann finished his tuna salad, folded his napkin, and, in his milquetoast voice, said, Good day to you all. Most enlightening.

When Ninos pushed his uneaten bowl of chocolate tapioca pudding towards the center of the table Stuart raised his eyebrows to ask permission to take it. Ninos nodded and groaned.

All this is so dispiriting. I never think myself so serious as this. I come here nineteen-thirty-three, thinking, okay, maybe this place is better. At first maybe so. I learn English, people seem nice, weather good. I live well. They pay me too much money to do almost nothing. No one is interested in plays I write before I come, plays that *make* me come because government back home thinks them so dangerous. Here, they look at my plays and say they can't read them because they are not in English and instead hand me script of some good picture another studio made, and tell me write like this only different. I am, what would you say? Legitimate counterfeiter. I watch a movie that makes money, and think how to tell it different. Instead of 'boy loses inheritance and struggles', my story is 'father decides to see if disinheriting son makes boy better, more moral'. Turn one story around, tell it from another direction. I learnt this from Maupassant, and nothing is wrong with doing it like that, but I think there is no real creation in it. Of course, what is real creation anyway? Only five, six, maybe one dozen plots in the whole history of mankind. Now I find someone to translate my plays, serious work, and when I show them to Cherry you know what he says? Too dark, too weird, not American. Write me a serious American story, very realistic, and maybe we try, this is what he says.

Johns folded his napkin and wiped the sweat blistering his forehead. His whole body was limp, as if wrung out by the conversation.

At first it seems okay for me here. I think, good, in America at least I can be political. I fight fascism and do not worry that someone bashes my head or sets my house on fire because I have different beliefs. But now I do not know. People like this – he gestured across the room as Jason d'Estes reappeared, dried and dressed in a clean suit – they remind me too much of Blackshirts and Brownshirts and everyone who does not care what shirt they wear so long as he gets to say which color good, which shape of head the right one, which art good, which books bad, who go here, who cannot go there. They make rules on backs of their hands and call this decree by divine right. *But come on*, my friends, this is ungodly dictatorship. Not dictatorship of proletariat, but dictatorship of bullies, of thugs.

Do not misunderstand. I hate Stalin. He is a bully, too. Bullies are everywhere. I turn one way and see it through clean glass, turn another and is only dense fog. Maybe best would be to disappear, go be farmer far away, where nobody bothers. Stop trying to be artist because all bullies think artists are dangerous. Maybe we are dangerous. Free radicals.

The hour for lunch was up and it was time to turn myself over to Krug and Cherry. After saying goodbye to Stuart and Bert and Ninos, Margaret drew me aside.

I wanted to warn you, Desmond. I hear you need a visa or visitor's card for Mexico now and such things are not Tenderloin girls, neither fast nor easy.

But people go to Tijuana all the time.

She shook her head. I have it on reliable authority the southern border is no longer good for a quick exit.

I smiled disingenuously. That might be true if you're going on business, or trying to settle permanently, but I'd be presenting myself as a tourist.

I wouldn't bank on it, sweetie. It'll take a plane to leap.

Forced by Fate…expelled and exiled.

I always thought you should be writing melodramas. Who said it anyway?

Take it to Research. They'll have it on a card.

What a schmuck you can be.

Love you, too, Maggie.

Oh blow off. That doesn't happen until the final reel.

Unlike a number of my more political friends, I still had a valid passport, which meant unless the Feds thought I was a genuine threat to the republic I could put myself on a plane to Paris without being stopped. But I knew that you had no passport, Myles. You'd never even been to Canada. If I was going to leave quickly I would be doing it alone.

Preoccupied by this, I walked back to the Executive Building just as you were coming out, and for the first time in the years I had known you, you looked afraid in a way I could see was no performance. Your face was pale, eyes cast down, and if I had not greeted you I doubt you would have noticed me there on the steps. Even after I had spoken your name you would not look directly at me, almost acting as if we did not know each other, making an impatient, dismissive gesture with your hand, not quite shooing, I think, but giving me warning. Myles, I said again, but you were walking quickly, back towards the soundstages, and I knew I should not follow or raise my voice. Something had happened and I began to guess what it might be, although even my ugliest fantasies fell short.

Behind you, in his oily shirt and panama hat, the man who called himself Hank stepped from the revolving door and spat on the pavement at my feet.

Gave you a chance, Mr. Frank. You can say that much.

As I entered the lobby the three receptionists looked up at me in a single synchronized movement. None of them smiled.

Kay

Because the water from the faucet smelled she washed her hair
at most once a week and never washed her face, only used cold
cream, as Mother recommended, and most days took a birdbath
because of bills and money being unpredictable, which is to say
whether there would be enough or not at the end of the month, and
sometimes well before that. Kay's hair was so fine it would take no
curl – even with hot rollers it fell slack after a few hours. Mother
would shake her head, her daughter's hair being so unpresentable,
and Ruth, who went to the beauty parlor twice a week, would have
been incandescent, because of the family's appearance and their
standing in the community being so important for the store and
Kay always letting them down. At least here there was no one to
let down but herself. The boy didn't care. Hank certainly did not
care. There were women in neighboring towns as far as care goes,
where Hank was concerned.

   That morning in the mail there was a letter, which Mrs. Smith put
under the door without knocking and then tiptoed down the stairs as
if she had been trying to catch Kay in whatever it was she imagined
Kay did. The gall of it. Another letter from Mother, postmark
and handwriting unmistakable – grammar, spelling, syntax and
punctuation more so. Surely a greater shame than flat hair.

   Dear Kay –

   will drop you a few lines to tell you must come home, we
   can get yours and the boy clothes here. and I don't think he
   will need a over coat. you folks talk like we were liveing at

the north poll. we have a better climate here than you have
there. I think when we want to pay for yours & the boy's trip
it is a poor excuse. I guess Hank does not want me to see my
grandson before I pass away. and I could not go to see you
when you don't have a place to keep me. I know it would
make Vernon happy to have you come home, Ruth also. you
don't know how hard it is when you have not been home for
8 yrs. I will not stand for any excuses. must close. love to all.

Your Mother

Kay folded the stationery and put it back in the envelope. Why did
one write 'must close', when there was nothing to hurry about?
Better to write, 'I have nothing more to say' and leave it at that
rather than pretending to be in a rush when a letter could be set
aside until all had been said that needed saying. And this excuse
about there being no place to keep her, as if Mother could not
afford a room in a hotel, which would be cheaper than Kay and the
boy going all the way back east.

The shoebox in the top left drawer of the desk was nearly full
with letters from Mother and Ruth and the odd one from Vernon. It
was time to find somewhere else to keep them, only that was the one
place she could lock and the boy not be able to get inside, or Hank
for that matter, since the key she kept – well, no one would think to
look where she hid it. She had not told Hank that Mother wanted
them to visit because every time he came home he was gone before
she could do anything more than ask him for money. No question
but he wouldn't care two bits whether they went to Oklahoma or
not. He would rather be done with them, probably hope the train
derail or they both be kidnapped on the way. If she suggested they
go all three together he would grumble about being too busy to leave

his work, whatever it now was, assuming it was. The problem was that she would not manage to make the trip alone with the boy, owing to not being able to handle him properly, not on a train with that so public as it was, and what would people think of them with their bags instead of cases? What would they eat anyway and the boy always hungry now? Mother did not realize she would have to wire money for the tickets in advance, not to mention extra for food, though she had tried to explain this as clear as she could in the last letter she sent but the words were sticky and she must not have said it right. Clear as taffy. As much as she might want to go home there was no way to do it. Communists traveled with packed food instead of eating in dining cars. Communists traveled with soft bags instead of hard cases. Communists traveled with everyone else, sitting upright like Bolshevist anarchists instead of taking a sleeper car or driving themselves, but Kay could not drive and even if she paid the tickets Mother would balk at a sleeper which is why driving would have been better, except then the motels. Mother had said someone like her did not need to know how to drive, but Mother drove and all her sisters drove and each had their own car. No one had ever even let her behind the wheel of a car. It was on account of her nerves said her father. Hank said, Better that way, so as you don't think you can go off on your own. No money to run a car anyhow.

From the desk she noticed the cushion in the middle of the couch was askew. As she pushed it back into place she heard paper slipping between upholstery and the clink and jangle of silver. She pulled the cushion out and underneath it there were three five-dollar bills and another six dollars in quarters, stuffed in the crevice between the seat and the back of the couch. The boy could not have been sleeping there without knowing, which meant he must have hidden it himself, using the couch as his personal bank and not telling her what he had, though he knew she was short. The audacity of it. He could not have come by the money honestly. Only question was how, whether stealing or – she supposed he might have picked up work here and there but it was unlikely, what with him being so indolent. Some months ago she caught him skipping out of the Smiths' house, such a spring in his step, and was certain he had been stealing and would need a whipping until Mrs. Smith came to the door behind him and said thank you in that sweet voice of hers she used for dogs and babies. Other times, whenever Mrs. Smith saw the boy moping, it was obvious she pitied him, which made no sense, because could the woman not see what he was? Turned out she had been paying him to wash her windows and Kay had to say thank you but he has schoolwork to do and I would not wish him to inconvenience you, he is clumsy, like to break things, and with your fine ornaments, the figurines and whatnot, we could not afford to replace them in case of an accident. And Mrs. Smith had drawn her lips out in a line that reminded Kay of the way Ruth performed those times she got highhanded with them when they were children. It was an expression that said, I cannot believe you are sassing me, and you a grown woman, with a boy so thin his pants won't stay up and in the wrong light you can see straight through his neck, like the skin shade on a lamp.

Kay gathered up the notes and coins from the crack of the couch and put the money in her purse. There was no lock on the door to the apartment and she was certain Mrs. Smith snooped when they went out, there being times when Kay returned from an outing and a cushion was not where she remembered, or papers on the desk sat with their smug corners square, and throughout the apartment lingered a perfume she could never place, a blend

of peaches and leather, like a fruit picker's shoes only ladylike,
churned up with flowers and fog. No doubt Mrs. Smith had a spare
key to the desk drawer, meaning she must have read the letters
and knew all their business and so would be sure to think them
Communists. Or worse. What is worse than a Communist? Any
kind of criminal. But we are not criminals. I am not, no. But? But I
cannot speak for my husband. And the boy? The boy, Lord, the boy
is the boy, he does what boys will, and I teach him a lesson when
I must. He has come by some money. Yes, I suppose, but it could
have fallen from Hank's pockets or the boy might have earned it,
and at least this solves the problem of groceries. For the moment,
only for the time being. Yes, I know, but can you not let me have
that relief, even for today? What about the rent, Kay? What about
it? What will you do for the rent, if Hank does not come back?
Hank always comes back, sooner or later, with the odor of sin so
thick on his skin.

On the shortest route into town there was the dog that growled
at a gate so she went north up Pratt then right along the alley,
which still smelled to her like DDT, that scent of almonds, but also
oleander, heavy and sickly. Branches of pink and white blossom
dangled over the high tops of fences all the way down to Van
Ness Avenue, except at the empty lot where in the evenings the
boy played with his friends. No idea of their names except the
Japanese one, Teddy he was called. She had told the boy not to
play with Teddy but they kept turning up together. There was
something wicked about the friendship. Boys should not be so fond
of each other, not by the age of twelve.

The glare from the dust on the ground made her squint, a
problem of being fair, unlike her siblings, all of them dark as

skunks except Vernon, so that some had suggested – Rosa in fact used to speculate when they were girls, playing dolls in her bedroom – Kay and Vernon might have a different father from all the rest, but such talk neglected that Papa in his youth was golden-haired as a Valkyrie, before he went bald. Hank was almost bald, just past fifty, growing fat where he used to be fine, one of the leanest most beautiful men she had ever laid eyes on when first he met her, one day in the family store, and removed his hat, showing his waves of rich brown hair combed so neatly, and the shine on his shoes almost blinding, and now there was no hair to speak of, the baldness hidden under that filthy panama hat, and his jaw undiscoverable in the drapes of fat that hung from his cheeks, and if there was a shine on his shoes it was most likely from filth. It seemed to happen to men.

Palm fronds rattled against one another, clattering as tanned animal skins stretched taut, and the breeze lifted her hair where she'd tried to make it tidy. Whatever the route it was just over a mile to the store but it took more than half an hour on foot because there was always something to look at, the oleander cascading over fence tops or dogs running along Owens Avenue that would give anyone a fright with their snarling. Probably belonged to those Mexican Communists one heard talk about, fruit pickers trying to put honest farmers out of business was what Hank said and she supposed he must be right.

The walk along Inyo made her nervous so she turned up D Street and then east along Kern, hurrying past the house where they had last lived, not wanting to pause because of the eviction and the shame of it and the neighbors all knowing. Mrs. Coffey was at her window watching but Kay kept her eyes on the pavement and did not even flinch or turn around when she heard a screen

door open and the woman calling her name in a tone that said
you still owe me for that cup of flour you borrowed three months
ago and the window pane your boy broke last year. Next time Kay
would remember and stick to Inyo.

Across the railroad tracks she came into town and found
herself passing the 202 Club, Save More Drugs, Palace Meats,
the bargain department store and grocery store and pastry shop,
past Linder's Hardware and the hotel where she believed Hank
stayed so often they could have bought a house with what he
squandered, and right into the bank at the corner. The teller took
half the money Kay had found in the couch and said good morning
but with a tone that also said I know you owe money all over
town. Everyone knew. The debts and eviction and whatnot. It was
impossible Mother should ever come, because then she would see,
and the shame of the whole family knowing Hank was just what
they warned when she said if they did not let her marry she would
run away, and then that's just what she did anyway. How could she
blame them for hating Hank when she did herself?

Kay wandered down the street looking in store windows until
she was standing beneath the twin Moorish towers of the theater
staring at the face of Randolph Scott, with a kerchief tied round
his neck and Dorothy Malone in blue jeans holding a rifle at her
waist and *The Nevadan* in black and red letters between them.
Scott looked like Hank before he started to lose his hair and
turn fat only Scott was more handsome. Even so, there was in
his bearing a quality – the way he held his tall frame and cocked
his head, turning his chin just off center as if using it to point
in the direction he was heading – that gave her a queasy feeling
such as she got when Hank drove too fast on mountain roads
or when he pressed his tongue deep in her mouth and was ripe

with the scents of ten thousand women. Westerns were not her preference and fifty cents was fifty cents but it being free money after a fashion she decided to treat herself, and Scott was a good Republican after all, so it was supporting the cause of justice in a way, in times such as this, when Reds were trying to tear the country apart from the inside out.

The ticket seller was a girl with spit curls and red nail varnish and a fat mole on her chin colored in with eyebrow pencil as if that would turn it into a beauty mark. Still looked like a witch and a slut. The girl was too busy reading *Modern Screen* to glance up, just handing over the ticket as if Kay was a ghost, not even saying anything. Insolence.

It being a weekday and still during school hours there were not that many others in the audience and no one else in the balcony. The newsreel flickered without its stories really settling because what was the point of it all anyway, the events of the world?

The picture starts with a bank robber hiding gold. He's called Tanner only it's Forrest Tucker in the part and his meaty face made Kay think of her father, cheeks pink as pork cutlets. Tanner is galloping across a valley, the Sierras in the distance covered with snow, which meant they'd shot the thing late last year most like. It was supposed to be Nevada but Kay recognized the landscape as just the other side of the mountains, over towards Lone Pine and the Alabama Hills. Lawmen on horseback are chasing Tanner, their guns drawn, and then out of nowhere there's another man, a dark rider who keeps following, even when the others give up. What message did it send, that the law would abandon its pursuit of a violent criminal? Except it was Nevada, or meant to be, so perhaps that was all the explanation one needed.

Tanner's crossing a stream and the dark rider follows like

they're dancing with each other, until you can see it's Randolph
Scott in a three-piece suit and homburg. When Tanner gets a look
at the getup he calls Scott greenhorn and forces him to swap
clothes, only Scott hesitates so Tanner wonders what he has on
underneath, ruffles maybe? A couple of men downstairs in the
theater guffawed but the ruffles tickled a memory, not about
ruffles as such, but about what Scott might wear. He has this
knowing smirk that reminded her of a look she had started seeing
on the face of the boy, a grin like the cat with the canary, head
cocked to one side, chin doing all the indicating. Every time she
saw it that expression made her want to broom the boy's legs.

Tanner and Scott ride together through the dust, and the sight
of them set Kay's heart beating faster so she was aware of it in
her chest and neck and the rise and fall of her stomach against
the weight of her cotton dress. The theater was cool and the seat
more comfortable than any in the garage apartment. Imagine
sinking between the rows after the movie finished and hiding
there, turning on a single light at night and eating popcorn, living
between the concessions counter, powder room, and auditorium. It
would be perfect, alone save the people on screen for company.

It seemed as though this picture was just one hold-up after
another, outlaws jabbering at each other while Scott stands around
wearing that smug smirk all the time. She had never seen such
a look on Hank or her father. Something almost feminine about
it, like expressions on one of Mother's church friends, full of the
Spirit and proud of her faith, judging in silence everyone around
her. She realized, staring at Randolph Scott's face, that this was
perhaps what made her hate the look when she saw it on the boy: it
seemed so unmanly.

Now Scott and Tanner are camping by a stream, water flowing

between their legs, around the fire, queer place to camp, any fool would tell you never to camp on water. They sit like men always do, legs splayed, as if it's the easiest thing in the world, water gushing between them, Scott wearing a pinkie ring on his left hand. Mother always said never go about with a man wears a pinkie ring, it would end in sadness even if the man was quality, only she didn't explain why. When Kay caught the boy wearing a toy ring on his little finger last summer she thrashed him until his legs were blue.

Head to foot, Tanner and Scott lie next to each other, and it's supposed to be night, although they must have shot the scene during the day, because of the blue sky and it just being deep shadow instead of dark. Always confusing why the pictures did that and not just shoot in the actual night when it was supposed to be night in the story. Undoubtedly something to do with working hours and the unions. That was proof the Communists were even dead set against reality – that is to say, making a picture during the day and calling it night.

Tanner sneaks off in the dark but Scott sees him leaving and like a woman who doesn't know how to stop her husband when she catches him ducking out for a floozy, he raises himself on his bedroll and follows, riding under blue skies meant to be black, shadowing Tanner through rocky land that was almost certainly the Alabama Hills above Lone Pine. Hank had wanted to buy a plot over there, put down a deposit, but somehow got the wrong idea about the deal, and then the deposit was gone and the land never theirs. That kind of disaster was always happening with Hank.

Scott's riding up to a ranch, two cowpokes staring like he's a Martian, and he meets the young woman who runs the place, Miss Galt, only at first he thinks she's a cowboy and is surprised when the boy steps from behind a horse and it's Dorothy Malone. She's small and slight like a boy, so it was understandable he might have been confused. A man downstairs made a rude noise. It wasn't clear what he meant by it but the sound plucked at Kay's gut and she felt herself flush.

Scott asks to trade his horse seeing as it's injured and Miss Galt says it'll take three weeks to heal. He says he'll wait, and she says not here he won't, and he asks where then, and she suggests in Twin Forks only she doesn't know what they'll make of him in his three-piece suit and homburg and he says probably more or less what folks would think of her if she showed up in his hometown dressed like a man and she says they'd probably think she was pretty sweet and that's what they'll make of Scott in Twin Forks, pretty sweet. Wouldn't a real man just lean over and show a woman like Miss Galt how sweet he was? It seemed queer. She tells the cowpoke Rusty to fetch the gentleman – that is Scott – a horse, and Rusty, who's been staring the whole time, is relieved to understand it's a man he's looking at, because he couldn't tell from Scott's appearance, what with the suit and homburg and cute womanly ways. As Scott rides away, Rusty stares as if smitten, whistling like a lovebird.

Scott did look pretty sweet though not half as much as back in the thirties when he and Cary Grant set up housekeeping together and all those pictures of them playing husband and wife and Hedda Hopper and others saying about it not being normal, but then they both had wives now, because how else could it be? Maybe that was why the reference to ruffles earlier.

Now Scott's wearing cowboy duds and next thing he's in this saloon looking at a sheriff whittling false teeth and sitting next to Tanner. The story was hard to follow, nothing explained, just one scene after another and still no idea what Scott's character was called. Why was it that in cowboy duds he made a person feel even queasier in the stomach than when he was dressed in a suit? He looked like a tall girl with no bosom, pants pulled up high, shirt pressed flat against his windowpane chest.

The saloon's owned by Dorothy Malone's father, that is the father in the picture, which is Mr. Galt, which is the actor George Macready, him with that terrible scar on his right cheek, like a sickle arcing up from the hinge of the jaw to his cheekbone. He's after the gold Tanner robbed and asks Scott to work for him but Scott's not interested and Galt's men rough him up, only it looks about as real as babies boxing. It made one wonder if this was how men really behaved when women weren't around, if they roughed each other up all the time and camped by streams and slept head-to-foot but would betray a fellow if there was money involved.

When her thoughts returned to the screen, Kay could make no sense of what she was seeing. The story seemed to be hidden behind the action, all of it baffling. But perhaps that's life, everything unexplained. There was no telling why Hank should disappear for days, turning up at night without warning or reason, then take off before dawn and only come home weeks later, sometimes with money, sometimes without, one month a farmer, the next one a salesman, sometimes alone, other times with a man she'd never met who would be his business partner for a week or ten days and then disappear leaving Hank to do whatever it was kept him away from her and the boy. She had seen thousands of miles adding up on the truck's odometer, never any reason given, no excuse made, and she did not dare ask, nor about the matchbooks from Earl Carroll's and Ciro's and all those clubs in Los Angeles she was certain only criminals and movie stars frequented.

Scott's asking Miss Galt for another horse and though

suspicious she gives him one as if she can sense he's not a bad man. Off he goes with both horses but now he's holding up the sheriff and the sheriff just moseys into the jail cell and doesn't even put up a fight. What was this picture trying to say about criminals anyway? Why did they want a person to root for the outlaws? None of it made any sense, it was like good and bad had been turned inside out, as if one was meant to cheer for evil and hope for its triumph. It was almost enough to make Kay get up and walk out of the theater but then she noticed a man and woman sitting downstairs. They were both young, and the fellow had shiny blond hair and the girl curly dark hair, and the man's arm was snaking around the girl's shoulder and as Kay leaned forward over the balcony railing she could see how he kept reaching for the girl's breast. She was shivering and pushing the man's hand away and then he reached across himself with his other hand and was gripping her arms and she twisting in the dark with the light of the screen on her face and trying to watch the movie. The first time Kay and Hank had been to the pictures he assumed so much and she had been too scared to speak. That had been the beginning of being stuck with him, and stuck with the boy who reminded her of Randolph Scott with his strange skinny ways.

When Kay turned back to the screen she thought she must have missed something again. Miss Galt's demanding to know what Scott's story is, and he admits he can't say but needs her help and she refuses him. Then he says he's not keeping the gold, that's not why he's working with Tanner, and he shows her something all wrapped up in a piece of cloth, which seems to change her mind.

The blond fellow downstairs had both hands on the girl's breasts and she was making a sound like a kitten crushed in a squeezebox. The sound punched Kay's stomach and lungs

together, made her hands shake. She was about to scream for
help, but then an usher came along the aisle swinging a flashlight,
and the blond man put his hands in his lap, acting as if nothing
had happened. The girl could have stood up right then and run
after the usher and Kay wanted to shout, tell her to do just that,
but she and the girl both sat frozen, caught in the light from the
screen. Mr. Galt is asking his daughter who Scott's character
is and Miss Galt says Scott's good and that means not like you,
daddy, and Galt slaps her and she says but Scott's a federal
marshal. So that it explained it at last. All this time Scott *was* the
law, so when the other lawmen didn't seem to be doing their jobs
in the full spirit of the law, well, it was a relief is what.

When George Macready slapped Dorothy Malone the slap looked
real, like Macready really went for it, and enjoyed it too. Kay was
certain she could recall every time Hank had slapped her. Each blow
stood out in space and time, the events of a given day providing
specific texture and force, bringing it into focus so she could pluck
a still shot from the blur of impressions that made up most of her
memories since the day she had been too afraid to stand up and
walk out of the theater when Hank did what he wished. That was
back in thirty-six, before they were even married. Fourteen years of
images smudged together, an undercranked silent film that caught
and froze in moments of pain or repulsion. She remembered the
picture, Katharine Hepburn, something about a woman in England
having a child out of wedlock and trying to go her own way, as if that
was a model for others to follow.

They're back in the hills again. Strange how places appear on the
screen and it feels as if you were really there, picking a trail through
rocks on the other side of the Sierras, no straight line to get there
from town, you'd have to drive south to Bakersfield, or maybe there

was a lumber road through the mountains, but here were the peaks, burning on the back wall of a room in the middle of the San Joaquin Valley, though she must be facing south, and the mountains were actually east. She tried to work out the directions, herself looking south at a view of mountains to the east of her, an image taken from the east looking west, but the thoughts made her dizzy as if the theater were on a lazy Susan. Hours seemed to pass, as if time had opened up, expanding and contracting, present into past. Tanner and Scott have reached the entrance to a mine, hidden among the potato-shaped boulders of the Alabama Hills, and the bags of gold are in Tanner's hands, coins running through his fingers. Kay knew what she would do if she found a bag of gold. Get the hell out of California for a start, and forget about Hank and the boy.

At last, Scott confesses to Tanner he's a federal agent, but warns him that Galt and his posse are trying to kill them and they better stick together. There's a shootout with Galt's men, and finally Miss Galt comes along and it's five hours later, time still expanding and contracting. She finds her father all alone, shooting at Tanner and Scott, and Miss Galt creeps up behind Mr. Galt and shoots over his shoulder to get his attention, so she's turned against family because this is a world where you can't even trust your own blood, forget about what side of right and wrong they might be on. Then Tanner shoots Galt in the back, dead, and it's horribly, horribly quiet.

The blood on the screen was nothing like real blood, more orange than red. When someone was shot there would never be just a little ketchup-smatter and no hole in the skin, and if you were shot in the face like one of the men from the posse, wouldn't you fall down dead right away instead of dropping so slowly? Seeing animals shot, horses and coyotes and deer, and the corpses afterward, there were always holes, but in the pictures when someone got shot, no holes, just the orange ketchup.

With the shootout over, Scott and Tanner struggle like a man and a woman in bed when the woman doesn't want it, dust and rocks raining around them so Tanner gets buried in the rubble and Scott has to pull him to safety as the mineshaft closes behind them, covering up the gold even though getting the gold seemed to be the whole point of the picture. Downstairs in the theater the blond man made a noise of disapproval, as if the gold should be everyone's priority, regardless of life or death, and the curly dark girl shushed him and tried to stand but he grabbed her hand and pulled her back to the seat.

At the end, Scott takes Tanner away, heading for justice, and Tanner's not even handcuffed, he's *happy* he's about to be punished. Miss Galt is there, and the little slut doesn't look at all unhappy her father is dead. She says to the sheriff that Scott will be coming back for his horse but it's plain as anything she means he'll be coming back for her, and then they can set up housekeeping, but with that cowpoke who's sweet on Scott it doesn't bear thinking about. Who was the 'Nevadan' anyway? Scott didn't seem to be. Tanner? Mr. Galt? Miss Galt? And what about the gold? Was it still buried up in that mine in the Alabama Hills? So many questions. Like life, what seemed to be resolved was actually not, in fact nothing was settled except Tanner, the criminal, not even the worst of the criminals, having to pay, and all of the other ones dead.

Bomba on Panther Island with Johnny Sheffield was showing next, but it was a picture for children really, and besides, there were groceries to buy, and time had flown so the boy was probably home already, alone in the apartment and getting up to goodness knows what.

The bag was so heavy Kay had to sit on the curb for a few minutes
as a firetruck went past. Not long before he died Papa sat to rest
on the curb walking home from the store and Ruth came along
in the car, stopped, and harangued him because of it being an
embarrassment to the family him sitting there and frankly quite
bad for business to let people think they belonged to the class
who sat on the street, the filthiness of it. The siren grew fainter
and then stopped like a bird choked mid-song and the strangled
mechanical squawk made Kay spring to her feet.

Turning down Pratt, what with the smoke rising from behind
the garage apartment next to the Smiths' house, she knew it must
be the boy. Devil take his squinty head and the pouting lip and the
way he'd *yes ma'am* and *no ma'am* but go on doing just what you'd
told him he'd not to. He was standing in the alley by the empty lot,
dead grass still half on fire and two firefighters pointing a hose
and another of them talking to the boy and his friends, other boys
she didn't recognize, but not the Japanese one, he was nowhere
around. Probably ran at the first sign of trouble. Not that she'd do
different. The scene made her want to turn and walk back in the
other direction and spend the rest of the afternoon at the soda
fountain until she could go to the State Theater and watch Betty
Hutton and Victor Mature in *Red, Hot, and Blue*. But the fireman
had seen her and the boy was pointing at her and she knew that
turning around and walking away was impossible because of the
authorities knowing she was responsible, in the end, as she was
the mother and Hank being such a ne'er-do-well.

What's he done she said as she approached the men.

Playing with match guns, said the firefighter. Just about

burned the whole block down if Mrs. Smith hadn't called it in.

The fireman spoke in a way that told her he was from back east. If not Oklahoma then Texas or Missouri.

Kay put the bag on the ground and clapped her hand across the boy's face so his head spun like it wasn't attached to the rest of him and all the other children, that firefighter, too, sprang back where they stood and the whole lot fell silent, just dogs barking some streets away and the sound of a car horn and a baby crying and a radio across the alley with the Andrews Sisters moaning 'I Can Dream Can't I?'. Lord, could they ever. The boy glared like he would kill her and damn him if he didn't turn that head slowly, lifting his chin, eyes always on her through the full arc of the turn, and present the other cheek.

You get upstairs now, she said, before I call the police to take you away, and the boy said You wouldn't call them, and a little girl snickered and then she slapped him again, slapped that other cheek harder than the first and this time drew blood where her fingernails caught his skin and she said You get inside before I blind you, and then the boy ran, skirting the smoldering grass and coughing through the smoke. Kay watched as he slowed and spoke to Mrs. Smith who was standing in her yard shaking her head and then he was up the stairs and inside, the door slamming behind him. They would get evicted for this and where to next? Motor Lodge this time. She had seen that in their future, praying at night, at the foot of the couch while the boy pretended to sleep, the image coming to her when her eyes closed and she wondered which bar or hotel room or flophouse Hank might be holed up in. Devil take him. And the boy.

What's a match gun? she asked the firefighter, I don't let him play with guns, and the man pulled from his pocket a wooden clothespin that had been taken apart and glued together with the pieces of wood back to back and a chamber whittled out of the center and the spring affixed like a trigger so a match pushed inside cocked the spring and all the boy had to do was trip it.

They light the match and it flies thirty feet in a fair breeze, said the firefighter. Know any of these others? He nodded at the group of boys and the lone girl, the dirty loose thing, all of them squinting in the evening light.

She shook her head. White trash, all of them, was what she thought but did not say. She picked up the bag of groceries from the ground and followed the path the boy had taken round the lot until she was standing at the fence between the garage and the Smiths' house and Mrs. Smith standing on her back porch coughed as if to say, I expect you'll explain this before you go inside the apartment I own on property I own next to a lot I own that your boy has seen fit to burn.

I'm sorry, Kay said. For what he did. I'll get him now, to apologize.

He already did. On his way inside.

Oh. Well, I'll make him clean it up.

Just a vacant lot. Nothing to clean up. Point is that fire could have spread and burnt down my garage and your apartment and my house and the houses of all the other folks on this block and then where would we be, Mrs. Knowlton?

Kay did not know what to say but, Yes, I see, it won't happen again.

And where were you, I'd like to know? Mrs. Smith said, crossing her arms over her bosom and looking down through the horn-rimmed spectacles she wore when she did her crossword puzzles in the shade with a glass full of ice and mint leaves and Kay did not like to think what else.

I had to go to the market.

Been gone an awful long while, I should think, said Mrs. Smith, just to buy groceries.

Yes, Mrs. Smith. I had errands. Thank you.

You are lucky I don't phone the police. That boy needs looking after. He needs a man about the house.

His father – he's a traveling salesman, you know.

Phone book says he's a rancher.

He lost the lease on the ranch.

And now you say he's a salesman.

That's to say – yes, I think so, Mrs. Smith.

Don't you know?

My husband's business is his business.

A husband's business is his wife's business first and last, in my experience, said Mrs. Smith. You would do well to take an interest or his business might just be the end of you, Mrs. Knowlton.

At that Mrs. Smith turned and picked up her paper from the porch swing and went inside letting the screen door slam behind her and Kay felt the force of the sound shoot through her so she had to clutch the bag of groceries tighter in her arms or else it would have fallen to the ground.

The boy was on the couch reading a comic book and did not move when the door opened and slammed shut again. Where'd you get that, she asked, and he said nothing so she tried to rip the comic from his hands once she'd put the groceries on the kitchen table but he held tight and tugged it away from her so that some of the pages ripped and when that happened he was on his feet and his face red and him blazing like this was the moment he was finally going to kill her.

Where's my money? he shouted, and she said What's ill-gotten is not yours to keep and he said It was not ill-gotten it was earned

and she said That is a very likely story. He screamed It's true! and
his voice was so loud her ears began to ring. That was *my* money!
he screamed, What did you do with it? It is someplace safe, she
said, and that is all we will say about it until your father gets home
and then you will explain to him how you came to have it.

The boy ran to the bathroom and slammed the door and since
there was no lock on that either she went after him, pushed it
open and cornered him between the door and the sink.

When your father gets home you will explain to him how you
came to have every last cent of that money and you will give back
anything you stole or took that was not yours.

I didn't steal! he shouted, pushing his face towards her so that
the place where her fingernails had caught his cheek bracketed
her vision.

You are a liar! she said, grabbing the bar of soap with one hand
and with the other pulling the hair at the back of his head and using
the soap to lever open his mouth, pushing it between his teeth.
When the jaw would not open she took her free hand and pinched
either side of the joint and the boy moaned and then she got the
soap in and pushed it deeper until he was gagging and the suds
came from his mouth like the chops of a rabid cat. In the mirror –
that other Kay on the other side with another boy, those other parts
of themselves in that other unreachable place – she saw herself drop
her hands to her side and the boy spitting the soap into the sink and
leaning over to heave and then he turned on the water and started
drinking from the tap. She hit the back of his head and heard his
teeth crack against the faucet and he was screaming now and there
was blood running into the water and rushing down the drain.

One way or another he would have to learn.

May 30, 1950

9

The clock in the middle of the third-floor corridor of the Executive Building struck two as I stepped from the elevator and its chime was still echoing by the time I arrived at the reception area of Leo Krug's office suite. Krug's private secretary, Anita Tinges, frowned as I approached her desk.

You were supposed to be here for lunch, Mr. Frank. Expected an hour ago. Appointment confirmed yesterday by phone. And yes, there will be a record of the call.

Because Anita knew everything about everyone many of us believed Krug had run a master line through her desk that allowed access to any call coming through the studio switchboard. Comments like this suggested we were not mistaken. When I first began working at the studio John warned me never to assume there was any such thing as a private phone conversation on the lot. If Anita said there was a record, I had to assume she was telling the truth.

But an hour ago Lucille told me Mr. Krug could only see me at two.

Anita removed her tortoiseshell glasses. Now, Mr. Frank, did Lucille prevent you from coming upstairs?

Of course not.

And did Lucille prevent you from speaking directly to me?

No, although I didn't—

And tell me, Mr. Frank, does Lucille keep Mr. Krug's diary?

I don't suppose—

And by your reckoning does Lucille know Mr. Krug's thoughts before he does himself?

I shouldn't imagine—

Well I do, Mr. Frank. I know Mr. Krug's thoughts before Mr. Krug has thought to think them. You were expected for lunch and now an unpleasant situation that should have taken an hour to resolve is going to take two. Mr. Krug is upstairs and presently indisposed so you will have to see Mr. Cherry. If you are lucky you will find Mr. Cherry in Mr. Cherry's office. If you are unlucky – well, if you are unlucky, you might think about clearing out your office and going home, Mr. Frank. Not that either Mr. Krug or Mr. Cherry has said anything to me, mind you, but I am not at present thinking good thoughts about you, Mr. Frank, not good thoughts at all.

The beaded chain that held the spectacles around her neck when they were not perched on the end of her nose swayed as she spoke so that the green and red rhinestones sparkled.

Now turn around, Mr. Frank.

I hesitated.

Only a masochist would make me say a thing twice, Mr. Frank.

I pivoted, sliding across the carpet but walking at an angle to her desk because the idea of Anita Tinges at my back was more frightening than the risk of falling flat on my face.

Now walk, Mr. Frank. One light little loafer in front of the other, and don't come back without an appointment, but frankly, Mr. Frank, given the thoughts I'm thinking about you, I don't imagine there will be any further appointments, ever again…frankly.

Porter's secretary Susie Cott was on the phone when I reached her desk at the other side of the building. Her eyes were focused on the front page of the *Los Angeles Times* and for half a minute she showed no sign of having seen me.

Of course I wanted to speak to him, but there was never anyone like that at Bryn Mawr… Well it isn't something one jokes about,

Donna. You can't walk all over people on your way up, I mean how would you like it if someone flattened *your* head to get another rung up? It's simply not cricket... No, not the insect. It's an English expression I learned from Mr. Grant... Something to do with not being square.

I cleared my throat and Susie flinched.

Don't scoot, Donna, I have to work, she said into her headset. You're not in the appointments for this afternoon, Mr. Frank. You were supposed to have lunch with Mr. Cherry and Mr. Krug upstairs but he, that is Mr. Cherry, said you didn't show.

Lucille told me—

Susie shook her head as if she pitied me.

Don't you know Lucille has a death wish for every writer on the lot? She thinks it's your fault she never gets to act. I told her it's the cameramen if it's anyone, or the directors, but she said if writers wrote parts she could play then she'd be a star.

Maybe I should write a movie about a two-faced secretary.

Susie narrowed her eyes to dark green slits.

Porter had recently had his office redecorated, creating a sitting area that resembled a family room with a porthole television, coffee table, and bar cart, a separate business area with a long conference table, a formal lounge section whose purpose eluded me, and the space around his desk itself, which constituted a region all its own. The whole room was the size of a small bungalow and could have housed a family of four. Whoever did the decorating had a taste for rosewood tables and low davenports upholstered in biscuit linen. From a record player in one corner a trumpet wailed cool blue notes and one wall of the office was filled by a single canvas splotched with black ellipses against a white field.

Porter was sitting on one of the low couches near the front of the room with his back to the door. He pointed at the painting as I walked in.

Just got that. Supposed to be a requiem to the Spanish Republic. Looks like a bunch of big black testicles to me but it lowers my blood pressure to stare at the thing. I suppose some would say it's subversive. Communist art. Porter turned to me and winked. The gesture seemed to mute the trumpet and draw a line between us. I liked the painting and the music and the furnishings but could think of nothing witty to say because I felt I had arrived unprepared for a fight. Scotch rocks or vodka neat, Frank? You'll need one or the other.

Nothing hard for me.

Porter pressed the intercom on the end table, asked Susie to bring us coffee, and then we waited, blasted by the trumpet. There was a humming noise beneath the top notes but I could not tell if it was coming from the record or Porter's throat. Since his arrival at the studio a year earlier our relationship had cooled, as if he believed he could not be openly friendly with a man who was supposed to answer to him, or perhaps he felt just as pained by our shared past as I did.

I must have told you that he and I were friends in college. We pledged the same fraternity at Cornell and lived in a rambling mansion overlooking a waterfall that froze nearly solid in winter. Our friendship had been cemented in the aftermath of a fire that destroyed the fraternity house, forcing the remaining members into temporary accommodation where Porter and I shared a room one semester. When I say that our friendship was cemented, I mean that I had long assumed this was the case, however much the fire itself was a traumatic memory. Every time I saw Porter the feeling of standing on the wet lawn in the dark and realizing with horror that someone was missing came over me, so that I could smell the burning house and feel the coldness in my feet and the heat on my face. His friendship at the time had helped me survive the aftermath of that loss, but working together at the studio and finding him so remote where he had always been warm in the past renewed the pain. Perhaps I never told you about this, Myles, or only shared what little I could bear to recount. By that afternoon, I had all but convinced myself that given the chance one of the most important friendships in my life might yet be reconstituted and the old Porter who had kept me company on long walks in Ithaca's gorges would return to kill off whoever this bogus stand-in might be.

On further thought, I suspect I never spoke to you about the history Porter and I shared because I was concerned that it would make you doubt your place in my heart. It should not have done, and I ought to have trusted I could convince you this was the case. This is another matter for which I must ask your forgiveness.

I'm sorry about earlier, Porter, I think Lucille—

Porter signaled me to be quiet as Susie brought in the coffee on a tray, placed it on the table between the two couches, and closed the door behind her.

She spies for Krug, Porter whispered. He poured the coffee, adding milk and sugar to his own, and leaned close to me. What neither of them know is that Anita spies for me, and I spy for the gentlemen in New York.

Not very honest.

One can't afford to be. But for the next hour you and I are going to make an exception to that rule. Let's put aside the recent distemper of our exchanges.

You mean to say this isn't about *She Turned Away*? It was a disingenuous question. I knew our meeting had nothing to do with the film.

Nick Charles has it in hand. The project will be fine.

But it's John's picture.

Marsh likes to think so.

Help me, Porter, I'm lost.

As I said, I'll be honest with you, and you will be honest with me, because we are old friends, and the times are exceptional.

A bell rang somewhere, but it was not the clock in the corridor. The fight had started and I tried to find my feet.

Round 1

Porter picked up a fat file from the davenport and dropped it on the coffee table, rattling my cup in its saucer.

The studio decided a while ago to undertake investigations of those among its employees about whom there might be some suspicion of political or moral irregularities. I am sorry to put it so baldly. This was instituted before my arrival, and while I might cavil about the subterfuge involved, believing it always better to approach the suspected individual directly and ask for an explanation, I can understand Krug's rationale. I know you think of me as a brother and I once thought of you likewise without giving it a second thought.

Past tense, I note.

I think of you now as a member of a larger family, like a cousin who has strayed. You cannot deny that you betrayed me, Desmond. You were never honest about yourself.

Through all the years of our acquaintance I had never heard

Porter's voice sound as it did then, his words flashing and cutting like steel through the music.

You've always known my politics, Porter. When we were students I'm pretty sure they were your politics as well. I hoped they might still be.

I am not speaking of politics, at least not yet. I am speaking of moral irregularities. Sexual betrayals.

Although you and I had taken people like John Marsh and a very few others into our confidence, I thought that we had managed to keep the truth of our lives sufficiently secret that this kind of confrontation might never occur, and yet I also always lived in the expectation of it happening one day, the result of a slip on our part, or some gossip's suspicion about my visits to your house under the guise of my friendship with Helen. It had not occurred to me that the studio itself might investigate those it suspected, or that such investigations would prove as intrusive as they did. Faced with such exposure, my heart thrashed between panic and relief, because having the secret out in the open between Porter and me was almost as welcome as it was terrifying.

You think Helen and I are having an affair, I said, resorting to the lie on which we had all agreed as our first line of defense. But it isn't true, Porter. I guess you don't believe in friendship anymore, is that it?

Porter scowled. I said this was a unique situation, Desmond, and you and I were going to be honest with each other. You know exactly what I'm referring to and it has nothing to do with women. His voice jumped, fighting the trumpet. It has nothing to do with Helen or any other woman because you've been tricked into believing you have no interest in women. I think you've been lying your whole life about the very nature of your most intimate moral character, about the way you have been warped and inverted.

How quickly I crumbled in the face of truth. I made no further effort to deny what I was, perhaps because the sense of relief quickly outweighed any terror I might have been feeling.

What did you expect me to do, Porter? Say to you, wringing my hands and sniveling, *I want to confess I'm a homosexual, but I hope you'll still be my brother and roommate?*

I had never used that word to describe myself before, and immediately it felt too restrictive, signifying in my mind a class of characters with whom I have always struggled to identify. I could not confine my body to the poses of a flouncing pansy, nor put myself in the clothes of a tart or varlet or queen, and whatever alternatives might exist were resistant to summons, as if they, like me, did not wish to answer the call of that spurious nineteenth-century epithet. I have penchants and predilections and desires, but those attractions and impulses, those orientations, do not make me some*one*, not in my own mind at any rate, even if they do in the eyes of others. I remain, to myself, always a subject, doing and acting, never an object, a thing, an example of a certain type. With few exceptions, perhaps that is why I avoided the secretive scene I could have chosen to frequent in those years, as I assume you also avoided it Myles. I wanted the freedom of not belonging to any group, even one that might have embraced me.

If I had spoken honestly to you, Porter, I continued, it would have been the end of my social life, if not the end of my actual life. If I had confided in you, you would have told all the brothers and the dean and I would have been hounded from the university. I might have killed myself if someone else didn't kill me first. How dare you demand that I should have been honest when you would have turned such honesty against me?

Despite the air conditioning, sweat bangled Porter's neck. You were trying to convert me, Desmond, I am certain of that. And you were not the first.

Nonsense. I never thought anything of the kind. You honestly believe I wanted more than friendship from you?

Isn't that what your type always wants?

Not for a minute! And what do you mean I wasn't the first?

You know who. I'm talking about Noah Roy. Before he died, he tried to get friendly with me.

Noah Roy.

Do you recognize the name, Myles? Even if I never spoke of him, and I am now convinced I probably did not, it should still be familiar to you. I had used it in my novels and scripts over and over so that there was always a character called Noah, often a Roy, sometimes just the initials N.R., and when it was too painful to use the whole name, parts of it, or even its variants, I resorted to describing the boy to whom it belonged, so that throughout my works there is often a young man with a *shy lean face*, or *deep blue eyes*, or a bearing that suggests a cadet expelled from the military for some dubious offense, who carries his shame like a poppy in the buttonhole. Porter saying his name that afternoon, however, awoke in my memory a more precise pattern of associations.

At Cornell Porter and I were in the same class, Noah a year behind us. He had pledged when we were already brothers. At some point I became conscious that Noah looked at me differently, and I knew on several mornings that I had dreamt of Noah in ways I did not dream about women. He was not the first boy I had found attractive, but he was the first I allowed myself to fantasize about, to imagine what I wanted to do with him, what I wanted him to do to me. We began playing tennis together, and although Noah was a superior athlete, naturally long and quick with an elegant forearm that returned a ball with easy power, I could not help feeling in those games a union approaching consummation. One weekend, when the rest of the brothers were away on a social exchange, I was in bed with a cold and Noah, who had remained in Ithaca for a tennis competition, stayed. I woke in the night, coughing and sneezing, and after a quarter hour of blowing my nose I heard the boards above my room creak, and then the murmur of Noah's feet tiptoeing down the stairs and along the hall. My door opened and Noah came in, sat on the bed, and put a cool hand against my brow. *You'll get sick*, I warned him. *No matter*, he said, leaving his hand where it was, *what can I do?* I knew he meant not only *What can I do to help you?* but also *I cannot help what I feel, so what can I do?*

It was the first time either of us had kissed another boy, and then Noah slipped into my bed. We didn't know what to do, no one had ever told us, so at first we just held each other, a little shocked by the way our bodies reacted, then fell asleep and woke again in the night, discovering that kissing was not like it was in movies, two closed mouths pressed together, but that it was possible to open the other person's mouth with one's own, that kissing was warm and wet and awkward, that teeth were always a part of it, that there were edges and sharpness to negotiate, but once the problems were known an arena of play opened where a game of repetition and experiment and variation became possible and pleasurable, that the game could continue until both of us were breathless and exhausted by it, and then rally and start again, so our exertion was both hunger and its satisfaction. There would be few times when we did not fear discovery, but as summer arrived we made plans to stay at the cottage on Lake George that my parents were abandoning that year in favor of Cape Cod. There was only a caretaker, a defrocked Jesuit who got drunk every night and went to bed early, leaving us alone in the drawing room overlooking the water with nothing to distract us but a collection of records and the walk-in bar. Each night we locked the door to the drawing room in case the caretaker should wake, turned off the lights, and wrestled around on the carpets, playing like children, except that the play, by degrees, turned into the most serious game of my life. We taught each other what to do, how to stimulate and soothe and subdue, and until meeting you, Myles, that summer was the most harmonious time of my life. In the autumn, we returned to tennis and had to be content with moments stolen in our rooms, knowing every time we kissed or touched, the few occasions that we chanced anything more intimate, risked discovery that would ruin us.

As I looked at Porter, I could see Noah's face as it had been before his death, pale and freckled, laughing and bright with promise, and then I remembered the boy's blackened skin after his body was removed from the ruins of the house. On the lawn overlooking the gorge, Porter and I identified him. It was only after Noah's death that the two of us became close. Sitting there in Porter's office all those years later was the first time I had heard anyone accuse Noah of being what he was. Why formulate it as an accusation, as if the designation itself were a crime? Because the label signified a certain catalogue of activities that were, in fact, against the law, I have to remind myself, perhaps also remind you. The only legal homosexual was an inactive one. If you and I had been caught in 1950 we could have been sentenced to twenty years in prison, placed on California's then newly created registry of sex offenders, and risked sterilization by the state lest we, in our non-breeding way, accidentally reproduce and make more men like us. Moral eugenics and nothing less. When Governor Warren signed

the bill in January that year, there were few voices of protest. A
social worker by the name of Mrs. Darryl Holmes – bless the dear
lady – wrote to the *Los Angeles Times* calling the laws against sodomy
what they were: medieval hysteria, no better than what the Nazis
had been doing only a few years earlier. Kinsey had the right idea
where sex was concerned, wrote Mrs. Holmes, and yet politicians
and lawmakers refused to listen to the good doctor because they
were all too ashamed to admit he might be right.

Porter was grimacing.

I can't speak for Noah, I said. As for myself, Porter, I sensed you
and I were not the same.

This was not the truth. Quite the opposite. I always suspected
Porter secretly might be like you and me and Noah and so many
others besides, whether or not he had a wife.

Men like me are not, despite what you might have heard, only
interested in having sex, I said. We like friendship – ordinary non-
sexual friendship – as much as you do.

You call it friendship. I call it mendacity.

I have always been as honest as I could, Porter. You never
asked me whether I loved women or if I intended to get married. I
thought there was a chance you understood, that you intuited the
truth about me and chose not to speak of it. I thought when you
married and chose someone else as your best man it was because
you had concluded I was not the person you wanted standing next
to you at the altar as you took your vows. It saddened me but I also
understood why that might be the case.

An honest man of your stripe would never have allowed himself
to be so friendly with normal people. You came to stay at my home,
Desmond, with my parents. You compromised every one of us in
doing so. You would have done better to settle down and find a wife

or live a less sociable life. Become a priest! I feel personally affronted by the − what shall I call it? − the platonic intimacies we shared as young men.

I'm still young, Porter. So are you.

I know men like you want to believe in eternal youth. This is part of your perversion, isn't it, this cult of adolescence.

Perversion! Sixty-four-dollar word. What perversion? What I do in private with other men, *adult* men, Porter, man has done for millennia and sometimes far less privately.

The trumpet across the room howled away at my nerves and I wished I could make it stop. Porter flipped open the folder in front of us.

You call this private?

The first items in the folder were a series of photographs: you and me on the pool deck of your house, both of us in swimming trunks, you straddling my waist, our mouths pressed together. Under other circumstances I would have been touched by the tenderness of the images but in that moment I felt my temperature drop. The pictures must have been taken only in the previous week because you were in a pair of stunning new trunks you had just purchased. We had never been so brazen before, but recently convinced ourselves that the fences and shrubbery surrounding your back garden were adequate protection. I picked up one of the photographs. The angle was poor but anyone could see it was your profile. There was a picture of me from that very morning, naked and emerging from the pool. When I saw it I caught my breath. This photo, all these photos, must have been what the man Hank was offering, what he was giving me the chance to buy before handing them over to Porter. How differently that day might have played out if I had taken the chance, if I had talked

Hank down from ten thousand dollars to some figure I could have managed to procure before the banks closed.

Beneath Porter's disgust I could see that he was almost pleased.

I won't ask you to explain it, Desmond. I don't think there's any explanation for this behavior. It's one thing if you keep it private, even if it still disgusts me, but another thing entirely if the truth gets out. The man who took these pictures may work for us but he's been threatening to find someone to pay him more than we're offering. This very moment Hedda Hopper is sitting on a story about your nightly sleepovers and these photos are all she needs to go ahead with it. You know what we've had to pay to keep this out of the papers? Your shenanigans are risking too much. I've already spoken to Myles, and he assures me nothing like this will ever happen again.

I did not know if he was bluffing, but I refused to believe it was true. If you had made such a claim it must have been only to make Porter leave you alone, or perhaps to protect me, but it explained why you had been so cold when I passed you earlier, and I wondered whether you blamed me for all of this. In a way, you would not have been unjustified in doing so. Was I not the one who was always testing your affection, even as I claim to have been anxious to protect you? Was I not the one who approached you on set, who convinced you earlier that week, when the photos must have been taken, that we could expose our kissing to the sky because no one could possibly be looking?

I shouldn't have to remind you, Porter continued, that both you and Myles have morals clauses in your contracts. Legally speaking, we have enough evidence to fire both of you and see to it that neither of you works in the motion picture industry ever again. We could even turn you over to the police, although that is not in our interests.

Myles makes this studio too much money, and frankly so do you, in your way. But there are too many homosexuals in this studio and it is my aim either to get them cured or get them out. I feel personally betrayed by you, Desmond. I feel betrayed by the way you seduced me into friendship when we were young men. I feel betrayed by the ways you've continued to trade on our friendship. I feel particularly betrayed by the way you corrupted one of our brightest young stars, someone who should be like a son to you.

Oh, Jesus, only if I had been a child bride, Porter.

Don't make such filthy jokes.

Let me assure you, Myles is old enough to know who he is, and believe me, he has always been a very willing partner.

Everyone knows the only way you people can survive is by recruiting the innocent. What's a homosexual but a sexual offender? It makes me wonder if you might have been the leader of that little cell at Cornell, if you were the one who recruited Noah, if in fact I should have feared you more than anyone else.

A *cell*? You think I'm a Verkhovensky or Nechayev? You're out of your mind, Porter. Homosexuals are not revolutionaries or terrorists, at least not the way you mean.

You've done a good job so far in recruiting Myles but it's not too late to rescue him. At least in Helen he has a wife who will support him.

I had to cough to cover my laughter. If Porter had no idea about Helen and Barbara I did not want to betray them.

Can't you see that Myles is what he is as I am what I am? And you are what you are!

Save your insults for your own kind. There's no equivalence of any sort. As soon as shooting is finished on this picture, Myles is going to take some time away in a clinic with a highly respected analyst who specializes in cases of coerced perversion. We've spoken about it over lunch and he is entirely in agreement.

If you don't mind, I'd like to hear it from Myles.

I don't want you anywhere near him, Porter said, but that may be a moot point because I have other, graver concerns about you. Matters involving morals can be fixed and managed when the individuals involved are willing to submit to treatment. Matters involving national security demand a higher threshold of investigation and cure.

National security? So I'm a pervert *and* a spy?

Your word, Desmond, not mine. But now that you've said it, I have to ask you, are you a Soviet spy?

The upper hook landed before I could block or parry and it stung more than the sexual accusations because it was so untrue. A laugh exploded from my throat but there was nothing funny about what was happening.

Round 2

Porter sat up straighter and pinched his lips together. I began to wonder what had happened since our undergraduate days to change him. As a student his thinking was nuanced, supple, so that I often felt as if I learned as much from him as from our professors. But now there was a bluntness and inflexibility that bewildered me.

First and last, a motion picture studio is a community, Desmond. And like any town or city or state or country, the citizens of that community have a responsibility to abide by and uphold its laws, to support its democratic processes, and to ferret out those who would seek to overthrow what has been democratically implemented by the community at large.

Come on, Porter, a movie studio is a business, nothing more or less, I snorted. It makes products that it sells to make money and so make more product, all to produce capital that makes a tiny minority of men at the top richer than all the rest of us combined.

Porter took the file to the long rosewood conference table under the black and white canvas. His hands trembled as he turned the photos of you and me face down on the folder before beginning to lay out clippings from newspapers, typed notes, and photostatic copies of a number of letters in a regular grid that covered the table's entire surface. When the jazz record came to an end he stumbled across the room, flipped it to the other side, replaced the needle with a scratch that tore through the speakers and was followed by the trumpet sobbing against a background of muted saxophones, the percussionist keeping furious time with brushes on the snare.

Friend at Capitol sent me this. Crazy stuff. Calms me down, though, just like that subversive painting. And boy, do I need calming today.

I glanced at the documents spread across the table. It was all so predictable.

This is your flimsy case against me, Porter?

I thought you should have a chance to defend yourself.

Is there an appellate body if I lose in this chamber?

Porter reddened and sweat flowed from his hairline. It was a perfect impression of those cartoon characters who pop with fury. All he lacked was steam shooting from his ears.

Why won't you take this seriously?

The problem is, Officer Cherry, I drawled, putting on a wheedling tough-guy voice, I don't see as there's nuttin' t'explain…

What about this? Porter fingered a copy of a letter. Blunt fingers, stubby ends. I imagined what those fingers might do. Greetings from

Desmond Frank to the Moscow Art Theatre. *Wishing you all the best for a long future of fine theatrical productions.* Ever been to the Moscow Art Theatre, Desmond?

No, but does it matter?

Item two. Profile of Mr. Desmond Frank in the *Daily Worker* from March 1944, describing you as 'Movieland's Young Bane of Oppression'. Isn't the *Daily Worker* a Communistic publication?

I'd have said it was Socialist myself but you're the one casting about for labels, so call it whatever you want. I don't see that it makes much difference what I think. Not to you at least.

Porter frowned. Item three. An Open Letter from the American Committee for the Protection of the Foreign Born. Your name is on their letterhead, right there. The letter itself, if *letter* you can call this hysterical screed, demands an end to the U.S. Department of Justice's deportation of alien nationals. Isn't it the belief of that organization that they must protect all foreigners on American soil as part of their revolutionary activities and in support of Soviet agents who have infiltrated the country?

As far as I know it has nothing to do with spies or infiltration or anything else you might want to call it. It's a matter of common sense and humanity, Porter.

I saw myself lean back on the ropes, protecting my head and taking the blows, watching through a fine audible haze of brass and percussion as my old friend picked up one item after another, evidencing my purported involvement with or support of organizations as diverse as the Civil Rights Congress, the Progressive Citizens of America, the Committee for the First Amendment, the Joint Anti-Fascist Refugee Committee, Friends of the Abraham Lincoln Brigade, League of American Writers, the Stop Censorship Committee, the Council on African Affairs, the

Artists' Front to Win the War, the Hollywood Anti-Nazi League, the Spanish Refugee Appeal, and the National Council of the Arts, Sciences and Professions, among others. The U.S. Government's Loyalty Review Board had condemned most of these organizations as Communist fronts, as you may remember.

With each piece of evidence, my smile set stronger roots. It was all too incredible to be taken seriously. Porter's jabs went soft and wide.

I put it to you, Desmond, that every one of these organizations is subversive, Communistic, or anti-pathetic to American values. Whenever you put your name to shit like this – Porter held up an open letter published in the *New York Times* from the Committee for the First Amendment – you betray this nation to the Soviets. Whenever you open your checkbook or host a party or march in a goddamned May Day parade you contribute to the forces of darkness and evil! Don't you understand that May Day parades are tools of the Communist International?

The Comintern was disbanded in forty-three, Porter. Now it's the Cominform. At least get the name right.

You are a *traitor*, Desmond. A true-blooded American loyal to his country wouldn't even know such Soviet lingo!

Stop gnawing and finish me off. I won't do what you want, so let's call it quits. I'm down. The ref is counting.

Porter raised the index finger of his right hand, twitching it so close to my face that eventually it made contact. Then, to my astonishment, he pushed his fingertip into the place where the softer tissue of my nose connected with the cartilage. For ten seconds that felt like ten hours, as the trumpet warbled, neither of us moved.

You don't get off that easy, Desmond. I want to give you the chance to recant and apologize and make good with the Feds. We're willing to help you do it, in fact we're going to *make* you do it, to atone for what you've done. Through your political activities you are taking bread not just from our mouths but from the mouths of our children. Take enough bread and we'll have nothing left, we'll be forced to turn ourselves into cannibals and infanticides, we'll have no choice but eating the children we bring into this world if people like you and your Communist spies have your way. Well I say it stops *here*, at this goddamned studio. Given what we know about your so-called private life and the ways you've betrayed this company and your colleagues, we want you to make an example of yourself. You'll be our reformed little Red, true blue by the time we're through with you. Thank God it's not too late.

All at once, as Porter was speaking, the editor of memory in my mind undid his work. The cuts were reversed, the original footage restored to a complete reel that ran through the Steenbeck, the subjectivity of time stripped away to reveal the uncut negative of that night when a fraternity house at the top of a gorge burned to the ground and killed a young man. What did you say, Porter?

I said *Thank God it's not too late.*

Round 3

I considered the possibility that Porter was not, in fact, entirely himself. Who knew what pressures the Head of Production at one of the world's largest movie studios might suffer? Such stress could produce any number of anomalous psychological effects, but that afternoon Porter was so unlike the person I thought I knew that it felt as though he was already absent, dead, and some diabolical force was animating his body.

You've lost your mind, Porter.

I am perfectly sane!

I took the uncut footage (the hard intimacy that had sprung up between us, the invocation of Noah Roy, the memories of the fire and its aftermath, the walks in the gorges with Porter, the tennis matches and love matches and freedom with Noah at Lake George, the present accusations, fragments of remembered conversation, rumors about Porter's wife, Yvette), chopped it up, rearranged it, and ran it all together in a montage (a + b = c, thesis + antithesis = synthesis) until the events of that night formed a narrative I could read, and in interpreting what I discovered, following the logic of one image juxtaposed against another in ways I had not previously considered, at last I understood, fourteen years after the event, that Noah's death was no accident, and in making sense of my first love's death (of what from then on I have always considered Noah's murder), the picture I had assembled and hastily taped together began to make sense of Porter as well.

How's your marriage, Porter?

That's none of your concern.

Then why should my relationship with Myles be any of yours?

Porter flamed back into focus. You're trying to trade in equivalents where there aren't any. You're breaking the law, you're breaking your contract, and you're perverting the vulnerable.

Oh nonsense. Myles is not vulnerable, at least not in the ugly way you mean. He's not a child, not by anyone's measure. But come on, Porter, answer me, how's your wife?

I won't discuss my wife with someone like you.

Yvette left you, didn't she? She's moved back to New York.

It's a trial separation.

You know the rumor I've heard, but which I've chosen neither to

315

believe nor to spread? People say she left you for non-consummation of the marriage.

Porter stumbled away from the table and let out a long, horrified sigh. *That is nothing but mendacious…*

A rush of air blew from the vents near the ceiling and it was so cold I began to shiver. *If anyone should make an example of himself, Porter, it's you.*

I know you're trained for this, how to turn an interrogation to your advantage.

You betrayed yourself earlier.

The only person who's betrayed himself today is you, Desmond.

I've been thinking about it since you said it.

Once more, I played back the re-edited footage, reviewing the night in the fraternity house, the smell of smoke, the way I woke Porter in the neighboring room, how we then woke all the other brothers and began evacuating. Noah's room was on the top floor, in the converted attic, and I had turned to Porter and said, *I have to wake Noah.* Porter had paused, his eyes flashed in the smoke, and he said, *Noah's already out, I saw him go.* Later, standing on the lawn in the dark, taking a count of the brothers, we discovered Noah was missing. I turned, running back toward the house as flame broke through the windows, wrapping tendrils around the high gable. Before I reached the front steps I found myself face down in the grass, tackled by Porter, who was whispering into my ear, *It's too late, thank God, it's too late.* When the firemen carried out Noah's body, Porter said he must have been mistaken. It was night, there was smoke, all the brothers looked the same in the dark.

You told me we were both going to be honest, so be honest, Porter. You knew Noah was asleep upstairs, didn't you? You thought, Sure, what the hell, let the faggot burn. Serves him right. *That about the* size of the crime? I remember what you said that night. *It's too late, thank God.* Why *thank God?*

Porter leaned against a couch and covered his eyes with one hand.

You don't know anything about it.

What did he do to you, Porter, that made you hate him?

I did not—

That sounds like a confession.

If I wanted a priest I'd convert.

You started the fire, didn't you, knowing what might happen. You were awake when I knocked on your door. You were dressed even though it was the middle of the night.

Porter's hands were shaking. I had won the round, and without considering the magnitude of what I was about to do, sat down behind Porter's desk and began opening drawers until I found one that was locked.

Give me the key.

You should be institutionalized, Desmond. You're sick.

I don't think you understand. I have nothing to lose because either way my time here is finished. I have no intention of cooperating with you or the FBI or the House of Representatives or whoever else might demand I betray my friends and principles to go on living a free life in this supposed land of liberty. You, however, have a great deal to lose, and if you don't cooperate with me, I will phone Hedda Hopper myself and tell her not only about your wife and your marriage, but also about Noah Roy and that fire fourteen years ago. And then I'll call the cops. So, give me the key.

Porter fumbled in his pants pocket, withdrew a set of keys, and threw it towards the desk. The record was over. I rose, flipped it, and set it to play once more.

Round 4

There was no gun, as I had half-expected to find in the locked drawer, but dozens of files on producers, directors, writers, actors, composers, costume designers, set decorators, and other staff. The largest of the files was on Krug himself. At the back of the drawer was a photo album. I placed each of the files on the desk and as I withdrew the album from the drawer Porter shouted at me to put it back.

The genre of photograph was not shocking in itself, not to me. Each page presented an array of young men in gymnastic poses. Some depicted two men wrestling, one carrying another, always wearing small posing-strap pouches if anything at all. In the back of the album were a dozen issues of so-called fitness magazines.

I have an interest in bodybuilding, Porter wheezed.

As do other men I've met in my life.

The personnel files were similar to my own, stuffed with photographs, documents, clippings, copies of letters, and notes from private detectives employed by the studio. There was a file for you, Myles, and ones for Helen and Barbara, although both of the latter included information only on their political activities. The nature of their personal relationship, as I suspected, remained unknown to the studio or its investigators. It was the Krug file that most interested me. Unlike the others, the case against the head of the studio was chiefly financial. There were copies of bank statements, bond certificates, financial records, deeds, rental agreements, invoices, and check stubs.

You'd have to be an accountant to make sense of it.

Laundering, embezzlement, bribes to city officials, organized crime. We're trying to figure a way to get rid of Krug, but nothing ever sticks. He's always one hand removed from the actual exchange.

You don't have a loyal bone, do you, Porter?

I'm loyal to myself and the men in New York who sign my paycheck. Krug is a child. He has tantrums. Someone has to keep him in line. I'm the person responsible.

That must be consoling.

Listen, I can help you if you just keep quiet. I'll arrange it so you sit down in private with a couple of fellows, answer their questions, and you'll never be bothered again. You can go away, spend time in that clinic. We'll get you well again. I've been there myself.

You call yourself well?

I manage my illness. They helped me understand I was an anti-narcissist who had no real interest in his personality and projected that interest outward. I have learned to redirect it inward. Bodybuilding has helped me love myself again, Desmond. It might help you as well.

Nonsense. I wish I could sit inside your head for a couple hours and see what picture you're running because I bet it's directed and produced and written by Porter Cherry with music by Cherry and gowns by Cherry and every part in the goddamn picture played by Cherry. Fuck your clinic and your files and your quiet meetings with G-men.

Porter took off his jacket. Underneath it his shirt was soaked. Whatever affliction he might have, the man was definitely sick. Under other circumstances I might have mustered the selflessness to feel sorry for him but I kept seeing Noah Roy's face after the fire. Save for Porter's deception, Noah might have lived, and the life I had known in the intervening years would have been a very different one. I might never have come to Los Angeles, I might never have met you, Myles, although that is only speculation. I regretted and grieved Noah's death and hated Porter for what I understood to be his responsibility, but I could and can still hold those feelings alongside gratitude for the years you and I spent together. My desire was always, from the moment I met Noah, from the moment I met you, from the moment I have met other men in the years since you and I were last together, a life of open companionship rather than isolation and subterfuge.

Porter coughed, propping his head in his hands. What are you going to do, Desmond?

I came here hoping that because of the friendship we once had, you would see your way to making a situation less difficult than it might be. I believed in your humanity. I can't say that now, and it saddens me to realize you've always been a stranger to me. You accuse me of deception, but you were the worse deceiver by far. I deceived only to protect my wellbeing, and the wellbeing of those I've loved. You deceived to advance your own position. So I don't know what I'll do, but you probably won't see me again.

Although I was tempted to take them all and make a bonfire in the hallway, I left the files on the desk and walked out the door without looking back. It was the sort of moment when, in one of my scripts, the character would hear the click of a gun and freeze, but there was only the susurration of air from the vent, the wailing trumpet, and the mechanical slaughter of Susie Cott's typing. I waited for a moment, hoping Porter might apologize, but neither of us said anything.

Susie grinned at me as I stepped into the hall. It was more unnerving than if she had frowned.

Mrs. Tinges called to say that Mr. Krug is waiting for you, Mr.

320

Frank. You're to go upstairs right away. You'll find Mr. Krug in the executive gym.

But the gym itself was deserted so I went looking for Krug in the locker room, wending my way through rows of steel cupboards until I found him near the back, by the showers, immersed mid-chest in an ice bath, bat-wing arms balancing on the rim of a roll-top tub. A chiropractor massaged his shoulders and with each palpitation Krug's chins jiggled, his whole face bloodless under a bristle of dyed black hair. Through tri-focal lenses, tears running down his face, he squinted and frowned. As I approached the bath, Nick Charles and an assistant appeared from behind a bank of lockers.

That's too hard! Krug snarled, reaching up to scrape his fingernails against the back of the chiropractor's hand. Give me the Pocketbook File.

Nick passed Krug a thick manila folder. He opened it and held up a photograph of a naked woman.

Whatcha think of that pussy, Mr. Frank? You might call it a beautiful beaver, don't you think?

I wouldn't know, Mr. Krug.

What about this one? Krug held up a second photograph. Ain't that a sweet fucking honeypot?

I couldn't honestly say, Mr. Krug.

Nick? What about you? Dig the shape of this privy pond?

Nick smirked. I'd say it's perfect, Mr. Krug. Swimmable.

Krug laughed, flapping his arms against the ice. This kid kills me.

The other assistant piped up, I'd swim it, too, Mr. Krug.

Et tu, Bruce? Krug laughed. Even little boy Bruce would swim it. What about this one, Mr. Frank? Heat your hands in a muff like that?

No, Mr. Krug, I would not, I said, crossing my arms over my chest.

And this one? Krug held up another photo, and another, and another. I thought I recognized each of the women from around the lot and began to wonder if the price of bit parts in the studio's films was posing for Krug's private gallery. When I failed to pass comment on any of them, Krug shook his head. What a waste.

How's that, Mr. Krug?

I assume Porter has explained the studio's position, and what will be required if you want to remain in our employment, although given your moral and political deviance I have my doubts about the wisdom of doing anything other than burning you at the stake. I don't believe Reds or queers can be reformed. Porter has other ideas. He's the pragmatist in this marriage. I'm the realist. You might be able to win him over, but I'll always see a Red Queen when I look at you. And after all I gave you. That's not gratitude on your face.

I think you'll find Porter has changed his mind.

I know he's as big a faggot as you, if that's what you're implying. Porter doesn't matter. I make the decisions here. I decide who stays and who goes. I'm a rich man. I'm the most successful movie man in history. I'm so fucking rich I could buy and sell everyone in this town if the fancy took me, and you are a peon, Mr. Frank, nothing more than that. You know how many novelists and dramatists and cartoonists and two-bit scribblers would bend over and let me fuck them blind just to set foot on this lot? You are replaceable, and I say you go.

I wanted to ask Krug if he had ever truly cared for someone other than himself, demand to know what he had done for the war widows, for all the fatherless children and childless parents apart from make money off their grief. I wanted to know what he did for the young men and women who came to the studio and earned so little they could barely survive. Instead I stood there in silence, but my silence seemed to anger him more than anything I might have said. His face began to turn red, so deeply red that it appeared nearly black in the low light of the locker room. The ice in his bath cracked and the meltwater sloshed. I thought of telling Krug that I spent every day inventing characters who were each, in some small respect, portraits of myself, and that when audiences across the country watched actors playing those versions of me they began to see the world through my eyes, legions of people like me weeping and suffering, laughing and delighting, just trying to live happily and prosperously, and that in time they would turn to men like Krug and condemn them, just as I do now.

Except I said none of this, because it seemed pointless to do so. I was not going to change his mind. I was not about to make him see himself differently or become a better person through my righteous indignation. He was too evil or too stupid, or both.

I took a breath and said, Oh go to hell, Leo. I quit.

When he heard this, Krug began to struggle, pressing his weight up and rising to stand in the ice. The moment he reached his feet, revealing the whole red and yellow mass of his body, he slipped and fell back into the tub, howling in pain.

Rather than feeling defeated, as I walked back to the elevator I imagined I could dance up the walls and across the ceiling. Never in my life had I quit anything, and the sensation was so strange, so liberating, that I both wanted something to happen, for there to be an immediate response, and feared it would be so dramatic that it would make me change my mind. That potential for undoing was as perversely attractive as the determination to continue on the path I had chosen was reassuring. I expected someone would come running after me to drag me back into that locker room – perhaps Nick and Bruce and the chiropractor, or even Leo Krug himself, naked and dripping meltwater, screaming for my head. But no one came, I was alone, and those halls that were supposed to signify wealth and glamor looked cheap, the paint applied hastily, boards joined roughly in corners, lights flickering and carpet riding up, everything smelling faintly of sewage and damp. The whole place was nothing but a pile of plaster and horsehair, bound together with sawdust and glue.

In my office, I picked up the phone and called Stan, who had been looking after my affairs since I first came to work for the studio. When he had finished screaming at me for five minutes he asked what I intended to do next and I told him I would go to Paris or Rome, although I had not at that moment decided one way or the other.

You and Julie Dassin, Stan sighed. Maybe you can shack up and make plotless po-faced pictures about the proletariat and put us all to sleep. I wish you'd phoned me before you went to see Cherry. You should have done what he asked. It would have made your life much easier in the long run.

He gave me no other choice, Stan.

Now, now, Desmond, he chided me, remember the first thing I ever told you when you arrived from New York? *Always you have a choice.*

It is no more than a reassuring fantasy to suggest that one always has a choice. Sometimes at least one of the choices presented is impossible, or appears impossible, because it would imperil the life or wellbeing of yourself or someone else, because it is ethically compromised or antithetical to everything you believe to be moral and right. I still say that I did not have a choice, that I could not have lived with myself if I had taken Porter's offer to submit to psychoanalytic treatment determined to harangue the queer out of me, or condescend to cooperate with a witch hunt I believed then and still believe was evil, however I might look back critically upon my own political beliefs at the time, however Marxism has been irremediably tarnished by the twentieth-century history of Communist states, however the Russia that was briefly our strategic ally in World War II has proven itself over the subsequent decades (notwithstanding the hopeful years of Gorbachev) to be hostile to freedom and democracy and America itself, hostile in more recent years to everything I hold dear, including the possibility of being a man who loves men openly, without apology, without risk of persecution.

As I sat in my office, I did not know whether to believe what Porter said about you, Myles. His suggestion that you had so easily acceded to the studio's demands was more upsetting than the discovery that our relationship was known to Porter and Krug, and presumably also to Nick Charles and others. I also felt pained that I had put you in such a position, that I had pursued you in the first place, that I had convinced you we could manage our secret if we were careful. I even felt pained that I had allowed you to straddle me by the pool in your own backyard rather than insisting we do nothing, ever, which might be captured by the lens of someone who wanted to destroy us. Thinking through all of this, I found you splitting apart in my mind, one Myles cooperating with the studio, perhaps even giving evidence against me, quick to agree to treatment you did not need, the other Myles a victim of my own selfishness, thrown into peril because I had done too little to protect you. I would not be so cruel as to compare you to Noah Roy. I am old enough to see that between two people one has loved there will always be an element of incommensurability. You were each your own person, absolutely, of such radically different origins and character that no comparison was truly possible except in the most reductive terms: your sex, your appearance, your way of being in the world. Nonetheless, as I looked around at the desk and the shelves I would soon begin packing, I thought to myself that Noah Roy would never have made me doubt his loyalty in the way that you suddenly had.

SHE TURNED AWAY

Part Three

EXT. HIGHWAY 99 - DAY

Faye's car stings along the freeway, zipping past
mountains and onto the desert where the shimmer of
afternoon light blurs its outline.

INT. FAYE'S CAR - CONTINUOUS

Orph digs his fingers into the steering wheel and
checks his watch, as if wondering how long this
adventure might take. From time to time he and Faye
turn to each other, every glance drawing them deeper
into their own shadows.

                    ORPH (V.O.)

     Thing with twins, even identical ones, you
     always like one of them more than the other.
     I'd married Ursula, but it was Faye who had
     something - not just poise and beauty but that
     strange quality a woman who's been overlooked
     most of her life always has, of recognizing
     when a man is low and knowing how to pick him
     up.

A jackrabbit runs across the road and, as Orph fails
to see it, Faye reaches out to turn the wheel and
save them from hitting the animal.

Her hand lingers on Orph's longer than it should and
he looks down at her fingers. Maybe he'd like them to
stay there and maybe Faye wouldn't mind obliging, but
she puts her hand back in her lap.

                    ORPH (V.O.) (CONT'D)

Ursula was all opportunity. For a while I
liked it, but Faye was the nurse in the ward
who bathes your cuts and dabs your brow and
even when she's low herself never lets a guy
think he's in danger of stumbling out of life
if he coughs too hard. I told her something
like that once, but it was already too late.

FLASHBACK TO:

INT. BALLROOM - EVENING

Years earlier, at the party following the joint
wedding ceremony between Faye and Jack, Ursula
and Orph, both couples share a champagne toast,
surrounded by friends. Orph wears his Army dress
uniform.

                    EMCEE

Now it's time for the best man's dance. In
this case, since the grooms are each other's
best men, the couples invite everyone to join
them.

Swapping partners, the two couples trip down to the
floor as the band whirls into 'Frenesi'. Faye and
Orph get caught up in the crush of their guests,
becoming separated from Jack and Ursula.

                    FAYE

Looking very handsome, Private Patterson.

                        329

                    ORPH

Come on, Faye, don't tease.

                    FAYE

Take a compliment, soldier. You're dashing.
Why, if I -

Stopping herself, she looks away from Orph, but
her feet keep moving as the tempo quickens, hand
tightening where it touches his shoulder.

                    ORPH

Faye, I want to tell you something -

Turning her head so gradually time might have
stopped, Faye looks at him as if she knows what he's
about to confess.

                  ORPH (V.O.)

I knew she felt it, too. We were both a little
wounded, both ready to look after someone
who'd been wounded in the same way. We were
the ones who were supposed to be together and
it would haunt us for as long as we came home
to the wrong person.

As they hold each other's gaze, Orph leads Faye
around the dance floor. They are far enough away from
the others that they can speak without fear of being
overheard, although they keep their voices low, as if
conscious of the danger.

FAYE

You know it isn't possible.

ORPH

Why shouldn't it be?

FAYE

We're married now.

ORPH

So we'll get an annulment.

Faye scans the other side of the room for her sister.
Ursula is the one she's worried about, not Jack.

FAYE

You could make a girl break her vows.

ORPH

So you feel it, too.

FAYE

I can't allow myself to feel it. Ursula would
- you don't understand.

ORPH

I'm no dunce.

FAYE

She'd kill me, Orph.

                    ORPH

    And Jack would kill me. So we run away where
    the killers can't get us. They're the ones
    made for each other, just like I'm made for
    you.

Faye falls into Orph's eyes. His passion almost
convinces her. Her body softens, she leans her weight
against his, and then, as though conscience has
slapped her awake, she blinks back tears and shakes
her head, composing herself before anyone can notice.

                    FAYE

    I can't do it, Orph. Not in this life. Maybe
    in another.

BACK TO PRESENT:

INT. FAYE'S CAR - DAY

As Orph and Faye approach the outskirts of Palm
Springs, the car's hot interior crackles with the
electricity between them. Orph loosens his tie,
unbuttons his shirt another notch, runs fingers
through his short dark hair. Faye keeps her eyes on
the vapors rising from the road.

                    ORPH (V.O.)

    It was so hot in that car it felt like it took
    us a week to get to Palm Springs, but once we
    were there Faye knew right where to go, almost
    as if she'd been to Woody's house before.

                        332

Driving through the western fringes of the town they
stop outside a modern house with flat roofs and slab
walls, mountains rising hot and sullen behind it.
From the street, most of the house is obscured by
shrubs and cactuses.

EXT. WOODY'S HOUSE, PALM SPRINGS - DAY

Orph and Faye ring the bell. A HOUSEBOY opens the
door.

                    MONTEZ HOUSEBOY
     I can help you?

                    ORPH
     We're here to see Woody Montez.

                    HOUSEBOY
     Mr. Montez is busy.

                    ORPH
     Tell him Corporal Orph Patterson wants to see
     him.

The houseboy looks anxious and squints at Faye. Her
face twitches, perhaps offering the kid a clandestine
message, but it's difficult to tell for certain and
Orph fails to notice.

                    HOUSEBOY
     Mr. Montez by the pool. I show you.

333

INT. WOODY'S HOUSE - CONTINUOUS

Orph gawps at the interiors: stark and ultra-modern,
furnished with slipper chairs and matchbox couches,
walls hung with abstract paintings. Irregular ceramic
bowls decorate rosewood tables, and a jazzy trumpet
wails menacingly from a record player. If this is the
future, Orph isn't sure he likes it.

EXT. WOODY'S HOUSE - CONTINUOUS

Outside, a pool surrounded by lawn stretches across
the front of the house. At the far end, a gazebo
shelters a gathering of MEN who make no concession
to the desert climate: they're a rubble pile of dark
suits in a world of white walls and sunshine.

As Orph and Faye approach the gazebo, the houseboy
runs ahead and speaks to WOODY, the tallest of the
men, a blond-haired goliath who is all muscle under
his charcoal suit. When he sees his visitors he
paints a nasty smile under his moustache and comes
striding across the lawn.

                    WOODY
    Ursula, baby, you finally decide to pay up?

                    FAYE
    I'm her sister, Woody.

                    WOODY
    Oh, right, right, Jack's stuff.

ORPH

That's Mrs. Plutone to you, buddy.

WOODY

C'mon, friend, don't get tough.

ORPH

I'd take it kindly if you treated my sister-
in-law with a little respect.

As the two men stand next to each other Orph can see
just how outmatched he is. Woody is hard and cool as
a highball.

WOODY

Since you're back in the picture, Corporal,
maybe you can sort out your wife's debts.
She's into me for a couple of Madisons.

ORPH

Speak English why don't you?

WOODY

Ten thousand dollars, friend. Ursula Patterson
has a little gambling problem and she made
the mistake of taking it outside the family.
If she'd done her business at your brother's
joint, maybe it coulda been worked out, but
Woody's not nice like a bank, and when folks
forget to pay Woody on time, I don't take
their house and their furniture, I break some
legs, or I get my friend there...

335

> (he motions to an even bigger and broader THUG
> in the gazebo)

...to break some legs, and other things too,
and maybe go pay a visit to the elderly
parents and little nieces and nephews and
whatnot.

                    ORPH

I'll call the cops!

                    WOODY

They'll be glad to hear from you. Every cop
in California is a friend of Woody Montez.
You can't touch me, _soldado_. Pony up or get an
appointment with the bonesetter.

Orph moves to swing at Woody but the men in the
gazebo are on their feet and holding Orph back before
his fist can connect.

                WOODY (CONT'D)

Don't be a dummy, baby. Let's talk about this
nice and quiet. Come inside. Have a drink on
me.

Woody points toward the house. They have no choice,
so Orph and Faye walk back up the steps into the
house as Woody, his men, and the houseboy follow.

                  ORPH (V.O.)

Sure they were tough but something wasn't
right about the set-up. I knew I oughta feel

336

like I was walking to my own execution but
instead I had the idea I'd wandered into the
middle of a play without I learned my lines or
even knew what character I was.

INT. WOODY'S LIVING ROOM - CONTINUOUS

Inside, the long vertical shades are angled against
the sun's blast. At a bar in the corner of the room
the houseboy mixes a pitcher of martinis. As he pours
the cocktails he slips a powder into one of the
glasses, taking care to place it in Orph's hand.

                    FAYE

    Haven't you seen Ursula, Woody? We thought you
    might know where she is.

                    WOODY

    Seen her? No, but I've been looking for her
    all right. Jack doesn't know where she is?

Orph sits on the edge of a couch. He sips his martini
and within seconds the world begins to blur. Another
mouthful to steady himself and then another, but
the conversation splinters and the house seems to
be tilting on its axes, furniture rising up at
impossible angles and the men around him laughing,
faces flashing in gruesome detail: sharp teeth and
hairy nostrils, gold caps and bleary eyes.

                    WOODY (CONT'D)

    - you know our Ursula, nothing but trouble -

                         FAYE

    - oh <u>yeah</u>, my sister, she can sure get into
it -

                         THUG

    - but once you're in, you're in -

                         FAYE

    - and when you're in it with Woody -

                         WOODY

    - or when you're in it with <u>Jack</u> -

Hyena laughter shakes the room and Orph reels at the
faces around him. He drops the glass and slumps over,
falling to the floor.

                    WOODY (O.S.) (CONT'D)
    Aw, that was too easy.

                    THUG (O.S.)
    He's ruining all our fun.

                    WOODY (O.S.)
    What a sucker.

                    THUG (O.S.)
    What a softy.

                    WOODY (O.S.)
    A first-rate <u>punk</u>.

FAYE (O.S.)

   Come on, Woody, don't be rough. Leave him
   alone.

From where he lies on the carpet, Orph can see
Faye's ghostly white heels walking away from him and
disappearing into a blur of darkness.

                    FAYE (O.S.) (CONT'D)

   Let go of me, Woody, or Jack'll put you in
   traction!

Just before Orph is about to black out, mammoth boots
approach his face. His eyes focus long enough to see
one of them pull back and aim before kicking him hard
in the gut as the lights go out.

DREAM SEQUENCE:

INT. MALAVITA - NIGHT

Orph wakes in a dim hallway lit by a distant glow.
As he begins walking towards the light, the walls
lengthen, stretching to tower above him. The more
he walks, the farther away the light seems to be.
Shadowy fists begin to reach out from the darkness to
batter him, his face exploding in bruises and gashes.
He starts to run and keeps running until his legs
wobble and he almost collapses.

A door appears before him, light bleeding around its
edges. It swings open and he steps onto the stage,
stumbles to the spot-lit piano, and sits down to
play. Drops of blood from the gashes on his face hit

the keys as he strikes the first notes. He begins to
sing 'Bewitched, Bothered, and Bewildered'. At the
chorus, Faye appears from stage left, singing along
with him.

Halfway through the song, from the opposite side of
the stage, Ursula steps from the shadows. All three
are singing: Orph at the piano, the two sisters to
his right and left. At the end of the song, Orph hits
a few jarring notes, single strikes of the keys that
echo through the room as the two women stare at each
other.

FAYE

Don't trust her, Orph!

URSULA

Don't trust her, darling!

URSULA AND FAYE TOGETHER

She's lying!

Dazed, Orph glances back and forth between the two
sisters. The lights come up, revealing other versions
of Faye and Ursula at tables around the room,
emerging from the wings, and dancing on the revolving
stage. There are dozens of them, all shouting at
Orph.

WOMEN IN CHORUS

She's lying!

They're lying, Orph. They're all lying!

340

She's lying!

No, she is.

She is.

No, it's Faye, Orph.

It's Ursula. It isn't me, it's not me.

It's her! She's lying!

Be careful, Orph!

It's your fault!

Can't you see, Orph, you did this! It's your
fault, all your fault!

She's lying!

Orph stands, holding his head as the stage spins
faster and faster. Three of the women close in,
fingers pointing at him.

WOMEN (CONT'D)

You left me to die!

You left us to die!

You let us drown!

You should have saved us!

341

You killed us! It was your fault, Orph!

Your fault!

Orph breaks through the circle of women and flees into the wings, running past the woman who seems to be Faye.

                    FAYE
Wait, Orph, wait! Don't go! You can't trust her! You can never trust Ursula!

Orph runs through the dark backstage area searching for a door. One of the women is behind him, calling his name.

                    FAYE (CONT'D)
Orph! Wait! I'm coming, wait!

EXT. MALAVITA - DAY

Orph bursts from the club into the bright daylight of the parking lot. As he turns around, one of the sisters is standing in Malavita's open stage door, her hands reaching out into the light, but she seems unable to step beyond the shadowy threshold of the club.

                    FAYE/URSULA
You can't leave me, Orph. Don't you see it was always me?

        (her voice softens, warms, begins to steam)

It was always going to be <u>me</u>, Orph.

Unable to see her face or what she's wearing, Orph cannot tell which sister it really is.

                    FAYE/URSULA (CONT'D)
It will always be me.

The door slams shut and Orph looks around at the empty parking lot, the empty street, empty skies. No one else is around, no cars, no birds, the air is still, the sky a white shell. Out of the silence he begins to hear a dragging gait and the tap of a cane echoing off the buildings. He spins, holding his head, squinting into the sun, but cannot locate the source of the noise.

Once again, Orph begins to run. He runs faster and faster but always finds himself back in the Malavita parking lot. Out of breath, he can't run anymore. As he stumbles into his own shadow, the sound of the dragging gait and tapping cane grows louder in his ears.

Beside his own, another shadow appears: the outline of a smartly dressed man with a snap-brim hat and a cane. As the shadow of the man draws closer, Orph stops, standing still, waiting, his breath ragged. The cane swings into the air and comes down hard against Orph's head. He falls to the pavement and blacks out.

EXT. BATTLE LANDSCAPE - DAY FOR NIGHT

A burned-out panorama of broken trees. It could be a
landscape of dream, or a waking nightmare: a warzone,
a battlefield, one of the incinerated territories of
the Asian continent.

Orph is dressed in his military uniform, carrying a
stretcher behind his back. As he trudges across the
charcoal sand, the stretcher becomes too heavy to
carry and at last he has to drop it.

He wipes his brow and turns to find three women
dressed in black feather dresses sitting on the
stretcher and reaching out to grab him. They rise
from the ground, silent but threatening as Orph
runs away through the trees. As he slips down an
embankment he turns back to see the women pursuing
him.

When Orph falls, he reaches up to a tree for support,
but every branch and limb he touches breaks away from
its trunk, and at the point of the ruptures, faces
appear, trapped within the trees. These are the faces
of SOLDIERS, American and Japanese, bleeding and
crying out to him.

                    SOLDIERS
    Why did you leave me behind, Corporal? Come
    back, Orph. Don't let me die here, Patterson.
    You have to come back. You said you wouldn't
    leave me to die alone!

A pack of black greyhounds appears on the horizon,
baying and gnashing their teeth. The largest of the
dogs raises its nose, sniffs the air, growls, and
plunges down the bank as the other dogs follow.

Orph runs but the dogs are quickly upon him, tearing
at his limbs. He struggles to fight them off, and
just as one of the dogs leans in to devour his face,
he wakes.

BACK TO PRESENT:

EXT. SOUTHERN CALIFORNIA DESERT - NIGHT

Night has fallen. Orph opens his eyes, rubs his
head, shudders, and shakes himself fully awake.
His face is almost as ravaged as it was in his
dream, clothes ripped, but his wallet is still in
his pocket, emptied of money although his driver's
license remains, as if Montez and his men wanted to
be sure he could still be identified. His watch is on
his wrist, keys in his other pocket. He struggles to
stand but steadies himself, planting his feet wide.

In the distance he sees car lights and begins walking
in their direction. At the side of the road his thumb
sticks out, catching the light of a truck that wails
past, choking him with dust.

Tumbleweeds sweep across the asphalt. Cars and trucks
speed in either direction, never slowing. Orph might
as well be invisible. After a dozen vehicles pass,
an old truck limps to the shoulder. A RADIO plays a
honkytonk melody from inside the cab. The driver, an
OLD MAN, cranks down the window.

                    OLD MAN

Gotcha gun?

                    ORPH

Nope.

                    OLD MAN

Knife maybe?

                    ORPH

You can search me, Mister. I'm all cleared
out.

                    OLD MAN

Going to the city?

                    ORPH

If you take me.

                    OLD MAN

Get in.

INT. OLD MAN'S TRUCK - NIGHT

Inside the cab the driver turns over the engine a
few times before it starts again. When it catches he
smiles, shining a flashlight into Orph's face.

                    OLD MAN (CONT'D)

    Been a mite unlucky.

When the man reaches out to finger a cut Orph
flinches.

                    ORPH

    Could be worse.

                    OLD MAN

    Where you bound?

                    ORPH

    You know that club called Malavita? On Sunset
    between Vine and El Centro?

The man whistles through his teeth, shakes his head,
and pushes the hat back from his brow.

                    OLD MAN

    Jack Plutone's joint? What you wanna go there
    fer?

                    ORPH

    Jack's my brother.

This time it's the old man who flinches. He looks
at Orph as though he wishes he had made sure his
passenger was unarmed.

                            OLD MAN

    If Jack Plutone's your brother and you still
    don't think you're unlucky, I guess you got
    more luck than sense.

Orph avoids the Old Man's gaze as the truck slides
through the desert night and back into the city.

EXT. MALAVITA - NIGHT

Malavita is a great white box lit like paradise. A
woman's head is picked out in lights on the stucco
façade, her right eye winking mechanically.

INT. MALAVITA BACKSTAGE - NIGHT

Orph enters the club through the stage door and
watches the performance from the wings. Modest Jones
is at the piano accompanying the Fury Girls on their
first number of the evening. The stage spins at the
rate of a second-hand and the three singers are in
the same feathery black gowns they wore in Orph's
nightmare. It's enough to give him the shivers.

INT. FAYE'S DRESSING ROOM - NIGHT

Without knocking, Orph opens the door to Faye's
private room. He finds her sitting before the vanity,
surrounded by bunches of white lilies, a gardenia in
her hair. Autographed photos from Montgomery Clift,
Tallulah Bankhead, Robert Taylor, Barbara Stanwyck,
and Clifton Webb decorate her table.

                            348

Startled by Orph's arrival, Faye turns around,
pulling closed her dressing gown.

                    FAYE

Oh, <u>Orph</u>, I'm so relieved. I didn't know
what to do. Montez threatened to kill you if
I called the police or told Jack. He said I
should just come back and act as if nothing -

                    ORPH

Shut up, Faye. You and Montez are in bed,
aren't you? That was the lick, wasn't it?

                    FAYE

What a way to talk to a nice girl.

                    ORPH

I never met one. You and your sister least of
all. Nice girls. I don't believe they exist.

                    FAYE

He must have hit you on the head harder than I
thought if that's what you believe.

                    ORPH

Maybe he knocked some sense into me.

                    FAYE

I'd say he knocked you blind.

                    ORPH

You knew right where to find him. Led me to
that house like you'd been there a hundred
times. I heard you talking after you thought
I'd passed out. What's the drift, little
sister?

Faye stares with a new sense of distance, but also
respect. She flicks her hair back over her shoulder,
turns to face the mirror, and touches up her
lipstick, eyeing Orph's reflection against her own.

                    FAYE

Sure, I knew where he lived, and I knew Ursula
had trouble with him, but Woody Montez is no
friend of mine. He's more dangerous than you
can imagine.

                    ORPH

I know how to deal with dangerous men.

                    FAYE

Not Woody. Montez thinks Right and Wrong
are two sides on a menu, choose a dish from
whichever you please, hold the gravy. Apple
pie grenades for dessert with a side of
arsenic ice cream.

                    ORPH

I'll call the cops.

FAYE

If you think that'll do any good you're as big
a fool as Ursula said.

Orph grabs Faye by the shoulders and pulls her from
the chair. He looks like he might hit her, then
realizes what he's doing and stops himself.

FAYE (CONT'D)

Just like Woody. Nothing but a lousy thug. At
least Woody knows which side he's on.

ORPH

I'm nothing like him. I'll show you. I'll go
to the cops.

Faye steps away from him, her right hand reaching
inside the dressing gown to fondle the butt of a
pistol. For now it sleeps where it lies, wrapped up
warm in Chinese silk.

FAYE

Cops in this town are so crooked they think a
girl walking a straight line is a criminal.

In the background, they hear the Fury Girls' number
come to an end and Faye slides her hand out of her
pocket.

FAYE (CONT'D)

I'd tell you to come play but you don't look
up to the job.

                    ORPH

Nothing wrong with my hands.

                    FAYE

Go home, Orph. Get some sleep. You can't fight
Montez. If Ursula's in trouble with Woody
we might as well forget her, but one way or
another you're gonna have to pay up.

EXT. MALAVITA - NIGHT

In Malavita's parking lot Orph climbs into Ursula's
white convertible coupe. He sits for a moment,
studying the war-zone map of his face in the rearview
mirror.

                    ORPH (V.O.)

I couldn't tell if Faye was playing me or
playing someone else. I had the idea she knew
more than she was saying about Ursula. Maybe
Ursula wasn't even gone and the two of them
were cooking up something together only I was
too dumb to see it.

INT. URSULA'S CAR - NIGHT

Driving through the streets of downtown Los Angeles,
Orph can't stop glancing in the rearview mirror - no
longer to look at his face, but to survey the traffic
that might be behind him.

ORPH (V.O.) (CONT'D)

Every corner I turned, I kept looking for the
little white bullet of Faye's car, expecting
it to hit me right between the shoulders
before I'd even heard the trigger. And if it
wasn't Faye holding the gun, I knew it would
be Montez collecting in the only way that
would give a guy like him satisfaction. And if
it wasn't him or Faye, then I had this feeling
my own big brother might be there, riding on
my back fender, waiting for the right moment
to catch me in his sights.

INT. URSULA'S APARTMENT - NIGHT

Orph opens the door to the Wilshire apartment, leaves
the key in the lock, and pours himself a drink.
Two fingers of bourbon, no ice, nothing to slow its
transit. He drinks it quick and has another, looking
out the window at the semaphore of city lights as if
trying to read the code.

ORPH (V.O.) (CONT'D)

That night I realized I was alone. There
was no one I could trust. Only person I had
on my side was me, and I began to wonder if
everything I'd been told since I came back
from the war was a lie.

When the doorbell buzzes, Orph puts down the empty
glass on the windowsill, steps into the bedroom,
finds his uniform in the closet, and from the pocket
of the jacket retrieves a key that opens a locked
drawer in the top of his dresser.

From the drawer he removes a .45 semiautomatic
pistol. The doorbell buzzes again and he tucks the
gun inside the waist of his slacks before cracking
the front door.

It's Faye, cocooned in black silk. When he sees
the glint of blonde hair he opens the door wider,
standing close as she slopes into the room, drawing
the hood of material away from her head. Orph keeps
one hand behind his back.

                    FAYE

    You can use both hands, Corporal. I'm a big
    girl...

Faye grasps his arm, he holds it firm, and then,
rising on the balls of her feet, she angles her face
up, brushing her lips against his. His shoulder moves
and Faye's expression turns cold as she feels the
pistol poking her in the ribs.

                    FAYE (CONT'D)

    I said hands, not arms. Thought you were
    honorable, soldier.

                    ORPH

    You want me to believe this is a fair fight?

                    FAYE

    Told you I know nothing about Montez.

                    ORPH

     Maybe you tell me what you do know, and quick,
     before my finger starts to twitch.

Faye slinks into an armchair as Orph keeps the pistol
trained on her. It jumps in his hand, as though it
needs a longer leash, but when he's satisfied Faye
isn't going anywhere he sits across from her, putting
the gun at his side.

                    FAYE

     I shouldn't be here. Jack will wonder.

                    ORPH

     Then go home.

                    FAYE

     Couldn't help myself, Orph. When I saw you
     again, I began to remember how it used to be
     with Jack and me.

                    ORPH

     You had your chance, Faye. I told you I'd go
     away with you, once upon a time, but it's too
     late for that.

                    FAYE

     What do you mean had my chance?

Orph seems surprised, as if Faye has forgotten a part
of the past he could never imagine forgetting, as if

                        355

the whole story of his life over the last decade was
starting to unspool on the floor.

                    ORPH

    I'm talking about the night of our weddings.
    We both felt it. I told you then we could go
    away together and leave Jack and Ursula to
    lick their wounds. But it's too late for that
    now.

Faye looks so startled she almost seems angry, and
then, a little too slowly for it to make sense to
Orph, she composes her face.

                    FAYE

    You and me - of course, I have to confess I'd
    forgotten.

                    ORPH

    Not exactly consolation.

                    FAYE

    That isn't what I meant. It was so long ago.
    You mean to say you've loved me all this time?

Orph strokes the pistol and looks away from her,
blushing.

                    FAYE (CONT'D)

    I see. Oh, yes, I see. Of course you're right,
    I can't go away with you now, but that doesn't
    mean we couldn't stay here. Sometimes sticking
    around can be just as exciting as leaving...

                    ORPH

Jack's my brother. That hasn't changed.

                    FAYE

You think he stays in nights when I'm not
around?

                    ORPH

Maybe you both need a little house training.

Faye slides across to the couch. Orph grips the
pistol and although he doesn't move the gun he has it
pointing in Faye's direction as she presses her mouth
against his once more. This time he responds, letting
her lean hard across his chest. He releases the gun
and moves his hand to touch her back, gripping her
tightly.

                  ORPH (V.O.)

Sure I was wondering what Jack was gonna
do when he found out, because I knew there
was no way this monster would stay locked
underground. We'd let it out and now we had to
deal with the beast. But I still couldn't make
myself trust her.

EXT. WILSHIRE BLVD - NIGHT

From the street, the lights in Orph's apartment go
black. Inside a dark telephone booth a flame darts,
illuminating the face of Eddie Majestic. He flicks
a lighter on and off but has nothing to burn as he
holds the phone receiver up to his ear.

                     357

EDDIE

Nah, if that chump suspected she'd a been out
the door already. I'll stick around. You know
me, I likes the night.

As he finishes the call, Eddie turns the flame on the
telephone cord, smiling as it starts to smoke and
melt.

EXT. WILSHIRE BLVD - NEXT DAY

Eddie wakes up the following morning in his car,
watching when Faye emerges from Orph's apartment
building. She gets into her own car and drives off.

Orph appears a moment later. He climbs into Ursula's
car and heads in the opposite direction. Eddie starts
his car and follows, a block behind Orph.

INT. URSULA'S CAR - DAY

Orph checks the rearview mirror and as he turns a
corner the traffic thickens. Eddie's car is just
visible in the distance, but Orph doesn't notice.

ORPH (V.O.)

I had a hunch that Rose Zapatero might have
more to tell me than she did before, so I
headed back to Pasadena.

EXT. PASADENA BUNGALOW - DAY

Outside the Zapatero house, Orph is surprised to
see a FOR SALE sign hammered into the front lawn.

358

He rings the doorbell and when there's no answer he
knocks, rings again, and finally gives up, walking
back towards the curb as a WOMAN in the house next
door shouts from her backyard.

                    PASADENA NEIGHBOR

    Oh mister! You looking for someone?

Orph turns around, walks to the other house, and
talks to the woman over her low picket fence.

                          ORPH

    Rose Zapatero still live next door?

                    PASADENA NEIGHBOR

    That house has been vacant for the last six
    months. They've been trying to sell but no
    one's biting.

                          ORPH

    Come again?

                    PASADENA NEIGHBOR

    I feel bad for the girl and her mother, they
    could sure use the money.

                          ORPH

    I don't understand. I thought Rose Zapatero
    lived there.

PASADENA NEIGHBOR

Used to be the Wesleys lived there, but then
the father, Mr. Wesley that is, he got killed,
shot right through the living room window
while his wife and daughter were upstairs. My
stars, I can hardly bear to think about it.
This was always such a quiet neighborhood,
too.

ORPH

But I was here a couple days ago. I met the
woman who lived there, Rose Zapatero.

PASADENA NEIGHBOR

You must have the wrong house, that's all I
can think. Such a tragedy, but then everyone
knew Ralph Wesley was mixed up in business
on the Strip, gambling and whatnot, and like
I always say to Mr. Darien, nothing good can
come of business on the Strip. It's getting so
I'm ready to move back to Iowa.

As Orph walks to his car he catches sight of a dark
vehicle parked down the street. Maybe it looks a
little out of place, maybe there's nothing suspicious
about it at all, but as he gets back in his own car
he keeps clocking the drag in the rearview mirror.
It's too far to see who the driver might be, too
distant to recognize Eddie Majestic, slumped low
behind the wheel.

360

ORPH (V.O.)

I had the right address, and I remembered
the house, but if Rose Zapatero didn't live
there I started to wonder if she even existed.
What with the murder and the connections to
the Strip, the smell was getting stronger all
the time. It was sweet and sour and a little
too familiar. And then there was the tail I
thought I'd grown, hard and dark and a hundred
miles long. I sat there for an hour, waiting
to see if the other guy would make a move and
when I finally drove off, he twitched to life,
wagging me all the way back to the city, and
Malavita, and the brother I was sure I oughta
know better.

Internal Memo

April 10, 1950

To: John Marsh and Desmond Frank
CC: Leo Krug, Nick Charles

From: Porter Cherry

Gentlemen –

Having spent this past weekend reading the most
recent draft of <u>She Turned Away</u>, I cannot help
raising what I feel are two quite grave concerns, one
of a political, the other of an artistic nature. I
hope you will consider these issues as seriously as I
take them.

First of all, I did not recall the very queer dream
sequence from any of your previous drafts and can
only imagine you must have inserted this at the last
minute to prevent it being overruled. It cannot, of
course, stand as it is, being too far beyond the
ordinary, too much in the realm of the surreal for
such a picture of daily life in the Los Angeles of
today.

Secondly, I must object in the strongest possible
terms to your inappropriate references to the bombing
of Japan. It seems entirely unacceptable to pervert
an innocent picture of this kind into some ugly
variety of pacifist commentary on what all reasonable
people would now agree was the legitimate and wholly
honorable end to a war that no one wished to see
prolonged.

The presence of Japanese soldiers in the dream
sequence, which you will have no choice but to modify
or eliminate, is beyond the pale of taste, as it

362

seems to suggest some equivalence between our own fighting boys and those of our enemy, whom you must not forget we vanquished.

The American picture-goer does not want to sit down in the dark and find himself smacked in the face with the unpopular beliefs of what our friends in England rightly deride as 'Percies' too scared to do their duty in defense of freedom. Be honorable, gentlemen, and change this rotten script.

Yours,

Porter

Internal Memo

April 10, 1950

To: Porter Cherry
CC: John Marsh

From: Desmond Frank

Dear Porter,

It was with considerable dismay that I read your
memo this morning. As for your accusation of some
late addition, all I can do is tell you to read the
earlier drafts: the dream sequence was always there,
as it is in my story, on which this picture is based.
The story, as you may remember (if you read it), is
even more political in its references to the bombing
of Hiroshima and Nagasaki than the screenplay we
have written. If, in your limited wisdom, you think
it impossible for our picture to examine issues
of equivalence between Japanese and Allied Forces,
even in the setting of a recently discharged and
traumatized soldier's dreams, then what can we two
lowly artists do but bow to your insistence of
superior knowledge and morals?

Where I would wish to draw the line is with your
insistence that a dream sequence of this kind does
not belong in a serious and otherwise realist
picture. Have you not seen Mr. Alfred Hitchcock's
Spellbound (produced, in case you forgot, by your
dear friend and erstwhile Svengali Mr. Selznick),
which includes one of the most extraordinary dream
sequences ever put to film and was made a scant five
years ago with the guidance of no lesser a figure
than the artist Mr. Salvador Dalí? Or, if that is too
recent for you, who seem ever more cemented in the

364

past, what about Georg Pabst's <u>Secrets of a Soul</u>, a
deeply serious picture with one of the strangest and
most unsettling dream sequences in the history of our
young art.

What makes such montages of the unconscious mind
(however imaginary) so distressing, and so uncanny,
is their placement in a picture set in and drawn from
the ordinary world around us, a world recognizable
as our own, and one that by its very ordinariness
allows us to distinguish our dreams as dreams because
they are so extra-ordinary. If dreams become ordinary
in art they are no longer dreams, because the world
of the dream is the world of our darkest and most
hidden self. That is all we are trying to do in this
sequence, to explore the depths of the character
Orph Patterson's tormented inner life. If the
unconscious is so distressing to you, Porter, even
when imaginary, then perhaps you should not be in the
business of motion pictures, which are about nothing
if not the subconscious and unconscious parts of our
tortured minds.

As for your imputation of cowardice, I resent the
suggestion. I, for one, presented myself to fight and
was refused as physically unfit, a clear 4-F case.
That is all I hope I need say on the matter.

Yours regretfully,

Desmond

10

Alone in my office I sat spinning a fountain pen between my fingers, an image surrounded by countless other images, myself no less an image than the framed photographs of you and Helen, no less an image than the pen or desk or door or my books or copies of the scripts I had written, no less an image than my typewriter or stapler. I touched my brow automatically, as I learned to touch it, blindly, as a child, discovering the arc required for my fingertips to find the precise place on my face where I wished them to rest, my body the center of all my perceptions, trained to understand its place, its association, with all the things, all the images of things, that surround it, those images received by my retinas, processed by my brain, two streams of information brought together into a single perception. The sense of liberation I felt on leaving Krug and telling Porter I would not submit to his demands that I prostrate myself before analysts and agents had evaporated and in its place was a sense of panic that debilitated me because I knew I had already left it too long in telling you what I intended, and yet a part of me still believed that if I kept delaying, willing everything to resolve itself so that by some magic I would find a solution that might allow me to stay without compromise, or could imagine a proposal that would convince you to accompany me, I might not have to tell you I had already purchased a plane ticket, or that my clothes were already packed at home, or that I had given the man who cleaned my house notice and a severance, or that I had instructed my agent to handle the sale and disposal of my house and its contents – in other words that I had already put my Los Angeles affairs in order and was ready to leave.

Sitting at my desk now, in Florence, rather than my desk at the studio in Los Angeles, I take up a different fountain pen, turn it

367

over in my shaking hands, and as when the images of all the desks I have ever sat before came to me recently, a succession of images of other pens, earlier pens, rises from the depths of memory and overflows to submerge and replace the pen in my hand now, the pen I can only understand as a pen because of the memories that tell me it must be such a thing, memories completing the rudiments of perception. There is always a moment of delay as I hold this pen, any pen, a moment in which, however unconsciously, my memory summons a catalogue of all the other pens I have handled over the span of decades. A pen is never just the utensil I use to write. A pen is what I was holding when I found myself paralyzed by the prospect of confessing to you that I was leaving you, and so all the writing I have done, every pen I have held in the years since last standing in your presence has been marked by the memory of my terror and guilt, my sense of not wanting to break your heart while knowing I must.

As I packed, the clock above the door of my office counted me towards separation from the years I had spent in Los Angeles, from love and grief, the self-excommunicate contemplating the hill before him. Somewhere it seemed a bell was always tolling. Copies of scripts filmed and unfilmed dropped into wooden crates, buried under a glass paperweight, photographs of friends signed with affection, my bachelor's degree certificate in an ornate wooden frame, a nineteenth-century bronze miniature reproduction of a Roman copy of a Greek statue of a man enthroned with flowing hair and beard that once belonged to my grandfather, a drapery of cloth round the lower body rising up across the back and over the left arm, extended but broken off above the elbow, the right arm snapped at the wrist and resting on the right leg, sandals on the feet, mouth open, nose missing, face fixed in judgment, bewilderment, or despair. A nose would have made his expression less equivocal. I wrapped the bronze in newspaper and stuffed it in the corner of a crate. At the time I could not imagine which among these possessions would be abandoned, whether in the end they were all no more than markers of defeat. The bronze now sits on my desk here in Florence, one of the few objects I brought with me.

Stan phoned and tried to talk me into retracting all that I had said to Porter and Krug, and then spent ten minutes naming all the other lots and producers where he could no longer get me work, asking if I would not consider television, if I would not entertain the possibility of letting someone else take credit for my scripts, until at last I sighed into the phone I suspected was tapped and said, It doesn't matter anyway, because by Monday everyone will know what I've done.

We can fix this, Stan insisted. I know some fellows. It can be done quietly.

I won't betray friends. I won't even betray enemies.

Forgive me for saying so, Desmond, but the people you think are your friends can do nothing to help you these days and your enemies would not do you the same fav— And with that the line clicked three times before going dead. The studio operator came on to tell me that she had been ordered to terminate all calls to and from my office.

I hung up the phone and glanced down at the photographs of you and Helen and John packed in the nearest crate. It meant nothing to hide the others' faces but covering yours was too much like shrouding the dead so I put your photo on top, face up. I was reminded of my grandfather, deprived of his wife at the end of his life, weeping as a New York summer roasted the skin on his brow. Grief had brought delusion and my grandfather looked up at me, still a child, and said, *Who are you? Why do you bother me? Where the hell have you come from? Why don't you leave me alone? Go jump off the balcony why don't you?* My mother gripped my shoulders, knelt down, and explained that the old man was deranged by sadness.

Deranged?

Disturbed.

To put out of order, to disarrange the mind, to misplace the identity of the familiar face, to replace it with another, a polite way of saying that grief had turned my grandfather crazy.

What should we do?

Revere him. It was not a sensible answer. How to revere the mad? *He's wholly in his grief, Desmond.*

Holy in his grief, the young Desmond heard, not *wholly,* and who's to say what my mother really meant? She had a difficult relationship with her father-in-law. I never asked her to explain and only thought to wonder about it once she was dead herself. My grandfather did not wait for me to throw myself off a balcony, taking his own life a week later by striding out onto the terrace high above Park Avenue, climbing the low wall, and before my father could rush from the living room to stop him, taking one final step off the parapet and into twenty-four stories of air. His impact killed a newspaper boy, and so our family, believing in restitution as an ethical imperative, paid the boy's parents a settlement the bewildered couple living in a cold-water tenement had never thought to demand.

Into another crate went my own attempt at adapting *The Argosy,* that first novel of mine about the two college friends, the younger of whom dies in a fire. Perhaps it was too close to reality, lacking the magic of artifice. The studio censors said the men could not share a bed unless it was made comic, with a female love interest to inoculate them against suspicion, but I could never manage it.

Too much artifice in that case, and lies of the heart are corrosive. That was also a factor in the decision I had made. The pretense of being nothing more than your friend was beginning to sicken me. I knew I could not spend a whole life in a state of deception, the only state I had occupied since discovering the direction of my desire. Truth could come out only in rooms with locked doors and drawn blinds. I wanted love that could live in the open. Love sequestered was no longer a love I knew how to sustain. Perhaps you would tell me that there was nothing wrong with our love, that we would have managed, that I was sacrificing real love for an impossible fantasy.

Following the funerals of my grandparents, so close together, the next one I attended was for Noah Roy, whose body was interred in the Ithaca City Cemetery just under the heights of Cornell, because Dr. and Mrs. Roy believed their son had been happiest during his short days at the university, and they anticipated that the cemeteries of Long Island would not for long be as tranquil as Ithaca's seemed likely to remain. Five fellow fraternity brothers and I served as pallbearers and along with the other members, the family, and additional mourners from the university, we stood around the gravesite making no attempt at stoicism. Porter, I remember, failed to attend. Everyone cried, there were bushels of white tulips, robins dug worms after an overnight rain. Two other fraternity brothers and I spoke. Every attending member of the Roy family was too stricken to form words and looking at them I found myself so overcome I lost control of my movements, sobbing from the hips and bending double when I had finished my speech. The act of putting earth over the body of that boy seemed obscene, because surely, if we opened the casket and breathed air into his lungs, he could be revived and transformed into a being unlike himself but still capable of living among us, a flower or horse or fast current of water running through those gorges where we used to sit and read. I fell to the ground and wept, conscious that my weeping was more intense than the tears of Dr. and Mrs. Roy, who stared at my sorrow and carried themselves across the grass to crouch down and comfort me as Noah's sisters, older, both married, turned away from each other, clutched their husbands, and wondered, I have no doubt, why a young man should be so rent by the death of their brother.

In the weeks after Noah's funeral I found no consolation in the Catholicism that my parents, of negligible faith themselves, had done little to encourage. Amens were hollow. I observed no rituals of grief, instead sinking my sadness into study. There was nothing holy about grief. Holiness was as imaginary as divinity. There was only the human, the profane, the everyday muddiness and saltiness in which grief could expand to be the whole world and cosmos, so that all I sensed and thought, the fullness of my body, mind, and experience of living, pulsed with anguish. In the passing years, sadness has never drained itself entirely from my sense of the world. Occasional transfusions of happiness have topped up the balance. While I was with you the steady drip of your affection was quick against the torpor that had left me stalking the underworld, but loving one who had died before his time also kept me tethered to death, carousing at the banks of the same dismal river. And that feeling of being drunk on death has never entirely receded through the many decades that have now passed, while the loss of you through my own actions constitutes a grief all its own.

Paused in my ruminations that afternoon, the door opened without a knock and you stepped into the orange sun that came through my office window. Out of costume, in your own clothes, makeup removed, hair swept with brilliantine, you seemed an arrival from another order of nature, a hundred different characters composed on your face as you closed the door behind you and fell into a chair, gaping at the empty shelves and open drawers of the filing cabinet, the crates stuffed with my career. The only sounds were the murmur of cold air passing over metal and the music of oil derricks pumping across neighboring hills.

I hear you've agreed to let them make a man of you, I said.

I wasn't given a choice, Desmond.

You should have walked out the door.

Don't you see it won't make any difference? I'll do whatever they want but it's nothing to us.

You knocked over the chair as you stood and though it startled us both you left it where it fell and tried to embrace me. Your eyes, bright with confusion and pain, jammed a knife in my brain because I knew that this was it, the critical moment, and I had so little to give.

I'm leaving, Myles.

I know! Jesus, everyone knows. Nick has been telling the whole studio you quit, and if you hadn't Krug would have fired you because you're a Red and a queer.

I had never hit anyone, not in play, not even in sport, but the temptation to destroy Nick's face struck me in that moment. I wanted to do irreversible damage, to tear the skin from his bones and poke out his eyes.

No, Myles, I mean I'm really leaving.

I saw one of my own expressions inhabit your features. That was your talent, being absolutely yourself at the same moment you could be a mirror for anyone else. I looked at myself in you, and then, by some magic, felt I could gaze at my actual self through your eyes, which reflected all the fear and desperation alive on my face.

Back to New York? But what about Helen and me?

Not New York, Myles.

To stall for time I rifled my empty desk drawers to be sure nothing remained. Put belongings into furniture and the vessels take on the qualities of their contents and the character of their owner. Even when I stayed in a hotel I could not place items in drawers because I would have to check ten times the next morning and wonder whether the end table or dresser might have adopted one of my many souls, perhaps one I could ill afford to lose. Once I walked out the studio gates they would never let me back inside, and whatever was left in the desk might be thrown in the incinerator or absorbed into the prop warehouse only to show up one day in a B-movie about an insurance salesman or a corruptible banker who thinks he's found the surefire loophole that will let him get away with a million. That stapler would be his, with its sleek engineered line and steel gray finish. Those guys, the banker and insurance men characters who thought they knew how to game the system, could never imagine they lived in a universe ruled by the laws of Joseph Breen and his Production Code Administration. The criminal always had to pay in the end. It was as solid a guarantee as death. Was I not, in my own way, the criminal who fails to see his place in a system rigged against him?

If you're not going to New York, then where? Lake George?

Maybe it's better you don't know. Easier for both of us.

You're killing me, Desmond.

Was it then that you picked up the chair and held it like you might throw it at me only to put it down clumsily and begin to cry? I reached across and touched your shoulder and felt you collapse under the weight of my hand.

Why don't you just stay here? You've got the money, and if you ever run out, Helen and I will look after you.

You don't get it, Myles. I can't stay in America. If I don't leave I'll end up with no choice but to walk straight into a federal prison or go on the run and I can't do either.

But where then?

France? Italy? There are other places to make movies. Maybe I'll finally write the book about this city I've been trying to start for years. Or maybe I'll just do nothing. Maybe I'll put away the pen.

Sun rotted the planes of your face. If you leave me I'll kill myself, you said.

That's a terrible thing to say. How could you threaten me?

I can't do without you.

Then come with me. I dropped to one knee, took your hands in mine and kissed them, covering my eyes with your palms. You cupped them around my head, pulling it against your body. This is what I remember. You asked what people would say if you left your wife and I told you to bring Helen, too, that the hunters would be coming for both of you and it was imperative we all climb out of this hell before it swallowed us whole.

When you let go of my head I knew it was never going to happen and for the first time I felt embarrassed before you, like taking off my clothes in front of a new lover. The sun hit my eyes and I flinched.

If you stay, we'll protect you.

This isn't a movie, Myles. The good guys don't win. Maybe in a few years things will get better, but one day they'll come back to finish the job. What does it matter if people whisper? Let them talk.

I'd be finished.

Find the right haven and no one would care.

We stood next to each other, silent. I remember thinking the wrong word would ignite the air around us. And then you said something that so stunned me I nearly screamed.

What if you did what they ask? What if you said you were sorry? If you could repent—

I don't believe in repenting for something I could never bring myself to regret, Myles.

But if you say you're sorry, no matter how you really feel—

You can't go around saying the lines you think people want to hear. Life's not a performance.

Isn't it?

Not for me.

But if you could just say you were sorry they might forgive you and we could go on like nothing's changed.

Do you love me?

Of course I love you, Desmond. How can you ask?

You were crying again, beating the air with your fists.

If you love me, how can you answer any other way but to say *I'm coming with you*? Learn your lines, I shouted. The words came out with such rage it shocked us both but we had no chance to react because at that moment the door flew open and Margaret Brookes tumbled into the office with Stuart Carmichael behind her.

What have you done? Margaret cried. If they see it's that easy to get rid of *you*, none of us has any hope! At least you could have told us first!

Leave him alone. He did what he had to do. He didn't have a choice, Stuart said.

I was aware of your uneasiness and the way Stuart seemed to notice the redness of your face, our mutual discomposure, and the fact that the two of us had been alone together. You made an excuse about an appointment and asked if you would see me at Mary's party that night, as if we had not already arranged that you and Helen would come to my house for dinner and drive over together, but we performed this planning again for the sake of appearances. Such habits were so engrained that even in crisis we stuck to the script.

Stuart and Margaret smiled, moving aside to let you make your exit. Everyone knew how to behave for the scene, remembered their blocking, managed to hit their marks as the sun captured us all in magic-hour light. Was this what you imagined we might do indefinitely? Play the parts society wrote for us?

So where will you go? Stuart balanced against the edge of the desk, absently picking through my old scripts.

My mother's family has a place in Florence.

I think you should go farther, said Margaret, spitting her words. Africa maybe. You're not made for civil company, Desmond.

What's so uncivil about Africa? I might like it there. I could join an independence movement.

You'd pick up a gun and try to write with it.

We talk all the time about revolution and do nothing but make donations and compose editorials for journals that only preach to the converted. Maybe it's time we were a little more active. Vanguard action, insurrection.

Hollywood could never be the home of revolution.

I'm not talking about Hollywood, Stu. You think you can stay here, either of you, and survive what's coming? The studio heads will line you up as human shields while the armies of Congress approach. Servile Hollywood! *A ship without a pilot* in the middle of a fascist storm!

Jesus, Desmond, calm down.

The industry has turned itself into a tool of the Republican Party and the Legion of Decency and every other crypto-fascist organ grinder. If we were properly organized, if the whole movie industry was suitably led *by* the people and *for* the people then we would have been able to defend ourselves, but it's already too late. Do either of you even realize? You can make yourself a martyr, turn traitor against your friends, or get out of here to save your own life. *Those are the three choices.* And once you get out, join the fight where there's actually some chance of winning a battle that might help us remake the world.

Margaret stared at me. Stuart shook his head. I could see I was never going to convince them.

You two think militancy is madness, but the other side is not just crazy, they're evil. They mean us ill. They will try to win at all costs. I'm leaving before they throw me in a windowless cell.

You should stay and fight, Desmond. We need you.

You can't fight a system that's been rigged against you, not without blowing the whole thing up. If either of you ends up testifying and they ask whether I called for the overthrow of this government, please tell them I did. Throw the whole thing on the fire and start fresh.

Their faces looked pitying and then both began talking, Margaret trying to persuade me to make a formal apology, Stuart convinced I could find a gig at a rival studio. Paramount would have you in a heartbeat. Or Universal! I know you said you'd never work there, but why not? And there's always Columbia…

They meant well but I wanted none of it. I glanced out the window in time to see you and Helen and Mary walking along the studio's Main Street. I tried to read your body language but you looked no different than you did on any other day, your shoulders relaxed, a broad smile on your face, one hand around Helen's waist, everyone playing their part. Then Mary waved goodbye to the two of you and headed towards the front gate with the twitching undulation of a snake.

Mary

– I never said you could come in, Mrs. Marsh.

– And I didn't say you could be late, Dr. Werth. It's past five already. I've been sitting here wondering what to think. Do you call that a decent way to treat a patient?

– Mrs. Marsh—

– It's Miss Dawn.

– Very well, Miss Dawn, you know I had to cancel an existing appointment to accommodate you.

– No reason to be so sharp. I make an appointment I expect the other person to keep it.

– Shall we begin, Miss Dawn, or are you just here to get my approval of your new scent?

– I know what you're like. Make me stop dead on time and still charge for the full hour. Sun's in my eyes. Can't you close the blinds?

– That better?

– Turn the slats a little more.

– Isn't that too dark?

– Don't like to feel I'm in a police interview. Smells like pipe smoke in here.

– My smoking bothers you?

– What's a pipe but a prop? Every analyst has to have one. Or was it cigars? Bet you all get them in the same place when you come out of analyst school. Whole store for analysts full of pipes and couches that look the same and come with the same sick smell. Reminds me of my grandfather. God it's like midnight in here now.

Can't you turn on a light or is this the blackout?

   – That better?

   – It's in my eyes again.

   – How's that?

   – It'll do.

   – What's so urgent you couldn't wait for your appointment next week?

   – I'm trying to decide if I should cancel my birthday party tonight.

   –

   – Well aren't you going to say something?

   – You came to ask me about your birthday party?

   – Don't sound so patronizing!

   – I didn't mean to insult you.

   – You don't understand what a shame it would be to waste everything, what with the band already paid. Guess I could go ahead with it and drive to Malibu later.

   – Are you going to Malibu tonight?

   – If you interrupt all the time how am I supposed to get anything said?

   – I—

   – That's a rhetorical question, Dr. Werth, you don't have to answer it.

   – Quite.

   – I keep wondering what I'll do about a maid in Malibu. I can't take Nathalie. Her boys make my hair curl. Suppose I could use my girl in the meantime, but she's such a grouch. You'd think she was white the way she puts up a fuss if you ask her to do anything she fancies isn't part of the job. I tell her, listen, you're my assistant and if you're assisting you do whatever I ask, even vacuuming and

dusting. Could you stop that? I don't like the way your teeth knock
against the pipe. Can't stop thinking about the bit in your mouth.

– What is it about the pipe that so disturbs you?

– I don't know – the bone between your teeth.

– Bone?

– Isn't it bone?

– I wouldn't know.

– The idea of sucking smoke through a bone. Doesn't it make
you gag?

– Ever know anyone else who smoked a pipe?

– Großpapa. I mean my grandfather. Grandpa Karl.

– Did his pipe make you sick?

– I remember feeling sick in the farmyard when he stood there
smoking, or in the kitchen, when Grandma went to town and he
smoked inside even though he wasn't to, and if she caught him
she'd whack him with a rolled-up newspaper like he was one of
us kids. Nothing worse than the smell of pipe smoke mixing with
coffee and eggs and fresh bread, cow manure on his boots, right
in the kitchen. She could always tell if he'd done it. She'd cluck
and lift her nose and hide all his pipes for a week. He had a dozen
of them, all from the old country. I knew when he didn't have
his pipes he'd go for the willow switches. Smoked a pipe just like
yours. Same tobacco I bet.

– Where was the farm, Miss Dawn?

– Where do you think? Oklahoma of course. Middle of nowhere.
The house and barn faced west and Grandpa Karl would stand
there in the evening looking at his wheat and smoking as the
sun went down. Said he was watching for the end of the world.
I always imagined he was thinking about Germany. I never had
any memory of Germany myself. Left when I was three, just after

the war. Not even my husband knows I was born in Germany. My brother knows and now you know and my grandparents knew but they're dead. My parents knew of course but they died before my grandparents. My friends at school didn't know. My grandparents thought we should keep it secret so I just always have. Only other person who knows is Leo Krug and that's why. . . What brand is that tobacco?

– What's the rule?

– You and your rules. I've never been a monologue actress. I need another person talking so I know what to say.

– I thought you didn't want me to interrupt you.

– I'm uncomfortable on this couch.

– Why don't you lie down? It's more conducive—

– Who would want such a shade of green upholstery, and why this awful knobby fabric? Did you choose it?

–

– Well it scratches, even through my gloves. When I imagine all the other bodies that must have been lying on this couch it makes me want to gag. I should buy you a couch to keep just for me, or maybe from now on you should come to the house. Where are all those certificates from? They're not in English, are they? Or German? I can usually tell German when I see it even though I never learned to read it.

– Does it concern you if my degrees are from foreign universities?

– Are you foreign?

– Does it make you anxious that I might be foreign?

– You sound American enough.

– Don't you speak German as well as English?

– It's un-American to speak any language other than English.

– There's nothing wrong with speaking other languages.

– I don't want to speak anything but English ever again. I think we Americans speak the best English of anyone. It's plain speaking. I worry sometimes I might have a German accent. What do you think?

– Why do you worry about your accent?

– The elocution lady at the studio taught me how to speak only sometimes I still have problems with my vowels. My grandparents always spoke to us in German even when I told them to stop and my r's roll sometimes without I want them to, and my s's sometimes turn to sh's and I get so embarrassed. One of my worst fears is sounding like Marlene Dietrich.

–

– I wish you'd say something rather than asking me questions all the time. Isn't the idea that you're giving me advice? You sitting there saying nothing makes me feel like I'm closed up in a coffin.

– Do you know what claustrophobic means?

– Don't patronize me. I make lists of words whenever I come across ones I don't know. The proper use of words, this is what the elocution teacher told me, makes a person sound more sophisticated. Most people think when they meet me I couldn't string a sentence together without a writer to make it up for me. What they don't know is if I didn't put some real life into the scripts the lines would sound like nothing anyone ever spoke in a million years, which is why I just say what I think the character ought to say and forget the writer. Men have no idea what a woman would say, especially the fairies. They don't even like women to begin with. Why should I have to say words made up by a pervert who doesn't even look at me twice?

– Do you associate language with disgust, Mrs. Marsh?

– I wish you'd not call me that.

– Why don't you want me to call you 'Mrs. Marsh'?

– Because I hate my husband.

– Is that really true?

– Not quite. Maybe I'm thinking through my characters. They're twin sisters and I play both parts in the picture. One character hates her husband, but she also loves him, and she hates the husband of her sister, but she also loves him. I don't think love and hate are so different. They're not even two sides of the coin. They're all part of the same metal, the same stuff, don't you think? Hate a person long enough and you grow to love him. It's awfully cold in this room. Trying to scrimp on heating?

– Why don't you say whatever comes into your head, Mrs. Marsh?

– I don't want to be called Mrs. Marsh! That's not who I am!

– Then who are you?

– I don't know anymore! I was Rosa Schumacher for the first eighteen years of my life until Leo Krug looked at me and said from now on, you're Mary Dawn. A new beginning, a new dawn for a new girl, that's what Krug said when I got my contract, and you know what he did then? Cupped his hand under my bottom and said, *Buttercup*, as if I was supposed to like it. You can't just stop being the name you were, it doesn't work like that, so for ages I wouldn't even turn around when someone called me Mary or Miss Dawn and they'd have to call for me more than once, or sometimes use the name of the character I was playing, and I knew I should turn around if they called out one of those names but it took years before I felt like Mary Dawn, and then you get married and what do they expect but you should take a whole new name. It's too much. I've been three people in thirty-five years and I don't know which one is really me, never mind all the parts I've played, not that I think I'm any of those gals, but they soak into your own character somehow, I mean you noticed it last time, the way I start quoting lines from my pictures. I know I've done it just now, part of what I said came out without me even thinking about it, but they were lines from the picture where I was a war widow who discovered her late husband was a German spy. You know the hell it was to play that part? That's what first got me thinking about going into analysis because the whole time I was acting that widow of a spy I was thinking, what else am I but the granddaughter of spies? Not that my grandparents were actual spies, but they were foreigners in this country, and I was born a foreigner and isn't a foreigner a kind of spy? I mean I know they weren't, not really, but no one ever thinks you're a real American unless your family has been in the country for several generations and we've hardly been here ten minutes as far as the history of America is concerned.

  – Would you feel more comfortable if I called you Miss Schumacher? Would that help in any way?

  – Oh no you don't. Call me Miss Dawn or Mary.

  – Perhaps you could answer my question by telling me why you don't want to be called by your legal name, why you would wish to call yourself Miss rather than Missus, and why you refuse to lie down on that couch?

  – But I've just told you. You aren't listening.

  – Maybe I'm asking the question in the wrong way. What I want you to think about is why you have an aversion to being identified as a married woman. Forget about names, and think just about that, what is it about being recognized as a married woman instead of a single one that makes you so uncomfortable? No, don't open your mouth. Think about it for a moment.

–

– Try to focus, Mary, think about why the idea of being married is so uncomfortable for you.

–

– Can you answer the question yet?

– You want me to say it's because of sex. You want me to say I don't like to be called a married woman because it means I've had sexual relations with a man and everyone can see I've had sexual relations because I have a daughter and I'm afraid it will make me look like a sex fiend.

– Is that the case? Do you think any of those things?

– I suppose you're going to say that because I've said them I must think them. Well maybe I do. What if it's true? What's wrong with not wanting people to think I'm a slut?

– Most people have sex, Mary. I would dare say almost all married people have sex, although I have met exceptions in my time. Why don't you want to be identified as a married woman who has sex?

– Keep asking questions like that, Doctor, and people might get the idea you're a sex fiend.

– Is it because you want people to think you're innocent, or childlike?

–

– Why is sex so shameful to you? Don't you imagine the president and his wife have sex?

– I'm sure it's none of my business.

– And your parents? They must have had sex at least twice in their lives.

– Maybe. Maybe not.

– Certainly. They produced you and your brother, as you must have had sex with your husband to produce your own daughter. How often do you have sex with your husband?

– It's been at least six months.

– Does he try to be intimate with you?

– He squeezes my arm like he's trying to take my blood pressure. Does that count?

– Do you have sex with men besides your husband?

– That's none of your business.

– People at the studio?

–

– Mary?

– Yes.

– And why do you do that? Do you not think that infidelity is shameful? Are you not afraid someone will discover you're an adulteress? Isn't that worse than being seen as a married woman who is intimate with her husband, a relationship sanctioned by society and religion and the government? It could be bad for your career if people found out.

– The way I manage things it's nothing but good for my career. When I sleep with a man I'm showing I own him. It's not the way you think. I'm showing I make the decisions and then he respects me. It's like staking my territory.

– Is that the real reason you don't want to be identified as Mrs. Marsh, because it makes you look less powerful to other men?

– Listen, it's not about sex. The truth is, I'm leaving my husband. I've already left him, only he doesn't know it yet.

– What about your daughter?

– Oh, I'll manage her later.

– You don't think she'll miss you?

– I'm doing this for my daughter, and really, if you must know

it, for the sake of the country, for the safety and security of every
God-fearing American who walks the earth this day.

   – You're quoting one of your films again, Mary.

   – You want me to talk or not?

   – Continue.

   – I can't go on living with that pig of a man. You know what I see
when I look at John Marsh? The face of a traitor. Even so, I don't
actually want a divorce, not because I think divorce is immoral,
although I do, but because it won't do me any good with my fans.
But now I have no choice, and when they come to know the truth
about John Marsh, about all he's done, then they'll understand.
You must believe me, I'm doing this because I have to do it, for my
own sake, and my daughter's.

   – You just described your husband as looking like a pig, and
the first time we met you described your grandfather as pig-faced.
I wonder whether you think that your husband and grandfather
share any similarities? Why don't you tell me about your
grandparents, both of them. Describe what they were like. Start
with their appearance.

   – They wore heavy clothes.

   – Why is that important, do you think?

   – I swore I'd never wear wool again if I could avoid it, or any
color darker than navy. When I remember my grandparents
they're always crossing themselves, genuflecting, praying their
rosaries, even as they worked the wheat fields and fixed up the
farm buildings and machineries and got up before dawn and went
to bed after dark. They almost never smiled. They were blocks
of wood. They only ever spoke German. My brother and I had to
do the real communicating, I mean with people in town, when
we went to market and whatnot. I hated how foreign they were. I

wanted them to speak English and dress like Americans and stop being so pious.

– And your parents?

– My mother, she was also called Rosa, she died giving birth to me, and my father died that same year, run over by one of the combines, or so my grandparents told me. My brother, Henry, he's five years older than me, he said Grandpa Karl was driving the combine. He's sure he remembers it that way.

– You mean your grandfather was responsible for your father's death?

– I'm not saying it was murder. Maybe it was just a bad accident. Maybe that's why they were so solemn. Is it possible for Henry to remember from such a young age?

– I've had patients with reliable memories all the way back to infancy. But let us continue with your grandfather. Perhaps you could tell me about your sense of him when you were a child, and what your relationship was like with your grandmother as well.

– I loved Grandpa Karl at first. My earliest memory is sitting on his knee, and his knee bouncing up and down, and him holding my hands in his. I was facing him, and his knee was going up and down, and he sang a song about riding a pony, and I remember laughing and him laughing and then he would tickle me.

– Is that a happy memory?

– I've never thought to wonder whether it was happy or unhappy. It's my first memory, and I'm laughing, so it has to be a happy memory. Most of my early memories are happy. It was only later that things started to change.

– Change in what way?

– He'd whip me, and whip Henry, even if we hadn't done anything. I had a dog, Kaiser, who used to protect us from my grandfather. That dog would put himself right between us and Grandpa Karl and bare his teeth whenever that old man came for us, and then I woke up one morning to a gun going off and when I looked out the window I saw Kaiser dead and Grandpa standing over him with his shotgun. Henry and me, we rode to town the next day and bought the meanest dog we could find, fed him up, made him loyal, and when he started protecting us Grandpa killed him too. I rode to school five miles in both directions with Henry on our horse and it was a one-room schoolhouse. All the way through school we had the same teacher, Miss Turnley. She was young when I started and gray by the time I finished. She must be dead now. Maybe not. I should send an autographed picture. People appreciate it when you remember them. We always got along well, Miss Turnley and me. That's how things stopped being so bad with Grandpa. Miss Turnley arranged so I started lodging in town when I turned twelve, and then I only saw Grandma and Grandpa twice a month on weekends and made sure I was on my best behavior so there was no risk of the willow switch. I hitched a ride with Okies coming west when I was only seventeen and made my way to Los Angeles and here I am. Well aren't you going to say anything, Dr. Werth? What's that look on your face?

– Are you making this up, Mary? I'm sure I recall that story from one of your pictures. There was nothing wrong with your grandparents, was there? They were perfectly loving. Perhaps a little strict, but not cruel.

– How dare you say such a thing? How dare you accuse me of lying? I know what my grandfather did! I hated that man! I laughed when he died. I laughed right in his face before he took his last breath and then I slapped his cold dead corpse! I slapped him and I danced on his grave! Phone my brother! He'll tell you it's true!

– That would be an expensive call.

– Charge it to my account. I don't care what it costs.

– Is it so important that I believe your story?

– No one ever believes it when I tell the truth! I can lie and lie and lie and people say I'm the most convincing actress they've ever seen, but as soon as I try to tell the truth people accuse me of making things up. I don't understand it. It's the worst thing in the world, to lie in a way people think is true and tell the truth in a way people always think is false. I know the difference between lies and truth and I'm telling one hundred percent truth. I wouldn't lie to you, because where would it get me?

– And if I said that I think you're lying to me even now? That I think you're a compulsive liar?

– You're about to make me cry, Dr. Werth.

– I've heard stories of violent parents and grandparents a hundred times before, Mary. I know when it's real and when it isn't. You're inventing. In the language of acting, you're improvising and extemporizing, because, and this is my medical opinion, you are still too afraid to admit what's really bothering you.

– And what is that, Dr. Werth, since you know so much?

– You've asked me the question you should be asking yourself. You're not here because you don't know whether to cancel your birthday party. You're not here because you think, whether or not it's true, that your grandfather was too strict with you as a child. You're here because of your husband, Mrs. Marsh.

– Stop calling—

– You're here, Mrs. Marsh, because of your husband and the ways you've betrayed him with other men.

– It isn't that at all. It's not about sex.

– What is it, then?

–

– Well, Mrs. Marsh? Or is it Miss Schumacher? No? Miss Dawn? Who do you think you might be, at this particular moment?

– You want it straight? Exhibit A: I wasn't born in this country. I grew up poor. My grandparents nearly lost the farm and then my brother gave up everything to hold on to the land and bring it back to life. I really did hitch a ride with Okies to California. I saw things on that trip you wouldn't believe, and if you know poor people and grow up poor yourself you believe in helping those who need it, but when you get a little success you want to protect what you've got and stop thinking so much about others. I tried to help people when I was younger. John showed me how to do that. I wrote letters and gave money and went to meetings and parades and I really believed I was doing something good. Plenty of us believed the same thing. Only now I start to see what a dupe I was and it was the Reds who were tricking me. Exhibit B: A foreign-born naturalized American can be stripped of her citizenship and deported. I'm not stupid. I can see what's coming. That fellow just a couple weeks ago, what's-his-name, committed suicide off Catalina because they were going to deport him. He was a naturalized American. And a German.

– That man was convicted of treason.

– You think they wouldn't do the same to me? You think I want to go back to Germany? My people came from what's now the East so who's to say they wouldn't make me go there? Sure, it's right to help people, but not the way the Reds want it. You work hard you should get to keep what you make. If I want to help people with charity, that's another question.

– You're afraid for your wellbeing, is that what you're saying?

– The only way I don't get deported is if I give up my husband.

– And what happens to Mr. Marsh?

– He's American born and bred. What can they do but put him in prison for a few months if he won't cooperate? Me they can stick on a boat with a one-way passage to the wrong side of the Iron Curtain. All John has to do is give the Feds someone else. It's easy. I don't feel guilty about telling the FBI what John used to do, what he still does. Gives money to all these causes and doesn't even know what they believe or where the money goes. He opens his checkbook every time one of his seedy friends comes asking for the orphans in Ruritania or the Spanish refugees or what have you. Exhibit C: If any of this goes public my career is finished. People don't like a wife who rats on her husband even if he's a traitor and they don't like a foreigner who's been keeping it secret. So, you see, I have no choice.

– That's what this is really about?

– That's it. It's not sex. It's not my grandfather. He didn't ever kill a dog in his life that I know of but he did whip me, and plenty. I don't care if people know I've had sex. I like it and I don't mind who knows it. Americans have a complex about sex. The whole country does.

– Extraordinary.

– And even still I can't help thinking that what I'm doing tomorrow is wrong. I feel as though I'm betraying John, and he's never – I mean truly never – done a bad thing to me. He is completely, boringly good, and faithful. Like a drippy-eared, tongue-lolling, wound-up springer spaniel.

– I understand, Mary, and I want to put you entirely at ease. You are doing what is right. Sometimes loyalty to one's nation trumps loyalty to one's marriage. Your husband has been, so it seems, disloyal to his nation, however unwittingly. You must present yourself to investigators as an innocent, unjustly influenced by his beliefs. It is only right that you do what you can to protect yourself, your daughter, and indeed the whole country.

– So it's okay what I'm doing, telling the FBI what I know?

– Absolutely correct. As you say, your husband will have the opportunity to clear his name and tell the authorities the names of others who have been disloyal. I will encourage him to do so at his next appointment. You must do what you know to be right, Mary. Choose nation over family, however high the cost. And now, I'm afraid we've come to the end of our time.

– How come I don't feel any better than when we began?

– Truth scours and chafes and leaves us aching. Tomorrow, you will cleanse yourself, and happiness will return.

– I wish I was as sure as you.

– Trust me, your sacrifice will not be forgotten.

– Thank you, Doctor.

– Thank *you*, Mary.

– I'll see you on Tuesday.

– Until then. In the meantime, I'd like you to try this, an experimental new drug sent to me by a colleague who works for the government. It shows intriguing therapeutic properties and I have a sense it may help you recover some of your repressed memories and may also assuage your anxiety. Strictly speaking I'm not supposed to give it to you to take home, but I trust you'll use it responsibly. I'd like you to try taking two a day to start, an hour or so before bed. It may help you gain insight into your past, and may also give you clarity about the present. I think you'll find its properties quite unusual.

– What's it called?

– Lysergic acid.

August 4, 1955

PART TWO:
Night

11

For Easter, Alessio and I throw a party. We invite Néstor and the American writer Paul, we invite friends of Alessio's, friends of mine, a Marchesa who brings with her a gaggle of actors and writers, so we are a gathering of nearly twenty for lunch, with hard-boiled eggs to decorate and legs of slow-roasted lamb and for the vegetarians a *torta pasqualina* so large it takes two people to carry it from the kitchen. Alessio and I sit at either end of the long table and in order to keep Paul within view I seat him next to me and Néstor opposite him, the two greatest rivals for my lover's affections, although I admit this rivalry may be only in my mind. Not long after we sit down, Paul says something that surprises me. My girlfriend would love all of this, he says, I wish she could be here.

His tone reminds me of the way you used to sound, Myles, in talking about Helen to journalists or strangers. In replying, I try not to sound incredulous. Your girlfriend, Paul? And what does your girlfriend do?

She's a teacher, he says, and then begins a tedious story about this girlfriend, her interests and how they met, how they are engaged to be married, and I think to myself, You are fooling no one at this table, my boy. We can see exactly what you are, and here, among us, you have nothing to fear, you can be yourself, be honest. So why not?

As Paul is talking I glance at Néstor and know that he, too, is skeptical, perhaps has heard much about this girlfriend already. When I ask to see a picture, Paul hesitates, whips out his phone, swiping through several photos until finding one he feels he can present. She looks very American, Néstor says, and Paul bristles, not knowing how to take such a comment. She looks lovely, I say, not wishing him to be too uncomfortable.

He helps himself to another piece of *torta pasqualina* and we change the topic, Néstor ranting about Roberto Benigni's spectacle *Tutto Dante*, which was on the television recently and that he finds, as so much else in modern culture, in exceptionally bad taste. How can Italians like this? he wonders, thousands upon thousands of them sitting in rapture as Benigni takes one of the greatest literary works in the history of civilization and makes of it something so cheap? And the audience clapping in time to the introductory music, it is all so *low*. Circus music! As if Dante were nothing but a clown. And that voice, Benigni's voice, it makes me want to vomit.

Perhaps it is not so cheap as you think, I say. Benigni takes Dante, he brings the work to life, he gives some satire on the present, and his popularity does something good, does it not? Can we imagine thousands showing up to see Robin Williams performing Walt Whitman in New York? I cannot quite imagine it, but perhaps I no longer know. Anyway, Alessio tells me that Matteo Renzi was there this year, for whatever it's worth.

Is the fandom of a politician a mark of aesthetic greatness? Néstor asks. No! It is horrible, but horrible, he says, and sticks out his tongue as if gagging.

Taste is subjective, Néstor.

I don't know, he says, I think maybe it is just *bad*.

Once lunch is finished, Paul excuses himself. He has duties with his university, some Easter event for those visiting students who have no idea whether Somerset Maugham was a man or a woman. He is grateful for our hospitality, and I thank him for the flowers he brought, although as soon as he is gone Néstor says, But doesn't he know that hydrangeas inside the house are bad luck? You don't bring someone hydrangeas, you must let me take them away, Desmond, he insists, and because Néstor is so forceful in all that he says and does, I cannot refuse. What is the story with Paul, I ask, did you believe what he said about the fiancée?

But not for a minute, Néstor says, and now Alessio is listening too, and the Marchesa, who laughs when she hears that Paul claims to have a girlfriend. But he's a homosexual, she says, does he not know it?

No, you see, I think maybe, how you say, he's in *denial*, says Néstor. He is a marathon runner. He runs and runs. Sometimes I go running with him, and I think, *vale*, it's going to be a nice five kilometers, and two hours later we're still running and I can barely take another step and he says to me, Oh it's so hot and takes off his shirt even if it's a cold day and says, Néstor, aren't you hot? And I say, What, so hot that you want to see me without my shirt? And he laughs and says, You gays are all the same, come on, don't be shy, I know you're an exhibitionist. So I take off my shirt, because anyway I *am* a little hot and I'm not shy, but not at all, and then he wants to stop for a rest before we run back into the city and he says, Here, let's sit on the grass, and he waits for me to sit down, and then instead of sitting down next to me he sits *across* from me, so he can look at me, and he stares, but I mean really stares – he can't keep his eyes off my tits or my crotch, and I can see he has an erection through his little marathoner shorts and I think, What, he wants me to suck him off right here in a field, although he's totally not my type, way too effeminate – there is the irony – and so I don't offer anything of the kind and when we finally get up to run back he touches my shoulder, his hand really lingering, he squeezes my muscle and says, Wow, you must really work out, and I think, You poor kid, you don't see what you are, and all the way back he talks about his girlfriend and he runs and runs and runs, runs so fast I struggle to keep up. What are you running from, Paul? I ask him one day and he looks at me like he just doesn't understand. But you know where his favorite place to run is? Parco delle Cascine, and we all know what happens there, Néstor says, raising his finger to punctuate the point.

But it astonishes me that a young man could find it impossible in this day and age to be true to himself, that he should feel he has to hide, perhaps most of all from himself, because of what other people might say. I thought that had all passed, that perhaps I belonged to the last generation for whom such charades were necessary.

If only that were true, Alessio says.

Néstor nods. And also, Paul is very Catholic, Desmond. Maybe it's no more than that.

So was I at one point, but it never got in the way of me being myself. I don't understand.

And think of all the sex the young man must be missing out on, the Marchesa says, laughing.

Néstor smirks. Or maybe not.

Maybe he knows exactly what he is, Alessio suggests. Maybe we don't need to feel sorry for him at all.

But if he knows, then why would he not be honest with us, when he can see what you and I are, Alessio, when it is obvious what Néstor is, when he should be able to understand that there is nothing at all to fear in our company. Even tell us, I have a girlfriend and she doesn't know and I can't decide what to do about it? Why could he not say that? Or do I forget the terror of coming out? Has something changed in the world that a man such as Paul feels frightened even among allies?

No one at the table can answer, no one explain. Of course I understand, I remember the terror of the closet, and I am not so lacking in empathy as to suggest that things such as faith and family and background have no effect on the way one does or does not come to accept oneself, but the encounter with Paul hurts, and perhaps hurts more, Myles, because that boy continues to remind me of you, with his physical quickness, his leanness and muscularity, and what one might call his affective softness, his tenderness and vulnerability. Even if he got it wrong, I was touched by the gesture of the flowers, not inexpensive either, and the box of chocolates that accompanied them, and the bottle of wine. I was touched by the effort he made to do what was proper, and not just proper but thoughtful. I find myself touched by the way he listens, by his eagerness to take in all that he hears, his determination to learn from people older than he, to be taught by the Marchesa not to pass a salt shaker hand to hand for fear of falling out with the other person. He took note of everything in a way that someone like Néstor, who perhaps is more magnetic, even more beautiful, arrives with a brute confidence that allows for little in the way of adaptation or evolution. Néstor will always be Néstor, and I do find him charming, attractive, but also, ultimately, unknowable. Whereas Paul, I think, is only Paul *for now*. In two years or ten he might have made himself into someone else entirely, into Paulo or Pablo or Pol. If I did not have Alessio, whom I love, who is a creature of evolution and tenderness in his own particular ways, I might look at Paul and think, Yes, *you*, in you I will recapture what I long ago lost, what I allowed myself through my own foolishness, my own terror of compromise and insecurity, to relinquish when I should have held fast to it — held fast to you, Myles.

As I continued to pack my office, I was preoccupied by our last words and the way you left when Margaret and Stuart arrived. I phoned Max at the house to remind him to prepare dinner for you and Helen and me, and then I phoned and left a message with your maid, Antonetta, telling her to remind you and Helen that you were expected for dinner at seven, and she said – always tart with me because she claimed I left messes in the guest room where I had never actually slept but pretended to stay for the sake of deceiving her – that no one had told her you were going out for dinner and what was she supposed to do with the boeuf bourguignon. They'll need a hearty meal after tonight, I said, so put it in the refrigerator and reheat it tomorrow.

I was closing the last of the crates when John knocked on my office door. He looked nearly as hurt and surprised as you had earlier.

Were you going to say goodbye? he asked, closing the door behind him. When I heard the news I thought it couldn't be true. I was sure you wouldn't leave without coming to tell me in person, but Nick said you quit, or you'd been fired, I couldn't make out which.

I explained Porter's ultimatum, my subsequent confrontation with Krug, and my sense that I could not possibly do what they demanded as price for remaining in the employ of the studio. The costs were simply too great.

If it was only the political matter, I said, I could almost imagine myself buckling under the pressure for the sake of being able to stay here with Myles. But if ending things with Myles is also the cost of staying, or knowing that I would have to commit to an even more byzantine performance of deception, pretending we are not what we are and what we would wish to continue being for each other, then no. It wouldn't be fair to either of us. Do you see how horrifying this is? They're forcing me into a position where I can do only one thing, because to stay under the conditions they demand would destroy me, to say nothing of Myles. Even my leaving won't save him from what they have planned.

That is what I told John, and I am sorry if you think I was unjustified in saying as much. Without me I feared that you would simply succumb and do whatever they wished, and that made it even worse, because in preserving my own self, even though I insisted to myself, and to you and John and others, that I was trying to protect you, to allow you to have your life, I secretly knew that I was doing the opposite. I was saving myself on the altar of your sacrifice. If I had stayed I am certain we would have faced other, different horrors, but I might also have saved you from disaster. I am equally certain that if I had found the courage to stay, that day would not have ended as it did.

John slumped in a chair against the wall. His color was bad, skin turning purple, as if he was on the verge of cardiac arrest. Isn't there anything we can do? His voice was choked and for the first time in our acquaintance he looked to me like an old man.

Nothing short of starting our own company.

No one would work with us, Desmond.

Myles would. Helen would. I can name a hundred people who don't look or act the way Hollywood expects and can't get the parts they deserve who would. Mozelle for one. I bet she could act rings around Mary. Imagine if everyone too black or brown or yellow or Red or queer teamed up to make movies like we wanted to make them. Movies that show America like it really is.

John stared at me as if seriously considering the idea but after a moment shook his head. No one would want to see them. Look at this country. People don't want to be forced out of their complacency. America will never see another revolution so long as the stores are full and a bare majority still believe they might be rich one day.

That assumes mainstream America is emptied out of people with sympathetic hearts, John, or that there aren't hundreds of thousands of people every bit as alienated as we are. This is not just a nation of Red baiters and racists and people who want to throw men like me in the fire. I have to believe at least half the population doesn't actually feel that way. We can't know how people will respond unless we try.

Maybe, but we'd still never get distribution. You know I'm right.

Well then, that's your answer, there's nothing we can do. I quit my job this afternoon hoping such sacrifice might save a few others but the truth is I doubt it. My own sacrifice means nothing to anyone but me.

And the people you might have named, John said, as if he meant himself in particular.

Names would have turned to ash in my mouth. I wouldn't have been able to speak. I would have gone to prison before naming names. And if I don't get out of the country in the next few days that might still be the outcome.

I hope I can be as brave as you.

I don't know that it was brave, John. I wonder now if it was just the opposite. Is running ever brave? It might be sensible or logical, but I'm not sure bravery comes into it. It takes courage to turn my back on what I have here, but part of me wonders if it's cowardly not to stand and fight.

From my desk I looked out for the last time at the falling dark and the glow of the studio and the lights on the streets beyond, lights illuminating bungalows and empty lots and the more distant lights spreading far across the city and into the hills.

Under the circumstances, I don't expect you to come this evening, John said.

It's my last Hollywood party. I'd be ashamed to miss the shame of attending.

Why don't we sneak in to watch the dailies one last time?

This was something John and I did whenever we were making a film together, stealing in through the back door of the studio screening room late in the afternoon as Porter and Krug reviewed the footage shot over the previous day.

I dialed the operator and asked her to arrange a messenger to take the crates back to the house. Empty, the room looked like it was in mourning, evacuated of hope and promise. It had the same look when I first moved into it, filthy with its previous occupant's defeat, but during my tenure I had tried to ignore that haunting energy and revive it with my own. I guess that's that, I said, and shut the door behind me.

Before we had turned the corner at the end of the hall Nick Charles was removing my nameplate and putting up a new one.

John eased the door of the screening room closed so the latch clicking into its slot would not attract the attention of Porter and Krug sitting halfway down the auditorium. Light from the screen flickered across the empty seats as we slumped into the back row, nodding at the projectionist who kept our visits secret in exchange for a bottle of scotch every Christmas.

On the screen, her eyes half closed, Mary was slinking across a silvery room towards a desk from whose bottom drawer she swiped a pistol, checked its chamber, and dropped it into her black patent pocketbook.

All movies should be in black and white, John whispered.

CLACK! went the slate between takes.

The scene changed and Mary was opposite Victor Grace in

another room. Close shot, over his shoulder, tight on Mary's face, a composition of planes and protuberances. I knew John was aspiring to a visual style reminiscent of *Double Indemnity* but the framing and camera movements were rougher, grainier, less machined than Billy Wilder's work. There was life and dirt and ugliness in John's films and that was what made them distinctive.

Krug hunched forward in his seat, shoulders bowed under the light pouring onto the screen.

Wait for me till I come back, baby.

What if you don't come back?

Eddie'll take care of things. He'll take care of you, too.

What use is Eddie if you don't look after me? Nothing good'll come of it, Jack.

From off screen John's recorded voice called *Cut!* and next to me the real John twitched. *CLACK!* went the slate. The next take started and Mary and Victor did the scene differently this time so it ran long enough for him to say his last line.

Don't worry, sweetheart. We'll have justice, and no mercy.

It was not how I had written it, but no matter. Porter's hand shot into the light, middle finger pointing at a corner of the image. Boom shadow against the stairs, he said.

Throw the wrong shadow and the audience knows it's a sham. John squirmed. Flaws in a film he directed were magnifications of the flaws he saw in himself. In the dark I could see him coming out in a sweat. *CLACK!*

Wait for me till I come back, sw—

Cut!

CLACK!

Wait till I come back for you, ba—

Cut!

CLACK!

The pictures used to look good. The pictures used to be beautiful, Krug grumbled. Rings of cigar smoke hung in the air, the world stripped down to grays, and *CLACK* a vision of nightmare sprang to life. Why do we make such ugly pictures now? Why can't you find me a director and cameraman who know how to shoot pretty? Would you fuck that girl? What's she wearing? Looks like a potato sack. Why do we make pictures like this?

People want to see real life, Porter sighed.

This is real life? A wimpish ex-soldier chased by chorus girls and trees that talk and hounds of hell and you think anyone's gonna say *that's* real life?

CLACK!

That's from the dream sequence, Leo.

Not like any dream I ever had. Why can't it be a nice dream? If a dream's a dream it should be a ballet with Gene Kelly and a girl in a cat suit. Not this mopey crap.

People aren't going to musicals as much these days. The numbers are down.

You think I don't know my own business, Porter? I was making pictures before you were sucking tit. Audiences want escape. They go to movies to see the image of a perfect life.

But people also want to see themselves. Ordinary people in ordinary apartments on ordinary streets with ordinary, grubby lives. They want stories about other ordinary people who struggle just like them, Leo. Even ordinary people have dreams.

CLACK!

At that moment your image flashed onto the screen, Myles, and Leo pointed into the projection. What are we doing about this faggot?

I am sorry to tell you he said this. I am sorry if this is news to you. I am sorry to bring back such painful memories. When he said it the word cut me as sharply as it ever has. I know that some young people now embrace it, make it their own, call themselves and their friends *faggots* with a sense of liberation and fun, but I cannot hear it without also catching the echo of men like Krug, or the countless strangers who have shouted the slur at me from behind, nearly always from behind, as if they were raping me with the word itself, sneaking up and plunging it into me bodily before I can even see the face of my attacker. I cannot hear it without recalling the way my mother used it to disparage the men who designed her gowns, who sold her jewelry and perfume, who kept her entertained. I cannot hear it without remembering the way my father turned it on me when he discovered what I was, never mind that he and my mother both repented, accepted me, would have accepted you as well, Myles, accepted us together as family if they had been given a chance – their ugly use of that word never disappears from my memory. It is always burning, ripe for recovery, presenting itself instead of all the other happier memories of my parents I would rather retrieve. I call them up and in their first appearance *faggot* is on their lips. And like all the most powerful epithets, it comes bundled with so many meanings that it will always be inescapable, it will not die, we will keep having to live with it until it no longer has any power or use.

A bale of twigs, bound, kindling for fires, fuel to keep warm, that is a faggot. Fuel to burn heretics, bind them alive at the stake, stack the faggots at their feet, light them bright, watch them burn, *what more cruel pain, I pray, than fire and faggot?* Or the embroidered image of one, a faggot, applied to those who might recant, a yellow star before its time, for heretics instead of Jews, a bundle of sticks in brown thread stitched to the sleeves: see what I was, what I am no longer, I have repented, admitted I was duped and then named my fellows, other apostates. The word was a lance between my lungs. Use it as a verb: faggot two heretics together, bound up, hand and foot, to stand on the pile of faggots where they'd burn. *Faggot them up together and faggot both on the pile of faggots.* Even better if they were, themselves, faggots. Faggot (recant) and you won't be faggoted (bound) for blasphemy on the faggots (bundles of fuel). Ornament your sleeve with faggots, you faggot. Perhaps we should blame it on the French: *fagot, fagoter. Look how poorly it's been faggoted!* one might cry. Or *Call the faggoteer!* Or even *Alas, the cupboard is faggotless! We shall have to look elsewhere.*

God, I hate faggots! Krug roared, and pain blossomed anew in my chest.

Or it can mean a simple truss, herbs and rushes, bundles of any ordinary thing: *My faggot of compliments, good sir*; a faggot of films, of actors, of motion picture executives, a parcel of rods, iron, steel, tethered together. A barrage of knives driven through the air and piercing my eyes.

Look at this faggot! Krug laughed.

And of course its use as a term of slander and violence was first directed at women, signifying some man's idea of a bound-up wad of a creature, an assortment of sticks or iron, a collection of household nothings, call a woman a bundle and dismiss her as such. Attach the word to woman, for instance Joyce's Mrs. Riordan, use it to mean the *womanly*, the *household* and *domestic*, *mean* and *miserly*, a *bore* and *devout*, make all those meanings signify women and then fling the word at men not male enough in the eyes of the many. *We should be more faggoty-minded* (disposed to burn them on a pile of faggots) *about the faggoty boys on the lot.*

Quiet, Leo. Someone will hear, Porter said. I was aware of him lisping, and conscious of myself thinking, even despite myself, *How faggy Porter sounds.*

I'll call any man I want a faggot, Krug snapped. Let's see the dumbshow with the talking trees.

We only have yesterday's footage. They reshot it today.

Roll it anyway.

From his red velveteen seat Porter shouted the order over his shoulder and the room went black as the projectionist changed reels. When the scene began to flicker I caught my breath at the sight of you stumbling, blood-streaked and pursued by the Arran Sisters in their black feathered gowns. Because music would be overlaid later John had shot the scene without sound. For a moment it felt possible to lean back and gaze forever at the silent gray movements of figures in space, placing my mind in your body, you as Orph, you as yourself, a man beloved and beholden to me. Then came a sudden freeze frame of you and me, removed from society, coming together in nature, noble savages joining only for pleasure – no child could be born, no risk of property or responsibility. Why should it not have been possible if our bodies were willing and our minds unfettered? The freeze frame, of course, was only in my mind.

You believe this faggot ever wanted to fuck a girl?

Porter sighed. He has a wife, Leo.

Put someone on Fairdale. I want to know what's the story with her. Oh Jesus, Krug groaned as the camera lingered on your face. Now every time I look at Haywood all I can see is him taking it backdoors from that Park Avenue pansy. They should put all those faggots on an island until they screw themselves dead.

Frank was a bad influence but we're getting Myles help, Porter said. At his age – there's every evidence it's a variety of mental illness, which with the proper treatment can be cured.

In the dark John turned to me, reaching out to squeeze my shoulder with such sympathy and tenderness I nearly cried.

A faggot's still a faggot, Leo laughed. Can't change their stripes. They're unnatural aberrations. We should throw them all into the fire, I tell you.

Such men as Leo take delight in restriction, in rules and law and regimentation, recriminating any slippage, any pairings of like with like. Continuity editing was a symptom of their psychosis: keep to a strict progression of shots or the audience has to think too hard, realizes the story on screen is a construct instead of real life, and so forget the unreality, fail to suspend disbelief. Perhaps a boom shadow was not so great a flaw. Show the joins in the artifice and make the audience think. Brecht would agree, Brecht the apostate who denied his own beliefs and fled: exile, it occurred to me, was the refuge of the self-preserving, flight the recourse of those too tired, too afraid, too ill-equipped to fight.

Our research shows that Myles is very popular with men and women alike.

Krug snorted. I can only imagine what kind of men like Haywood. Kind I wouldn't want to be alone with. You, Porter, you're the kind. You know a faggot stands up to me I'll knock the fucker flat. What's going on with this wasted footage? Are we running a celluloid charity? Who's the cameraman?

Between two takes the camera had kept rolling and, in the background, while one of the young assistants touched up your face, I watched myself shy into view. As you and I spoke my hand rose to touch your forearm, then you pulled away from me, glancing around to see if anyone had noticed. From his seat Krug belched with disgust. Right under our noses! These perverts have no shame.

If Frank hadn't quit I would have taken out a hit on the faggot. Maybe I'll do it anyway. Can we trust him to keep quiet?

It's not in Frank's interests to say anything, Leo.

The next take was rolling and then, at the end of it, the operator had failed again to turn off the camera and as places were reset I wandered back into the edge of the frame. This time you and I spoke at length, faces turned away from the lens, heads inclining towards each other, the makeup boy there again, correcting the shading of your cheeks. Who thinks he can waste film like this? Krug shouted.

Before the next take began, you and I moved alone in the frame. I was the shorter, and although still a young man myself at the time, I was visibly older than you. From certain angles we could have been brothers, hounded by the same avengers, one perhaps suffering more than the other, but both condemned by the same foul court, while from other angles you appeared so young that we might almost have been mistaken for father and son. Faggots aflame for each other, faggoted together. How gentle and equal a gesture it was, my hand on your sleeve, so sensitive and unpossessing. That is what I saw.

Once John asked me whether in a pairing of men we were both equals or if there was, as between a man and a woman, the risk of imbalance. I knew it was his way of asking me which of us was the woman and which the man, only he could not bring himself to say it so directly. If he had I would have told him it was not nearly so straightforward, our experience was not directly comparable to his with a woman, that we were both always men, assuming whichever position, active or passive, as suited us both in the moment. If only you and I could have turned from our private conference on screen to look out on the audience we did not know we had, and address

John from the other side of our projection. *There's always the risk of imbalance,* I would have said, *human relations are nothing but negotiations of balance. It's a game of give and take. I take and I give, I receive and I offer, Myles takes and he gives, he receives and he offers. You have taken and given, but you must also receive and offer, John. That is the formula for balance. It is not unidirectional, uniplanar, unitemporal, it is balance in all directions, ongoing, through time, and we will each of us fail.* Certamen prosequitur. A luta continua. *The struggle for balance.*

John shook his head, *CLACK!*, and the scene changed. You were alone on screen, a close shot of your face, such delicacy of structure, brows carved, cheeks sculpted, as if by magic throbbing with life: a Pinocchio or Pygmalion. There was no pride in you, not the kind religions condemn. You moved with grace and humility. Pride of that kind is a gift.

Are we making horror now? Krug howled, the shadow of his hand fisting an image of you devoured by dogs. On the set, the mannequin had appeared artificial, but in black and white it gushed with realism.

The takes ran on, scene to scene, *CLACK, CLACK, CLACK.* I hoped that come Monday John would arrive at the studio assuming his right to finish the film until someone presented him with an ultimatum similar to the one Porter had given me. Even prior to the threat of Mary cooperating with federal agents, the net had been closing around us both for the better part of a year, every time our names were mentioned in the wrong company. If John failed to cooperate it would be impossible for him to keep working. He would have to kill the John Marsh he had been up until that day if he wanted to continue. I could guess what he might be thinking, sitting in the dark next to me, perhaps imagining how others had already sacrificed themselves, so it would not be so immoral to give their names to the authorities. Maybe he convinced himself there was no harm in implicating people already known, in throwing another faggot on the fire burning the Communist heretics even if John would have to wear the sign of his apostasy on white sleeves for the rest of his days: in place of an embroidered bundle of sticks a small black microphone.

Where's Nick Charles? Krug bellowed.

Nick opened the back door as if he had been listening just outside and light tore across the screen for an instant, whiting out half the image. John and I slumped lower in our seats, trying to make ourselves invisible as Nick darted down the aisle to take his place in the row behind Krug.

Take a memo, Nick. Addressed to all producers, directors, cinematographers, writers, costumers… Strike that, address it to the whole studio. Title of the memo: *Shooting Pretty*. No – *Shooting Patriotic*. No, strike that, *Shooting Pretty and Patriotic*. Got that?

Shooting Pretty and Patriotic, yes, sir, Mr. Krug.

Once upon a time this studio made beautiful pictures. Now and then, too rarely these days, we still make a beautiful picture. I'm talking about movies full of magnificent ladies in well-appointed rooms and lavish gardens pursued by handsome men in Savile Row suits who aren't strangers to a razor and comb, who rise to the occasion and never wait for the girl to make the first move. Over the course of the last several years, however – and I, Leo Krug, date this development to the period immediately following the end of the war – an ugly new species of picture has been made on this lot which must now be eradicated. I'm talking about movies where everyone looks like they haven't had a square meal in a week and only bathe once a month and mend their clothes when they wear out instead of buying new ones. This is not a Poverty Row studio.

We are not grubbing for the dirty dimes of the down-and-out. If John Q. Public can afford to see one of our pictures after he's paid his rent and fed his kids and made sure none of them is running around buck naked then of course we would not turn him away from the door, but we are not making movies *for* him, and we are not making movies that show him how miserable his life already is. We are making pictures that give him a vision of the life that could be his if only he worked a little harder and had not been stupid enough to bite the first fat tart who wandered past his porch and had six gimping kids before he was twenty-five. You got that, NC?

Six gimping kids before he was twenty-five, said Nick. Got it.

You take shorthand?

Gregg method. Self-taught.

You some kind of faggot, NC?

No, sir, Mr. Krug. Think of me as a court stenographer.

Never tell me what to think. Where were we?

Six gimping kids before he was twenty-five.

Bingo. Mostly we're making pictures for people like us, and unless poor people are funny, noble, patriotic, or devout, people like us do not want to see them unless they happen to be wearing a uniform. The rich mostly want pictures about other rich people facing small hurdles but ending up happy in the end. Happiness is reassuring. Happy stories make audiences go home and try to live happier lives, which means they work harder to make more money, to spend more, to contribute to the economy, to pay admission to see our pictures. Poor people, on the other hand, have a crisis and first thing they stop doing is going to the pictures. But poor people only have a crisis if the rich have a crisis, which is why you have to look after the rich first. It is in our interest to keep the rich audiences happy and motivated to work harder, because then everyone benefits. Got it, NC?

Everyone benefits.

Your hand isn't sore?

No, Mr. Krug.

I can tell from the way you write, your hand gets a daily workout. No girlfriend yet?

No girlfriend, Mr. Krug.

Keep giving that hand a workout. Get a girlfriend next year. I'll rent you one. Where were we?

Everyone benefits.

They should make me head of the Federal Reserve. Strike that, they should make me President. This country would never have a crisis again if I made the decisions. I'd make it what it was before the Great Depression! America first! Just like Lindbergh said. That should be the ethos of this studio, which I don't have to remind you is an *American* motion picture studio, founded in America by Americans, employing Americans. We believe in the American way! In liberty, equality, fraternity! Indivisible and inseparable! Independence or death, from sea to shining sea, under God our vindicator! Work, family, fatherland! One, great and free! All for one and one for all, In God We Trust, *E Pluribus Unum*! Freedom or Death! Since the Waldorf Agreement, to which this studio is a proud signatory, we have made it our policy not to employ known Communists. This continues now and will forever be our policy, throughout the universe and until the end of time. Effective immediately all employees of the studio, contract and non-contract, are required to sign a loyalty oath to retain employment. All pictures currently in development, pre-production, production, and post-production will undergo review for subversive content. Any project found to be employing or asserting anti-American sentiments will have to be revised or canceled...

Krug was still talking but listening to his nonsense over the footage of you made me sick. I whispered to John that I would see him later and crept out the back door. Then, just as I turned towards the front gate, every light in the studio went dark. A scream tore the air. Men began shouting. I heard Krug thundering from inside the screening room. Doors swung open and slammed shut again. People bumped into one another and I tried to steer clear of the dark passing shapes. In the blackout the world dissolved into violet grays. There should have been a waning crescent moon but in the canyon of sound stages I could not see it.

At the gate it became apparent that the electricity failure was the studio's alone – the neighboring houses were bright, street lights all burning. I began looking for a cab but as I turned north, rounding a corner, a red-headed kid in jeans and T-shirt came tearing along the sidewalk, nearly throwing me to the ground before glancing back for an instant, then running faster again as a gang of older and bigger boys arrived in pursuit, some reaching down for stones in the road and flinging them in the running boy's direction. 'Hey faggot!' one shouted, and a fist-sized rock hit the red-headed boy square in the back. I tried to shout *Stop* but nothing came out. The boy flinched as other stones caught him, one grazing his shoulder, but he kept running, panting, until a rock the size of a baseball smashed into the back of his head. Mute, I watched as he faltered, stumbled, and then dropped to the ground like a marionette whose strings have been cut.

I couldn't move my feet. The flash of a switchblade cut the voice from my throat. No sound would come out. My heart was racing. I smelled the sourness of my own sweat. It all happened in less than a minute. The red-headed boy lay dark and torn on the pavement, the gang staring at his unmoving body, their black denim legs shining in lamplight. The shortest of the gang members laughed with the wild-dog cackle of a child horrified by his power. Then the others started laughing, kicking at the red-headed boy as if they were trying to wake him, and I could see that they didn't realize what they had done until one of them leaned over to flip the body and the fallen boy's face stared sightless into the night. A gasp went up and the gang looked at one another as if already trying to apportion blame, to judge who might be held responsible. Someone was going to snitch.

When I made the mistake of shifting my weight in the shadows the short kid noticed me, and then, coalescing into a single malevolent beast, the gang began inching across the pavement in my direction, leaning over to pick up stones in their path. I started running, screaming for the cops, reaching out to balance myself as I skidded around corners, the sound of the gang's footsteps following, *blocka blocka blocka*, flying down streets until I was deep at the end of an alley surrounded by smoke swirling in acrid clouds from a burning pile of trash. Behind me the gang shouted threats and kept moving closer until I could see their faces just as clearly as they could see mine. I imagined bargaining for my life, telling them I would say nothing, I would never snitch, they could count on me, all the inanities of the cornered and cowardly. Just as they raised their hands, rocks gripped and ready to throw, the shriek of a police siren sent them scattering into the night.

I know that I should have waited for the police to find me, but I ran, stumbling from the alley and into a street bright with traffic, jumping clear as a taxi screeched to a stop at my feet.

Night was down as the cabbie sped from the city's flatlands and into the hills. He followed Westwood to Wilshire, made the gradual rise along Bundy to Sunset. I knew it was the last time I would ever travel that route so I watched the houses pass, the dark palms above them quaking like idiot giants out for an evening stroll, heads lolling on limbless bodies, waiting to be cut down, felled on the pavement. The cab was hot and every bump juddered through my spine. I wanted to forget the day, forget what I had just seen, forget that I had only told you half the truth, Myles, that there was still the worse truth to come.

You look like you just got canned, said the cabbie, peering at my reflection in the rearview mirror.

Nope. I quit. First time in my life.

Bosses!

Got that right.

Be your own boss. Like me.

That's what I aim to do, I told him.

Only way to be free. The Reds want to put men like me out of business, take away our freedom, regulate every goddamn step we take, the cabbie continued, hectoring me as I stared out the window in silence.

When I got home I phoned the police to report what I had witnessed and they said they would send someone the next day to take a statement.

There was no point in telling them I would already be gone.

SHE TURNED AWAY

Part Four

EXT. MALAVITA - NIGHT

An oily Los Angeles evening has fallen but Sunset is
ablaze with the gaudy street-life of neon lights as
Ursula's car pulls into the Malavita parking lot.

Orph slips out, shuts the door, and glances around as
if expecting to be jumped. The day's fever is turning
to night sweats as he hunches inside his jacket. A
thought stops him and he skulks back into the car,
locking himself inside.

                    ORPH (V.O.)

    I'd been avoiding the club all afternoon,
    finding any excuse I could not to look my
    brother in the face. I went to the library,
    as though I'd find any truth in books. I found
    plenty, but not in books...

FLASHBACK TO:

EXT. LOS ANGELES CENTRAL LIBRARY - DAY

Orph hurries along the walkway to the Central Library
entrance, sky clear above the pyramid at the top of
the tower, statues of Phosphorus and Hesperus looking
down upon him.

INT. CENTRAL LIBRARY - DAY

Beneath the high dome of the Rotunda, a LIBRARIAN
helps Orph search back issues of newspapers.

                    ORPH (V.O.) (CONT'D)

Not three months old, right in the pages of
the Times, I found all I needed to know about
Ralph Wesley, the dead guy from Pasadena
in the house Faye told me belonged to Rose
Zapatero. Only there was no Rose Zapatero, and
I was sure there never had been.

A headline in bold type shouts across the lower
right-hand corner of the front page: PASADENA MURDER
TIED TO SUNSET CLUB. The byline, as with the article
Ursula was reading in Union Station, belongs to Noah
Roy.

                    ORPH (V.O.) (CONT'D)

I knew what I'd find even before I read the
story. The Wesley stiff had been working at
Malavita and someone put lead in his nut
while he was home watching boxing one Tuesday
evening. First house on the street with a
television, easy to find the window from the
flicker outside, but he was that kind of guy,
fast car, sharp clothes, always the showboat.
You could tell from the quotes the reporter
had wrung from the neighbors no one was sorry
to see Wesley gone.

Before closing the Times, Orph's finger travels down
the second column of the article, landing on the
final line: 'deceased man is survived by his wife,
Lillian Wesley, and a daughter, Nancy Jean Wesley.'

                              425

ORPH (V.O.) (CONT'D)

After everything Woody Montez said I didn't
see how I could go to the cops. Even if
they weren't crooked I knew they'd never do
anything to help me. Sure, I was a chump.
Someone had been dragging me on a string ever
since I got off that train. The reporter
seemed like a better stake. From the tone
of the story I guessed there was something
he wasn't saying, or didn't think he could
say, and that got me thinking maybe the right
questions would start him talking.

INT. LOS ANGELES TIMES LOBBY - DAY

A giant globe spins in the middle of the lobby as
Orph approaches the GUARD at the reception desk.

                    ORPH (V.O.) (CONT'D)

I told the mug at the front desk I had a hot
tip but I'd only talk to the reporter, Noah
Roy.

                    GUARD

Everybody's got a hot tip, buddy. Sell it
somewheres else.

                    ORPH

It's about that living room murder in
Pasadena. Roy wrote the story but it's a
bigger bomb than he knows. And I've got a
match to light the fuse.

The guard stares at Orph as though he's heard it
enough times to write the authoritative guide to
fast-talkers but something about Orph's face makes
him pick up the phone.

                    ORPH (V.O.)

    It was a bluff, but I didn't have time to
    lose.

Orph waits in the lobby and then the elevator doors
open and NOAH ROY, too young to have been in the war,
smart and good looking and hungry for opportunity,
crosses the floor and takes Orph's hand.

                    NOAH

    What's your name, sailor?

                    ORPH

    I'm Army for one thing, kid.

                    NOAH

    Oh, pardon me.

                    ORPH

    I'm Jack Plutone's brother.

Noah's face swings a hard right to caution.

                    NOAH

    I didn't know Jack had a brother.

Orph looks suspiciously at the Guard.

                         ORPH

    Maybe we should go somewhere more private.

EXT. DOWNTOWN LOS ANGELES - DAY

Noah leads them around the corner and a few blocks
away to a dive on Broadway.

INT. DOWNTOWN DINER - DAY

The diner WAITRESSES are all younger and tougher than
the men on the other side of the counter. Noah and
Orph each take a stool.

                         NOAH

    Two coffees, Maggie.

                       WAITRESS

    Wid or widout slugs?

                         NOAH

        (to Orph)

    Drinking?

                         ORPH

    Too early for me.

                         NOAH

        (to Waitress)

    We'll take 'em unleaded.

                         WAITRESS

                (shaking her head, disgusted)

What a coupla pups.

Noah raises the back of his hand as though he might
strike her if he didn't know better, but the waitress
makes a fist to show him just how stupid that would
be. She pours two cups of coffee and slams them down
on the counter.

                           NOAH

                (to Orph)

I take it you're not here to walk me down a
dark alley.

                           ORPH

I don't work for my brother, but I got an idea
you might know some people who do.

                           NOAH

You mean the Wesley case.

                           ORPH

That's the one. Jack's wife drove me out to
the house and showed off a dame I come to
discover doesn't exist. No relation to Wesley
or his wife but I'd bet money she works for my
brother.

                              NOAH

     Shade's all over this case. Just printing
     that story nearly got me killed. Someone cut
     my brakes but I jumped clear before the car
     crashed off Mulholland. Went over a cliff.

Noah demonstrates with his hand, drawing an arc in
the air and whistling.

                              ORPH

     You know where to find Wesley's widow?

Noah studies Orph as though deciding whether he can
trust him. He takes a slurp of his coffee and turns
to the waitress as if to ask her opinion. She leans
across the counter, stares openly at Orph, looks back
at Noah and gives him a nod.

                           WAITRESS

     I reckon this sprout's too green to lie. I'd
     almost trust him with my kid sister. Almost.

                              NOAH

     Promise you don't work for your brother?

                              ORPH

     I play piano at Malavita only that's not going
     so well since a guy named Montez left me for
     dead on the desert.

NOAH

Montez is one of Shade's goons. Bet you didn't
know that. Pretends to work for himself but
all the numbers rackets he runs belong to your
brother. Montez is just the enforcer.

ORPH

I'm guessing one of them did away with my wife
- maybe Montez, maybe Jack himself - only I
don't have it all figured out. I need to know
for sure Jack's behind the Wesley case. If he
is, that'll mean I can't trust him - not him,
and not his wife either.

As Orph starts to tell his story, Noah pulls out a
reporter's notebook and begins furiously writing.

ORPH (V.O.)

It was a relief to tell someone all about Jack
and me as kids, everything I knew about Jack's
business, about Ursula and Faye and the way
Ursula disappeared in the mountains. Roy knew
where to find Wesley's widow, and I convinced
him to take me there, a few blocks away, to a
hotel where they rent by the week and you'd be
wise to bring your own sheets.

INT. FLEABAG HOTEL - DAY

Noah shows Orph into the dingy lobby of a residential
hotel on East 5th. They take the rickety elevator up
to the seventh floor.

                    NOAH

    Folks check in to die here. Sometimes they
    mean to do it, sometimes it gets done for
    them. Guess who owns the joint?

                    ORPH

    Don't tell me.

                    NOAH

    Deed's registered to Shade Enterprises. Could
    only be one man...

INT. FLEABAG HOTEL - CONTINUOUS

Noah knocks on the door of Room 704, and when it
opens LILLIAN WESLEY is standing there pointing
a revolver in their faces with little NANCY JEAN
jumping around in the background smacking her chewing
gum.

                    LILLIAN

    Whaddya want? Thought you said it was
    finished. I'm trying to get back on my feet
    and the last thing I need is you turning up.

                    NOAH

    Calm down. I'd like you to meet Corporal Orph
    Patterson.

                    LILLIAN

    I don't need no protection, least of all from
    punks like you.

                    432

NANCY JEAN

We don't need no protectin'! My mama's gotta
gun! And she knows how to use it!

LILLIAN

Hush up now, Nancy Jean!

ORPH

Could we come in?

LILLIAN

Got somethin' to say, say it right here.

ORPH

Know who killed your husband?

LILLIAN

Got a fair idea.

ORPH

Was it Jack Plutone?

LILLIAN

Shade's letting us live here till I can find a
place of my own. I got nothing to say against
the gentleman.

Keeping the revolver trained on Orph and Noah, she
nods them into the room. Once they're inside, she
pushes the door shut with her foot.

LILLIAN (CONT'D)

(lowering her voice)

Maybe it was Shade and maybe it wasn't. Folks
said Ralph was skimming and Shade found out.
To teach people a lesson he showed what he was
prepared to do. I didn't see nobody, only the
car driving away while I had Ralph's head in
my arms. I gotta think about myself and Nancy
Jean. Now you've heard it, so scram.

ORPH

You don't work for Jack, do you?

LILLIAN

Me? You must be outta your mind, soldier. I'll
take his money but I wouldn't raise a finger
to save his life, let alone do his dirty work.
I know what my husband was and I know what
Shade is. Less I got to do with people like
him the better.

Lillian opens the door and, pointing with the barrel
of the gun, motions Noah and Orph out of the room.

LILLIAN (CONT'D)

Don't come back, see? Next time I'll answer
with lead.

She slams the door, leaving Noah and Orph standing
alone in the hallway.

NOAH

Checked in to die, only she doesn't know it
yet.

ORPH

Maybe she does.

NOAH

Doesn't know half what she thinks she does.

ORPH

The girl's no slouch. Did she tell you the
license plate number?

NOAH

Sure, and guess who it belongs to?

ORPH

My brother.

NOAH

Naw, Jack's not that dumb. Car's registered to
some thug calls himself Eddie Majestic.

ORPH (V.O.)

Eddie had been Jack's boy since before the
war. Those two were twisted together tighter
than iron cables on a man-of-war. If Jack
twitched, so did Eddie. I'd always made a
point of not knowing too much about Jack's
business but it was clear only a dupe could

think he was on the up and up. I thanked Roy
and told him I'd be in touch.

                    NOAH

Call if you need me, Orph. I know some fellows
who can help if you find yourself in a tight
spot.

BACK TO PRESENT:

EXT. MALAVITA - NIGHT

In the Malavita parking lot with the world going
crazy on Sunset only a few feet away, Orph snaps open
the glove compartment, retrieves his .45, slips it
inside his jacket, and looks up at the blinking white
box of his brother's nightclub.

                    ORPH (V.O.)

I didn't have all the knots tied together but
I knew Jack was the string, and I was pretty
sure Faye had a grip on both ends.

As Orph enters the club's back door, Eddie Majestic's
coupe slams to a stop across the street, parking
close enough that Eddie can pump down the window and
train his cold gaze on Orph.

INT. MALAVITA - NIGHT

In the shadowy corridors, Orph dodges DANCERS and
Fury Girls, sticking his head where no one wants it.
At the end of a dark hallway, he catches sight of a
woman he recognizes.

                    ORPH

    Rose! Rose Zapatero!

The woman tries to ignore him, but then, almost in
spite of herself, her head half turns in Orph's
direction. It's Rose all right. She scrambles around
the corner and down a flight of stairs into the
basement.

Pushing aside chorus girls, Orph stumbles down the
dark staircase until he finds himself in a cavernous
room full of costume racks and moldering pieces of
scenery.

He turns on the lights and at the far end of the
basement where the liquor is stored there's another
set of stairs leading up to the stage. The place is
quiet and then he hears movement from the other side
of the room. A mannequin falls over with a crash.

                 ORPH (CONT'D)

    Rose! Wait! I just wanna talk!

Rose slips up the other set of stairs. Orph dodges
around the costumes that fill the room but as he
turns a corner someone knocks him out from behind.

INT. FAYE'S DRESSING ROOM - LATER

When he wakes Orph is lying on a chaise behind a
folding Chinese screen that shields him from the rest
of the room. He grips his head in pain and can barely
keep his eyes open, let alone sit upright.

A door opens on the other side of the screen, and he hears the two voices he knows better than any others.

                    SHADE (O.S.)

Where is he?

                    FAYE (O.S.)

On the couch.

                    SHADE (O.S.)

Awake?

                    FAYE (O.S.)

He'll be out for hours.

Faye sits in front of her mirror to apply makeup as Jack slouches against the dressing room's closed door.

                    SHADE

Gotta wait for me till I come back, baby.

                    FAYE

What if you don't come back?

                    SHADE

Eddie'll take care of things. Take care of you, too.

                    FAYE

What use is that mug Eddie if you don't look after me, Jack? No good'll come of it, not

ever. Eddie'd throw me over for two bits and a
hot walk.

SHADE

Don't worry so much, sweetheart. I'll make
sure everything's square before I ankle. In
the end, I promise you, we'll have justice,
and no mercy.

FAYE

And a double-sawbuck to go with it. That's
what worries me.

SHADE

It won't be twenty. It'd be life if they
didn't think you were short of gas. But you
don't have to worry. We got heavy sugar behind
us. We'll take a mope if we gotta and plea
down to a little sleeping time.

FAYE

No soap, Jack. I want out. I'm not gonna risk
a fitting for a wooden kimono. I look too good
with a pulse.

SHADE

You'd look good in anything.

FAYE

I like the fit of living too much to risk
death might suit me.

                              SHADE

    Don't worry, baby. You'll be burning for years
    to come.

                              FAYE

    That's what scares me, Jack.

                              SHADE

    What do I always tell you?

                              FAYE

    Leave the scaring to you.

                              SHADE

    You always know your lines – my ones too. So
    just remember, we're fireproof. Square?

                              FAYE

      Square, Jack.

    Jack takes Faye in his arms and kisses her, but her
    gaze wanders to the other side of the folding screen.

    Orph is awake, listening. He hears the door open and
    close and as Faye's shadow approaches the screen he
    snaps his eyes shut. She sits down on the edge of the
    chaise and leans over to kiss him until he opens his
    eyes.

                         FAYE (CONT'D)

    Feeling any better, soldier?

                              440

ORPH

Basement floor reached up to smack me. How'd I
get here?

FAYE

Eddie found you when he went downstairs to
get a crate of the good stuff. We've got VIPs
tonight.

ORPH

How come I think maybe Eddie was the one
knocked me out?

FAYE

Eddie's a thug but he's all right.

ORPH

What's the game, sister? What do you know that
you're not saying?

FAYE

It's not safe for you here. You have to get
out of this stinking town and find somewhere
you can live a quiet life. That's what you
deserve.

ORPH

Maybe it ain't what I want. Maybe I like the
fire.

FAYE

It'll burn you up, baby. Some of us are built
to weather it, but not you. You're too good,
and goodness flames out fast. Promise you'll
leave.

ORPH

Not till I find out what happened to Ursula.
I got this funny feeling she's right here, in
this very building, and maybe the two of you
are fooling the rest of us, swapping parts.

FAYE

You're talking crazy, Orph. You don't know
what you're saying.

ORPH

For all I know <u>you're</u> Ursula.

FAYE

Ursula's gone, can't you see that?

ORPH

And <u>I</u> gotta find out what happened to her. No
one else seems to care.

FAYE

You'll get yourself killed, soldier. It'd be a
pity to lose what you spent so long trying to
save.

442

                    ORPH

Sounds like a threat.

                    FAYE

Take it how you will.

                    ORPH

You're not the Faye I used to know.

                    FAYE

I haven't been that little girl for a long
time.

She leans over and kisses him again.

                FAYE (CONT'D)

You better get lost now... Much as I'd like to
keep you right here on my couch.

                    ORPH

I'm nobody's lapdog.

                    FAYE

And I don't have time to clean up after
puppies.

She stands, turning away from him. He rises from the
chaise, holds his head, and steadies himself. He puts
his hands on her shoulders and turns her back around
to face him. They kiss again and this time, Faye
seems to be losing control.

                         ORPH

How 'bout we both get lost?

                         FAYE

Jack would kill me. He'd kill you, too.

                         ORPH

You once told me Ursula was the dangerous one.

Faye looks surprised.

                         FAYE

<u>Did</u> I? I don't remember that.

                         ORPH

Said I had no idea what Ursula was capable of.

                         FAYE

Well I was right. You didn't know her at all.

There's a knock at the door and from the other side
the STAGE MANAGER calls out.

                    STAGE MANAGER (O.S.)

Places, Mrs. Plutone.

                         FAYE

I have to go. And I suggest you do as well.
Get out of here, Orph, for your own sake.

ORPH

What about you?

FAYE

Me? I'll go on burning till there's nothing
left.

She checks her makeup once more in the mirror then
opens the door, waiting for Orph to make his exit
before she does. He pauses, brushing his lips against
hers, but she turns away.

After he leaves the dressing room, Faye closes the
door again and lifts her hair to reveal a small
birthmark on the back of her neck, a mole in the
shape of an oak leaf. With a sponge she covers the
mark with makeup until it disappears.

INT. MALAVITA BACKSTAGE - NIGHT

Orph watches Faye's performance of 'The Night We
Called it a Day'. It might have been written as a
ballad but she bites into the lyrics as if it's a
battle cry.

From the wings, Orph peers out on the audience. Eddie
and Jack and Woody Montez are entertaining a table
full of hard men in cheap suits.

ORPH (V.O.)

I didn't stick around for the end. I knew what
Faye was telling me, and I knew I'd be a fool
to expect anything different. But I wasn't

445

gonna give up so easy. Ursula was out there
somewhere, and if she wasn't, I knew someone
close to me had a good idea what had happened
to her.

EXT. MALAVITA - NIGHT

Orph slips out the stage door into the parking lot.
Eddie Majestic's car is still parked across the
street but there's no sign of Eddie as Orph folds
himself up inside Ursula's little coupe.

EXT. WILSHIRE BLVD - NIGHT

On neon-lit Wilshire, Orph parks outside his
apartment building.

Across the street another car pulls to a stop as
though it's been tailing Orph without him knowing it.
The door pops open and out jumps a clean-cut YOUNG
MAN in a dark suit and snap-brim hat. A blind man
could pick him out as a federal agent.

                    AGENT

    Corporal Patterson!

Orph wheels around, peering at the other man as he
slips from one pool of light to the next.

                    AGENT (CONT'D)

    Corporal Patterson? Wonder if I might trouble
    you for a word?

                    ORPH

  Who's asking?

The man reaches into the breast pocket of his jacket
and pulls out a slim-line wallet that flips open to
reveal the glinting badge of an FBI agent.

                 ORPH (CONT'D)

  I haven't done anything. Told the Fresno
  Sheriff all I knew. My wife just disappeared.

                    AGENT

  This isn't about Mrs. Patterson. It's your
  brother...

Orph looks around anxiously.

                    ORPH

  Better come inside.

INT. URSULA'S APARTMENT - NIGHT

Upstairs in the apartment, Orph pours two glasses of
bourbon without asking the Agent if he'd like one.
The Agent shakes his head.

                    AGENT

  Water for me, Corporal.

                    ORPH

  You understand talking to you could get me
  killed. And if not me, then my wife, assuming

she's still alive. Woody Montez threatened to
kill her if I went to the cops.

                    AGENT

We'll look out for you, Corporal. Nothing will
happen, not to you...

                    ORPH

Bet you say that to all the stoolies.

                    AGENT

Only innocent ones. I can't speak to your
wife. We were following her for a while but
lost her some time ago.

                    ORPH

Following Ursula? Why? I don't get it.

                    AGENT

We thought she might be open to persuasion.
Friendly persuasion, of course. Someone who
might know things she'd be willing to share.
About your brother.

                    ORPH

Ursula doesn't know anything.

                    AGENT

You've been away, Corporal. I think your wife
knew more than it was safe to know.

                    ORPH

You're suggesting Jack killed her?

                    AGENT

I can't say that exactly. But if you could
help us, we might be able to help her as well,
assuming she's still alive.

                    ORPH

Where do we start?

                    AGENT

With a list of everyone your brother knows
- not just now, but from way back, even when
you were kids. We think he's running his money
through connections so old we don't know where
to begin.

                    ORPH

This could take a while.

The agent pulls out a notebook and pen and slides
them across the table.

                    ORPH (CONT'D)

Suppose you want last names as well.

                    AGENT

Wouldn't be much use without.

                    ORPH

     I feel funny about all this.

Orph begins to pull away, but the Agent puts a hand
on Orph's and the force of the other man's touch
is enough to make him sit down, compose himself,
and take up the pen. He begins scribbling a list
of names. He writes for a long time, drinking his
bourbon as the Agent watches.

                  ORPH (V.O.)

     Every name I wrote down I heard kids from
     the old neighborhood yelling 'Stoolie! Rat!
     Informer!' When I was finished the agent took
     the notebook, slipped it in his pocket, and
     gave me his card.

                   AGENT

     If you find yourself in trouble, or you think
     of anything else, just phone this number and
     I'll come right away.

After the Agent leaves, Orph starts trying to knock
himself out with the contents of his personal bar. He
slides against the window and stares now and then at
the picture of Ursula propped on an end table. When
the phone RINGS it tears open the silence. Orph's arm
jerks to lift the receiver.

                    ORPH

     Not interested.

                    URSULA (O.S.)

Orph? Darling?

                    ORPH

What do you want, Faye?

                    URSULA (O.S.)

No, Orph, it's me. It's Ursula.

                    ORPH

Ursula, baby, where <u>are</u> you?

                    URSULA (O.S.)

You have to get away, Orph. I can't talk. It
isn't safe. Leave right now. Before they kill
you.

                    ORPH

Before who kills me? Ursula, just tell me
where you are and I'll come get you.

                    URSULA (O.S.)

You can't trust Jack. I have to go. Promise me
you'll leave. I'll find you one day.

The line goes dead and Orph puts down the phone.

                    ORPH (V.O.)

All the instruments playing solos in my head
started chiming in unison and for the first
time I could almost work out the song. For

                    451

whatever reason, Jack and Woody were trying
to keep Ursula away from me. Maybe she ran
because she was trying to protect me, or maybe
she ran just to get away from my thug of a
brother. Maybe she didn't run fast enough. I
tried to tune it in my head but every note
came out sharp. Jack wouldn't hurt Ursula. I
was pretty sure he loved her just as much as
I loved Faye. But at least I knew Ursula was
still alive, and maybe I could save her...

Looking out the window on the street below, Orph
notices a car sleeping in the shadows, and then the
blaze of a match that lights up the face behind the
wheel. Even in the state he's in, Orph can see that
it's Eddie Majestic.

Orph puts down the glass, grabs his coat and thunders
out the door.

EXT. WILSHIRE BLVD - NIGHT

When Eddie sees Orph coming straight for him, he
starts the car and skids off. Orph jumps into
Ursula's car and follows close behind.

INT. URSULA'S CAR - NIGHT

Too much booze in the brain: Orph knows he shouldn't
be driving. He struggles to keep the car in the lane
as he pursues Eddie east along Wilshire, the two cars
speeding through the canyons of the Miracle Mile,
on through Macarthur Park and down into the city's
forest of skyscrapers.

Eddie makes a sudden left turn on Olive and Orph
accelerates to keep up, driving so fast he begins
to lose control of the wheel. Running a red light,
STOP sign flashing, he careens into the back end of
Eddie's car.

In the rearview mirror Orph catches sight of a police
car's lights switching on from a couple blocks behind
him.

EXT. DOWNTOWN LOS ANGELES - NIGHT

Orph stumbles from the car at the same time that
Eddie jumps out of his. For a moment it seems as
though the two men can't decide who might be chasing
whom. Then Orph, judging Eddie's height and the gun
sticking out from his waist, decides he's the one who
should run and takes off, heading up towards Bunker
Hill. Eddie scrambles behind him. Police sirens grow
louder as they approach the accident.

Orph darts across Pershing Square, running through a
cluster of SHARP YOUNG MEN who scatter and disperse
into the trees when they see the police in pursuit.

Pausing to look back, Orph spots Eddie behind him,
the thug's hand reaching for a gun and aiming from
his waist. A SHOT goes off and Orph ducks, racing
past an OLD WOMAN knitting under a streetlamp and
continuing up Hill Street, running pell-mell until he
reaches the Angels Flight funicular.

Eddie is a block behind him as Orph fumbles to pay
his nickel and hops into the car just before it
departs.

INT. ANGELS FLIGHT FUNICULAR - NIGHT

Orph's breathless presence in the crowded car causes
a commotion and the other PASSENGERS move away from
him.

EXT./INT. ANGELS FLIGHT FUNICULAR - NIGHT

Eddie hurls himself through the entrance arch at
Hill Street and begins scrambling up the tracks, gun
clenched in his right hand, the left pulling his body
closer to the ascending car.

As Eddie closes the distance he fires a shot that
pings off the roof of the car and makes everyone
inside scream and drop to the floor. Another shot
breaks a window and then the descending car passes,
rolling towards Eddie, who is blinded by the
approaching lights.

Eddie slips, loses his footing, and before the driver
of the descending car can brake, Eddie Majestic is
crushed beneath the wheels of the funicular.

CLOSE UP on a WOMAN's screaming face, a MAN shouting,
a LITTLE BOY clutching at his OLDER SISTER and hiding
his face in her arm. But this is the city, and this
is what happens to thugs like Eddie.

The COPS arrive at the bottom of Angels Flight as
Orph's car reaches the top of Bunker Hill and the
Olive Street exit. Turning himself into just one
more passing shadow in a hot Los Angeles night, Orph
disembarks.

                    ORPH (V.O.) (CONT'D)

I told myself the cops wouldn't know who
I was, they hadn't got a good look at me,
but there was still the car. I took myself
back to the accident and watched from across
the street as the police tried to put it
all together. By the next morning they'd be
wondering why Ursula's car was bulldozed into
the wrong end of a dead man's. I went home
and tried to figure out what to do but found
myself tapping the bottle back into my arm
until the phone started ringing on the wrong
side of midnight. Sure, you know who it was.

INT. URSULA'S WILSHIRE APARTMENT - NIGHT

When the phone RINGS, Orph draws the receiver to
his face, and Noah Roy's voice purrs down the wire.
The screen splits in two as the men talk, Noah in
the darkened newsroom of the Times, a few EDITORS
and all-night COPY BOYS pounding away at their
typewriters in the smoky background.

                    NOAH

Listen Patterson, the cops cast a line and
reeled in a body.

                    ORPH

Eddie Majestic. I know. I was chasing him. Or
he was chasing me. It wasn't my fault.

                       455

NOAH

I'm not talking about Majestic, Corporal.
You've got bigger problems.

ORPH

I've had a bottle glued to my arm. Spell it
out.

NOAH

Corpse answers the description of your wife,
only she's not talking. They found her ditched
in the river.

ORPH

Ursula can't be dead! She phoned me just a
couple hours ago.

NOAH

Must've been her ghost, because this one's
been dead a lot longer. Listen, Patterson, I
don't think you did it, but the cops aren't
so sure. I suggest you get yourself somewhere
they aren't gonna find you for a while until I
can round up some help.

ORPH

Why help me?

NOAH

Despite myself I like you, and the cop who
gave me the tip is a buddy of your brother.

                    ORPH

I don't see it.

                    NOAH

Find a straight cop in this town and he'll be
at the hot end of your brother's gun. They're
tipping me because they've got it in for you.
That means your brother does, too.

                    ORPH

.Some family I landed.

                    NOAH

In your shoes I'd go to the Feds if you know
anything useful.

                    ORPH

I mighta done that already, kid.

                    NOAH

You turn snitch?

                    ORPH

Don't say it like I done wrong. They make a
fella feel he's got no choice. In this case
I don't think I did. If Jack is responsible
for half of what I think he is then he should
spend the rest of his life behind bars. No
one's gonna make me feel guilty.

Orph puts down the phone and pours himself another.
He's worked his way through most of the bottle and

has to fight the urge to finish it. Good sense is
fighting to win but keeps getting hit with sucker
punches.

                    ORPH (V.O.)

It was still early by Malavita standards but I
hoped Faye might have gone home for the night.

Orph puts through the call and the screen splits
again. This time Faye is unrolled across a chaise in
her home, windows flung open and the dead glittering
eye of a swimming pool reflecting city lights. She's
shed her evening gown and slipped into a different
identity. Holding the phone with one hand, she rubs
the other across the back of her neck.

                    FAYE

You know how late it is, Orph?

                    ORPH

Is my brother there?

                    FAYE

Still at the club. What's this about? Thought
I told you to get out of here.

                    ORPH

Something's happened.

                    FAYE

Orph, what's wrong?

                    ORPH

Can I see you?

                    FAYE

Why don't you come over here?

                    ORPH

I wrecked Ursula's car. Can we meet somewhere?

                    FAYE

There's a little place at the corner of Sunset
and Doheny that's open till four.

INT. VESPERS NIGHTCLUB - NIGHT

Vespers is a low-key joint with modern furniture
and low lighting. Orph speaks to the MAÎTRE D', who
directs him to a booth in the far corner of the club.

From the darkness a white hand emerges and as Orph
approaches he begins to make out the lines of Faye's
arms and the crown of golden hair, like jewels in a
paste market. She's nursing a martini and mimes to a
WAITER to bring one for Orph.

                  FAYE (CONT'D)

Get a girl out of bed this time of night you
better be charming.

                    ORPH

Majestic's dead.

Faye's shoulders draw back and she takes a swallow of
her drink.

>FAYE

You'd need an A-bomb to get rid of Eddie
Majestic. That goon isn't human.

>ORPH

He was tailing me. I turned the tables and it
got messy.

>FAYE
>(whispering)

You mean you killed him?

>ORPH

Do I look that tough? He got rolled by the
funicular at Angels Flight. Wasn't my fault.

Faye lights a cigarette, drinks a little faster, and
her arms start to shake. A hand flies to the back of
her neck as if it's trying to wipe away something
that shouldn't be there.

>FAYE

Has Jack heard?

>ORPH

Dammit Faye, how should I know? That's not
what I came to tell you. Who cares about
Eddie?... The police have found her.

                        FAYE

Who, Orph? Found who?

                        ORPH

Ursula. They pulled her body from the river.

Faye puts her hand back on the table, finishing the
martini as the waiter brings another.

                        FAYE

      (to Waiter)

You better pour a couple more.

                        ORPH

Got a tip from a friend at the Times. The
police are looking for me. I need somewhere to
stay until I can prove I didn't do it.

                        FAYE

But how, Orph? How can you prove it?

                        ORPH

I don't know yet. I gotta think it out. I was
pretty sure Eddie mighta been the one that did
it, but they don't put dead men in the chair.
Maybe it's Montez.

Faye puts a hand on Orph's arm and glances around the
room.

                    FAYE

You wanna be careful how loud you say that,
Orph. Woody has friends everywhere.

                    ORPH

Friends like Jack? Sure, I know they work
together. I know Woody's one of Jack's boys. I
got a feeling everyone I've met since coming
back to this rotten city works for my brother.
Maybe including you, too, sister.

                    FAYE

I don't work for anyone but myself, Orph,
let's get that clear. You always did see
conspiracies against you. Anything to believe
you weren't responsible for all the mess,
after you left Ursula with hardly enough to
live on. It was all the fault of everyone
else, never your own.

                    ORPH

If you don't wanna help me, I'll let you go
back to bed. Thought you'd like to know your
sister was dead but I can see you don't care.
You didn't happen to phone me earlier, did
you?

                    FAYE

Of course not.

                    ORPH

I had Ursula on the line only it couldn't have
been her because she hasn't been talking for
at least a week.

                    FAYE

Now you're trying to frighten me.

                    ORPH

I'm trying to flush you out if you're the one
plotting against me. Or maybe it's that Rose
Zapatero, who isn't called Rose and happens
to work at Malavita. Maybe she does a line in
impersonations, a little housewife here, a
little Ursula there. What do you think of that
theory?

                    FAYE

I don't know about that. If I were you I'd be
grateful Ursula's out of your life.

                    ORPH

What kind of sisters <u>were</u> you in the end?

                    FAYE

Sisters in name only. We couldn't have been
more different.

     (thoughtfully)

Listen, Orph, I want to help you. There's a
little house I keep, just my own. You can

                     463

hide out there for a few days. It's only a few
blocks away.

                    ORPH

Does Jack know about it?

                    FAYE

    (shaking her head)

Sometimes when Jack gets in a mood I need to
escape. It's my secret insurance policy.

                    ORPH

Jack gets rough?

                    FAYE

There are a lot of things you don't know about
your brother. I've had to learn to protect
myself, Orph. You should, too. Don't sleep
without a gun in your hand. If the doorbell
rings you better assume whoever's on the other
side wants to plug you.

Internal Memo

April 12, 1950

To: John Marsh and Desmond Frank
CC: Leo Krug, Nicholas Charles

From: Porter Cherry

Re: <u>She Turned Away</u>

Dear Marsh and Frank,

I have had further correspondence from the Breen
Office about this unhappy picture of yours and
additional issues are now being raised, about which
I would appreciate your opinion, notwithstanding
the hostility of your recent responses. Mr. Breen
is concerned that the picture's suggestion that
all police officers in the State of California are
corrupt and in the pay of organized crime is in
direct contravention of the Production Code. It does
not seem to me that this is necessarily what the
picture means to convey, as the only representatives
of the law in the picture are not apparently corrupt
(the unnamed FBI agent and county sheriff) and are
treated more or less sympathetically. It is my belief
that Breen's concerns can easily be put to rest
by the addition at the end of the picture of some
incorruptible Los Angeles police officers.

Breen's larger concern (and it is one I increasingly
share) is with the language of the characters, and in
particular the criminal slang used by the female lead
and her husband, your primary antagonist. Some of
your dialogue is sufficiently arcane that neither Mr.
Breen nor I is quite certain what is being expressed
and dictionaries are of little assistance. Could you
tell me definitively what a 'double sawbuck' might

465

be? I was under the impression it was old-time slang for a twenty-dollar bill, but that does not seem to be the way your character uses it.

Mr. Breen is also now concerned by the amount of hard liquor consumed by Orph Patterson, whose characterization suggests a potentially chronic case. Mr. Breen and I both have serious reservations about how this treatment of our veterans might be interpreted by audiences, particularly given that drinking is also presented throughout the picture as socially acceptable in the characters' wider milieu (for women and men alike, I note with some distaste), which it is safe to describe, despite the criminal aspect and the money associated, as those of the common man rather than the well-to-do. It is quite unacceptable to suggest that the diner waitress might serve alcohol illegally, even if this is only implied.

The one point about which Mr. Breen is quite insistent is that the characters Lillian and her daughter Nancy Jean either be eliminated or moved to a more salubrious setting, such as a charity home for the indigent run by a church. In no circumstances may Lillian brandish a gun, or have her daughter insist upon her mother's knowledge of firearms.

Yours truly,

Porter Cherry

Internal Memo

April 11, 1950

To: Porter Cherry

From: John Marsh and Desmond Frank

Re: <u>She Turned Away</u>

Cherry,

A double sawbuck is a twenty-year sentence. The other
changes you suggest are impossible. Lillian is in the
employ of the picture's criminal mastermind, so it
would make no sense to the picture or to audiences
to place her in the hands of the church, and without
her we both feel that something would be lacking.
As with the character of Rose Zapatero and the
diner waitress, Helen Fairdale's comic and careful
performances in each of these roles - as well as
in the role of Lilian Wesley - guarantees that the
audience will understand them as fiction, even as a
single criminal character reappearing in multiple
disguises. It is part of the essential fun of the
picture, if you can imagine that fun might be an
aspect of the business we are in. If you don't like
it, you can cut these scenes, but Desmond and I will
both take our names off the picture if you do. Have
you ever even read the script from start to finish?
You and Mr. Breen have such great ideas about <u>She
Turned Away</u> maybe the two of you should make it and
let us poor jerks get some rest.

Yours,
Marsh

Nathalie

In the kitchen at Summit Drive, Nathalie, or, as she thought of
herself still, Charlotte, although she had not used the name for
nearly a decade, not heard it spoken for years before those men
came to visit that morning and pronounced it with the cynical glee
that came from revealing to her the secret she had been keeping
all this time, put down three nearly identical plates of food – pork
chops, a pile of boiled potatoes, a side of cabbage sautéed with
butter, a salad of cucumber sliced so thin the rounds were almost
transparent and then dressed with vinegar and dill – for Iris and
Siegfried and Franz. She would have liked to give her boys larger
helpings than the little girl but Iris kept such a close eye on the
proportion of every portion and had such a penchant for reporting
any slight to her mother, who cared about such matters in a way
John Marsh did not, that Nathalie had learned always to give her
boys less than the girl and still, never mind the cruelty of such
shorting after all Siggie and Franz had suffered in their brief lives,
the displacements and alienation of migration, the vilification of
their people and family, the entire nation damned by the victors,
the assassination of their father by men so much worse than
he, the threats to their own lives by the British, such stresses
as should have made them permanently lean and lithe as their
forefathers, they got fat. It was something in the blood and yet they
were all of them distantly related, the Beckers and Schumachers.
Mary, that is to say Rosa before she forgot herself, was spectrally
thin, the child Iris, too, and that thinness, the ease with which the
Schumacher women remained slender despite eating whatever

468

they wished, kindled a brilliant hate that was enough, as far
as persuasion goes, to make Nathalie accede to the demands of
Agents Leopold and Loeb and set her mind to snooping as she had
in the past. Little doubt that Mary had once been, if not an actual
Communist, the kind of leftist agitator or nincompoop fellow-
traveler McCarthy and Hoover and their associates would judge
left enough to be leveraged, and yet surely the U.S. Government
must already have whatever evidence they needed, so why come
to her? Perhaps it was a test of her willingness or capacity to be
useful, and if she cleared this easy hurdle there would be other,
more challenging assignments. Work that would lift her and the
boys out of their position of servitude and penury into the sort
of life she remembered with both angst and longing, a life of her
own car and money, of being surrounded by important rather
than ridiculous men, receiving gifts of rare beauty and reveling
each night in the uncorking of a fine champagne, although that
had never quite been the life she lived as a general's daughter in
the years of her youth. Yet such power and affluence as had once
seemed her birthright might – assuming she played by the rules of
the game those agents had declared open with their visit, the first
run of hands revealed, scores already being tabulated and her own
points at nil – be hers once more.

Since the agents' departure that morning she had thought on
her social decline since coming to America. Her light mood, the
mood in which she started the day because there was going to be a
party and she enjoyed the merriment even if she thought her cousin
ridiculous, had darkened until she was consumed by rage and a
desire to kill as she had killed in the past, truly, with the fervor
and skill of one born to the job. No sooner had the agents left than
people from the studio began arriving to install the lights in the

garden and the scenery on the terrace, to test the sound system
and the cast of the pageant Mary had orchestrated to practice their
parts, with a stand-in who looked nothing like Mary throughout the
afternoon repeating Mary's lines into the microphone connected to
the loudspeaker, so the neighbors, if not the guests, knew exactly
what was coming that evening, and there had been complaints
already, the Stevenson woman ringing the bell, the Albright woman
phoning, the police stopping round to ask how late these festivities
were likely to last and suggesting that really there should have been
a permit and Nathalie had said to all of them that they would have
to ask her employer, John Marsh, who was ultimately responsible
for anything that happened on his property. He had done nothing to
her, was kinder by far than Mary, and yet she hated the man.

Although she pretended to the boys and to Iris and even
to Mary and John that her work increased by many orders of
magnitude as a result of the party, it was mostly the studio people
who did what was required for the pageant, and Chasen's staff
attended to the food and drink and had even arranged for the
hired dishes, cutlery, and glassware. Nathalie carried on as usual,
picking up the children from school and seeing to it that they did
not get in the way through the balance of the afternoon. All that
time she felt the rage crackling through her body. She drove from
the house and across Beverly Hills and everyone she saw she
wanted to kill. She picked up the children and while she did not
want to kill the boys she had a vivid sense of how it would feel to
garrote the girl with a length of piano wire affixed to two small
pieces of wood, as she had done in the past, although not a child
but a man nearly twice her size, and how much easier and quicker
it would be with the girl, and how she would have to be careful
not to twist the wire so tightly that the beast's head came clean

off. Seeing the boys again as they marched out of the school and climbed into the back of the car, she knew that she had no choice, and must do what the agents demanded, even if it meant betraying Mary, who, apart from being a monster, had done nothing that Nathalie would describe as truly awful, and she could say this, definitively, because Nathalie knew what horror was. Horror was her own province and métier, not Mary's.

Now, she left the children to eat, warning Iris not to boss the boys and the boys to stand up for themselves, though she had little confidence they would, given how Siegfried and Franz both loved the brute in their pitiful ways. She knew the evening would be a trial. Whenever there was company the ties of family were vigorously denied, Nathalie and the boys presented as a charity case. On multiple occasions Mary had even suggested to her guests that the Gebharts were gypsies or Jews as a way to curry favor or imply a nobility of spirit that was as far from Mary's actual personality as Nathalie could discern, and this happened most often with John Marsh's friends, with those Communists, the suggestion that she and her sons were refugees and not Mary's own blood, because to hint otherwise was to invite curiosity. And yet Mary had taken them in, and Nathalie could not be sure entirely why such generosity had seized her cousin, unless it was no more complicated than strengthening the attenuated ties of family and blood, and perhaps that was enough for some people, even people like Mary who was less than fully human, for whom fans and the public and her career were and would always remain paramount.

Of course, Mary knew Nathalie's real name, because she had always known her real name. What Mary did not know, what Nathalie hoped she would never know, were the precise

circumstances under which Charlotte Becker began calling herself
Nathalie Gebhart, nor did Mary know the quality of English that
Charlotte-Nathalie could actually speak, the strudel-English, as
Agent Loeb, or was it Leopold, had put it so ungenerously, being the
only version of English Mary or Iris or John Marsh or her own sons
had ever heard come out of her mouth, the BBC English reserved
for very particular times and places, quite specific space-times as
she came to think of them, in Britain, and even Germany, on one
occasion in France, and today, in America, in the California house
of her distant cousin, the house where she had thought to hide out
for the next decade, until she could find her way somewhere safer,
less obtrusive, Brazil or Argentina, although no contact from her old
compatriots had been forthcoming, and the more time passed the
more anxious she became about what eventualities might yet unfold.

Sometimes it happens in the course of a woman's life, Nathalie
had explained when she met Mary for the first time as an adult,
that she must leave behind one name in order, you understand my
dear, just to survive and make her way in the world after a time of
trauma and, like a lioness, safeguard the future of her young. Mary
had looked at her pityingly, cupped her face in her thin cold hands,
and held her gaze, nodding. In retrospect it occurred to Nathalie
that perhaps Mary had only been affecting understanding, as if
closeness, for her, were always a performance, but if Mary had
questions that troubled her conscience (assuming she had one)
or if she guessed that perhaps the substitution of one name for
another was not simply a matter of historical necessity, or of career
(as it had been for she, herself, Rosa Schumacher, who became
Mary Dawn), but of the erasure of an identity compromised by
crime – great, historical crimes, as the world now saw them, as
even Charlotte, that is Nathalie, accepted they must have been,

notwithstanding her participation in them – in favor of one more innocent, she asked for no clarification or justification. Instead she cooed, dovelike, I am sure that whatever you did was done for the sake of your boys. And so Mary had given Nathalie and her sons not only a job, but home and harbor and life, when others might have turned them over to the authorities, and not without reason.

Upstairs, in the bosom of the master suite, Mary was in the marble bath, preparing for her guests. Nathalie knocked on the door and Mary called for her to come in without asking who it was, as if she knew already, or assumed no one other than Nathalie would intrude on her toilette, which was true, John Marsh being too afraid, the boys indifferent, the child Iris too self-involved to bother with the ablutions of her mother, whom she openly despised. There were bubbles and foam heaped in hillocks around Mary's body, piled up to her shoulders, revealing in other places a bare stretch of skin or line of clavicle glistening in the soft light that reflected off the pink tiles. Balanced on the side of the bath, a martini glass containing two pearl onions caught the light from the bulbs that burned around the mirror above the sink.

Is Iris ready? Mary asked.

She would not wear the white dress. Insisted only on the blue.

But she wore the blue one to the last party! People will remember.

Yes, but she says it is her most favorite party dress. I tried to make her wear the white but no matter what I say she will not change. Perhaps coming from her mother, but you know, your daughter, she is so, so stubborn with me.

She says she wants you to take her to the movies again. You, not me.

Of course. It is always my pleasure.

Nathalie folded a towel that had been left on the floor crumpled and smeared with makeup and powder and pretended to occupy herself tidying up the perfumes and lotions in bottles and jars already ranged along the counter in regiments, alphabetical by type: cream for cheeks, cream for eyes, cream for neck and body and hands, scent for day, scent for evening, scent for seduction, celebration, and sorrow.

Will you need me tomorrow, Mary? Only I was thinking of taking the boys for an outing, maybe to see *Cinderella* once more, I know it must seem ridiculous, as if there is nothing else to see, but you understand that Siegfried, I mean Seth, please forgive me, my Seth cannot see this picture enough times to satisfy his little heart. I sometimes think, imagine such a horror, that he wants to be Cinderella. Of course I would take Iris, too, if she wishes to accompany us, only perhaps now she is bored with this picture.

She wants to see *The Third Man* but it can't be tomorrow. Mary smiled and her eyes were arctic. I meant to tell you earlier something has come up. I'll give you a day off next week to make up for it but tomorrow I need you. The children can play in the pool.

Oh? What is this thing you say has. . .come up?

Mary turned the hot tap and let it run for a minute, then turned it off again, doing this entirely with her toes. The dexterity of the movement was so nauseating Nathalie felt her gorge rise. It reminded her of something she had seen a decade earlier, was connected in her mind to that event, distant though it was, and the way it recalled to her mind the unnatural, twisting conjunction of flesh and steel comingled with the proximity of extreme electrical heat.

I have to speak to some gentlemen, Mary said in a new voice. Downtown. Men from the government.

But this does sound serious. It is not some problem with taxes perhaps?

Mary chewed her lip. No, but it is serious.

You aren't in any trouble?

That's why I'm going to talk with them. To avoid trouble.

Nathalie wiped the sink and looked at herself in the mirror, then shifted to focus on the reflection of Mary behind her. The toes were out again, turning the hot water tap. Nathalie put a hand to her mouth.

Forgive me for thinking of myself, but you understand, I worry only for my boys. It's nothing to do with me, is it, Mary?

Of course not. But I have to take precautions. I want you to pack the cases in my closet with enough clothes for two weeks and while I'm downtown you take the other car. Marsh won't need it, he won't be out of bed before dinner tomorrow if tonight goes how I plan. Take the cases to Malibu and unpack them once you're there. I can't explain more than that. I hope to be able to ask you and the boys to join me, and you'll bring Iris with you, though the truth is I'd rather leave it here and it'll probably object and want to stay with its father when it gets wind of it but I'll have the studio send a car for you and the children if it comes to that, whether it's just the boys or all three of them, that being my preference, you understand, because a child such as Iris, you have to keep tabs or it's bound to rumble.

Are you and Mr. Marsh. . .?

It all depends on him. Will you turn on that heater?

Nathalie switched on the chrome electric heater that had recently been installed, and its metal coils quickly turned orange. The coils, the dry electric smell as they heated up, the proximity of her own skin to intense heat, brought that unwanted memory back into focus, and then there were Mary's monkey toes and the taps and the steam from the bathwater, and in combination all of it made her gorge rise once more.

I have often wondered since I arrived here, Mary, whether you ever still speak your mother tongue? Without calculating its likely effect, Nathalie had switched to German and with this shift Mary's expression changed, the pinched hardness smoothing out, her brow clearing, the usually distant gaze drawing closer, focussing on Nathalie in a way that felt charged with a different energy than she had been conscious of emanating from Mary up to that point.

When I speak to my brother. When I write to him. We always communicate in German, Mary said, also switching languages, although her German was stiffer, with the quality of a poor girl striving for sophistication but falling short. You know, I still dream in German. I do not think in German now, not day to day I mean, unless I come to a thing or a problem that requires it. Most often this is a feeling or an abstract thought that I cannot communicate automatically in English, or I do not know instinctively how to say such a thing in English, and so I must pause and consider, and sometimes find my way around the problem, or I must let it go entirely, meaning that I cannot express what I might be thinking, because I do not know how to say precisely what it is that I am feeling in English, and, of course, the greatest problem is that no one knows this, about who I really am, that my first language is not English, not even John Marsh. Dr. Werth knows and my brother knows and the head of the studio knows, but no one else, you see, no one but you. You understand how much I trust you, how I could have no choice but to trust you when you first came here, and presented yourself to me, and demonstrated that you knew me, and where I came from, do you see? To be honest, I panicked. I thought, this is someone who can ruin everything that I have taken so long to build.

Yes, I appreciate that, Nathalie said, and understood at last why Mary had taken them in: keeping the threat close, lest Nathalie be tempted to tell the world that Mary was someone other than who she pretended.

I trust you more than just about anyone, Nathalie. Or maybe I should be calling you Charlotte.

I think you should call me Charlotte only if I should call you Rosa.

No, that name is only for my brother. No one else calls me that.

As you wish. I hope you know that I did not mean to offend. That's the last thing I would want, darling Mary.

It does not offend me, but Rosa cannot be the person I am here. Rosa is for elsewhere. If only I hadn't lied in the first place. I might have been a Hedy Lamarr or a Marlene Dietrich and maybe no one would have cared. But now it's too late. If the truth came out now, people would say I'd been trying to hide who I am.

Mary stood up in the bath and took the towel from Nathalie, who looked at the body of the other woman and marveled at the transparency of her complexion, the blue veins racing beneath the rosy skin, and the line of her hips, the bones jutting out. The towel went almost twice around her body as Mary stepped from the water onto the pink bathroom carpet where she unfurled the towel and vigorously swept it back and forth across her back, along her arms, between her legs and genitals and under her breasts, daubing at her neck, and carefully attending to the skin rising up to her hairline before dropping the towel on the floor and pulling the shower cap from her head, allowing her hair to fall around her shoulders. Nathalie picked up the towel, hung it over the rail next to the heater, and watched as Mary stood at the sink, applying different creams to her feet, her legs, her neck and hands and face.

Shall I bring your gown? Nathalie asked, still in German.

Not yet, thank you, Mary said, also in German, and so they would continue in German until, in a few minutes' time, Mary left the master suite. You are indispensable to me now. You have made yourself that way. I wonder, Nathalie, was it calculated?

My dear, I don't have the slightest idea what you mean. I should have thought it was obvious that I'm absolutely devoted to you.

Mary stared at Nathalie's reflection behind her in the bathroom mirror. She took a white puff from a box and dipped it in the scented talcum powder and began dusting her body all over, waiting for Nathalie to hold up her hair at the back before powdering her nape.

I see that. And do you know, I do not think I could trust anyone else like this. What is family if not the people one trusts most? The woman Mozelle, for example, I could never be like this in front of Mozelle, so naked, I mean. She has seen me out of makeup but I could never be more exposed than that. And yet with you, darling Nathalie, it is like we are sisters. I feel as close to you as anyone in my life. Perhaps to you I am closest of all. I feel that truly. I hope you see that, she said, applying foundation to her neck and face.

I feel close to you as well. I'm grateful that you trust me so deeply. I will always do my best to live up to that trust.

Yes, I believe that. Mary finished applying the foundation before attending to her eyes and cheeks and lips, powdering her face to finish, and then scenting herself all over, one of her scents of seduction. She stood, painted, a column of ivory. I am ready for the gown, Nathalie, if you would be so good as to help me with it. I must be on time for my guests.

Mary strode from the bathroom to the bedroom where she stepped into her underpants and Nathalie helped with fastening the corselet, then waited as Mary drew on her stockings and buckled them to the halter. The gown, by Balmain, was navy with a scattering of golden stars across the skirt, and another constellation at the bust, which struck Nathalie as in rather poor taste, tacky, but then Hollywood was a place where bad taste was often the pinnacle of fashion. Nathalie secured the gown's closure and noticed the fine hairs on Mary's back stand erect although the room was warm, and she wondered what caused this, whether it was the slight touch of her own fingertips that produced such an effect, Mary's body alerting itself to the proximity of someone in possession of a secret about her, a secret that seemed to Nathalie so inconsequential in comparison to the kind of information she hoped to discover, the proof one way or another that Mary might have been a Communist, if that was what the agents wished her to procure. It seemed unlikely, if not absurd, to suggest such a thing, and she wondered why those agents would ask her to spy on Mary if Mary was already preparing to speak with them tomorrow? Would that not be enough to satisfy them? And then it occurred to her that these American agents might be quite unlike any others she had encountered in the past, and cooperation, or perhaps cooperation especially, would make them no less suspicious of a person than if she resisted. Cooperation might, it occurred to her now, be interpreted as a sign of guilt.

You must tell me how I look. Mary adjusted the bust-line of the gown and swept her hair onto her left shoulder, revealing the small birthmark on the back of her neck, a chestnut-brown spot in the shape of an oak leaf. I always fear there might be something I'm not seeing.

Nathalie turned Mary by the shoulders to look at her face, tucked a strand of blonde hair behind her ear, and handed her a tissue. There's the tiniest shadow of lipstick on your left incisor. But otherwise, you are perfection.

Mary took the tissue and, looking close in the mirror, found the red streak, wiped it off, and again considered her reflection, breaking into a dozen different smiles and expressions, as if testing each for its effect. Before the hairdresser arrives I just want to be certain that downstairs everything is ready. Would you mind if I left you my cases to get packed?

Not at all, darling Mary. Leave it to me.

And would you not tell Marsh about the cases?

No, of course not. You can trust me absolutely.

Yes, I feel that. Mary took her hand, squeezing it and smiling, and Nathalie knew she had seen the expression before, in one of Mary's recent pictures, and that whatever flicker of genuine connection might have passed between them earlier had been replaced in an instant by the performance of feeling, what Nathalie thought to call its artful simulacrum.

Alone in John and Mary's bedroom, the door closed, Nathalie began opening drawers and closets. If the order was to pack, then it was reasonable to conclude that everything had to come out, and who could say what might be hidden in the hat and shoe boxes, beneath the corsets and girdles and underwear, tucked away at the backs of cupboards or under the bathroom sink, in the trunks and suitcases themselves, even, perhaps, in the fireplace or behind the mirror or beneath the painting of Mary gazing down upon the room? Nathalie allowed herself to search such as she never had before, scouring for clues, hoping for a trace that Mary might have forgotten or clung to, a Communist Party card or a list of members

or notes from a meeting or some other scrap of memorabilia that
would tie her indisputably to the Reds and suggest, in its singularity,
precisely the species of evidence that would be wholly new to
Agents Leopold and Loeb. She piled clothes onto the bed, opened
the cases, began packing what she thought Mary would want in
Malibu, emptied shelves and reorganized, opened and tipped out,
knocked against the closet walls and ripped the drawers out of the
dressers until around her was a chaos of furniture and garments.
Struck by how reckless she had been in this search, how careless
about the placing and position of what she had removed, Nathalie
tried to fathom what had compelled her into this frenzy, how it
was that a search of this kind, in this place and time, should propel
her into such haphazard methods, for if Mary walked in now, quite
apart from anger and surprise, she would know that something
was not right, for Nathalie had always, in folding and putting away,
in packing and unpacking, in laundry and cleaning and household
organization, ever since she had entered Mary and John's home,
demonstrated in all such matters the height of methodical precision.

And then there was the child Iris standing in the open door.

What are you doing? Iris, with the sole of her left shoe, pushed
the bedroom door closed behind her as silently as she had opened
it. Did Mother throw one of her nervous fits and leave you to clean
it up?

I suppose you must think yourself so terribly clever.

I suppose I must.

You should know that clever girls have difficult lives.

I don't think that's a very intelligent thing to say in this day
and age.

I was a clever girl like you.

You can't have been that clever if you ended up a maid.

That is not a nice thing to say. People do not always have happen to them what they expect or deserve.

That's what I'd call a fatalist attitude, said Iris. I believe in self-determination. Have you read Schopenhauer?

No.

But you're German, aren't you?

Not all Germans read philosophy.

That's not what I heard.

Don't you want to get married?

I don't think it's for me, said the child.

Then you will have to be very clever indeed.

My teacher says I read at a college level already and have done since I was eight, so I'm well on my way. But is this Mother's mess or yours?

Never mind that.

Then I suppose I'll have to ask Mother.

Nathalie looked at the girl and looked at the door and calculated the distance she would have to cover to block Iris from leaving the room.

That would not be very nice, Iris.

I guess that means it's your mess.

Your mother asked me to pack some bags.

You didn't pack like this when we went to New York or Hawaii or Havana, so I'm guessing either you've lost something Mother entrusted to you or you're looking for something and you don't know what it is. Which one?

Nathalie smiled and thought about what it would take to get rid of the girl. The latter, she said.

Well if you want to know where the bodies are buried you're too late. She's already burned them.

Excuse me?

I'm speaking metaphorically. You think I haven't been snooping too? Grow up in a house of secrets and you have to spend all your free time figuring out what's hidden. Mother burned a pile of letters and some other stuff, pamphlets and whatnot, in the fireplace.

Iris pointed at the hearth above which Mary's portrait glowered down at them.

When was this?

A few weeks ago. She cleaned it up herself and flushed the ash down the toilet. She didn't know I was watching.

Have you seen anything else?

Not so far. But I'll keep looking until I find something incriminating. Should I tell you if I do?

You are a strange child.

Look at the parents, Iris said, and turned on her heel to leave the room.

August 20, 1955

King and Quisling

– At least we won't need to eat.

– Just as well. The food at the Marshes is always terrible.

– That cook's like something out of *Hitler's Madman*.

– Straight from the bunker.

– Conrad Veidt in a dress.

King and Quisling sat in the living room of Professor Adelram Morrow, noted biologist, botanist, zoologist, everyman scientist, red-blooded American gainfully employed at the University of California Los Angeles, a prominent and vocal supporter of the university system's contentious loyalty oath (students had been rioting all week and now subversive faculty members were joining the fray), member of the Native Sons of the Golden West (he was born in Bakersfield), and across-the-street neighbor of Mr. Philip Desmond Frank. King and Quisling were drinking black coffee served by Dr. Morrow's wife, Phyllis, whose maid had baked a red velvet cake earlier in the day, decorated with cream cheese frosting and blue sugar sprinkles.

I told her it was practically a desecration but she gets these ideas in her head, Phyllis apologized, I hope you won't judge us too harshly, gentlemen. You know the Morrows hold the flag in the highest esteem. Edna was only trying to be patriotic.

King and Quisling ate their cake and smiled, or rather Quisling smiled, for King's hearing was impaired by the headphones connected to a wire that picked up the signal from the microphone placed in Desmond Frank's living room by means of a hole drilled through the exterior wall. Recordings were being made, but it was important to have agents there during waking hours in case anything out of the ordinary happened. It was just a matter of time before a subpoena was issued.

– Dessert?
– I couldn't, really, Desmond.
– Max?
– Yeah boss?
– Do we have any ice cream?
– All we got is sherbet.
– What flavors?
– Pineapple or orange.
– Sherbet anyone? Myles?
– I wouldn't say no.
– You should watch your figure, darling, American girls don't like their idols fat.
– Who's fat? Myles isn't fat.
– Not yet he isn't.

King and Quisling had been monitoring the Frank residence every evening for the previous two weeks while another pair of agents covered the days. For the most part it had been easy, tedious work, no surprises. Frank was a bore when it came to his domestic life, except for the obvious perversions, although the microphone was little use once people left Frank's living room, so a fair amount of conjecture was involved in determining what might be happening elsewhere in the house.

For dinner, Mrs. Morrow's maid had prepared steak with a dressing made from corn chips following a recipe printed in the

Times earlier that week. She was trying to wean Edna off *What Cooks in Hollywood* since Adelram had grown tired of David Niven's fishcakes, Eve Arden's meatloaf, and Joan Crawford's hot buttered bread, which was nothing more than an ordinary loaf minus the crusts smeared with half a pound of butter and put in the oven for a quarter of an hour. No one apart from the professor had been able to finish the corn-chip steak, so the cake, no matter its color, was received with relief.

King watched Mrs. Morrow lean over to cut her husband another slice. Professor Morrow was a fat man with a pink bald head who should not have been eating cake. Although better than the steak, there was something chemical about the cake's flavor and King put down his fork, leaving half his piece uneaten as he transferred his attention to the sounds of Desmond Frank, Myles Haywood, and Helen Fairdale talking in the house across the street. It had been a dull evening so far, as if the targets of his surveillance almost suspected someone might be listening. The Reds were clever, and the pansy Reds cleverest of all because they had to hide being Red and pansy from the rest of the world and even hide being pansy from their hidden Red colleagues. It was a tortured little cell—

– I suppose we should go fairly soon.

– They never get started before nine.

– Are we even welcome?

– Of course we're welcome. Have you told Helen about my suggestion, Myles?

– Listen, Des, maybe now isn't the time.

– What suggestion? What are you two cooking up?

—and then all at once the room across the street went silent
and King held his breath trying to discern if the shuffles and
other movements picked up by the listening system might
mean anything significant. Just when he decided he had heard
whispering a jazz trumpet blared into the microphone. It was so
loud he had to fling the headphones back from his ears.

Drink, Agent Quisling? Agent King? Professor Morrow asked
from his reclining chair, second plate of cake balanced on the globe
of his stomach. I couldn't persuade you last night, but seeing as
it's a Friday, he droned, I thought perhaps you might join me in a
nightcap.

Quisling glanced at King, who nodded. Two weeks with these
people and they both felt the need of a stiffener, although Quisling
knew he should not be drinking on duty. No telling when a situation
might change without warning. There was a gas fire in the living
room and although it had made it into the 70s that day, following
the red rays of sunset the evening shrank into chill so Mrs. Morrow
turned up the flame. Two red flares flashed in the faces of Professor
Morrow's spectacles and the fired red tiles around the hearth gave
the room a cozy ambiance, radiating heat so that, within a few
minutes, everyone's cheeks had a healthy red glow that made the
red of Mrs. Morrow's lips look quite muted by comparison. On the
wall above the fireplace hung a reproduction of an Italian painting of
the Visitation of the Virgin to Saint Elizabeth, Mary leaning forward
in a blue cloak over a scarlet gown that spilled out along the ground
as the cousins necked. Light flickered across its surface and it was
easy under the chemical influences of the dyed cake and the steak's
corn-chip dressing to imagine the Virgin martyred aflame. Mrs.
Morrow's mother had sent it to them after her recent stop in Italy,
where she claimed to have seen its original in one of the Florentine

galleries. Mrs. Morrow could not, herself, imagine traveling outside
her own country, especially somewhere people did not speak
English, and the fact of her mother's incautious tourism made her
worry that men like Agents King and Quisling might soon take an
interest in her husband or herself. It was part of the reasoning
behind allowing the authorities use of their home, believing that a
certain candor would prove the Morrows' willingness to cooperate
as patriotic Americans trying to uphold the rule of law in such
an age of darkness, when fifth columnists implanted themselves
even in the best neighborhoods. She liked corn chips, but while it
had sounded promising in print the reality just wasn't very tasty.
Tomorrow, she decided, they would go back to Lauren Bacall's
reliable beef stroganoff.

Professor Morrow poured fingers of the single-malt whiskey his
mother-in-law had sent from Edinburgh, believing its equal could
not be found in Southern California. There was a family rumor that
his wife's mother had fallen in love with a red-bearded Scotsman
and would not return to her own country. It had driven his wife
into such a red anger he felt forced to consult a friend in the new
medical school about getting her a prescription for secobarbital.
They first took samples of her blood – Professor Morrow had
sat holding his wife's pale hands as the blood, a terrible red, ran
into vials – to see that her system could handle the effects of the
tranquilizer because she had always been in fragile health. Even
after starting the pills (small and red and so glossy they might
have been shellacked with nail varnish), something, Adelram
was convinced, was still amiss, for far from calming Phyllis the
tranquilizers energized her, as though her body were scripted to
respond in the opposite manner to that expected. A woman of the
reddest blood would not be so highly strung, he was certain. Her

ring flashed in the firelight, its band bright against tapering white fingers. Phyllis had inherited the ring as well as the fingers from her mother, who claimed to have inherited all her jewelry from a grandmother, who herself claimed to have been an intimate of the Romanovs, so Phyllis insisted on describing the ring as 'pure Russian red-gold' even though Adelram had told her there could be no such thing as pure red-gold because the substance was almost certainly at least half copper and to advertise its Russianness, however fictional, however pre-revolutionary, was ill-advised. Lately she had taken to calling it, simply, her 'red ring', which, with the ruby inset, it might justifiably be described, although the stone itself was likely synthetic, and the whole thing no older than twenty or thirty years. Pure it was not, and could never be. It had become one of the points of small disagreement that threatened to eclipse the ordinary happiness of Adelram Morrow's domestic life. His mother-in-law, who on occasion practiced geomancy and had been a radical suffragist in her distant youth, jailed on two continents and given to pamphleteering, predicted some months earlier (and communicated this prediction by telegram from Cape Town) that Phyllis would evolve into her opposite: DEAR PHYLLIS RED AFRICAN EARTH REVEALS TERRIBLE FUTURE STOP YOU FATED TO BE AGORAPHOBIC STOP LEAVE ADELRAM NOW STOP RETURNING AMERICA NOT BEFORE CHRISTMAS STOP LOVE YOUR MOTHER. Adelram had burned the telegram before his wife could read it but nonetheless took note of his mother-in-law's prediction, and since then had become conscious of Phyllis's giddiness each time she left the house.

Adelram sucked the crumbs of his cake. I've long been suspicious of that Mr. Frank, he said.

So you've told us, said Agent Quisling.

489

Don't think I'm abasing him for my own advancement. I have nothing to gain from this cooperation with you gentlemen except the honor and satisfaction of serving my country in however small a way. Hospitality is a form of service, after all, I think you gentlemen must agree.

Quisling nodded and sipped his drink. Cooperative Professor Morrow and his wife might be, but they were a tiresome pair.

Is Mr. Frank a Jew? Do you gentlemen know? No? If he is, I suppose he must be what they call a Red Jew, red in more ways than one, of course, but I speak of the racial type, the redness of hair and complexion, as though, from a scientific point of view, biology had dictated ideology. My father always said the Red Jews will bring about the end of the world, Gog and Magog, the Ten Tribes and what have you. Worth considering when one encounters the type.

Quisling drank his drink and wished it were stronger. These people pushed him to the edge of his patience. If the Morrows were the kind of Americans who called themselves patriots and about whom nothing subversive would ever be suspected, he began to wonder if he might be on the wrong side, politically speaking, or at least on the wrong side of his own conscience.

My father has red hair but he's no more a Red than I. My dog is red, too, red as a chestnut, but your theory, I suppose, doesn't hold for animals or vegetables or minerals that occur in the natural world. I mean, they can't all be subversive, Professor Morrow, said Quisling.

Adelram Morrow chuckled so that his sphere of gut bounced and jiggled as though it might separate itself from his body and roll away to crush a path of ruin across the floor. I do not say that biology, or indeed chemistry, is the last word in loyalty, only that in the particular ideological perversion of Communism,

a red complexion or red hair might, now that red has been
elevated – or we might say denigrated – as the chosen color of
the Soviets, incline the red-haired individual to sympathy with
the ideology that celebrates red as the apogee of beauty. I have
always preferred white myself, and beige, and blue. Red is not
a color of calm or rational thought. Red is something that must
be harnessed and controlled to keep its particular power from
ranging unchecked.

My mother always used to call my father Red, though his name
was Frederick. I told her she shouldn't do that now. People might
get the wrong idea. Quisling finished his drink. He wanted another
and put the empty glass on the table hoping the professor would
get the message.

Another whiskey for Agent Quisling, Phyllis.

Mrs. Morrow swept up the glass in one hand while the other
poured from the open bottle of single-malt scotch. Whatever it was,
unpronounceable name, older than Quisling was himself, it smelled
like culture and was heady and warming and he wanted as much of
it as he could drink because he was unlikely to be offered its equal
again. There was bound to be a box of Cuban cigars somewhere,
and if he waited long enough those other gifts of hospitality might
emerge.

Of course it is not just certain races of Jews we might describe
as red. There are the Red Indians of our own great continent, not
to mention the red races of the Caribbean islands, no doubt the
product of miscegenation, and again, as my theory holds, entities
that must be carefully controlled and managed, put under the
balancing yoke of whiteness. No, I think it is fair to say that except
in the case of the Celtic, Scandinavian, Aryan, that is to say the
Northern European Germanic races and their brethren, any

other race exhibiting a red complexion has inherited this through
the undesirable breeding between racial groups and ought to be
regarded as fallen in a biological sense, prone to any number of
infections. You notice how in the Germanic, northern-European
red, there is always a balancing white complexion to keep the fire
at bay – the purest of white skin, in fact. Like you, Agent Quisling,
except you've no red hair. What is your family?

Norwegian on my father's side. Swedish on my mother's.

The professor nodded. Unfortunate name, given recent events,
but then a man is more than the name of his fathers, only. . . I seem
to have lost my train. Ah yes, it is only when that true whiteness is
absent that the real problems begin, with the sallow and the black
and the brown pigmentation that allows red to run rampant across
the psyche.

Quisling wrinkled his nose and sipped his second glass of
scotch. Since the war he had been teased and taunted for his name
and it had been insinuated that perhaps, really, he ought to think
of changing it to one less compromised. He took another swallow.
He would rise the next morning with bloodshot eyes, red as fire
with the weeping that tormented him when he woke and knew
himself a man alone in the world. King had a wife blonde as he and
there was no doubt King took comfort in this twin-like company,
but Quisling knew that, for him, woman was not his province, while
man remained forbidden. As these unsummoned thoughts mobbed
him, he was conscious of flushing red. Some careless nights he
had allowed himself to drive downtown, hang out at Cooper's
Doughnuts or wander through Pershing Square, knowing what
possibilities lurked in the shadows, visible in glances drawn to him
by the angles of his own body, the contours of cheeks, planes of
chest, his girder legs. Loitering was illegal and he was a lawman.

Temptation had to be suppressed. Consciousness of temptation was
the only thing that kept the fires at bay. It had nothing to do with
the pigments of the human species or its many races. He had fallen
into this job, fallen like a fool.

If you like that whiskey, I've got something you'll like even
better. I suppose you've never tried port, have you, son? Professor
Morrow crooned. Quisling shook his head, finished the scotch,
and put down the glass on the coffee table. Well go on, Phyllis, you
know what I'm talking about. Get the port for our guests.

Yes, dear, she said, hurrying into the dining room to retrieve
the correct glasses and the dusty bottle from the liquor cabinet.
She was unsure whether Adelram meant the good port or the
cheap port and decided he could only mean the former. Would
you like a glass yourself, dear? He failed to hear and she poured
the red liquor into four small crystal glasses, arranging them in
a grid on the silver tray her mother had sent from Morocco last
year. On high heels she wobbled back across the carpet and into
the living room, taking the tray first to her guests, bending over
so the men could reach the glasses without having to stand. Agent
Quisling looked her in the face and thanked her politely but she
was conscious of Agent King taking the opportunity to glance too
long at her bust. She straightened her back and placed a glass
between Adelram's dimpled fingers and kept the last for herself.
How nice it would be to go home with Agent Quisling, who wore
no ring and had a sensible leather-strapped watch and probably
lived in a sensible bungalow in Pasadena or Glendale and ironed
his own shirts and made sensible dinners for himself. Quisling was
the sort of man she felt she should have married, quiet and blond
– so very blond – and tanned and muscular and yet apart from the
beauty, that very particular California beauty she knew was made

from the best of the American races coming together in a white European ideal, he also seemed a sensitive and intelligent man, she could tell from the way he moved and sat and spoke, the care with which he treated her furniture and possessions. Later, once Agents King and Quisling were gone, there would be a suffocating hour under her sweating husband, pretending a tenderness she had never felt for him. She flushed and wished to be alone with Agent Quisling, whose first name she had never learned. He looked like a Peter or a Phil. What if these men were not spying on sweet Mr. Frank but were really there to spy on them, or what if the men were not agents of the Federal Bureau of Investigation but instead members of a criminal organization undertaking an elaborate surveillance of the Morrow home before breaking in to steal everything they owned, including all the jewelry her mother had given her, which she had been wearing ever since the men announced themselves?

King sipped at the port and listened to the music that came through the headphones from the house across the street as Mrs. Morrow squinted in her chair on the other side of the room, hands sallow and disunited against her lap, feet two badly butchered cuts of beef. After a moment the woman seemed aware of King's gaze and rearranged herself, tidying her legs, drawing herself erect, and folding her hands. She was not unattractive, still young, although her dress was dowdy. Nice tits, without question, two good handfuls of fun. Through the headphones a woman's voice began to sing and King imagined, as Mrs. Morrow's mouth moved in a conversation he could not hear, that it was she who was singing so enchantingly into his ears. It was not a song he knew but the music kept him mesmerized, so fixed on the face of his hostess that he was unconscious of tightening his grip round

the crystal glass, hardly aware of the pain as the shards cut into
his fingers. Everyone jumped at the sound he had not heard and
the red blood that fell, mixing with port, into the beige carpet at
his feet. He removed the headphones and Professor Morrow was
speaking in an agitated way, Here we are talking nonsense, all
of us crying Peace, Freedom, and Liberty, and poor Agent King
has fallen victim to the glass with a crack in it. No, don't trouble
yourself about the carpet, Agent Quisling, our girl will see to the
stains. Red rain will not blight this private acre of land, Adelram
laughed, although the carpet would most likely have to be replaced
and he intended reporting to the FBI's Los Angeles field office just
how inconvenienced he had been by this whole affair. The stain
darkened the longer it stood, red as their steak dinner but less
appealing, and he thought of raising his hand to fling a red coal
from the fire and suffer each of the agents to take it into their
mouths, to tie it inside against their teeth and watch their tongues
sizzle. No, no, no, Adelram, you could never do any such thing, but
what a pleasure it would be to see authority taking the hot rump of
chastisement for casting itself about so indiscriminately, as if he,
Adelram Morrow, did not have better things to do in his evenings
than entertain a couple of towhead schoolboys while they poached
the privacy of the whole neighborhood. No, no, no, Adelram, of
course, you believe entirely in their cause. It is only right the Reds
be flushed out of the country just as quick and hot as your bowels
void each time Phyllis administers an enema.

Phyllis, get Agent Quisling another glass of port and call Edna
to come attend to this stain.

Of course, dear, Phyllis said, bobbing out of the room.

Agent King was red with shame, cheeks as red as coals. What
fun it would be to plump them full with real red coals, a tortured

little chipmunk, two chipmunks, these agents, one crafty, the other an idiot, although often difficult to tell which was which, no gap-toothed grin to identify the dumb one.

What about my hand? Agent King's cuts were continuing to bleed, dripping on the redwood coffee table.

Funny, isn't it, Agent Quisling, that if the Red Army had its way the whole world would be drinking white spirit. Just goes to show how flawed their philosophy is. A sickness as vile as any pestilence. Even they know the beauty of whiteness, but are simply too afraid to admit it.

You don't have to convince me. Agent Quisling placed his empty port glass alongside the empty scotch tumbler as Edna bustled into the living room with a sponge and a bucket of warm soapy water and the saltshaker. None of what the professor said made the least sense to Quisling. If only their host would shut up and let them do their job and go home. Perhaps if you have a bandage, we could attend to my colleague's injuries.

Phyllis, won't you see to Agent King's hand?

With his uninjured hand King passed the headphones to Agent Quisling, who placed them over his ears as King rose, and, taking only a step or two, fell to the floor in a swoon and lay face down on the carpet. The maid screamed and Mrs. Morrow ran into the room, hand at her mouth.

Oh! she cried. I'll get the smelling salts.

Don't bother with salts, Mrs. Morrow, said Edna, better call the ambulance.

That won't be necessary, said Agent Quisling, kneeling over his colleague. It's just that he has an aversion to blood. The wounds aren't serious. We need the smelling salts, some rubbing alcohol, cotton balls, gauze, and tape. Do you have those items, Mrs. Morrow?

I think I must have some bandages in the first-aid kit.

As Quisling had spoken the sound of a woman singing flowed
out through the headphones, behind which he was certain he could
hear faint conversation. The music was comprised of longer and
shorter notes. Red notes, he thought, the short ones, in contrast
to black ones. He had sung in the church choir and remembered
the director telling them about the two different kinds of notes
in early musical compositions. Red full and red void. Full of red,
empty of red, but still undeniably red. The Reds on the other end
of the headphones were trying to empty and shorten their sound
but Red they remained, or so he had been trained to believe. The
training was beginning not to stick. What was the logic of redness,
of seeing redness everywhere one looked? And then, all at once,
the music stopped and the people on whom they were meant to be
eavesdropping began to speak.

– I don't see how it can work, Desmond. A quartet is no less
obvious than a duo, or a solo for that matter.
– And if we say that the four of us, being the best of friends,
couldn't bear to be separated?
– Is it really necessary? I don't know that the whole thing won't
lose steam in a few months. People will get tired of it. Does the
nation really care whether we believe one thing or another? I
can't see it carrying on myself.
– Don't be naïve, Helen. This is only the beginning. You have to
believe the words of the demagogues. They will do what they
threaten.

In the pantry Phyllis found the kit with a large red cross on its
white surface. It reminded her of the red she had run earlier that

day trying to make way for an ambulance, how worried she had been that a police officer might have seen her but somehow God was on her side, she had got away with the infraction and proved once again how unadvisable it was to go out alone. She did not know how her mother did it, traipsing all over the world in strange company, and at her age. Next to the first-aid kit was a supply of Adelram's red oxide stropping compound and a set of new straight razors. The glint of the blades made her think and the thought was unpleasant and she hurried back into the living room where Agent King was face down on the carpet with Agent Quisling leaning over him like mother to child, the headphones balanced on his ears seeming to accentuate the delicacy of his jaw. There was supposed to be boxing on the television starting at 8:30, live from the Hollywood Legion, and she had hoped to see the Richardson and Cracknell bout if she could get the agents out the door, because Richardson and Cracknell were both so handsome. What a pleasure it would be to see Agent Quisling in satin shorts and shirtless, squaring up to Adelram and slugging until he knocked him cold and then she could lean against Quisling's arm, touch his bare chest, and run off with him to a cold hotel room.

No, that particular thought was impossible. She put it away and indicated to Agent Quisling that he should return to his work while she tended Agent King's cuts. Since the man was prostrate on the wall-to-wall carpet his lacerated palm was conveniently facing up. She lifted it into her lap and as she began daubing the cuts with alcohol the man burst back into consciousness and cried out in pain, really very like a woman's his voice sounded, and Phyllis had to stop herself laughing. They had all had too much to drink.

Now your ordinary Red, by which I mean any of the citizens of the Red Empire, Adelram said, would leave his fellow to die. They call themselves the heroes of brotherhood but they are more

self-interested than all the robber barons combined, and this is
the result of their infernal system. If you're told everyone must
be equal and the government steals all the money you earn, or
doesn't let you get paid in the first place, then you have to fight
tooth and nail to keep ahead of the fellow next to you. Makes for an
inhumane society. Feeling any better, Agent King?

Yes, I'm sorry. It happened so suddenly. I don't usually faint.

Do you want me to phone the doctor?

No, thank you, Mrs. Morrow, you've done a very capable job. I'll
be fine now.

Funny, don't you think, how quickly our sense of the Red Empire
has changed. Only a few years ago the Englishman would have
looked at his map of the world and known that all the countries
colored in pink – which of course is only a diluted shade of red –
were his own, and most of the globe they covered, too. No bad thing
it was, I'd say, as our country was coming into its maturity, waiting
to take its place at the top of civilization. Truth is, I blame the
English for the rise of Communism. They gave safe harbor to that
villain Marx and their particular failure to control their colonies
and dominions has led to the sorry rise of the new genus of Red.
Power vacuums, gentlemen – the English left a great yawning power
vacuum when they retreated from the dark places of the earth and
now the Soviet is rushing in to fill the gaps. But by God we will not
let him win. We must fight to control the planet or risk falling into
a new dark age. That Attlee fellow, however reformed he may be,
is undoubtedly a menace. From what I can tell, he was at one time
a possible Soviet agent, turning England into a staging camp for
the worldwide march of Communism. Look at what he lost for the
forces of freedom: India, Burma, Ceylon! They have made a mess of
Palestine, and now Malaya is falling almost without a fight. South

Africa is the one bright spot, secured for freedom and prosperity, but the English had no part in that. We have only the white Africans to thank for that particular success and we can but hope the South Africans and Rhodesians roll out a model of organization and commerce that will whiten an entire continent. No, the new curtain of Red sweeping the world is one that must be cut to shreds before it blackens out the light that brings prosperity.

Edna was scrubbing the blood and port from the carpet, watching the pale skin of her hands redden with friction and salt. She knew how much Professor Morrow enjoyed having her on the floor, hands and knees, her backside shaking in his direction. More than once he had caught her like that, hiked up her dress and done the unspeakable, one of his chalky fat hands clasped over her mouth if she tried to make a noise. She would quit the job if she did not have a kid to feed. Every time it happened he took the opportunity to educate her, whispering suitable words: rapine, noun, as defined by Noah Webster, meaning 'plunder, pillage, violence'. Language will unlock you, Edna. And then the judder and the spasm and the wet withdrawal. Play a game with me, he would say, you be red and I'll be black. Chips laid on the table, Mrs. Morrow playing bridge at the home of some other lady, house twisted to a battle zone. Edna always beat him at cards, but he took his revenge in other ways, seemed to enjoy being beaten as excuse for punishing the woman he paid to cook and clean. I would have you here eternally, down to the ground, as it were, Professor Morrow might chuckle, my bête rouge. Edna never spoke to him, or spoke as little as she could to save herself while the punishments were delivered. The stain was lightening, but the carpet would have to be replaced. The trick was to make it look insignificant long enough that a new one could be installed while Professor Morrow was at work one day. Nothing more idiotic than a beige carpet unless you were only going to eat and drink white foods. She had read a library book in which the characters did just that, and it had not ended well, not well at all, the man left for dead in a South American jungle, the woman without one red cent.

King was relieved to see the stain begin to disappear as he noticed that some of the port had splashed onto his pale socks, staining them red, and he laughed to himself that he, a lifelong supporter of the Cincinnati Reds, should be made something like an honorary member of the team through such a dumb mistake. He had high hopes that Sewell, the team's new manager, would put them back on the road to the pennant, and then there was the hotshot pitcher Ewell Blackwell, with his whipping right hand (although there hadn't been much sign of it so far) and long lean body, who looked like a fellow with whom you'd want to have a beer and maybe throw a few balls back and forth, though King had no arm to speak of, but still, it was distraction from life, the ballgames, and he liked to imagine himself out there in uniform, the cap with the red C emblazoned on its front, and the funny red stockings that didn't look so comical on guys who wore them with purpose, the six-foot-six pitcher so tall and trim it would be possible in the right circumstances to shimmy up his body like climbing a coconut palm. If he were a baseball player, if he'd been born with the talent, King knew he could have made it to the top, been a celebrated pitcher or hitter, found out what gold really tastes like, eating caviar off 14-karat spoons instead of stuck in this dead-end job doing the bidding of a man no one liked. Boy, that Ewell sure knew how to play, he'd put Jackie Robinson in his place like no one else, told that—

Mrs. Morrow floated into view again. She had put red on her lips in a haphazard way that made her look so fuckable it unsettled King's equilibrium all over again and he began to swoon where he sat. At least a decade spread between them in age, as if she were an older sister or junior aunt, and the slight drainage of his blood seemed to hurry its passage to his groin so he began thinking about what else he might break or upset that would require Mrs. Morrow to lean forward and down, to give him a glimpse of the pink marble blush of her cleavage, Tennessee marble, hacked out of hillbilly soil and polished into a gleaming soft mausoleum. His boxer shorts would not long hold, he adjusted position, clasped his legs tight round his cock and thought of his father, fastest way to tame the lion, that lipstick on the woman's face, smeared just wide of the left corner of her mouth, it was like the red marks on a sheep, ruddled for property, he could be minded to shepherd her into a quiet fold of field—

Agent King, perhaps instead of port, you'd prefer a nice bold red to see you through the rest of the evening. Adelram had taken note of the way the injured agent leered at his wife. He wondered if Phyllis's reds had come or if there was still cause to be worried about another pregnancy. One child was quite enough, a further would be too great a burden and ought to be grounds for divorce. The first time he had encountered the detritus of his wife's cycles, Adelram mistook the sanitary pads for a variety of household dye test, perhaps to see which reds had greater permanence, or the offcuts from some WPA art project for the inhabitants of the local red-light district, commissioned in the mistaken belief that art would get the nation out of the red. Only war could do that, only war could put the nation in the black, and war must be the footing on which the country set itself forever after, on constant red alert against the Reds.

502

– Are we taking separate cars, Desmond?

– I might want to leave earlier.

– You're welcome to come with us. We could drop you on the way home, or perhaps you'd like to come back to the house tonight.

– I wouldn't want to risk you two more than I already have.

– Don't be like that.

– I'm stating a fact as well as a sentiment, Myles. I don't want to do either of you any harm. Clearly, that is all I've ever done to anyone. So let's go.

– Desmond, please. . .

– I'll be back in a few hours, Max.

– Have a good night, boss.

They're leaving, said Quisling, taking off the headphones. I think we're done for the night. He and Agent King rose, left the Morrows and their maid in the living room, and from the darkened study at the front of the house watched the two cars across the street roll out the crescent of driveway. The street was quiet. From the living room came the sound of the Morrows whispering to each other and dismissing Edna for the night, leaving their empty glasses for her to retrieve and wash the next morning.

We should follow. We know where they're going.

We think we know where they're going.

Half of Hollywood will be there.

It's a party. Why do we care if the man goes to a birthday party for a lady we know is cooperative? Quisling asked.

King raised an eyebrow as if Quisling's question contained its own answer. I think we should follow.

I want to go home. I've had too much to drink.

You've hardly had anything.

Two scotches, a glass of port, another glass of port. I think I might be sick. Do you have an antacid?

King shook his head. Light from the street glanced off his blond hair. Quisling wondered if the man loved his wife. They had been partners for only a month and he was already considering asking for a reassignment to someone whose face had been more disfigured by life.

I'll drive, said King, clapping a hand on Quisling's shoulder. We'll sit outside the Marsh place. We'll confirm Frank is there. We're supposed to follow him until the next shift.

I'll go if you let me sleep. Tomorrow, I don't know, I might just follow Mr. Frank's lead.

What are you talking about, Quisling?

I'm talking about – Quisling clutched the edge of Professor Morrow's desk. He had definitely drunk too much. He was about to reveal himself a doubter. A doubter was as good as a subversive. A subversive was a fellow traveler. A fellow traveler was as bad as a Communist. A Communist was un-American, scarlet, crimson, red, fire out of control, blood flowing, warnings unheeded, intoxicants derived from grapes, an alert he was ignoring. His parents would weep. He would spend the rest of his life weeping. There was a special penitentiary in hell reserved for agents of the Federal Bureau of Investigation who expressed doubts about the nature of their assignments, who spoke against the Director, who mistrusted the presiding wisdom of the nation. Who knew what the nation thought? Where was the nation located? He had lived in America all his life, never been outside its borders, and if aliens asked him tomorrow to show them the nation he would not have known in which direction to point. It was all going to hell. The vortex pulled not from the feet but from the head, drawing him down, dizzy, and the only thing to do was to plunge forward if he wanted to live.

Never mind, King. Let's go.

May 1, 1950

John

Although the volume on the television in John and Mary's den
was turned up the music from the terrace was so loud that John
struggled to hear the dialogue at the beginning of the Edward
G. Robinson picture airing on KTLA. It was one he had not seen
before, its title card showing a shadowy pre-war London with Big
Ben and St. Paul's and *Thunder in the City* splashed across the sky,
promising something other than what the story actually seemed
to be about since it started in New York with a montage of street
scenes, decent location shooting and quick-cutting, but had taken
a turn to the ridiculous as a squadron of advertising blimps flew
through clouds over the skyscrapers and acrobats went swinging
beneath one of them without harness or net. It was obvious
that the acrobats, three slender men in dark, figure-wrapping
costumes, had been hanging in a studio and the city beneath them
was no more than a cheap rear projection. Robinson was a decent
fellow, but *Thunder in the City* did not look like an example of his
better work.

Daddy, why aren't you at the party? Iris said.

I *am* at the party, Marlow, I'm right here.

No, I mean why aren't you out there with all the grown-ups?

I'm waiting for my own friends to arrive. Most of those people
out there are your mother's friends. They wouldn't say hello to me
if we were alone in the last room on earth.

Since before seven the room that opened onto the pool terrace
at the back of the house had been showing a reel of Mary's favorite
clips of her past performances. Anywhere a person stood in the

506

backyard it was possible to see the flickering image of Mary Dawn
in dozens of different guises and moods, one flowing into the other
like a procession of ghosts.

Isn't there anything better to watch?

One of Nathalie's boys – in the dark John could not see which
one – pushed himself up on his elbows.

Wrestling, Mr. Marsh. And boxing from the Legion. And
Versatile Varieties.

It was the older of the two, the one whose 'w's flattened out into
'v's and whose 'v's even more often pouted into 'w's. Vrestling and
Wersatile Warieties.

Not that, Iris shrieked. It's not even a real nightclub.

Shush, Iris, we're missing this lousy picture.

They pretend as if it's a real nightclub but it's just in the studio.
It gives me the creeps.

When John clapped a palm over his daughter's mouth she
squirmed, removed his hand to the arm of the chair, and played
with the metal strap on his watch. She was too old for this behavior
but a little more childishness a while longer was not such a bad
thing in a town where kids were expected to be adults off stage and
innocents when the cameras were rolling. He hoped Iris never got
it in her head to ask for a screen test.

In the movie's first scene a group of senior businessmen
criticized the Robinson character's advertising tactics: too much
hullabaloo and shemozzle (Blimps! Circuses! Parades!), not
enough gravity and restraint. What a thirties picture. The head
and namesake of the fictional company, a Mr. Snyderling, was
convinced it was just such hyping that had caused the Great
Depression. The office set looked artificial, and John was sure
Iris would be making a mental tally of all the ways the film failed

to achieve verisimilitude. He did not know how his child had
formed this passion for realism. He himself made ostensibly realist
pictures that always shaded over into the expressionistic, the
dreamlike, or the surreal, and it was these flights into the human
subconscious, into the realm of the possible rather than the real,
which Iris consistently disdained.

Of *White Heat*:

Iris: Is this supposed to be now or sometime in the future? I
don't think police have these kinds of machines. The person
watching the picture shouldn't have to wonder. It should all
be obvious it's from real life if it's a picture about real life.

John: The 'machines' as you put it, are a sophisticated
new form of radiolocation device and even if every police
department in the country does not yet have them they
most certainly do exist. This is not science fiction.

Of *Notorious*:

Iris: Is that a dream he's having? I don't think dreams
belong in movies about everyday life. Dreams are for fairy
tales and myths.

John: How many times have you woken in the morning and
told me what you've dreamt the previous night? And how
many times have those dreams been versions of fairy tales
we've read the night before, or myths you've been studying
in school? Isn't that a part of everyday life?

508

Of one of John's past productions:

> Iris: Is it raining because she's sad? You shouldn't have weather to show the way people are feeling. That isn't the way it is in real life, and certainly not the way it is in Los Angeles. Sometimes people are sad when the sun is shining. It's too obvious if the rain is supposed to tell us that she's sad, or is it supposed to be symbolic?

> John: It is raining, Iris, because we were shooting on location and it was the end of the shoot and I was over budget and it would have been more artificial to make the character happy. Sometimes these things happen, and sometimes people are sad when it rains. Sometimes the weather accompanies emotion. Sometimes weather even creates emotion. Try not to be such a literalist.

On the occasion of a visit to the set of *She Turned Away*:

> Iris: I don't think a voiceover is playing fair. If you can't make the story just with people saying their lines and doing stuff, then maybe you should write a book.

> John: Well you've got me there. Chalk it up to stylistic choice.

To her mother Iris simply said things like, You looked very pretty, Mother, or When you cried I cried, too, Mother, but John knew from the calculated, disingenuous way she spoke that Iris loved Mary about as much as a lost sock. The way she told her father what she disliked about his films meant, he was certain, that she

respected and loved him enough to be honest. Mary did not invite
honesty. Honesty should never be punished but that was what
Mary invariably did. Tell the truth and get a smack.

On the television the cityscape outside the office windows was
obviously an assortment of cheap miniatures made from cardboard
because whichever studio produced the picture must not have had
the cash or know-how to do more convincing model building. It
looked fake and it was fake and the fakeness could not be blamed
entirely on it having been made more than ten years ago, nor did the
fakeness have enough artistry about it to pass as interestingly fake,
not like *The Wizard of Oz*, for instance, where you could see that the
Emerald City and most of the backgrounds were matte paintings,
or even Fleming's other big winner, *Gone with the Wind*, where
everything was so beautiful it scarcely mattered if it registered ten
degrees wide of reality, but both those movies were fantasies of a
kind: a fairytale fantasy and an historical one. *Thunder in the City*
was a cheap fake and an artless one.

Perhaps Iris was right, and the hyperreal or the surreal
could never mix convincingly with the quotidian. But no, surely
not, because the Germans knew how to take the ordinary and
the fantastic and churn the two together in a way that was both
hellishly unsettling and utterly convincing on its own terms. John
wanted to toss out Hollywood's rulebook and write a new one in
which the first and most important rule should always be to break
all the rules found herein and ignore those who say otherwise.

When he was passing the room earlier he had caught the three
children playing. Iris was being Cinderella and Franz – whom
they were all supposed to call Fred – was Prince Charming, while
the younger one, Siegfried, renamed Seth, had been dressed up
in one of Mary's discarded pink chiffon dressing gowns as the

Wicked Stepmother. Mary was the one who insisted the boys
should have what she called 'American' names instead of German
ones, but everyone knew that when the lady of the house was
away the originals returned. John felt sorry for Seth even though
the boy's skulking made his skin crawl. On weekends and during
school vacations the lives of the three children blurred so it was
impossible to say who was the child of the house and who the
children of the maid. Nathalie had taken all three of them to see
Cinderella no less than four times at Pantages, and John was
certain he had paid for all of them each time, simply because it was
what Iris demanded. There was puppy love between her and Franz
and it seemed innocent enough for now, but he suspected Siegfried
suffered for it. Last summer he had come home from the studio
one day to find Iris instructing both boys to swim in the nude after
having made them remove their matching fig-leaf bathing suits,
which were themselves, John thought, a kind of obscenity. Iris
had stood there filming the brothers with her home movie camera.
He had spanked her and tossed the film and given a lecture on
propriety and human dignity. But Daddy, she had cried, Adam
and Eve went naked as the day. I don't see why Franz and Siggie
shouldn't go naked, too. Does the same go for you? he had asked
his daughter. Oh no, I'm playing God and God doesn't go naked. He
always wears a robe. The child was born to direct.

The Robinson character, in a slim-fitting gray double-breasted
suit, was getting fired as the boss, Mr. Snyderling, suggested he go
learn some modesty from the English. Off he heads, fastest ocean
crossing in the history of cinema, and arrives in London, where
his distant English cousins – rich in property, title, and class,
but church-mouse poor in cash – hearing word of his arrival, are
only too keen to sell off their stately pile in the misapprehension

that because he works for the Snyderling Company he must be a millionaire. Everything in England is always for sale. They would sell the Crown and the two little princesses if they could get away with it, then shift the blame for any tastelessness onto the buyer.

Why would they want to sell their house? It seems a lovely house.

Because rich people in England don't have any money.

And what about the poor people?

They don't have any money either.

Then why would Mr. Robinson's character go to England to learn how to sell?

I suspect that's the point. The American is going to teach the English how to sell and be proved right in the end.

You're so clever, Daddy.

Nathalie appeared at the door in the gray and white uniform Mary insisted she wear whenever they had guests. It made her look like an agent of the Gestapo.

Your friends are here, Mr. Marsh. What I mean is, Mr. Frank and Mr. Haywood and Mrs. Fairdale, they asked me to find you.

On the television, the German actress Luli Deste was in an open-top car on a fake street built in what appeared to be the tiniest of soundstages. Strange that she never had a bigger career with that face and laugh, those dark, penetrating eyes. Historical timing had not been in her favor. Just when she might have had a breakthrough in America Hitler happened and then you had to be like Dietrich or Lorre and learn how to play on the Germanness in a way that was sufficiently sinister and seductive so American audiences would understand the actors themselves knew there was something tarnished about their nationality, which made it okay to find Dietrich glamorous and Lorre darkly serpentine and that frisson of the verboten was enough to keep audiences lined up at the door. Luli, aristocratic and elegant, a real-life baroness by birth, was too comely a German to be comfortable, and that was why, John guessed, she had not appeared in a film since 1941. Word was she lived in New York these days, on her second or third husband, writing a book, but she kept in touch with the German exiles in Los Angeles. That bad-tempered Adorno fellow was supposed to have been a friend, part of the Mann and Chaplin sets, but he had left now, too, saying poetry was finished because of Hitler. No one with brains stayed in Los Angeles for long or if they did they never stopped complaining about it.

John lifted Iris off his lap. If she had her way, the kids would be watching boxing as soon as he left the room and she would get Nathalie's boys to strip to their skivvies and mime the bout in front of the screen. That had happened once before as well.

The clothes stay on, Iris. You hear me?

I always keep my clothes on.

You know what I mean. And no boxing, he said.

But this is just as bloody, Iris said, pointing at the television screen where Robinson was struggling to ham his way through the two-bit script.

Watch your mouth, brute.

The living room was choking with people who were supposed to be friends but most of them John would have traded for a night alone. Since Chasen's had catered the party it was trays of barbecued spareribs and soft-shell crab flown in from New England. John was certain it would be the last party he and Mary hosted together unless he changed his mind and turned informer. What he really wanted was to absent himself entirely from the whole mess, let the right and the left fight it out. If he could keep quiet in public and speak in private, pronounce the names of friends in self-preservation while telling them he'd said nothing, then that might be the way to do it and keep everyone happy. All John wanted was the quiet life in the house with the wife and the child, weekends at the beach, a simple career making movies. He knew it would be better for him in the end if he surfed the dominant tide, no sense fighting the current, a riptide takes you down, drags you south along the coast to Mexico, and drops you in a trench from which you never rise. He was inclined to surf, to do what was necessary, so that he could still come home at night having worked an honest day and feel pride in what he had done – the work, not the squealing. Pride itself was an achievement, a rising above his roots. How could pride in good work be anything but a blessing? Cora and Zebulon Marsh had tried to beat the pride out of him, his mother's hand raised as she shouted, You prideful boy. She caught him by his collar, put him over her lap, and spanked him until he could wriggle away from her and run to hide in the apple orchards, scurry through manzanita bushes and shimmy up the flaking bark of madroña trees where Cora could not reach him except with a pitchfork. He had watched her shoot a rattlesnake that split open releasing seven hungry babies and his mother had gone after each of those with an axe, lopping off heads and rattles before throwing their remains on a fire. At the end of John's seventh-grade year, on the final day of school, hot and dusty from the walk up the hill, Cora had put him over her knee, yanked down his pants, welted corrugations into his ass. Why such a beating? He had come home proud of his good grades. See how well I did! See how hard I worked! But no, You prideful boy, you should come home saying, I could work harder. I must not think myself greater than I am. I must know my place. I must always be humble.

With each adult success, his father had sent John a telegram with a single line: HOW WILL YOU KEEP HUMBLE? No word of congratulation or indication that the old man might feel any pride in the work of his son. HOW WILL YOU KEEP HUMBLE? Keep your head down, shoulders slumped, affect inconsequence. Be the sad-sack do-gooding dummy who lies down as doormat to every other man. They thought it was Christian, living by the example of Jesus, but Jesus was never humble. The man was a megalomaniac, any Freudian could see it, one more Oedipal son claiming he had no father but an invisible ghost! Poor Joseph, denied his paternity! What a son, what a horror!

John's parents espoused a spirit of abject humility, ungenerous, mean and denying, all the worse for believing so jealously in their own righteousness. Proud John had been, but prideful he had never felt. Beset by doubt, he was anxious of his own looks and talents, his performance as husband and lover, attentiveness as father, dutifulness as son. Cora and Zebulon, I beg your forgiveness, affection, and care. Wife and parents could give him no love and yet John went on asking for less: see how little love I can live on, see how I will still try to flourish, to be more vigorous for the drought, except that his hunger for love was so great it kept him returning, always hoping to find what would never be there. Nothing prideful about him, never had been, proud only in what he did well, and even still squirming with doubt that he might be delusional. Nothing he made would ever be good enough. Even if he achieved what might seem to him a near-perfect work, someone else would inevitably sneer: How slick, how trivial, how flawed.

April 21, 1950

12

In the midst of thinking back on that distant April day, returning to the scraps of speculative narrative I wrote in the weeks and months – and in some cases years – after my departure from America, trying to imagine the moments for which I was not present, could not have been present, but which I was certain bore on the outcome of that day even if only indirectly, a thought catches the back of my mind, a half-recalled memory, one I imagine might even be retrieved to wholeness if only I were able to locate its origin. It leads me to thinking about memory in a more abstract way and I know there is a book I should consult to help me. The shelves in my study are organized alphabetically, and by chance this means that the Bs are too high for me to reach. I ask Alessio to fetch the volume I have in mind, Bergson's *Matter and Memory*, because it has occurred to me that there may be something in it I have been trying to recall. Alessio smiles, an indulgent smile that says, Why don't you just relax, you don't need to read something so heavy at this time of night, pick up a thriller or watch another old movie, do something you would actually enjoy rather than what you feel you ought to do. But he says none of this and asks me to repeat the title and author. I watch him climb the ladder, his olive hand leading his eye along the spines until he finds the right one. Lips pursed, he gently blows the dust from the top of the book, handles it as if it might fall to pieces, and climbs back down the ladder.

Right at the moment he is about to put the book in my hands he snatches it back, smiling. But only for an hour, he says, wagging a finger, it is getting late and you should go to bed. He means that I should let him put me to bed, although he does little but tuck me in like a child, make sure I am comfortable, and give me a kiss.

Sometimes the kiss lingers, sometimes I think there might even be a surge of desire and not just affection. Once he has put me to bed, he will be free to go out with his friends for a late dinner, perhaps even just around the corner, to the trattoria that makes the most delicious stuffed carciofi. You can go now, I tell him, I will look after myself. Are you sure? he says, and I can see how badly he wants to go, how there must be someone he would like to meet but he has put him or her off because of his sense of duty to me. Go, I say, enjoy the evening. You don't want to come? No, I laugh, you must have your fun. He blushes and I know that I have made a misstep in this bare acknowledgement of the life he lives when I am not present, and the fun that he has. Perhaps with Néstor or someone else like him. This is not the life I imagined when I was with you, Myles. I envisioned us growing old together, loyal to each other until the death of one or the other. I believed that there would be no going behind backs to see younger men. I was sure that we would, in our eighties or nineties, still be kissing each other with desire, if only the memory of the desire we felt as young men. I did not imagine being the elderly child of a beautiful younger man who calls me his partner but goes out at night to fuck other men. I cannot really blame him. I have no stamina for sex these days, as much as I might wish for the pleasure of arousal and consummation. It is enough to be able to look at his beauty, a voyeur in my own home, but it is not how I hoped to end my life.

I page through the book, reading passages I underlined in pencil some years ago, until I find what I think I was trying to remember. Bergson writes that *we can speak of the body as a moving limit between the future and the past, a moving point that our past incessantly pushes into our future.* I find this a beautiful image but also a terrifying one, the idea that for each of us our own private past is the engine propelling us into the future, or not an engine but a tide, a flood. I see myself sitting here at my desk, writing to you, my body driven forward into an unknowable future by the rising tide of my past, a tide always coming in and never going out, pushing me forward, climbing onto an ever-diminishing strip of land, the little crescent of life remaining ahead of me. Before the land runs out and time has drowned me, can I not convince you to join me here, or if you can no longer travel then allow me to visit you? If the idea of my physical presence is more than you can bear, would you at least allow us a conversation, the chance to look at and listen to each other while we still have tongues to speak?

You understand I did not wish for that day in 1950 to end as it did, but every time I opened my mouth to tell you what I was planning only a portion of the truth would come out. The full truth twisted and died, rotting on my tongue. When, over dinner, I described to you and Helen my idea that we should all leave the country – that it was just a question of you securing passports and there was no reason to believe you would be denied them, although I had no idea if this was true – I was surprised by how stunned you both looked because I had fooled myself into believing your love for me was great enough that you could not refuse me, no matter what I asked. Perhaps this is a sign of narcissism, of egoism, my failure ever to see you as a subject in your own right.

Although I had little right to feel aggrieved, I was still hurt that it took only ten minutes for you and Helen to conclude that what I had described was an impossible proposition. *Crazy*, Helen said, and I remember how she hooted, a bitter laughter, as if she resented me for failing to see how such a decision would affect the two of you. I knew you were planning something but I never would've imagined anything so extreme, she said. What were you thinking, Desmond?

You both acted as if I did not understand the gravity of what I was suggesting, as if I did not appreciate what it would mean for your careers, assuming everyone would have believed the fiction we might offer as explanation. I knew that people would talk, that the four of us picking up and starting over in Paris or Rome would lead the gossip columnists to speculate in ways it would be difficult to deny. You acted as if none of this had occurred to me. Of course it had. And it made me angry that you both insisted there were no other places in the world where you could stand before a camera pretending to be people you were not, pretending to inhabit times and places you had never visited, would never visit.

Because this was your response, even before I had started the car I was again questioning my decision to leave. You had just driven away, and I sat behind the wheel, my eyes red with tears, trying to think what to do, how to frame the further revelation I had to make, that I was not only leaving, but leaving the very next morning. As I turned the key in the ignition I felt a surge of music before hearing what song was playing. Someone had been fiddling with the dial of the car radio, leaving the volume turned up so high it almost deafened me with the blast of a trumpet. I quickly turned it down but that sudden cacophony brought back a dream from the previous night, one that I must have had while trying to work at the table in your living room, falling asleep between bouts of writing, my head dropping forward on the typewriter keys. In the dream I kept hearing static as I sat in my living room, and the sound was so persistent that I began tearing at the fabric of my house to find its source. When I pulled down the curtains from the bay window I discovered floor-to-ceiling microphone panels cemented against the walls. I started ripping at the wallpaper and underneath it I found more microphones, plastered near the crown molding. When I removed the expansion leaves of the dining table, I found balanced on the central pedestal a microphone the size of a bathtub, as shiny and black as the eye of a giant horsefly. In the dream I ran my fingers over the plastic mesh and it vibrated at my touch, crackling with static. This was the source, these were the sources, of the static that had bedeviled me. I shouted threats, pushing my mouth against that surface, crying out *You bastards, you fascists, you Nazis! I'll get you! I'm an innocent man!*

I'll get you: stock phrase of wicked witches and half-baked villains. I needed a different script, or I needed no longer to rely on the words of others. It was time to go off book, to stop being predictable, to begin improvising and extemporizing in order to shake the tail that refused to leave me in peace.

On my drive to the Marshes I thought I might catch up to you but I could never see your car in the traffic chute of Sunset. In the Los Angeles night one vehicle looked like another, black or kidney or hunter green, curving scallops of metal catching the glow of twin-headed streetlamps before shooting again into darkness. We should have taken one car. If we had taken one car, what happened later might not have happened. I should have accepted your offer that you would drive me, but your refusal of my suggestion had raised a wall between us and I needed that time to be alone, to think how to move forward. Desperation led me to imagine concocting a lie, perhaps an illness or mysterious diagnosis that required me to seek treatment from a specialist in Switzerland, and I was sure for the space of five minutes that if you heard such a story you would instantly agree to come with me, would apologize for failing to see how ill I obviously was, promising to stay at my side for the rest of my days. It is a wonder I did not have an accident driving to John's house, I was so lost in my reveries about the life we might build in an Alpine chalet, surrounded by snow all the year through.

At Summit Drive a car stopped short behind me and killed its lights. I waited to see who it was, thinking it might have been you, but no one got out. Of course I knew what this meant, that the men who had been watching me for weeks were following now, even as I made my appearance at that odious party.

The two of you were there already, waiting for me at the gate, and we entered the house surrounded by other late arrivals bickering through their marriages of convenience and mutual advancement. In that crowd, even though I was with the two of you, I felt lost and alone. Still in shock from the extraordinary violence I had witnessed as I left the studio that evening, I was guilt-stricken that I had been unable to stop it, and convinced that such attacks were a portent of what awaited me if I stayed in America. I longed to be alone with you for the hours that remained to us, even as I was anxious about what you might do when you heard I was not just leaving in a notional sense, but had already bought a plane ticket and would be on my way to New York the next morning.

Although it was the last thing I felt like that evening, Mary's party finally brought my position into focus, making it possible to see clearly where I stood, who stood with me, who against. I accepted that there were no absolutes. My vision would always be relative and partial and perhaps I was failing to see an obvious detail that would have cast the entire situation in a different light. But already I understood that you were not prepared to come with me, and that my decision to leave would have irreversible effects on the two of us. Given a different run of events – the failure to witness the stoning of a boy who would have been killed with or without my presence, the failure to speak aloud to you and Helen what I was envisaging, the failure to take separate cars to and from the party – I might not have trusted my own perception. I might still have dithered and equivocated, failing to commit to the course of my own future. Everything that happened made my decision possible. All the small decisions, accidents, and coincidences led me to the place where I knew I had no real choice but continuing as I had planned, and that meant leaving whether or not you were willing to accompany me.

Because we were late most of the guests were already drunk and getting drunker. I thought if we stayed together we could protect ourselves from Mary's fascist friends – Disney and Cooper, Reagan and Menjou, Stanwyck and Wayne, Ginger Rogers and her mother, all of them so hard and varnished and pleased with themselves. There was no sign of Hepburn, Bogart, or Bacall, each of them too sensible to show up for the slaughter. Other people, friends and acquaintances I knew for a fact were Communists or fellow travelers, slunk around as if they hoped being seen at such a party might wash them clean of suspicion.

It may take centuries before America finally sees what it did in those years, assuming the country does not tear itself apart before such understanding becomes possible. Americans have the shortest sense of history of any powerful nation on earth. We think ourselves both young and eternal. There is no national memory of centuries of darkness, of those great long lapses in reason that mark the millennial histories of older civilizations. For Americans, embarking on a hundred years' war is taken as lightly as coming to the aid of distant allies. There is no ability to see that a step in the wrong direction cannot be corrected overnight but may take epochs to put right. True Liberty is imperiled by the drive towards oppression fueled by greed, marching nonetheless under the banner of Liberty. True Liberty is nothing like what Mary and her friends imagined, but instead an assurance of total equality among all people, of whatever race, creed, or national origin, including those who remain marginal or liminal because they cannot or will not fit inside the available categories. Is such liberty possible? What if you are not either/or and could never bring yourself to be one thing or the other? What if you feel like a socialist in the morning and a capitalist in the afternoon? What if you go to bed with a man every night but still notice the beauty of women and your mind runs along tracks of fantasy that you never intend exploring while always wanting to hold open the route to alternative destinations? What if you cannot be content with the limited choices at the automat of life that offers only pre-packaged portions of identity and purpose?

I will not be cottage cheese or cling peaches.
I will not be rice pudding or lime Jell-O.
I will not be roast beef or chicken salad.
Oh, Barbara Stanwyck,
I want to write my own goddamn menu,
So please sit down and shut up.

John met us in the foyer with that unfocussed cerebral expression he always wore after mixing alcohol with other drugs. I knew that the evening would not end well when he spoke and his words came out with the sticky viscosity of rubber cement. I'm an exile in my own home, dear friends, he said, so take a bottle if you can snatch one. You're in time for the fireworks.

In the backyard a chrysanthemum of red and blue sparks exploded overhead, revealing couples in the shadows, arms pawing legs, hands reaching under dresses. They call us perverts, I laughed, but look how decorous we are compared to them.

You glanced at me anxiously, as if you were afraid I would expose you. I had noticed that look more and more in recent weeks, every time I approached you on the set or spoke too loudly in public.

Nick Charles raced past, chasing a young actress. It was obvious she was not enjoying the pursuit.

Rapist! Helen screamed, and a few men near us laughed. Goddammit, it's not a joke!

Even this made you look anxious. Calm down, Helen, you said, trying to take her arm, but she jerked away from you.

As soon as New York promotes Porter, just watch, he'll make Nick Charles Head of Production and then that little schmuck will do whatever he likes, she said.

The band played the fireworks towards a finale that was only the first of the evening. Half the guests were in thrall to the pyrotechnics, half to one another, and all of them looked stoned.

The irony is, half of this crowd is queer, I said, only their husbands and wives don't know it.

Again I was aware of you flinching away, trying to distance yourself physically, as if you feared being seen next to me.

Over the years, as I have thought of what followed and read accounts of the party in histories of the period and in the memoirs of those present, my own recollection becomes complicated by the feeling that you had already turned against me. You moved to accept a glass of champagne from a young waiter and then stepped to one side so that Helen was standing between us. You took a glass for her as well, but left me to take my own. No matter, I could do it easily, but you had never been so unsolicitous in the past. Coldness marked you, your face froze, there was no glimmer of pleasure in your eyes or mouth, not the least performance of happiness. Of course I understand that this was my fault, but it did not make it easier. Maybe I should have left that very moment and allowed you to discover for yourself that I had gone when I did not answer the phone the next day. That would have been cruel as well, but perhaps no more so than drawing out the revelation as I did.

The evening's spectacle, Mary's carnival of Red-baiting, has stuck in my mind as among the most surreal moments of my life. It took a certain audacity to turn her own birthday into a Nuremberg Rally for the Republican Party. I assume you remember the grotesqueness of it, but I cannot trust you to appreciate what role it played in confirming to me that only one choice remained, and that was flight.

As a drumroll reached its crescendo, the lights dimmed and a spotlight picked out Mary in the center of the terrace. I noticed that she was gazing directly at John, who was standing to my right. The costume she had put herself in, a blue gown adorned with golden stars, her shoulders draped with an ivory silk shawl, suggested an attempt to present herself as a secular Madonna. It would have looked ludicrous anywhere else in the world, at any other time, but this was Mary's own little blockbuster production and the guests in the garden were ready to buy what she was selling. Her voice crackled through the speakers as she told us that America was God's guarantee of peace in the world, not just in our own time but for all time. Until the return of Christ, America would be God's standard bearer and swordsman. The tone was saccharine, humorless, lacking all irony, and it reeked of Nick Charles.

This is a nation of light, she continued as searchlights swept across the garden, picking out the roofs of neighboring houses and pushing night beyond Holmby Hills and Beverly Hills and the Hollywood Hills, out to the valleys, to the cities of the plain where audiences of stricken Americans quaked in expectation of their judgment day, huddling in blackened movie houses to watch every patriotic spectacle we fed them, praying against atomic holocaust and blaming their state of terror entirely on the tidal wave of socialism and unbelief sweeping from the east, as if their own country had nothing to do with it, as if we had not dropped the first atomic bombs ourselves. That is what I saw, and when my eyes had adjusted to the brilliance, registering the group of men and women in white processing behind Mary, the silver chariot drawn by a man dressed as a griffin with a giant fiberglass eagle's head on his shoulders rolling in to receive her, I recognized in the crowd a hunger to watch such fantasy and not just suspend disbelief but actively to believe that what they were witnessing must be true. Such shifting from mere openness to set aside rational thought for the space of ninety minutes' entertainment to a more permanent and simple-minded openness to embracing fantasy as the substance of everyday life was what made Hollywood so lucrative, and the America that followed it such a dangerous, childish place.

This was Mary's enthronement, her apotheosis, and her cleansing of herself before the community that might decide to turn against her if she did not sacrifice the people who had once been her friends. One of the men in white placed a crown of laurels on her head and another thrust a blazing torch into her left hand, while a third wrapped her in a green robe and placed a tablet in her right hand, transforming that secular Madonna into Lady Liberty, uniting Church and State in one diabolical costume change. If it had all ended there it would have been bad enough, but then the music shifted to a medley of patriotic folksongs cuing the entrance of the three blonde girls in red, white, and blue dresses, spiraling as Mary stepped into the chariot, all of them whirling round the terrace, dancing with conviction however badly choreographed they were. If this was meant to be a vision of American beauty, as seemed the intention, it suggested despite itself a place of chaos that should have been easily swept aside by the four other dancers, women in black wigs and red babushkas wielding scythes, who entered with a crash of cymbals. What will happen? I wondered. Will the poor American girls succumb to the Soviet handmaidens? No, of course not, because like every movie made in that era the plot was rigged to punish the villains: Mary intervened, holding her torch and tablet aloft and chasing the black-wigged dancers off the terrace and into the dark.

I wonder if Mary ever considered that the historical pageant ending her spectacle was in bad taste, that having actors dressed as George Washington and Abraham Lincoln speaking about *revolutions just and revolutions vile* and the need for *the just to vanquish what is evil lest darkness conquer the earth,* and choreographing Washington to go charging off stage with his sword raised, or Lincoln speaking about the ways that *mature revolutions seek to liberate those left behind, to bring light to the dark and so uplift mankind* might be hubristic. Did it ever strike her that employing four black extras from the studio to play slaves whose chains would be broken by Lincoln's own hand might be a desecration? Or that having the men sit at Lincoln's feet staring adoringly over at Mary, their white savior, as a piccolo played a spiritual melody might be flagrantly racist? I doubt it. My stomach churned as Mary smiled at those four men, the music becoming rural and folksy to accompany the approach of an elderly actor dressed as a farmer holding a Bible above his head. How moved so many people looked, how tearful and *credulous* when Mary took the Bible and held it out, calling on us to Behold! The book of our nation, our faith, and our progress! The book that shows us the way!

When I turned to you and Helen I hoped to see some hint in your expressions that you found it as disturbing as I did, but you were rapt, Myles, and seeing your face, the tears welling in your own eyes as the band began playing the opening bars of 'The Battle Hymn of the Republic', watching you join to sing along with everyone else, I thought: I do not know him at all, not at all. I have only tricked myself into believing that I know this man whom I allow to enter my body, whose own body he allows me to enter, but such entrances and caring do not mean that we actually have any idea who the other person is. That you could be moved rather than disgusted by what was unfolding before us suggested I would never really understand you, that your boyhood in Montana – if that's even where you were from, if I can actually trust that the stories you told me about your origins were true – was so remote from my own America that even if I thought I understood you I would never be able to predict what moved you or frightened you or gave you consolation. Perhaps, over a lifetime, I might have come to understand. Perhaps it would not have taken even that long. A decade? How many years until I knew what your weaknesses were, what would make you cry or compromise your own ethical stance, assuming you even had one?

By that time I was long past ready to leave, but Krug and Porter stepped to the microphone to do their tiresome double act, that standard of Hollywood variety and award shows, straight out of vaudeville, patronizing us all, Dear friends, ladies and gentlemen, it gives us great pleasure to be here tonight to celebrate the birthday of one of our family's brightest stars, Porter starts, the straight man (ironically) to Krug's joker, *it's so bright I need shades*, and the polite smattering of laughter for the first of his gags, not loud enough to drown out Porter as he tells us that Mary has spent her entire career at our great studio, reminding us that she came to Los Angeles looking for stardom like everyone else, arriving at the studio gates as one more extra with a dream, but unlike so many others the studio recognized her native talent and cleared the path for her ascent to the stratosphere, to become one of America's most beloved leading ladies, and though he would like to tell us how much Mary is worth to the studio Krug nails the timing and interrupts, *but we don't want her to ask for a raise*, and the crowd laughs more genuinely but again not so loudly that they interrupt the flow as Porter doubles down on the patriotism, telling us all how much Mary *means* to America, how she herself, if you can believe it – this coming from a man who loves Miles Davis and Robert Motherwell and *Physique Pictorial* – is a symbol of liberty and freedom, a representative of what is best about our nation, an unelected senator of common sense, fighter against tyranny, totalitarianism and oppression in all its forms, a patriot on the side of the angels, and there is Krug's third cue, allowing him the biggest laugh of the night, *but what a devil when it comes to contract negotiation!*, and the whole place erupts because *everyone* knows that Krug is the one speaking the truth, revealing just how canny and conniving and strategic Mary is. She plays her part as well, blushing and laughing and shooing them with her hands as if it's all too embarrassing, the jokes so ridiculous they couldn't be further from the truth, Porter's sentimental stuff so true that she could only be humble in the face of such praise, and this continues as the two men harangue us into singing 'Happy Birthday', and as she listens, watching the hired maître d' wheel out a three-tiered cake decorated with sparklers, Mary clutches her hands to her chest as if genuinely surprised, but I could see how she was glowing, how it was coming off precisely as she planned. It was time for the final act of her performance.

I turned to Helen and she whispered to me, You have to hand it her, she always cries on cue.

Were you still in thrall, Myles? Were you among those who believed in the fantasy? Was it too difficult to watch a fellow actor putting on such a brazen performance of falsity and *not* believe it? Would not believing it have revealed something to you about yourself that you could not have stomached? Would it have been too destructive to your own illusion of yourself?

Mary paused a moment to be sure we were listening. She stared at John, her gaze always returning to him after it had flitted across the crowd. All this had been for him. I could see it at last.

A great many of you know I grew up on a farm, she began. Like the farmer in our little pageant tonight, I have always turned to the word of God as guide for the way I live, and as a prophesy of what is yet to come for all people. My grandparents were immigrants who sought freedom in this great nation, and thanks to their courage I have grown up in the land of the free. I feel it my duty to defend this country that has given me everything: my success, my family and friends, and most of all my fans. What would any of us be in this business without our fans, those ordinary Americans who look to us as examples and guides, who learn how best to live from the stories we tell, who understand from the struggles we depict what one should do, and what one must never do, the pleasures of doing good, and the perils and punishments that come from doing what God does not intend. It is our responsibility as practitioners of this young art to live unblemished lives, to work in the service of liberty, to make ourselves embodiments of the goodness enshrined in the founding of the greatest country in the world. We cannot falter in our fight against tyranny, whether it be the tyranny of Nazis or the far greater tyranny of those Communist agents bent on infiltrating and undermining our nation from within, like the parasite that will feed on its host, those monsters who wish to destroy this country, and our great history. We must search out and eliminate the subversives among us, either by converting those wayward souls to the holiness of liberty, or seeing to it that they pay for their evil beliefs, pay for what they have done and hope to do by putting them in prison or, in the case of foreign agents, deporting them as swiftly as possible. America cannot rest on its laurels, we cannot falter in our vigilance, either at home or abroad. We are the envy of the world just as we must be the keeper of the world, and knowing that position and responsibility we must guard against attempts to dilute our strength or distract us from our mission. I thank you all for coming tonight, and invite you to celebrate but also to reflect on what each of you good people might do to make this nation safe for liberty, for all those ordinary Americans out there, in places like Oklahoma and Ohio and Wyoming, people who can only dream of the lives we are privileged to live in this little colony of light, and know that each of us has a duty to our fans to be examples and guides, to take our place in the political life of this nation. Think for a moment, she said, softening her voice, just think…

I looked around at the faces of the people I knew and did not know, some of them, like you, appearing transformed, a few like me sneering, others visibly alarmed. When Mary lit the silence with laughter it caught in the microphone and exploded as a whine of feedback that made me jump. I guess I forgot this is a party, she said. Let's not be solemn now. Have a piece of cake and fill your glasses. Please enjoy yourselves, and thank you for coming, my friends. It means so much to this simple country girl.

Thunderous applause, cheers from the men, polite smiles from the women, an orchestrated chorus of 'For She's a Jolly Good Fellow', and then I watched as John pushed through the crowd, charging up to the terrace and into Mary's arms. He took her face in his hands, kissed her, and the crowd cheered. For the handful of press photographers who had been admitted, John and Mary posed, smiling. You said that we should congratulate her, and I said I'd rather not, and Helen said it would be bad form not to, and I said I've never cared much about form, and she said that's the privilege of never having had to think about money, and I said is that a criticism, and she said no, Desmond, I'm just being honest. Not all of us grew up so liberated.

I lost you and Helen in the crush and by the time I reached John and Mary I was alone and the three of us stood apart from everyone else. What Mary said next I believe she would have said if every microphone in the country had been recording her words. I'd like you to leave, Desmond. My husband invited you but this is my party and you're not welcome. Then she turned, walked across the terrace and down into the garden, her face cracked in two by the breadth of her smile.

When I turned to John he looked away from me. She wants me to come with her tomorrow, Desmond. I think it might be the only good choice I have.

I told him I didn't think he was feeling himself, that he was tired from the shooting, he'd been drinking all day, the bromide and bourbon this morning and champagne this evening and the stress of all that had happened was deranging him. I know I failed to choose my words well because he turned to stare at me with a look I had never seen from him before. It told me we were finished. Maybe I am deranged, he said, but maybe I should just do what she says. Life will be easier that way.

What you're proposing would mean I could no longer be your friend, John.

Unlike you, I'm a family man. I have to consider that, too.

Is that how it is?

That's how it is, Desmond. The abruptness in his voice surprised me.

Then don't expect to hear from me again. I have to find Helen and Myles and then I'll leave. I won't make any trouble. Don't worry.

Desmond…

No, that's okay. Good luck finishing our picture. I hope they let you.

This time I did not wait for John to reply. He had bent and twisted so many times over the course of the day, so many times over the years we had worked together, that I no longer had the patience to see if he would change direction again. Flexible and feeble as his beliefs so often proved, I had nonetheless hoped that he would be sensible and good-hearted enough to see through the distortion and ugliness of Mary's Red-baiting, a campaign that was, at its charred heart, about greediness and thuggery and fear of a world in which everyone was as free as Mary imagined Americans already were but in truth could never be unless they were rich and happened also to believe precisely what she and her cadre of fascists espoused. People like Mary, the poor-made-good who had struggled and strived to hunt with the native-born wealthy in their own habitat, could never see their own position. You had to be born rich to understand how the advantages accrued through generations of wealth were engrained in ways that the impoverished, the middle classes, and even the newly rich could not wholly imagine. It was not just about what you could buy but all the things you never had to think about buying, the world of possessions and property you never needed to acquire in the first place, the doors that opened without force, the ways access could be assumed rather than requested, the ease with which outsiders could be policed, expelled, or expended. This was something you yourself could not see, Myles, and your own naïveté always pained me.

I could not find you so I took another glass of champagne from a passing silver tray and slumped at the foot of a tree. Other guests were glancing in my direction and I wondered if I had been speaking my thoughts aloud. It would not have been surprising since I spent so much of my waking life with an interior monologue, passing comment on the people around me, people who would have been horrified to learn what I really thought – not just about them, but also my desires and prejudices, the way that despite myself epithets of race, national origin, and class struck automatically in my mind like notes on the roll of a player piano plinking a score composed by my parents and grandparents, by the society that surrounded me, and even though I could instruct it to create more interesting and varied music, melodies of nuance and heart, the roll would always eventually return to its beginning, to the first chords that, even within their lovely if simple melodies, contained notes of fear and self-justification inherited from the people who brought me into the world.

Overhead I searched for that night's waning crescent moon but it was inconstant as John Marsh, swayed by the first passing star, lit and extinguished and lit again, according to its fancy. If memory could fade as easily as the moon one might lead a happier life but certainly not a truer one. Golden in a white tuxedo, Apollo walked across the lawn, the passing image of Noah Roy, always wandering out of reach. I bit my cheek and tasted blood. It is now a struggle to capture what remains of my memories of Noah, to hear the score of our love for each other, though *love* is an inadequate word, *romance* as well, *partnership* too businesslike. *Passion* might come closest, since *passion* contains both beauty and horror, pleasure and suffering. *Passion* can be either noun or verb: my *passion* for him, the *passion* of his martyrdom, the *passion* between us, the man who was my *passion*; and then, in action, I was *passioned* by him, this too can be said, or we *passioned* our voices together. I stood looking at my reflection in his polished tombstone beneath the cedar tree, wherein I *passioned to see myself escap'd from so sore ills*. That was Keats before I took it as my own.

This music of memory plays in spurts and squalls of noise, like a film pieced together from unrelated clips or scenes edited without regard for continuity. The challenge is always to keep the story of Noah – or you, if I am thinking of you, Myles, as I have been throughout these pages – contiguous in my head, writing it over and over to keep from losing it now at my death. Agon is all that remains, the contest of remembering, replaying, and containing without loss the little I yet grasp. How was Noah different from you? It was never only a question of appearance or physical attraction, since you were objectively the more beautiful, but of a flawless synchrony and understanding, the sense of never needing to translate ourselves to each other. If I spoke what I felt, Noah would respond in a way that made clear his complete understanding of that feeling. I cannot remember us arguing, although perhaps time and grief conspire to erase what was imperfect, and the first love is always the one we wish to magnify beyond all others, the love for which one feels oneself capable of total sacrifice, of being willing, literally, to give up one's life for another. I had never felt this for you, Myles. I must confess that. Noah read me as I read Noah, two minds reading each other as the self reads itself. I do not think I can say that of you.

Lanterns swayed across the lawns, their light turning faces into waxworks wet with insobriety. I tried to stand but my legs buckled and I sat down again hard on the grass. I did not want to leave without you, whose body and tenderness, whose capacity to reflect my desires and dreams, might let me pretend Noah was still alive, one last time. Perhaps that was all you ever were to me, a vessel for memories of someone else.

A full moon of two hands, one clear and pearlescent, the other mottled gray, joined together in front of me, reaching down out of darkness. It was the man and his daughter who had given me a lift that morning, standing above me.

What are you doing here? I asked them, staggering to my feet. I didn't imagine I'd see you at a bloodbath like this.

They are friends of friends, the daughter explained. We do not really know anyone in fact. Schoenberg was supposed to come I thought but he must have heard what was afoot. We cannot find him anywhere.

No, my dear, the man corrected, they are *friends* of friends of friends. The Feuchtwangers, around whom all else revolves I think, they know the husband. Who can keep track with so many spheres of connection. Always there are too many.

Or sometimes not enough, I said, conscious of the laughing faces around us, cheeks ripe, like background figures from Beckmann or Dix, ready to transform from louche to goose-stepping in the space of one night.

Chaplin told us to come. He said it would be grisly.

And of course now he does not come. This is so like him. Unreliable. Unpredictable.

But so very charming.

I think these American fascists are preparing their own book-burning squads, do you not find? Exhibitions and dismissals of *Entartete Kunst*, how do you say in English? Obscene art?

Degenerate.

Degenerate art, yes. They do not see how degenerate they are themselves. What trouble they make. And this time also it will be motion pictures. Mountains of celluloid smoking in this desert. It is a nice image, perhaps, but a horrible one. As I told you this morning, I go to Scandinavia soon. Maybe I do not come back. At least there they do not think I am aiding in plots to overthrow western civilization. Imagine, the old man sighed. These people are philistines.

Don't, Papa, the woman said, touching his arm.

I told them I was sorry to leave them, but I had an early start the next day.

Once again you are in no state to drive, Mr. Frank, the daughter said. Perhaps we could give you a lift? We have always our car.

I came with friends. I have to find them. I hope I'll see you again in a more sympathetic setting.

As the man and his daughter made their way towards the house, there was a sudden clattering, shrieks of laughter and alarm, and then a disturbance of bodies making way for a man, bumbling and slow, one arm outstretched and swinging. It was not Frankenstein's monster, as it first appeared, but John Marsh, pursuing Nick Charles, who sprinted pale and erect through a bed of tulips.

You know there's a rumor Nick Charles killed his own mother, a woman near me said.

A man next to her laughed. Not killed: *sold*. That boy's got ambition. Slick as mercury.

Waiters and waitresses passed through the garden planting blue and white lanterns, softening the party into a vision of wonderland. I wandered around hedges and pergolas until I came to the tennis court where you had been hiding. At first I did not see you amid the clusters of people sitting on that close-clipped lawn, but then your face caught the light, angled towards a lithe young man who might have been Montgomery Clift or Farley Granger, the two of you reclining and chatting, nothing more than that, but in such an intimate way that it looked as if you were already lovers. My heart throbbed with jealousy. I picked a path through the other people until I was standing above you.

Where have you been? you asked, all innocence.

Looking for you, Myles. It's time we left.

I turned around earlier and you were gone. That pageant, whatever it was, wasn't it the limit?

The limit, laughed the lithe young man.

You can say that again, I said.

I just did, laughed the lithe young man.

Ha-ha, I said, deadpan.

You're as funny as Myles said, laughed the lithe young man. I wanted to hit him but as my fist rose I lost my balance and had to lean against the court's chain-link fence. The waiters and waitresses were installing torches around the perimeter and I began to see that the tennis court contained everyone Mary would have wanted to eliminate from her vision of America, all the Jews and queers and blacks and yellows and browns, all the people who had come for John's sake rather than hers, writers and philosophers, directors and designers, most of them exiles from places they had thought darker than the one they chose as refuge, a novelist whose whole family had been killed in Dachau, a philosopher who had fled Berlin days after the Reichstag fire, a playwright who had done the same and arrived in Los Angeles with a contract from Paramount, a satirist who had smuggled himself out of Paris in a steamer trunk, a cinematographer who was traveling in America at the time of the Anschluss and had never been able to return to Vienna, a screenwriter fired from UFA along with all the other Jewish artists, a composer and impresario, a couturier, a Talmudic scholar, a poet, a romantic versifier, a cultural critic. One of them, a philosopher, turned sharply in my direction. How can you laugh? he demanded. There's no humor now. How can you laugh about anything? Who are *you* to laugh?

I'm laughing at what people like our hostess would choose to do to people like us, given the chance.

Gallows humor, the philosopher said, almost spitting. He sat up straighter in the flickering torchlight. I do not think enough time has passed for gallows humor. I do not know that enough time ever will have passed for gallows humor. I try to laugh at innocent jokes and the air inside me turns to poison. This whole place is toxic. I came here believing every myth this country makes up about itself, more fool I. I thought I had escaped into a land without darkness. You see the pictures of American faces, so innocent, so clean and hopeful and earnest, and you think: This is a place for hope to flourish. And then you get here and see that while it might not be like the place you escaped, there is just as much darkness, only the darkness here is only now returning. Cycles of night. I cannot live in the dark.

But where's safe? I asked.

Nowhere, the man said. The mistake is believing anywhere is safe from darkness.

It's time to go, you said, taking my hand without hesitation and pulling yourself up from where you were sitting. You said goodbye to your lithe young friend and I tried to tame my jealousy as we picked our way through the crowd on the tennis court and back across the garden, finding Helen inside, already in her coat, looking as if her world had ended.

She was almost tearful when she spoke. I've been waiting ages for you two. I thought maybe you'd left without me. Let's get out of here. Who's too drunk to drive?

I am, I heard myself say.

You drive him, Myles, I'll take our car.

I felt your hand reach inside my pocket to retrieve the key.

Outside, idling on Summit Drive, a dozen limousines were lined up waiting for passengers who refused to come.

SHE TURNED AWAY

Part Five

EXT. FAYE'S HOUSE - NIGHT

Faye's secret house is a squat bungalow that sits in
a long narrow lot on Cynthia Street where jacarandas
wave in the moonlight.

Faye parks in the driveway at the back of the
property and she and Orph slip in through the kitchen
door, checking over their shoulders to be sure they
haven't been followed. The bell of a church tolls
once, sad and hollow.

INT. FAYE'S HOUSE - NIGHT

Faye brushes past Orph to lock the door from the
inside, her movements slowing and smoldering as her
hand rests against the knob.

                    ORPH
     Don't you have to get home?

                    FAYE
     Jack won't miss me. The guest bedroom is down
     the hall. I'm upstairs.

                    ORPH
     Not afraid of me?

                    FAYE
     Plenty afraid, Corporal, but I'm not a fool.

She opens her purse and shows him the butt of her
gun.

                        FAYE (CONT'D)

No fast moves. You have your room. I have
mine.

                        ORPH

Hot and cold, sister. Last night I was ready
to run away with you. I thought you felt the
same.

                        FAYE

If the world turns cold, so do I.

She pulls down the blinds, switches on a light over
the sink, pours herself a glass of water, and stands
looking out the window. Outside, lamplight filters
through the fans of plumose leaves.

                        FAYE (CONT'D)

There's a shower off the kitchen, but if you
want a bath you'll have to wait until morning.

                        ORPH

I want to thank you, Faye.

                        FAYE

You're not safe yet. You won't be until you
get out of Los Angeles. I hope you understand
we're finished. Jack would never let me get
away.

                        ORPH

Supposing I could take care of Jack?

                          FAYE

Don't be a fool. Eddie may be dead but there's
a whole pack of other thugs, not to mention
Woody Montez. If Jack wants you gone you'll
wake up on the other side before you even know
you're in trouble.

                          ORPH

Did Jack kill Ursula?

Faye swings around, back against the sink. The light
hits her eyes and there's something half-crazed in
her face.

                          FAYE

Jack? No... Jack didn't kill Ursula. Why don't
you give up on her already?

                          ORPH

Maybe I loved her.

                          FAYE

I thought you loved me.

                          ORPH

The truth is I could never tell you apart.

                          FAYE

That's a rotten thing to say.

                    ORPH

Maybe I wanted you both.

                    FAYE

You're just a spoiled kid, aren't you?

          (a beat as Orph smirks)

You can stay until tomorrow and then you're
gone. Find a taxi to the station and get a
train as far as you can go. Keep traveling
until you're at the end of a road that goes
nowhere, then step off that road and walk
through the fields as long as your legs will
carry you. Only then can you sit down and
stop. Build a house, find a wife who doesn't
already have a husband, play your music, have
some kids, raise a white picket fence. This
one's not for sale.

Orph starts to speak but Faye puts a hand over his
mouth. He takes her fingers from his lips and kisses
them. Faye pauses, feeling his breath on her skin,
and then, slow and cold, she pulls her hand free.

Watching until Faye disappears up the stairs, Orph
finds his way through the darkened hallway to a
little bedroom at the back of the house. Still half-
drunk, he collapses against the mattress.

                    ORPH (V.O.)

Only way I could see clear of this mess was
confronting Jack, face-to-face, brother-to-

brother. If I could look him in the eye and
ask him to tell me the truth, then I'd know
for sure. I didn't care what Faye said, I was
already certain they both knew the truth about
Ursula, and I'd put all my money on Jack being
responsible. I couldn't sleep and then I heard
Faye moving around above me.

Orph leaves the guest bedroom and goes upstairs where
he finds Faye coming out of the bathroom, wet hair
knotted in a towel. She edges past him, turning her
back and walking towards her bedroom. On the back of
her neck, Orph notices a distinctive birthmark in the
shape of an oak leaf. He looks once and looks again.

In a flash, everything makes sense. He grabs Faye by
the shoulders, twisting her round to face him.

> ORPH

I said I could never tell the two of you
apart, but there was one thing I always knew
to look for to be sure it was you.

> FAYE

I don't know what you're talking about.

> ORPH

That birthmark on the back of your neck. A
little oak leaf. Faye didn't have one, did
she, Ursula? It's been you all this time,
hasn't it? It's not you who's been missing,
it's Faye!

Her eyes flare as she whips off the towel, hair
falling across her shoulders.

                    FAYE

     You're crazy, Orph, and you're drunk. You
     don't know what you're talking about. I am
     Faye.

                    ORPH

     Like hell you are. Faye was too good to do
     half the things you've done since I came back.
     Faye was a saint and an innocent. And Faye had
     a neck like a sheet of silk. She didn't have
     this –

He grabs her again by the shoulders, pulls the hair
away and looks hard at the birthmark, pinching it
between his thumb and index finger.

Ursula, for now it is undoubtedly Ursula, swings back
from Orph, slaps him hard in the face, and rushes
into the bedroom, locking the door behind her.

                ORPH (CONT'D)
            (banging on the door)

     Does Jack know who you are? Is that Faye lying
     dead in the morgue? Did you throw her in the
     river or was it Jack? Tell me, Ursula! I'd
     like to hear the truth!

The bedroom door squeaks open and the barrel of a gun
pokes through the crack. Ursula pulls the door wide,

stepping into the hall as Orph backs towards the
stairs.

                    URSULA

You've been trouble ever since you came back.
I don't know why someone couldn't have dropped
a bomb on you over there. It would have made
everything simpler. Eddie could have taken the
fall for Faye and it would have been neat and
painless.

                    ORPH

What kind of monster kills her own sister?

                    URSULA

I'm the victim more than she was. I'm the one
who's suffered! When she found out about me
and Jack she threatened to tell you!

                    ORPH

What do you mean, you and Jack?

                    URSULA

We're in love, Orph. Always have been. It should
have been me and Jack from the beginning, but
somehow... If only things had been different we
wouldn't be in this mess. I couldn't let Faye
ruin what I have. It should have been simple,
but Faye loved Jack more than you can imagine.
She fought for him, and she lost.

                              ORPH

But how? How did you do it?

                             URSULA

We were at Woody's place in Palm Springs...

FLASHBACK TO:

EXT. WOODY'S HOUSE - DAY

A bright afternoon at the modern desert house. In
matching swimsuits, one black, one white, the twin
sisters lounge by the pool as Jack and Woody and
Eddie and some other HEAVIES play poker in the shade.

There are other people in the background, Modest
Jones and the woman who called herself Rose Zapatero,
even little Nancy Jean and Lillian Wesley and the
waitress from the diner where Orph met with Noah Roy.

                          URSULA (V.O.)

Only it's not Woody's place. It's Jack's.
Everywhere you've been, everything you've seen
since you came home, it all belongs to your
brother. The apartment where I lived, the car
I drive, the clothes I wear, the club, the
house in Pasadena, the flophouse downtown,
even this house, Jack owns it all. Everyone
you've met and spoken to, everyone who's
chased you and helped you and led you along,
they're all paid by Jack. Faye, too, she got
paid just like the rest of us, only she didn't
want to keep quiet.

                              551

From beneath her sunglasses Faye looks across at her sister, and then, past the pool, to the gazebo where the men play cards and smoke and drink.

Jack makes no attempt to hide his interest in Ursula when she turns over on her stomach.

                    FAYE
          (whispering to Ursula)

What do you suppose you're doing?

                    URSULA

Don't be such a prude.

                    FAYE

You forget I have a husband. And so do you.

                    URSULA

He's on tour, didn't you hear?

                    FAYE

But mine isn't.

                    URSULA

If you did more to keep him interested you wouldn't have to worry so much. Besides, there's plenty of Jack to go around.

Faye sits up, looking as though she might be ready to hurl a brick at her sister. Jack notices, smirks, and

turns his back on his wife and sister-in-law. Faye's
fingers twitch as she stands.

                    FAYE

    I'm going to get a drink.

Ursula blinks into Faye's backlit face: a gray oval
of skin surrounded by a mane of fire. The two gape at
each other as if calculating their next moves.

                    URSULA

    Didn't Mother ever tell you not to drink
    alone? I'll join you.

INT. WOODY MONTEZ HOUSE - DAY

In Woody's living room the blinds are drawn and
everything is heavy and silent. Ursula carries a bag
over her shoulder.

                    FAYE

    Afraid someone's going to mug you?

                    URSULA

    No honor among thieves.

                    FAYE

    I'm warning you, Ursula. Leave Jack alone. If
    you don't, I'll go to the cops and tell them
    just what business Jack's into. He thinks I'm
    such an innocent, sweet little Faye, but I
    listen all right. I know where the bodies are
    buried, I know how he cooks the accounts, I

know names and numbers and times and places.
I've been watching and remembering since I
first realized what Jack really was. And I'll
tell them everything they want to know. I'll
bring all of you down.

                    URSULA

You wanna watch out, Faye. Talk like that
might get you sieved.

Faye begins mixing martinis. She fills two glasses
while Ursula removes her shades and drops them into
her bag. They clatter against a bottle of pills.

                URSULA (CONT'D)

What, no olives?

Faye pouts and leaves the room. While she's away,
Ursula pulls the pill bottle from her bag, crushes up
several tablets under a spoon, and stirs the powder
into one of the glasses until it dissolves. Ursula
picks up the other glass as Faye returns with a jar
of olives.

                URSULA (CONT'D)
            (leaving the room)

Changed my mind.

Faye scowls, opens the jar, and drops an olive into
the drink that Ursula has spiked, then follows her
sister back outside.

EXT. WOODY MONTEZ HOUSE – DAY

Faye, still holding her martini, steps into the
water, puts her drink down at the side of the pool,
and climbs onto a floating air mattress.

                    URSULA (V.O.)

  I just wanted to scare her a little, put her
  to sleep for a few hours and disappear with
  Jack. I couldn't have known what would happen.
  You have to understand that, Orph.

Faye retrieves her martini, drinks it in one long
swallow, returns the glass to the side, and pushes
herself away from the edge.

As the afternoon dissolves into twilight and Ursula
frolics with the other guests in the garden, Faye
falls asleep, and sleeps, and continues to sleep. And
then, once everyone else has forgotten her, she turns
over and slips into the water.

                URSULA (V.O.) (CONT'D)

  We didn't find her until it was too late.

Ursula is the first to notice her sister floating
face-down in the pool. She takes a long drag on her
cigarette, drops it to the concrete, and stubs it out
under the toe of her sandal. For a moment her hands
rest on her hips, and then, without any sense of
urgency, she calls for her dead sister's husband.

URSULA

Jack, I think your wife had one drink too
many.

Jack, Woody, Eddie, Modest Jones, Rose Zapatero, the
whole group of them come over and stare at the body.
Lillian covers her daughter Nancy Jean's eyes. Woody
and Eddie wade into the pool and pull Faye's lifeless
body onto the patio.

URSULA (V.O.)

I wanted to phone the cops but Jack said he
couldn't have his wife dying right under his
nose. We invented a story that she'd gone
away, and I carried on as myself until you
came back. But for me to become Faye, Ursula
had to die. I was going to go on being Faye
for the rest of my life.

BACK TO PRESENT:

INT. FAYE'S SECRET HOUSE - NIGHT

Standing on the upstairs landing of the little West
Hollywood bungalow Orph looks stricken.

ORPH

Drowned girls don't run off through the trees.

URSULA

Always trying to save a life, aren't you,
Corporal? Maybe you should have thought more
about your own. Now move.

556

                    ORPH

Where are we going?

                    URSULA

Back to the club. Jack'll know what to do.

Ursula pushes him with the barrel of her gun, nudging
him down the stairs.

INT. URSULA'S CAR - NIGHT

Ursula forces Orph into the driver's seat of her car.

                URSULA (CONT'D)

    You drive. And if you've got any ideas left in
    that sentimental head of yours, you'd better
    lose 'em quick.

Orph reverses out the drive, Ursula's gun still poked
in his ribs. He turns a corner, accelerates up San
Vicente and turns right on Sunset. Even though it's
the middle of the night the street is pulsing with
cars and people on foot coming out of clubs.

                URSULA (CONT'D)

    I was sure you'd forget about me when you
    thought I was gone. You never loved me, so why
    stick around? Why not get lost?

                    ORPH

I didn't know what was bad for me.

                    URSULA

    Shut up why don't you?

                     ORPH

    You're doing a foolish thing, Ursula.

She jabs the barrel of the gun deeper between his
ribs.

                    URSULA

    You look a little flushed. Maybe you need some
    ventilation.

                     ORPH

    Nothing but hot air in here.

Orph pulls to a stop outside Malavita. He and Ursula
slide off the car's front seat together, both exiting
on the driver's side.

EXT. MALAVITA - NIGHT

Doing a double-take over his shoulder, Orph sees a
car pull to a stop down the block. There's a snap-
brim hat inside that suggests the G-man Orph met
earlier.

INT. MALAVITA BACKSTAGE - NIGHT

Inside the club, the last act finished hours ago and
nearly everyone has left for the night. Ursula steers
Orph through the deserted hallways, keeping her gun
in the small of his back. As they climb stairs and

                      558

slouch down another long corridor, it starts to feel like a maze, recalling the nightmare Orph had after getting knocked out in Palm Springs: the endless hallways, the door, a disaster waiting on the other side.

At last they stop at a door with light bleeding behind it from the crack along the floor.

> URSULA
>
> Go on, open it.

Orph turns the knob. Inside the room, the club's business office, Jack and Woody are poring over a stack of ledgers. The sound of the door opening startles them, and they pull their guns. When they see Ursula has Orph under control, they crack nasty smiles.

> URSULA (CONT'D)
>
> Soldier boy solved the puzzle, Jack.

> JACK
>
> Took you long enough, little brother. Maybe all those bombs rattled your brain.

> ORPH
>
> I didn't want to believe you could do it, Jack, neither of you. What would our mother say?

JACK

Ma's been dead a long time. In this life you
have to make your own family.

ORPH

Not the way I learned it.

JACK

Always a choirboy, Orph. Reading the good
book.

WOODY

Where I come from, we gag the choirboys.
They're likely to sing.

ORPH

I don't care anymore. I've seen too much to
stick around in a world run by men like you,
Jack. You don't know the difference between
money and love.

JACK

Aw, you hurt my feelings. Money's just as
important as love. Ain't that right, Ursula?

Nodding once, Ursula draws close to Jack.

JACK (CONT'D)

Problem is what to do with you now. Put
a bullet in you and people start to ask
questions. Maybe you write a suicide note
and stumble into the river, confess to your

560

wife's murder, say you found out she was
cheating with Eddie. We'll find someplace nice
and quiet where you can wade down into the
water...

                    ORPH

I thought we were brothers, Jack. You promised
to look out for me.

                    JACK

What a little punk.

        (to Woody)

Tie him up.

Orph struggles but Woody is bigger and stronger and
with help from Jack they quickly bind Orph to a
chair.

                JACK (CONT'D)

Don't go anywhere, kid. You got a letter to
write.

Jack and Woody leave Ursula alone with Orph. The
little pistol in her hand doesn't look as though it
could do much harm but she keeps it trained on Orph
all the same.

                    ORPH

You don't wanna do this, Ursula. You're not
rotten like them.

                    URSULA

I'm snake-bitten, remember. Venom goes
straight to the heart.

                    ORPH

We could leave now and start over.

                    URSULA

You think you can escape? Jack's got friends
everywhere. He's the future, sweetheart.

                    ORPH

Then let me go. I'll disappear.

                    URSULA

You'd just snitch to the cops.

                    ORPH

It's all over anyway. I've told them
everything they wanna know.

                    URSULA

What do you mean?

                    ORPH

I mean the G-man who gave me the choice that
wasn't a choice. I sang all the notes he
wanted to hear, told him everything I knew
about Jack. Wasn't much, but it was enough.

                    URSULA

You rotten stoolie!

                     ORPH

There's two kinds of snitching, Ursula, the
right kind and the wrong kind, and what I done
is the right kind, the kind that looks out for
the little man and rats out the big one. If
you think it's anything different you're as
big a snake as Jack.

Ursula swings an open palm across Orph's face,
drawing blood with her fingernails. Orph winces, head
bending forward, hair falling into his eyes. When he
looks up again his wife leans over to kiss him.

                    URSULA

Why do you have to be so damned good?

She starts unknotting Orph's restraints.

                URSULA (CONT'D)

Now get out of here.

                     ORPH

Come with me. I won't leave you.

                    URSULA

How can I? I owe Jack more than you could ever
guess.

ORPH

Money can be paid back.

URSULA

Not only money. It's true I was in debt to
Woody. I went to Jack and Jack bought him out,
made Woody part of the family, turned my debt
into his... The debt I owed Woody I now owe to
Jack.

ORPH

No honor among thieves.

URSULA

It's all I have left. Now get out of here
before they come back.

At that moment the door opens and Jack and Woody
enter, guns drawn.

JACK

What's the idea?

URSULA

I went to powder my nose and when I came back
he'd got loose. Can't you mugs tie a knot?

WOODY

He couldn't have got free. I like that she let
him go.

                    URSULA

   It's not true!

                    ORPH

   Leave her out of this.

Orph tries to push past Jack and Woody but Woody's
gun goes off, hitting the lamp and shooting out the
window. The lamp falls to the floor, exploding in a
cloud of sparks that catch along the curtains.

A fire starts to crackle and smoke fills the room.
From the street there's a ripple of static and then a
voice comes across on a bullhorn.

                FEDERAL AGENT (O.S.)

   This is the FBI. We know you're in there,
   Plutone.

In the shadows Jack looks wildly at his brother and
sister-in-law.

                    JACK

   What is this? What have you done? Who's the
   rat?

            ORPH AND URSULA (IN UNISON)

   I am!

The fire spreads up the drapes and along the wall. In
a minute the whole office will go up and all four of
them with it.

                     565

ORPH

She had nothing to do with it, Jack. You want
a stoolie, well I'm the one, and I'd do it
again because it was the right thing to do.
All you want is to get rich no matter how many
lives you ruin. I don't care if you wanna kill
me, just do it quick. I got nothing to live
for. You took my wife and you took Faye. You
even took the brother I loved. You took away
everything that kept me alive.

Woody and Jack might have their guns trained on Orph
and Ursula, but no one has noticed Ursula's hand
reaching for her pistol.

FEDERAL AGENT (O.S.)

You've got one minute to give yourselves up
and then we're coming in!

Ursula raises the gun and dumps a slug into Woody's
chest. As he falls backward his own gun goes off
twice, shooting Ursula in the shoulder and Jack in
the leg. Ursula's own shot was true, and Woody slumps
to the floor, dead, Jack sprawling next to him.

EXT. MALAVITA - NIGHT

On the street outside Malavita, half a dozen cars
have stopped traffic. FEDERAL AGENTS are poised, guns
drawn, as the shots ring out inside the club.

The Agent who interviewed Orph is at the back, and
alongside him is the Times reporter, Noah Roy. Smoke
billows from the top floor window of the club.

                    AGENT (CONT'D)

Good thing you followed him.

                         NOAH

Newsman's hunch. What now?

                        AGENT

I'm taking Plutone out of there dead or alive.

                         NOAH

Look out for Patterson. He's on the level.

                        AGENT

              (to the other agents)

Okay boys, we're going in.

Another shot fires inside the building, and the
agents rush the stage door.

INT. MALAVITA - NIGHT

Ursula holds her pistol, barrel still smoking while
across the room Jack is clutching his stomach where
she's just shot him. Orph scrambles to get the gun
away from his brother.

                        JACK

    They'll put you inside, baby. Send you to the
    gas chamber.

                         567

                         URSULA

        I don't care what happens to me.

A line of flame shoots across the floor, dividing
Jack and Ursula from Orph.

                         ORPH

        We've gotta go, Ursula.

Orph fights through smoke to the door, opens it, and
when he does the fire triples in height.

                         URSULA

        I'm right behind you!

Orph leans into the flames, pulling Ursula off the
floor and into the corridor. She's bleeding badly
from the shoulder and they can already hear the
slamming doors and pounding feet of FEDERAL AGENTS.

                         ORPH

        You never did nothing, Ursula, you hear me?

Ursula, gasping as they struggle along the corridor,
flames licking out of the office and into the
hallway, pauses and looks steadily into Orph's face.

                         URSULA

        The thing is, baby, I did. Jack and me, we're
        two of a kind.

From the office, Jack screams in agony. Ursula turns
and starts stumbling back towards the fire.

                    ORPH

   Ursula! Let him go!

Ursula looks back over her shoulder at Orph. She
shakes her head.

                    JACK (O.S.)

   Ursula! Don't leave me! Ursula!

                    URSULA

   I can't do it, Orph. Not in this life. Maybe
   in another.

Ursula disappears into the office as a ball of flame
explodes into the hall. Orph turns away, running down
the stairs and into the drawn guns of a group of
federal agents. The Agent who interrogated Orph steps
forward.

                    AGENT

   He's okay, boys. Where's your brother,
   Corporal?

                    ORPH

   Upstairs in the office with my wife.

                    AGENT

   Police think your wife's in the morgue.

                    ORPH

   They've got the wrong sister.

                        569

(a beat)

So did I.

The Agent leads Orph out of the building as sirens
whine in the distance.

EXT. MALAVITA - DAWN

At the stage door, Noah Roy is waiting, notebook in
hand. When he sees Orph, his face shines. The sun is
starting to rise.

                    NOAH
    Am I glad to see you, Patterson.

Orph smiles, but his expression quickly twists into
sadness.

The two men walk across the parking lot as an
ambulance and fire engines arrive.

                    NOAH (CONT'D)
    What'll happen to them?

                    ORPH
    Nothing, they're already dead.

                    NOAH
    Maybe you could tell me your story, from the
    beginning... I have a feeling people will want
    to know.

                    ORPH (V.O.)

And that's how we ended up here, me all alone,
spilling my guts with my whole family laid out
in the morgue.

INT. THE TIMES - DAY

Orph sits in the newsroom of the _Times_ as Noah Roy
writes down everything he's said. The notebook is
full and both men look shaken by Orph's story.

                    ORPH

Sure, I was a chump, but I was a chump who
wanted to believe people were good, who wanted
to think that when a G-man knocked on the door
it was a soldier's patriotic duty to help.
I don't regret that. My brother got what he
deserved.

                    NOAH

And your wife?

                    ORPH

I'm not so sure about Ursula. She fell into
Jack's world without realizing there was no
way out.

                    NOAH

Will you go to her funeral?

                    571

ORPH

Sure, I'll be there. I'll always be there. I
wouldn't know any other way. Funny thing is,
I still feel loyal to her, and I don't think
that will ever change.

FADE OUT.

Kay

In the kitchen in the apartment above the Smiths' garage in the
dark of the evening under a naked incandescent bulb, because it's
that kind of place and that kind of story, Kay is standing at the
stove staring at the frying pan and holding a spatula in one hand
and the other hand's fingers tapping her teeth and the elbow of
the arm of that hand tucked into her waist and her hair a limp
mess in the steam of the kitchen and the boy sitting behind her,
at the table, and the two of them wondering, for the boy must be
wondering – was, she knew, always wondering – where Hank was
and when he would come home. The hamburger patty was black
on the outside and red on the inside and the smell of char filled her
nostrils but she was not going to waste good food so scraped it out
of the pan and onto an enamel dish, sliding it next to a spoonful of
green peas and a slice of bread. If the boy was not so insubordinate
she would have made shirred eggs because of him loving that
dish better than anything else she could cook never mind it being
dinner instead of breakfast, or chipped beef, or creamed tuna,
never mind that Hank called both of those shit on a shingle, but
tonight it was a hamburger patty and peas and for dessert half a
canned peach, never mind that the boy did not deserve to eat after
what he had done. There was still a lesson to be learned, always
a lesson to be learned, and different modes of instruction to be
employed. She had learned about pedagogy in teachers' training
and knew that the stick, as opposed to the carrot, was often more
immediate in its results even if it required greater reinforcement
over the longer term.

Against his mouth the boy held the bag of ice and blood was staining the cloth and there was an old towel laid on the floor under his chair to protect the linoleum and though he had stopped crying hours ago his eyes were still red and swollen as she had not seen them before and though it gave her a flutter in her stomach she sat down at the table with the enamel plate and the hamburger and the peas and ate her dinner and then the boy understood, she could see, that she had cooked only for herself. His fingers scrunched the bag of ice and a drop of meltwater mixed with blood dripped along his hand, rolled past his wrist, along his bare arm, down to his elbow where it sat against his bare ribs, and trickled around his waist, disappearing into the folds of the second old towel, the one she had told him to wrap round himself for decency, him having had to undress otherwise his clothes might have got stained, never mind that they already smelled of smoke from his treachery and would have to be laundered before he had worn them twice. She would be sure to make him do the washing.

Take it away, she said, the ice. He moved the bag from his face. Open your mouth, she said, and he did and she watched to see whether any new blood would come, and when it didn't she said for him to go wash himself and put on his pajamas and then it would be time for bed. But, he started to say, and she looked down, took a bite of the burned hamburger patty so raw inside it was oozing blood onto her plate, and with the hand not holding the fork she held up a finger and the boy knew better than to speak again when she did that, and he stood and quietly pushed the chair back under the table without knocking it and went quietly to the bathroom and closed the door just as quietly and she heard in all that silence more anger and terror than she had known from the child and it made her feel glad.

One lesson learned.

She finished her food although almost choking, and listened as the boy washed, and listened as he pulled pajamas from the dresser in the living room, and listened as he returned to the bathroom. At a lower setting than before she heated the frying pan and poured in corn oil and when it was hot enough dropped in another patty and reheated the peas and took another plate from the cupboard and when the meat was cooked and the peas hot she put the food on the plate and the plate on the table, so when the boy came back to the kitchen he saw the food and his face was like morning. She smiled at him and they sat together at the table as he ate, chewing each bite slowly because who knew when the next might come, a good lesson to learn, one she had taught by giving him nothing but water for two days a few months earlier, and when he was finished she took out the crystal sherbet glasses that Ruth had sent her and in each glass spooned half a canned peach and another spoon of the syrup and she and the boy ate their peaches, smiling at each other in silence, and she knew the lesson had been learned, at least for now, and he would not soon cross her or misbehave or disobey and in time she might even begin to trust him a little.

You can wash up, she said, and the boy said, Yes, Mother, and carried the sherbet glasses to the bathroom, then came back for the forks and knives and the two enamel plates and the frying pan and spatula and the pot for the peas and the bread knife and she listened, there, sitting at the kitchen table, as the boy ran water in the bathtub and washed the dishes and placed each clean dish in the bathroom sink and then looked up and smiled at him when he came back in the kitchen and took the cloth from the rail on the stove and walked back across the living room to the bathroom, and let the water out of the bath and dried each plate and pot and pan and utensil and then carefully brought them back to the kitchen, the glasses each on their own to be especially careful, the plates stacked together with the cutlery on top, the pot on the pan and the spatula and knife last of all, the blade held down for caution, and then she listened as the cloth dropped with a wet settling whip onto the handle of the oven door and she said, Now you can watch the television, if you like, until nine, and then it will be time for bed. What will you do, Mother? the boy asked and she said, I will read the paper, by which she meant Mrs. Smith's newspapers saved from the trash, and that morning's copy of the *Los Angeles Times*, which she had bought for herself with the money hidden in the couch, the money the boy claimed was his own, rightfully gotten, and that was something she should not forget, although that particular lesson would have to wait.

The boy turned on *Pantomime Quiz Time* and Mike Stokey and the guests were sitting in a living room with Adele Jergens, who had that funny squint, and Frank De Vol, who looked like he might be a Communist, and Hans Conreid, who had played a Communist in that awful picture *The Senator Was Indiscreet*, and then there was Vincent Price, as sinister a man as she had ever seen. On top of her pile of newspapers was the clipping from earlier in the week about the wedding of Generalissimo Franco's daughter and the Marques de Villaverde, and the new Marquesa in a Balenciaga faille dress and there having been footmen to carry the train, it being five yards long and all of it happening at the Pardo Palace outside of Madrid. The people on the television were playing charades and laughing and it seemed a little off-color and the boy laughing along with them but also at them in a way that seemed a little off-color too, but the boy was happy and what with how rare it was to hear him laugh she turned back to that day's paper and

read about how the awful Dr. Robert Gordon Sproul, president of
the University of California, had allowed an active member of the
Communist Party to remain at UCLA, the woman having registered
three times as a Communist in Los Angeles County, so there could
be no doubt about it, could there, that Dr. Sproul was in no position
to defend his position. It only went to show that Senator McCarthy
was right about the Communists and their fellow travelers being
everywhere, at every level of society and in every profession, even
the universities, trying to indoctrinate and recruit the innocent
youth of America.

The boy laughed and it came out so shrill she thought there
was a girl in the room and looked up and knew it was the boy
and it made her so angry she flipped the page of the newspaper
so it almost tore. There was a story about that nasty man Dalton
Trumbo, the Hollywood scriptwriter and Communist, and that
other one, Lawson, and how their lawyers were trying to keep
them from having to go to prison as they were meant to do, but
luckily the Supreme Court, Kay read, had refused to reconsider
its judgement that the men were, in fact, in contempt of Congress,
them having failed to answer the questions put to them three
years ago about being Communists, in point of fact. She cut out
the article and underlined words like routine and refusal and
postpone, which although she knew them did not use them often
enough in her letters or everyday speech. *Pantomime Quiz Time*
was finished and there were commercials and then it was 8:30
and time for B.F. Goodrich's *Celebrity Time* with Conrad Nagel,
who was not very good because he always stuttered and hesitated
when he was speaking, as if he was not sure what he was supposed
to be saying or even, sometimes, what it meant, and that did not
give a good impression. Ilka Chase and John Daly were on the

program and she didn't like either of them, too smart for their own good, so turned back to the newspaper and the first story that really unsettled her, it being proof if ever she needed it that the Democrats really were no better than Communists, since President Truman had said something to the effect that Senator McCarthy was the Russians' most important asset in the United States, and Senator Taft said how that was libelous and now the President was asking whether libeling Senator McCarthy was even *possible*, which is to suggest, as Kay understood it, that the President himself was suggesting that Senator McCarthy was such a terrible man through and through, in every facet of his life, public and private, that a person could say any vile thing about him and it wouldn't be libel because it was true, and that seemed to her the most outrageous thing she had heard said about anyone, tantamount (a fine word that made one sound sophisticated) to calling Senator McCarthy the devil incarnate, a man of total sin, and not just a stooge of the Kremlin. It made Kay so angry she stood up and went to the desk and took out a sheet of paper and a pen and began writing a letter but she became distracted by John Daly's voice on the television and the sound of his vowels, there was something about them that reminded her of that rogue Roosevelt but it was stranger than that, almost as though it were not entirely American but not British either, it was so strange that she began to wonder if perhaps English was not his mother tongue, and he might have been one of these very well trained foreigners who can sound almost American but never be altogether convincing because of being born into another language. She made a note on a leftover envelope to write to CBS about it.

She turned back to her sheet of stationery and was about to address the letter to the White House when she heard the

downshift of gears and a clunk-clunk-throb coming around the
corner, recognizable as the sound of Hank's red pickup, so she
put away the pen and paper in the desk drawer. Should I turn
it off, the boy asked and she said No, it will be fine, because of
it being a Friday and Hank bound to be in a good mood and she
tried to remember how many days it had been since she had seen
her husband and then the truck's brakes squealed and when she
looked out the window she could see the truck parked outside, but
right in front of the driveway, blocking the whole span of it such
that Mr. and Mrs. Smith would not be able to get in and out of the
garage in the morning, which she knew would be a problem, Mrs.
Smith always preferring to go to the grocery store on a Saturday
and Mr. Smith to go fishing, and often early, some weekends
leaving before dawn to drive up into the foothills and on occasion
all the way to Kings Canyon. She waited for Hank to move the
truck into a more appropriate position but the lights were still on,
and the engine running and it stayed that way for some time until
the lights and the engine both went off but the door of the truck
had not yet opened and the boy looked at her with his fretting
expression and she said, You had better stay here.

The air was still warm as she went down the steps, noticing
the television was on in the Smiths' living room and the curtain
moving as if Mrs. Smith had been checking to see what was
happening and then the Smiths' back door was opening and Mrs.
Smith standing there and calling out to Kay, Your husband will
need to park his truck elsewhere than in our driveway, I've said
it before and I will not say it again, and Kay said, Yes, Mrs. Smith,
I'm just coming to remind him, but when she reached the truck
and saw Hank's head leaning forward on the steering wheel and
the smell of whiskey coming out of the open window and beneath

the booze, rising up from around Hank's feet, the sourness of vomit and on top of it all cigar smoke and a strange perfume, a perfume she did not recognize and knew was not hers because she had no perfume, she knew that Hank would not be moving the truck himself. Mrs. Smith was watching as Kay stepped up to the truck window and said, Hank, Hank, you have to move the truck, and Hank murmured and she said it again, Hank, Hank, you cannot leave the truck there, and then Hank began to snore. She turned and looked at Mrs. Smith, the woman standing at the gate that separated the yard from the garage, and her hands on her hips. Mrs. Smith was a substantial lady, and not at all intemperate usually, but Kay could see that she had had enough, what with the boy setting fire to the vacant lot and now this and the rent coming due and who knew what Mrs. Smith might have discovered in the apartment while Kay was in town that afternoon. She said to Mrs. Smith, I'm sorry, I just have to get my boy to help, my husband isn't well. And Mrs. Smith dropped her hands, and the woman's face was sympathetic when she said, He's already in bed, but should I ask my husband to help? And that was the worst of it, actually, the sympathy, and Kay said No, I'll just get my boy, and she tried to run up the stairs but tripped and fell forward, and had to reach out and brace her hands to keep from hitting her face on the steps, and as her palms hit the risers splinters went into her skin and she twisted her left wrist and the air was knocked from her lungs and she had to stop a moment but then righted herself and reached the landing. As she came through the door the boy sat up on the couch and turned around, craning his neck to look at her and she said, Your father is – that is – your father needs your help.

The boy put on his slippers, the ones his grandmother had sent, and followed Kay down the stairs and the two of them stood at the side of the truck and the boy's face lost its fretting and became angry again, and then she opened the door and Hank was in a dark suit she did not recognize and there was vomit at his feet, around and inside his shoes, which she also did not recognize, shoes of fine dark leather, and she said, I'm going to pull him forward and you're going to support one side while I support the other, and she thought how she wished her friend Vivian could be there to help her, because Vivian was strong and could corral a pack of hunting dogs and get them to do just what she wanted and would have been able to hoist Hank out of the truck without any more bother than lifting a sack of potatoes. Looking at her husband Kay tried to make herself into Vivian, the way she imagined Vivian would have been, and pulled at Hank's arms, turning him around, and when that didn't work, she pulled his legs to the left and out from under the steering column, so she could then turn his shoulders and get her hands up under his arms and lift him out and the whole great weight of him fell on her so that she staggered backwards, but he was out of the truck and she could prop him against the side of the cab and the boy was there to support his father on the left while she took the bulk of his weight leaning to the right and he was starting to come around, though still drunk. Lucky the stairs were wide enough the three of them could walk abreast, and they took it one step at a time, practically lifting Hank the whole way up to the apartment and Mrs. Smith watching them all the while. Kay felt her face burning and it was a relief to get inside the apartment and maneuver Hank to the couch where the boy usually slept, and watch as he collapsed, face down against the cushions, and she angled his head to one side, in case of there being more sickness to come, and found a paper bag and an empty coffee can and put those next to him and the boy was sitting at the table watching, and the child looked so small and thin and his father so fat and white and she said, I have to go back outside again for a minute. If he's sick use the bag to catch it, and the boy nodded and she could see his eyes were red again and she didn't stop to think about it but went out on the landing and down the stairs and into the truck and the keys were still in the ignition and she took herself to the Smiths' back door and knocked and Mrs. Smith opened and said, Are you all right, Mrs. Knowlton? And Kay said, Yes, thank you, but you can see my husband is not well enough to drive, and I don't drive myself. The keys are in the truck, so if your husband—

My husband came home early today with a case of the flu, so I will move the truck myself, said Mrs. Smith.

I don't think you understand, said Kay. The truck, it is not—

I am capable of driving a truck, Mrs. Knowlton, and Mrs. Smith came out of the house, pushing past Kay and down the walk to the gate, and then along the driveway and to the truck and when she reached the truck and opened the door Mrs. Smith held her breath and covered her mouth and turned away, saying, Yes, I see. Do you have any newspapers? as if she knew Kay had been taking them from the trash, and Kay nodded and ran back up the stairs and in one of the stacks against the wall found some newspapers from February that she had finished reading, and brought them back to Mrs. Smith who put the papers down on the floor of the truck, covering the vomit so that it squelched under the newsprint, and then she got in and started the engine, and put the truck into reverse and backed it out of the driveway and parked it across the street. When she got out of the truck she wiped her shoes on the grass and handed Kay the keys and said, It is a sorry business, Mrs. Knowlton.

I can only apologize, Mrs. Smith.

It is a good thing my husband has not seen this, Mrs. Knowlton, because if he had, I cannot promise what he might have done, but I will keep it to myself. There are doctors, I believe, who specialize in your husband's condition.

Yes, I understand, said Kay. Thank you, Mrs. Smith.

I am not unsympathetic, Mrs. Knowlton, but it is my and my husband's lives as well as yours and your boy's and your own husband's. We all of us feel it when someone near us is ill, as your husband is ill. All the people around him feel it, you see, not just his family, and I have to wonder—

Yes, I see, said Kay, I will do something about it.

Kay and the boy sat watching Hank as he slept, snoring, sometimes talking, the two of them waiting for him to be sick, although he was not, or to wake, which he did not, and Kay looked at her palms and with her fingernails tried to pull the splinters, and when her fingernails wouldn't do it she went to get the tweezers and by the time she was finished her palms were red and sore, prickling as with heat rash. After a while the boy began to drowse, his head bobbing forward and then righting itself, but she did not want to tell him to go sleep in her bed, lest Hank wake and find this the case, him having nearly killed the boy once a couple years ago when she said he could take a nap one afternoon in the bed and Hank had come home early and said, What is this filthiness, but tonight, now, she eventually said to him, Go get a blanket and try to sleep in the armchair, and the boy drew himself up, his limbs loose and dangling, and trudged to the sideboard, where his bedding was kept, and he found a blanket and a pillow and settled himself in the green armchair, the pillow against one of the wings, blanket drawn up to his neck, tucked around his chin, and in minutes he was asleep. She leaned back in

the hard dining chair watching the boy and the man, thinking how
her father was never like this, and her brothers neither, how they
had always kept their decorum and never got more than tipsy, not
in her presence, and if there was bad behavior it was confined to a
world outside of the family home, where women and children could
not see it, at least not women like she thought of herself, perhaps the
women Hank courted when he was not attending to his wife and his
child, those women might like a man out of control, but Kay did not.
When still in school, long before Hank had appeared in her life, she
wrote a story about a young woman who marries the first dashing
man who pursues her only to find too late that he is an embezzler
and a cheat and a failure who brings shame on his family. There are
times, watching Hank now, that she wonders if she did not write her
husband into being, if imagining an unhappy marriage had brought
Hank to life, summoned him into her own life, and condemned
herself to this.

Past midnight Hank stirred in his sleep and then, opening his
eyes and seeing where he was, sat upright. How did I get here?
he mumbled, and she said You drove home and we helped you
out of the truck and up the stairs. You collapsed onto the couch
and I thought it better to let you sleep here than try to move you
to the bed. You're not strong enough, he said, and she said, The
boy helped me. Hank and she both looked at the boy and the boy
had an expression on his face that was fey and, though asleep,
almost happy. It must have done something to Hank, this look, its
girlishness, or else hearing that the boy had seen him in the state
he'd been in, because he stood up and walked across the room and
lifted the boy by the shoulders until he was standing and said You
wake up now. The boy flinched as he opened his eyes and tried to
pull away from his father but the man's fingers dug into the child's

bony arms so that he squealed. It was the same crushed kitten
sound made by the curly haired girl when the blond man squeezed
her in the theater.

What are you, a girl, sleeping in a chair? You can sleep on the
floor if there's nowhere else to sleep. The boy did not reply. Are you
soft? said Hank and the boy shook his head and Hank said I think
you're as soft as a girl, and then, before she could think better of
what effect it might have, Kay said, He set the vacant lot on fire
today, as if that was proof, is what she was thinking, of how tough a
boy he really was, but the boy looked at her as if she had betrayed
him, and she knew, in a way, that she had. How's that? Hank
asked, and the boy still said nothing, and Hank put his nose almost
against the boy's and bellowed, Explain yourself!, his voice so loud
the furniture shook.

It was an accident, the boy whispered, and Kay, again, spoke
before she thought about it, and said, He used a match gun, as
if that were further proof of his boyish ingenuity, of his very
ordinary boyishness, and Hank said, Is that right? and then he
turned back to the boy and put his nose once more almost against
the boy's own and hollered, Get the broom, and then he released
the boy's shoulders and the boy stood there, shaking, and his face
wet now, but he did not move and Hank yelled again, even louder,
his voice tearing itself apart, Get the broom!, and the boy turned
and walked to the kitchen, and when he came back with the broom
it was shaking in his hands and it was then that Kay herself went
into the kitchen and tried to find something to do.

The Bon Ami was under the sink and she got it out and began
sifting the scouring powder onto the counters, listening as the
broom fell against the boy's body and the boy whimpering and
Hank silent except grunting and she got a cloth from the sink and

then remembered the kitchen faucet didn't work, so she spat into
the Bon Ami and began scrubbing the counter with the powder,
only it caked because she had used too much and there was not
enough moisture, and there were mounds of Bon Ami in little drifts
that rose and fell, undulating across the kitchen counter between
the stove and the sink, drifting like snow across flat fields. She
scrubbed in circles and spirals and straight lines but seemed never
to progress from one end to the other. There was always a section
she had missed and the thwack of the broomstick against skin was
awful in her ears and made her see lightning as it struck above the
plains of Oklahoma, each thwack a great white bolt that branched
and connected to the next and they came so fast and in such great
numbers that the sky above the fields was white and the counter
white and her hands white, her palms burning from the scouring
agent, and she knew she had done it, too, the beating with a broom,
but usually through pants, and this was not through pants, not
this time, she could hear it. It seemed that she had been scrubbing
the counter for an hour but it could only have been a few minutes,
possibly less, when the boy came back into the kitchen, walking
so slowly it seemed as if he was not really moving, and he put the
broom back in the broom closet and quietly closed the door. Again
she heard the rage in his silence, but did not turn to look at him
and did not speak when he paused, waiting, standing behind her,
his breath uneven. Go to bed now, she said, go to bed, and the boy
left the kitchen with a silence she felt would shake the building
to its foundations. She wiped the cloth across the counter and did
this a dozen more times, shaking the Bon Ami from the cloth into
the sink, but still there was a white film of powder and she decided
it would have to wait until morning because the light of the single
bulb was too dim, and the bathroom on the other side of the living

room, and Hank in the bathroom now, his stream thundering into the water and reverberating through the apartment like her father and brothers never did because they had been taught better, and the only working taps the bathroom sink and bathtub itself, was the excuse she gave herself.

The boy's face was turned into the cushions and a sheet almost covering his head, but the blanket only coming halfway up, so she fretted about him catching cold before morning but did not draw it up higher because that was something he would need to learn for himself. In the bedroom, Hank was sitting on the end of the bed in his underwear, a cigarette between his lips and an ashtray in one hand.

The rent is due at the end of the month, she said, and Hank gave her a look like he thought she was ridiculous and also that he hated her and she wondered why he came back, if that was the case, why he did not stay out with his women, whoever they were. What was it about her or the boy made him keep coming back when it was obvious to anyone that he did not want to be there, not with them, him preferring wilder company than she could provide.

What about your movie star friend? Ask her for the rent.

It isn't like that. Would you ask your friend Don for the rent? Why should I have to do it with mine?

She could afford it. Don couldn't. She could buy us a house for Chrissake.

If she bought us a house every other friend who needed a hand would be at her doorstep. That is not what friendship means. It does not mean you ask for handouts from the richest person you know.

Maybe not where you come from.

I am asking if you have the rent, she said. You are my husband.

And what is the date today, tonight? he asked.

She looked at the electric clock with its glowing blue-green dial on the dresser, the clock that was plastic but painted brown to look like wood and which she had bought without realizing it was not wood, and the realization had made her hopelessly sad because her brothers and sisters would have said that was predictable, Kay making an error like that. The clock said it was long past midnight, almost two in the morning. How had it got so late? How long had Hank been in the bathroom? How long since he had been beating the boy? How long had she been scrubbing the counter? How much time had passed between Hank waking and going after the boy? How long had Hank been asleep on the couch? How long had it taken them to get him up the stairs? When had all of it started? She could not account for time, found it impossible to fill the hours that had passed since he drove up outside with what she knew to have happened, but perhaps she was forgetting, perhaps he had slept for longer than she knew, perhaps she herself had slept while he slept, or they had watched other programs, the wrestling, and then *Petticoat Parade*, perhaps she and the boy had spoken while Hank slept, or played cards, the boy beating her at rummy as he always did, hand after hand, or counting his cribbage runs with such precision and inventiveness that she was sure he was making up the rules, pretending that some combination counted when it did not, because he was like that, bending the truth to fit what he wanted from the world. It is the fifteenth of the month, this day coming, she said. Hank laughed and the sourness of the sound warped the walls of the room.

Then there's time, he said. What day is it due?

The last of the month, the last working day. There are thirty days this month, only. Today is Saturday, the fifteenth—

Which means the thirtieth is a Monday. And that means there's time.

You don't have the money now.

Maybe I do and maybe I don't.

If you have it now, you could give it to me and I could put it in the bank.

You'd like that, wouldn't you?

If we don't pay on time, this month, Mrs. Smith will say we have to go.

I'll get it, he said, but then he stood and started putting on clothes, and he was dressing like he was going to work, wiping out the filth from his shoes and the smell spoiling the air.

Are you leaving already? she asked.

Back to Los Angeles.

What are you doing there?

Working.

But what is your business? You are no longer a farmer as far as I can see.

The men I work for will pay me.

If we don't have the money—

That's enough, he said, and he was putting on his suspenders and a brown cotton jacket and she looked at the pile of dirty clothes on the floor and wondered when he would be back but knew not to ask.

We could come to Los Angeles, she said. We could all live there, if that's where your work takes you.

Sometimes it does. Sometimes it doesn't, he said. I have to be alone when I work.

Why do you come back to me?

Then again he looked at her like she was stupid and she remembered the invitations for their wedding, how they had been married in her parents' house and the gifts of china and silver and

crystal from her family, the way no one from Hank's family had
even come to the wedding or sent so much as a card, how Vivian
had been there as her maid of honor and Hank had no friend to be
best man, so one of her brothers had done it even though he hardly
knew Hank, and before the ceremony Vivian had taken her hand
and said, That Hank is lucky, you know, I'm almost jealous, and she
had kissed Kay on the cheek and Kay had blushed and they laughed
together and had to stop themselves laughing because the peach
chiffon would get stained if she started crying with laughter as so
often happened with Vivian, the laughter taking them over, and
Vivian now had a shoe store with her husband, and raised hunting
dogs, and Kay imagined how she and Vivian might have run a shoe
store themselves, Vivian managing the books and the business while
Kay met the customers and chose what shoes they would stock and
how she could have seen her family every day, and might have been
there when her father died, and that would have been a happier life,
wouldn't it?

Hank did not answer her question. He walked past her. Do you
have nothing to give me, she asked, to pay for groceries at least?

Hank did not answer.

She heard the door to the apartment open and close and the
sound of his shoes going down the stairs and across the street, the
truck door open and close and the engine turn over and the clunk-
clunk-throb as it shifted into gear and took off around the corner
in the middle of the night. There was a motel on the other side of
town, and she knew they would be there come May, in a single
room, the three of them, assuming Hank came back at all, and if
he did not, if there was no money, she knew she would have to find
work or take the boy back to Oklahoma and swallow the shame of
it all.

The boy had slept through it, she supposed, since his head was still turned to the cushions and covered by the sheet and his breaths deep and slow. There were no pictures of Hank as a boy so she could not say whether he took after his father, but the boy, she knew, looked like she had as a girl, skinny and blond, his head cocked to one side in the way of her family. Did he learn the trait from watching her and his aunts and uncles, or was it a habit written into him?

She knelt at his feet and pressed her hands together in a position of prayer without actually praying, because she did not know what to pray or to whom, but was muttering words that came to her, as random as rain on a roof, and her voice rose in pitch and volume until the boy pulled the sheet from his face and cocked his head, looking at Kay as if he could kill her, and his father, and every fresh thing on the earth.

May 30, 1950

13

My eyes open in the dark, and I cannot tell whether it was the nightmare that woke me or Alessio getting back from his evening with friends. In the dream I was driving a car in Los Angeles, but everything about the situation was confusing. The car was moving in reverse, driving at considerable speed, and at first I did not realize this was the case, perhaps because I was driving with the flow of traffic, but I alone was going in reverse, looking where I was headed in the rearview mirror, and it only gradually became apparent to me that I was running stop signs, one after another, and every time I approached a stop sign by the time I had noticed it I was already in the middle of the intersection, and the car would not slow down, I could not reach the brake pedal for some reason, and I feared that a collision was both imminent and unavoidable, it was only a matter of time before another car rammed into the side of my own, and when I took my eyes off the rearview mirror, exhausted by this always inadequate vigilance, I looked at the streets that were in some sense behind me, because I had left them, but also in front of me, because I was still facing them, facing the past I had just come from, unable to change gear, and borne backwards into my catastrophic future.

After a dream like that I cannot go back to sleep. I pull off the duvet, put my feet on the floor, and sit up on the bed until the dizziness stops so that I feel able to stand. My cane leans in the corner of the room and with it I walk down the hall to the kitchen where I find Alessio standing at the open refrigerator. Desmond, I'm sorry, I didn't mean to wake you, he says, tenderly touching my shoulder. I assure him he didn't. It was my own bad conscience, my fatalistic mind, no fault of yours. I can make you some warm milk, he says. Yes, that would be nice. I will be in my study, I say. But you cannot read now, he says, like a nurse to a child. Tell me, my dear, what else can an old man do when he finds himself awake after midnight? If I return to bed right away I will toss and turn. I have to read myself back into sleep.

The dream bothers me because I know it is not original. Or, rather, the dream might be original but it is obviously marked by my recent reading, by Benjamin's *On the Concept of History*, and in particular by his ninth thesis, in which he writes about Paul Klee's *Angelus Novus*. For Benjamin this figure, the *new angel*, became an angel of history, 'face turned toward the past', viewing the past not as a sequence of events (as the ordinary person might view it), but instead as 'one single catastrophe' that piles its rubble, its 'wreckage', before him. This angel is motivated by an impulse to restoration, to pause and pick up those chunks of rubble, even to 'awaken the dead, and make whole what has been smashed'. But despite such a desire, he cannot do this, for a 'storm…blowing from Paradise' throws him forward, hurtling him 'into the future, to which his back is turned', making it impossible ever to pause long enough to reconstruct what would always resist reconstruction.

Is it hubristic to think I might be like that angel, or is it merely realistic? I wish to take the ruins of my particular past and make them whole once more, to revive my own personal dead and remake what is shattered, while recognizing the impossibility of this task and knowing I am always driving forward in reverse, incapable of braking at each potentially calamitous intersection of time and space, destined to gaze at what I can no longer touch, this pile of wreckage, these fragments at my feet, fated always to fly backwards to my own irreversible shattering.

Or have I simply read too much and slept too little these weeks that I have been writing to you, Myles?

Alessio brings me the warm milk with a spoonful of honey, a piece of the sweet *colomba pasquale* I should not be eating, everything presented with such care on a tray with a cloth, a grating of nutmeg on the surface of the milk. His thoughtfulness moves me, touches me. Was it such an awful dream he asks, that it makes you cry? Yes, it was that awful, what it makes me feel on waking is awful. Have you finished the letter to Myles? he asks, coming behind me, massaging my shoulders, draping his arms around my neck and nestling his cheek against my own. I breathe to see if I can catch the scent of our Spanish novelist friend but smell only Alessio himself. No, I tell him, not yet – almost. There is not much left to confess. I don't know why you can't just phone him, he says, if you have so much to say.

Maybe it is because so much time has passed.

I feel the roughness of his stubble against my cheek, a prickliness that reminds me of my father, so that I am flung backwards in time and find myself a boy again, crying in my bedroom, stubbornly staring out the window when my father comes up behind me and takes me in his arms, resting his unshaven face against mine. Who knows what might have made me cry so long ago. So many years, Alessio says. I know that he means it is because I am so very old and no longer think clearly, or because I am so very old and people of my generation still believe that a letter has a certain value or power, particularly when it is a matter of defending what one has done, even and especially if that action might be indefensible.

Go to bed, my dear, I tell him, and Alessio turns my chair on its casters, drops to his knees, kisses me on the mouth, this beautiful man, with an intensity that is not only the mark of affection but the symptom of desire, if desire be sickness. How could he desire me when there are handsome men his own age to entice him? Or, perhaps the better question is, how can his heart be so great that he can be enticed by those other men, muscular and lean and smooth, unblemished and bronzed, quick with passion, and yet still desire me as well? I do not write this to you, Myles, to inspire jealousy or aggrandize myself, this old man still attractive to the beautiful young, but to suggest in my maladroit way that you and I, given the chance, might discover our desire for each other still alive if we were able to find a way beyond the decades of silence and at last stand together once more in the same bright room. I would kiss your scars to heal them, I would kiss your mouth with desire as Alessio kisses my own. I would be penitent and patient. Even in these last weeks or months or years, whatever may remain to me by the grace of the universe, I would strive to undo the wreckage of more than half a century.

Believe it, won't you?

On Summit Drive that night, Mars trembled in the southwestern sky, glowering red at the world. Space aliens, I said, still very drunk as we walked to the car. They might already be on their way. You rolled your eyes at me, but I meant it. I would welcome them, America's update on avenging angels, warriors of the faith transformed into invaders from a red planet, proxies for the more prosaic fear of invasion, also from the air, and of devastation by bombs whose genesis we must blame on the greatest minds of the age. I read somewhere that America's idea of Mars owes more to Ares, Grecian bringer of chaos, than to the Roman god whose warmongering was always in the service of peace. If the hawks and Red-baiters had any sense they would have adopted Mars as their own. H.G. Wells was responsible for that shift, and Orson Welles as well, marshaling Martians to cook up a national panic of interplanetary war in 1938.

In the history of cinema up to 1950, Martians had usually looked like us, if a little more sinister, elegant, and – typical of the racism and xenophobia endemic in Hollywood at the time – they were often implicitly Chinese. Over fifteen episodes in 1938, Universal Studios sent Flash Gordon to Mars to fight Ming the Merciless and his Martian queen who had designs on Earth. It would only be a matter of time before another studio decided Mars should take a hostile interest in its blue neighbor, so transmitting a message into theaters across the nation about the many varieties of red menace. Though I had only heard about it from a Russian cameraman working at the studio, even the Soviets, back in 1924, in Protazanov's silent film *Aelita*, had seen the symbolic potential of Mars as 'Red' planet, dispatching a Soviet scientist in a rocket to lead the enslaved Martian workers in revolution against their bourgeois alien masters. When the revolution triumphed, the scientist returned to Earth, and Mars remained red in the most beautiful Soviet sense, which made it, of course, anathema to America. Mars could only be the enemy *because* it was red and warlike and just close enough to our wet blue rock to constitute a convincing threat.

I don't follow, you said, stopping at the car.

All I mean is they should cast you as Flash Gordon. You're much more beautiful than Buster Crabbe.

You're drunk, Desmond. Get in the car.

What do you see when you look in the mirror? You don't see yourself as we do, do you? Who was that boy on the tennis court?

Just another actor.

People across the street were watching us but I no longer cared. I pressed myself against you. Who, Myles?

His name was Roy.

My heart plunged at the sound of that name.

First or last?

First of course, you said, helping me into the passenger seat. After the door thumped closed it was quiet and then you opened the driver's side and I could hear music from the party bawling away behind us.

Close it quick, Myles. Beneath the leather upholstery and vapors of gasoline I could smell champagne and tobacco, your cologne, but also other scents I could not place. What's his last name?

I don't remember. Leave it alone.

You had never spoken to me with such sharpness. We sat in silence for a moment as a man and woman ran laughing past the car. The man tripped, falling against the hood, and the woman lunged to catch him. When he noticed us watching it made him so angry he pulled away from the woman, aggressively shaking her off before disappearing around the corner.

Where's Helen?

Remember, she's taking our car. I'm waiting for her to come down the hill and then she'll follow.

Who is this Roy?

Goddammit, let it go, Desmond. You're drunk. He's just a bit player at Universal. He had one line in a Raoul Walsh picture a couple years ago. That's all I know.

They won't let you keep him. He's only a child.

He's my age as a matter of fact.

Like hell he is. You think because I'm leaving you can take up with someone else before I'm gone?

You're not leaving. Stop talking like that. There's Helen.

You turned over the engine and pulled away from the curb as lights swept across the dashboard. Friend or foe? I mumbled, squirming around to look into the blinding face of the car behind us. How can you tell if it's friend or foe?

I know my own car. I can see the license plate. You're paranoid.

But behind Helen I saw another car, a dark sedan, and then another still, a police cruiser. On the nights we were occasionally apart, I wondered if you had ever gone cruising, heading to that notorious gas station on Hollywood Boulevard or hanging out in the shadows at Pershing Square, meeting men who might not recognize you in the dark, or in returning to some Skid Row flophouse and discovering in the light of a naked bulb who you actually were believe they were hallucinating an angelic visitation. That was what you always seemed to me, descending from above, not entirely human, weightless and sheathed in golden skin. *Where did you come from?* I asked you the first time we went to bed. *You're not human at all.* Forgive me for ever saying that. I was young enough to think it was a compliment, then saw how it nearly frightened you away, you who wanted to believe in your ordinariness even when most exceptional. *Come on, I'm just a farm boy*, you told me, *I'm shy.* Such a quality of the American west, willful modesty even in the throes of sex.

When we slowed to the intersection with Sunset I looked behind us again. Helen waved while the two other cars, the sedan and police cruiser, hung farther back, as if out for a stately midnight parade. So long as I stayed in America, this is how it would be, an over-the-shoulder life, always wondering whether or not I would make it home a free man.

Black trees swept past the car and I rolled down the window to listen to the night, the world whispering that the hour was late, I had to tell you I was leaving tomorrow and would not be coming back. Do you understand that I never wanted to leave? Do you understand how tormented I was because it meant leaving not just you and Helen but everything I loved about our country, everything that remained good about it, with no guarantee I would see any of it again? Perhaps if it had been my luck and choice to return to America once it became possible, I might have been able to recapture that sense of complete belonging and familiarity, although I suspect I would have remained always at least half European, unable to see the country of my birth entirely from the inside again. I was resisting telling you because to confess the imminence of my departure was to render myself exile in every sense. I knew, staring out the car window, listening to the words on the wind, inhaling Los Angeles in its early days of night, that the men in Washington would take pleasure at my escape because it would appear to them an admission of guilt. In public they would bluster over my flight from so-called justice, never mind that for someone who loved his country as much as I, who adored America despite the hatred it had shown him for his politics and the valence of his desire, notwithstanding the ignorance and fear that has flourished so often in its borders, there could be no punishment worse than exile.

I say that and yet I claim I could not bear to stay because of what might have happened to me. These feelings cannot be resolved. The punishment of leaving was worse than anything, and yet the punishment I might have suffered had I stayed would have been worse still. In the impossible space between those feelings I have spent the rest of my life.

I laughed, although none of it was funny, and you glared at me.

What is it, Desmond?

I'm going tonight.

Yes, we're going home.

No, I'm taking a taxi to the airport. I'll wait for the next flight to New York. There's one tomorrow morning. I have a ticket already. Pan American. A stewardess was nearly sucked out the window of a Pan-Am plane earlier this year, but it's a risk I'll have to take—

Desmond—

—the window blew out over the Carolinas while the flight was en route from New York to Miami. If that happens to me I'll have to flap my arms and just hope I stay aloft. The poor thing was asleep when she nearly went out the window. They had to pull her back inside.

But what are you going to do in New York? you asked, and I could hear your voice breaking as if you were beginning to understand what I was trying to tell you.

I'll get another plane.

Another? But where to?

Paris. Rome maybe. Whatever's leaving first. It's Holy Year and I could claim to be doing research about a man who's strayed but comes back to the fold. The Italians would love that.

But how long will you be gone?

The passing blur of black trees had started to nauseate, or maybe it was the conversation. I closed my eyes.

Myles, I've told you.

I don't know what you mean.

I'm not coming back.

You accelerated, gripping the wheel. You're talking stupid.

I want you to listen, Myles.

No, you're drunk.

I'm quite sober now. I need you to hear me—

You can't leave! you shouted, whacking your palms against the wheel so the car swerved. An oncoming truck honked its horn and you steered us back into our lane.

In the dark your cheeks reflected every passing headlight. Outside of a script it was the only time I had made you cry. I told you earlier, Myles, I have to leave. You can follow me once you have a passport. You and Helen and Barbara, all three of you. We have enough money between us to last a long time doing nothing at all.

But what would we do for the rest of our lives?

You needed a convincing plan for our future, and the truth is I did not have one. I tried to extemporize, like you or Helen might. They love you already in France, I stammered. Imagine, this beautiful American boy who cares about European cinema. There's no one else like you! We'll start our own company, make our own movies. Please, say you'll come.

You were shaking your head, fingers clenching and unclenching the wheel. I sensed the car moving faster, your foot pushing against the accelerator and then one hand abandoned the wheel, flying to your face to rub tears from your eyes, elbow propped against your torso, black sleeve disappearing into the drape of the tuxedo jacket.

Pull over, I said, but you drove faster, your eyes closing because they were overflowing, and then you swerved to the right, veering in and out of the other lane, following the curve of Sunset around the university, accelerating again into the sharp left as we approached the intersection with Bellagio Drive and Bel Air's West Gate. There were lights from a car turning across our lane, and then your hand cranked the wheel hard to the right, the right hand crossed over the left, and your foot pounded the floor but I could not see which lever you hit. With a sudden lurch I was thrown forward and fell back into night.

When I opened my eyes there was light all around, the front end of the car buckled against the shattered windshield, and ahead of us, bleached by headlights, the column of the Bel Air gate with a crack rising through it. Stupidly, I worried about the crack. It would have to be repaired, maybe the whole gate rebuilt, and what would that cost, and how would the press cover it, what would they say about us, how drunk we both were. In my lap I felt a wet heaviness and when I looked down I saw through the gathering smoke that it was you – your head, your neck, the line of your shoulder, buckled like the front end of the car. You had not been wearing your seatbelt, you must have nearly gone through the windshield, which had shattered into a million bright prisms.

I screamed because I could not find your face.

At first you did not respond and then the blood in my lap parted and I saw your lips.

Help! I shouted through the open window.

You closed your mouth and I screamed again as the door opened and Helen's hands reached in. She was shouting too and then your weight lifted from my lap and Helen was pulling you by the shoulders out of the car. I tumbled onto the street and tried to follow, watching in wonder as she lifted your slender body and carried you in her arms, put you down in the grass, and propped your head against her fur stole. Kneeling over, your head between her hands, she screamed for an ambulance.

I looked up to see a police officer running, and behind him two men in suits, which meant we had been followed, just as I suspected, and for an instant I was so furious I forgot about you and thought only of the cop and the circumstances and wanted to blame the accident on that, as if being followed had caused the crash, which in a sense it had, of course, and the rage I felt was so great that I screamed when the cop reached down to hustle me away from the heat of the car. Sirens were shredding the night as he sat me down on the other side of the gate. I crawled towards the sound of Helen's voice and knelt on the grass next to you. Ruby gloves, I thought when I saw Helen's hands, she's wearing ruby gloves.

We should get further away from the car, I said.

We can't move him, she shrieked, her face turning as red as her hands, and I saw that she was fighting to hold your head together because it was coming apart like a cracked ceramic bowl. I reached out and took one of your limp hands in my own, clutching it, but you did not respond. Smoke hissed under a blast of water and the flickering became more mechanical. You seemed half underwater, your head submerged beneath Helen's hands, and I could no longer bear to look at those red gloves or the broken skull they held together so I focussed on the fury of Helen's face. She did not look away from you, not for a second.

Hands reached down to lift me again, pulling me away from you as men in white slid your body onto a board, floating you through the mist and the smoke. Hands pushed me to follow your hovering bier, propelling me into the white open mouth of an ambulance. Inside I watched fingers go to work on your head, pressing, applying gauze, trying to staunch the bleeding. Helen was next to me, both of us sitting upright though the paramedics said I should lie down. No, I said, I will not lie down. I needed to keep watch over you even though I struggled to focus with the siren ringing in my ears, the sound circling and spinning as the wheels circled and spun beneath the vehicle, propelling us west along Santa Monica Boulevard. The hands of the medics held together a head that kept straining to come apart. All the king's horses and all the king's men, I thought. But you were no egg, you could be healed, you were capable of breaking apart and patching yourself together again. You did it every day.

I reached to touch your hand and you screamed, then fell silent when they put a needle in your arm. The white bandages on your head turned red and then brown. Surely it was makeup, special effects cooked up by a group of talented technicians, nothing more, just an illusion, all would be fine. It had to be. Your eyelids fluttered open so I could see the clear whites beneath, blue irises focussed on me, and then they closed once more.

That was the last time we ever looked into each other's eyes.

At the hospital, in the waiting room, under the blue-white wash of ceiling lights, Helen and I sat. The doctor who examined me said I was bruised but nothing worse and recommended a neck brace in case of whiplash. I told him I'd take my chances, but what about Myles? The doctor told us you were still in surgery. Helen's hand trembled in mine and I stared into the nearest light, unblinking, the image of your eyes fixed in my vision. After thirty seconds or a minute or even half an hour – I can't say because time split and slowed and sped up again so that I had no sense of duration or chronology – it felt as if I was gazing down on the earth from outer space, watching a schoolroom globe bobbing in a frothy white sea and wondering about the fate of its inhabitants, as if I were no longer one of them. Perhaps I was trapped on Mars, in a waiting room in the palace of the war god. Perhaps this is no longer life, I thought, and I can count myself free.

The lights flickered and Helen dropped her head against my shoulder, circling her arms around my waist. You can't leave, Desmond.

Across the waiting room three nurses were chattering about boyfriends and movie stars and the minor dramas of their lives. I wanted to shout at them to keep quiet but then the doctor returned. He was standing in front of us and I realized he had been talking for a while.

—confident his vision will return.

Can we see him now? Helen asked.

He's under sedation.

We won't disturb him.

The doctor glanced at me as if I posed a problem, then nodded and led us out of the waiting room, past the gossiping nurses, and down a long blue corridor at the end of which he paused before a door.

From the threshold we stared at you. Your face was blackened from bruising. White bandages made a turban around your head. Your chest rose and fell in a steady movement and a drip was stuck in your arm. There was a heart monitor and a nurse sitting on a chair in a corner reading an issue of *Modern Screen* with Elizabeth Taylor on the cover. The nurse looked up at Helen and opened her mouth as if she might ask for an autograph. I wanted to tear the bandages from your head to see what they had done to you. There were stitches across your face where the skin was exposed, and again I had the ridiculous thought that it was makeup and we were not actually living through this, but stuck on a soundstage and the scene had gone on too long and if someone would just call *cut* I would fly across the room and rub the makeup from your skin and rip off those fake stitches and we could go home and get on with our lives. Helen's hands trembled and a whimpering sound came from her throat. I knew then, perhaps for the first time, that whatever you and she had, it was more than I had appreciated, not as simple as a convenient relationship for the sake of the press, and realizing this made me so hot with anger I wanted to remind her that she had no claim on you, that you were mine and not hers. But she was the one who had carried you to safety, not me. She was the one who found the strength and clarity in that moment to make sure you survived. I took her hand and she clasped it so hard I thought my fingers would break. All this happened in less than a minute, and then the doctor with his lean grimace, his godly smugness and odor of Brylcreem, urged us back into the hall.

Has he spoken? Helen asked.

The doctor flicked his eyes back and forth between us, again looking at me as if I were a complication. He did, the doctor said, but he wasn't making much sense. We're hopeful he'll make a full recovery. And then he turned to Helen, taking her arm. Could I speak with you alone, Mrs. Haywood?

In the waiting room the three nurses had moved on from men and movie stars.

No, I heard she cut her throat, the poor thing, said one of the nurses. Such a shame.

Must be a person has no hope if they do that, said another.

It's the children we should feel sorry for, said the third. How can you believe in God when your mother goes and does a thing like that?

Whatever relief I felt that you were alive was instantly undercut by the realization that I had made this happen. My selfishness had done this. If only I had been able to see the venality of my choice a few hours earlier, if I had understood how my egotism could destroy everyone I loved, perhaps that would have been enough to make me face whatever injustice awaited me, however unthinkable and unbearable it seemed at the time. And yet, if I had stayed, I am certain our secret would have come out, and would that not have ruined you, ruined us both, in its own catastrophic way? Or else the struggle to keep what we had secret would have eaten away at us in ways just as destructive. In that hour in the hospital I knew for the first time that I would give my life for you, Myles, even if it meant lying down right there on the hospital floor and letting everything go, or being stoned by a mob, or sitting before a panel of men in bad suits and refusing to betray all the people I counted as friends. I wanted to die that you might live.

Some nights now, alone with Alessio, who is sweet to me but with whom I have so little in common, about whose faithfulness I have constant doubts and yet no sense that I have the right to demand his fidelity given my age and decrepitude, I regret that I did not manage to pull off such a bargain, to give my life to make you whole.

Helen came back into the waiting room and pulled me to a corner away from the nurses, turning her face so that they could not even read her lips as she whispered.

Myles was talking about you before the operation. He was asking for his husband. The doctor thought it was shock or delirium, but I could see he wondered if there wasn't more to it.

What did you tell him?

I told him it was for a part – a psychiatric patient who thinks he's his own wife – but I don't think he believed me. She sighed and looked over her shoulder at the nurses. I wish Barbara was here.

Give me your keys. I'll pick her up and be back before dawn.

Helen mangled inside her clutch and pressed the keys against my palm. When I said that about the doctor, I didn't mean you should go, Desmond. If anything, I think you should stay. Barbara could always get a taxi.

The three nurses were silent, watching our little drama unfold.

No, I whispered, it's better I go.

John

John stared at the pink bedroom, the princess canopy in chintz
trimmed with eyelet embroidery flowering above the headboard
to the height of the ceiling, the oil portrait of Mary in an ermine
stole regarding him from its place above the hearth. Since she had
redecorated the room earlier in the year he no longer felt there
was a place for him in it.

Mary pushed the bathroom door closed and he heard the lock
turn. One day the fire department would have to break down the
door to get her out. It would be sleeping pills or a slip climbing
out of the tub after too many martinis. He used to assume the
recklessness was benign and accepted that while she was not
faithful to their marriage she was in every other way loyal to him
and determined to advance both their careers. After this day
he was no longer certain. It felt as though the partnership had
turned into a rivalry and she had arrived the better prepared.
Constancy and familiarity were all he could offer. He demanded
nothing in return but a convincing performance of devotion
for the cameras and the press, her shenanigans kept out of the
gossip columns, a certain decorum before their friends and
colleagues. The liaisons he knew about had mostly occurred
during working hours at the studio or at parties where she would
disappear for an hour and resurface looking like a bobbysoxer
on heat. Since their wedding, at least until six months ago, they
had slept in the same bed each night and had never been apart
for a whole day. It was in the contract, page 4, paragraph 6,
or so he liked to pretend. Both of them had morals clauses in

their contracts with the studio, however, and there was nothing imaginary about that.

When Mary opened the bathroom door again she jumped at the sight of him. What are you doing in here?

Following you. Explain something to me. What is it about Nick Charles?

She blushed and John knew he had been right.

Choice.

I don't follow, Mary.

We all have choices, right up to the moment we act, and then the old set of choices dies and a new set is born. Each choice leads along another path. In the end, at the close of your life, you find yourself in the place that you've chosen, accompanied by those you've picked along the way as your companions. I've chosen Nick because he represents radical choice. But I've chosen you as well.

I'm not enough for you?

I could ask the same of you, John.

I've never had an affair.

You've had an affair of the heart, and of the mind.

I recognize that line, Mary. It's on the showreel downstairs. You're even playing it the same.

Mary scowled. When you lost interest in me you fell in love with that counterfeit belief. You realize you can't call those people your friends anymore.

Because they don't fit in with shows like you put on tonight? That was straight out of 1933. I was ready to call Riefenstahl.

They're enemies of America.

Your America isn't one I recognize, Mary.

Then you must be blind. We're at war, even if bombs aren't being dropped and soldiers aren't fighting. America is always at war.

Earlier tonight I thought I could love you again.

I don't care about love.

No, I can see that. Just tell me what you're doing tomorrow.

I have an appointment downtown.

I guessed that much. And they'll ask you some questions. I want to know what you're going to say.

I'll tell them you and I used to attend meetings. I'll give the names of everyone I remember who was at those meetings, and at the end of the discussion the authorities will have me on record, and anyone who wants to make trouble will be told I'm clean, and nothing more will come of it.

What happens to me?

You have the same choice. We don't even have to do it downtown. I could phone first thing tomorrow and ask them to come to the house instead. All you need do is give names and dates. Nothing could be simpler. Do that for me and I have the rest of our future planned.

John sat on the edge of the bed so that the real Mary and the oil portrait of Mary were both in his line of sight. What kind of future would that be? My friends wouldn't speak to me.

You can get new ones.

And my work?

It doesn't matter if people like you or not, the studio will be on your side. You'll spend another ten years making good, honest, American movies before retiring. Then, after a few months' rest, you'll announce your candidacy for office. We'll start small, with the State Assembly, and then move on to Senator or Governor. After that, we'll look to national office. I see a great future for us together, John. Part of what I've realized today is that I need you as much as you need me. Just imagine: *President John Marsh.*

A Technicolor montage flashed through John's mind: the whistle-stop campaign tour of California, speeches from the back of a caboose, an open-top Cadillac in a Raisin Day parade in the San Joaquin Valley, talking to fruit packers and migrant workers, aerospace engineers and longshoremen, rubbing shoulders with the titans of California commerce, and then the first oath of office, speeches from the floor of the statehouse, ribbon cuttings and cocktail parties, his governorship of California, flights between Sacramento and Los Angeles, a barnstorming campaign for President, speaking up and down the country in small towns and big cities, addressing both the common and the great, and then the night of the election, awaiting the results, waking the next morning to find himself elected, the months of preparation before the inauguration, Washington transformed into the best version of itself, America in the morning of its third age, and Mary always at his side, a Madonna for the nation, Liberty made flesh.

The vision almost convinced him, but gazing at the two Marys, the living one and her varnished image on the wall, he thought of all the arguments over the years, her betrayals and duplicitousness, the hungry striving.

I wish I could remember what was good between us, he said. I wish bad memories could be wiped like chalk from a slate and only good memories remain. I wish you could be faithful to me as I have been faithful to you.

Oh, John—

It's true. If we're going to do this we have to do it together, as you say. If I must be faithful to my country then you must be faithful to our marriage. That has to be the contract.

Mary raised her chin and looked down at him. He tried to envision her in black-and-white. Bled of color she was most convincing, the good part of her just as present and visible as the bad – Faye and Ursula, Light and Dark, two halves of the same person. That had been his contribution, splitting what had been a single character into two, twins dividing the dual aspects of Mary's own personality and then, perversely, casting her to play both parts. The experience had nearly driven her mad, he knew, and he blamed himself. Standing before him now in triumph, a goddess or a vampire, light and dark were comingled so that John could not say if darkness was the mate of logic or superstition. All he wanted was for Mary to smile as if she genuinely cared for him, as she had in the past, without derision or irony.

I wish I could forget everything that has ever pushed us apart, Mary.

She did smile, but not without irony.

Dr. Werth gave me something today. A new medicine. He said it would help with remembering what I've forgotten. I haven't tried it yet. Maybe we should take it together.

She floated back into the bathroom and returned with an orange-brown bottle of pills.

How many do we take?

Two to forget all the bad, she said, and two to remember the good. She placed the pills in his palm and he put them on his tongue.

Sweet. Probably a placebo.

They lay down next to each other on the bed, he in his tuxedo, she in her blue gown, listening as bass notes from the music outside rattled the windows. John began to drift into sleep, eyes closing as colors and shapes mutated, metamorphosing against the backs of his eyelids. He thought of the man dressed as the griffin in Mary's pageant and imagined the monster turning unprovoked to attack her, throwing her from the chariot, and he, John Marsh, dashing forward to save her only to find as he drew closer that Liberty was a harlot, cheaply painted and scuttling across the terrace to embrace the feet of Nick Charles, grown to the size of King Kong and towering over Los Angeles. Nick reached down, plucked Mary with one hand from the terrace, stepped through the hedge surrounding the property, and tramped off into the eastern hills.

John opened his eyes. Mary had one arm flung against her pillow, the other resting across her abdomen. Posed, even in repose.

Daddy? Iris called from the other side of the bedroom door. I can't sleep.

You better put her back to bed, Mary said without opening her eyes.

John craned his neck to taste Mary's lipstick, the smoke and alcohol on her breath. Her mouth moved against his in a way that was almost convincing.

In the hallway Iris looked wide awake and flushed, as if she had been drinking. It would not have been the first time.

You should be in bed.

It's too loud, she whined.

You can sleep tomorrow.

As John opened the door to Iris's room he glanced over his shoulder in time to see Nick Charles slinking into the master bedroom.

Who's that? Iris asked.

A snake.

Maybe you should kill it.

Yes, I suppose I should.

Long past midnight, meandering in a maze of text, tripping over slabbed Sunset Boulevard pavements, his senses pulsating under the influence of the drug Mary had given him, having run and cabbed and hiked, footsore, far from home, John believed he was the star in the heavens and everyone else mere planets in his orbit. Nick Charles was just ahead, slouching in a brown cloth jacket adopted for disguise. Lamplight glinted on streetcar tracks, flashing orange yellow red in the gaseous bonfire of twinkling neon signs.

S
E
C
U
R
I
T
Y

B
A
N
K

T
A
F
T
B
L
D
G

WARNERS' THEATER
THE DAUGHTER OF
ROSIE O'GRADY

El Capitan

ROOSEVELT
HOTEL

B
A
R
K
E
R
B
R
O
S

P
A
N
T
A
G
E
S

Johnny
Weismuller in
CAPTIVE GIRL

GOOD NIGHT LADIES
SEXSATIONAL STRIPTEASE

GRUEN WATCH TIME

A pale blue car screeched to a halt at the traffic light as the STOP arm swung into place, the letters S-T-O-P picked out in white bulbs beneath the colored trio of lights, and then, as red pulsed to green, STOP's white letters against red fell back into the mechanical gray body and the GO flag, black on white, swung up to the perpendicular. John stood mesmerized before the changing sign until he noticed SECURITY BANK winking in his direction.

Two girls burst from the shadows beneath a marquee, one in a mint-green smock dress over white blouse with puffed short sleeves, the other in a white dress with ruffles in a V falling from her shoulders to waist, white bow tying up her hair, white patent shoes, white ankle socks.

How's about it? Mint Green asked.

Two fer one, said Ruffled V.

Yer place or ours, Minty drawled, her accent Bronx-like so it came out owwwahhhs.

John shook his head. The girls stuck out their tongues and cycled on. Time stood rooted in front of Warners' Theater, a clock sunk in concrete, smiling at the green fabric awnings batting simpering scalloped eyelashes. All the world was in love with John, all trying to seduce him. Nick Charles in brown jacket turned around. He was wearing a mask, didn't look himself at all, and gave John a come-hither pout.

Streetcar cables hanging above the pavement buzzed harmony with the antennae pulsing from building tops, all that electricity relaying spirit and girdling the world, singing a love song to John Marsh. Time branched, pushed forth leaves, flowers, and fruits, the concrete cracking from time's growth, searchlights slowing, their golden echoes sweeping skyscrapers, shilling for men massaged in dark back rooms by skillful catamites. Irving Jakobson jacking off the Junior Senator from Wisconsin. America First! That's what Lindbergh said, the Nazi.

The color of the world was too distracting. Everything should be in black and white, grayscale for clarity. Cars cakewalked streets in Sunday best: drab green, sky blue, kidney red, ink black, canary. A yellow cab with fat red face shook its tail, compelling John with its soft rubber purr: Pursue, Pursue, Pursue.

Walking for hours that split into lifetimes, contemplation at last became possible.

John's Chemical Contemplations (A Speculation):

1. To snitch or not to snitch, that is the question.

2. Stick by friends and say nothing and so lose everything. Lose wife child house work. Lose everything but life. Lose country. Lose parents. Lose home. To end alone with friends, thus not alone. To start again with nothing but friends. Are friends everything or nothing in the end? To leave with shirt on the back, one suitcase, wallet of bills, talent of one's eyes. Individual talent as passport and papers. Create a new life as an American no longer American. Live off the backs of friends. Can friends be trusted more than wife?

3. Choose Mary's side and keep all but friends. Sacrifice friends for wife child house work. Keep everything except for friends. Keep country parents home livelihood. Never be trusted by friends again. To arrive in a room and be the traitor who repented, the comrade who snitched against innocent men.

4. Do one thing (choose Mary's side) while pretending the opposite. Speak in private and pretend silence. Have it both ways. Hold cake in hands and eat it whole, one mouthful. Sit both sides of the fence. Impale oneself on falsehood. Live a double life. Lose nothing and be unlivable to oneself, unfathomable to anyone else.

5. Take the child and run with friends: Mexico Argentina India Italy France England Russia: turn against Mary and America: render oneself fugitive but not bereft of family: take the child and raise her right. Only left is right. Fault of the French and tennis court revolutions. Failure of language. Fault of Latin. Nothing sinister about the Left. Nothing correct about the Right. Redirect the debate. Right and Left are meaningless. Above and below. Those on top, those beneath. With one or with the other. Possible to be on top but still with those beneath? Possible to be beneath and support those who would oppress?

6. Find new friends. Become someone other than what one has been. Run for office play the game climb the ladder sit the summit rule the world. No different fundamentally than 3 or 4.

7. Go underground. Fake one's death. Run solo. Trust no one. No choice there. No different fundamentally than 2 or 5.

8. Suicide. Killing of the self. Real or figurative. Real the only real way out. To do away with in order to escape, to stop.

9. How'd he get away with it?
I always heard he was a Commie.
Why wasn't he subpoenaed with the rest of us?
Assume he made a deal.
When you assume you make an *ass* of *u* and *me*.
Commies don't get deals they get punched against the wall.
It's his wife made the deal.
Two for one.
Don't work like that.

I just don't get it.

Two fer one I tell ya.

I'd a swore he was a Commie spy.

I'd a swore he's one of ours.

I'd a swore he'd never turn.

I'd a swore it was a two fer one.

One of owwwaaahhhs. . .

You can't trust him either way.

Can't trust him won't trust him.

Never could trust him.

Dozens of better directors.

He's had his day.

Hire someone else.

Smells fishy.

Smells funny.

His ears stick out.

He's gaining weight.

Oily.

Greasy.

Probably a queer to boot.

Give that Commie faggot the motherfucking boot.

10. Murder.

Contemplations were a drain whirling down, blue shot-silk planet
at the bottom of time's drain. Not as shot as he, dragging his feet
with soles pressed on cool concrete. All of it shot to hell, this
paradise and he, circumnavigating, shot-up without needles.

Nick? Nick Charles? John called out. Mumblety-peg he'd play
between the blades of that brown-cloth back. A new Brownshirt,
Nick Charles. Again the young man clocked him over his shoulder,

checking John was still at heel. He ducked his chin in affirmation, maintained the pace, afloat on currents of wet goodwill. He would kill in love.

Sure, I'll be Nick, says the Brownshirt, you can call me whatever you like.

A red-brown streetcar stopped to vomit mouthfuls of lovers and John swerved out of their way, teetering as a man hustled him back on his feet.

Woah now, you'd better get a taxi, mister.

A taxi, yes, he could follow Nick faster on four wheels.

You know where you're going?

Always. I'm the director. The prime mover.

A woman in red waylaid him, hand on his chest. He liked the shape of her face but not the stubble sprouting through peach foundation.

We could go somewhere, she said.

I'm not sure what I'd find down there. John reached between her legs, got a face full of fingers and a scream.

Monster! she shouted.

Bulbs shone so brightly he had to cover his eyes, but the light wormed between his fingers, vibrating into blazing rings spinning in different directions, burning his irises – what would become of his Iris? – until he had to turn away and, keeping Nick Charles in his sights, fell into the back of a cab. Nick danced just ahead, scooting atop the hood, flexing his supple form into feline chrome ornaments as they progressed along the Boulevard, turned north on Vine – he could see the lights of Earl Carroll's, head of a woman on the nightclub's side outlined in white lights, beckoning John to come inside – then roll left to Franklin, flow up Los Feliz, north on Vermont – Live around here? Park's closed, said the cabbie – and

when Nick flew from the hood into the air John shouted STOP. He
opened the door before the wheels were still. Slapped his wallet
into the driver's hand, the man palmed bills and coins, shook his
head, and cuffed the wallet back into John's breast pocket, hand
flexing a moment to feel the beating of his heart.

A cop at the park's entrance slept in his car so John slipped
past, patent leather jogging on concrete as the road climbed to
the Greek Theatre. A coyote paused ahead of him, raised its paw,
and trotted away into darkness, glancing over one gray shoulder.
Paranoiacs, coyotes, always checking what's behind them.

From beneath the pines on either side a scree of teens tumbled,
boulder boys in black, rubble girls in white with matching red
leather shoes and motorcycle jackets curving over wheel-well
busts and biceps. Seeing him in his monkey suit, one of the girls
shook her head, harping, Get a load of *that*.

Woman-hater, wailed another.

A high young man stepped forward, spit, lit cigarettes end to
end. We're the Angels, and this is our circle, he said, nodding at the
girls in red and white, and who is you?

John Horatio Marsh.

Never heard of him, coughed a barrel-shaped girl with ropy
black hair.

You live at RYC?

Sure he don't. They don't got fine livin' up there.

Too old to be a vet. He's a cop!

I'm not a cop.

Vice squad I bet.

On the wrong end of the squad maybe, laughed Ropy Barrel.

Said he was a woman-hater.

In the distance the coyote stood on its hind legs, stretched tall as Mount Hollywood, gingerly stepped over the hills and disappeared into the valley on the opposite side.

What are you kids doing here in the middle of the night?

Kids he calls us! High Angel fogged smoke in John's eyes. We're here to play. Ain't that what kids do? We plays.

You haven't seen Nick?

I said he was a woman-hater.

Nick your son, old man? High Angel sneered. Or just your punk?

Nick's the man who makes me cuckold.

We don't like no dirty talk here, Mister!

I didn't – I said cuckold.

Ohhhhh! It hurts my ears. . . cried squawking girl.

Why I oughta warsh his mouth wid soap.

That's some kinda queer somethin' he's sayin'.

Sure looks queeroo.

Hey, Bea?

I'm over here.

Well I wants you over here, Cicone.

Yeah, yeah, keep it in the icebox.

Queer him if he's queer, Bea.

They wants I should queer you if you're queer, said the one called Bea, flicking a finger at John's chest. So is you queer or ain't you?

Don't know what you mean, John said.

He's trying to queer us, plain as starlight. Queering our fun.

Queering the pitch.

Queering our plans.

Surely, madam—

Hey, buddy, I ain't no pro!

Honestly, I don't understand you, John cried.

Hear the way he speaks! I said he was a queerer.

Fumbling closer to the theater as a rock came flying from deep in the crowd, John staggered wide of the missile and watched it thump to the ground at his feet. Poor John, said the rock, forgive me.

Man, look at him. His head's queer. He took sumpin'.

Look at the hands flutter. Patron of the Waldorf. I said he was a woman-hater.

The Waldorf? Where's that?

Place your pops used to go.

Why I oughta. . .

Why's he lookin' at me like that?

Are you Nick? John asked High Angel. It's a very good disguise.

You queer for me or sumpin', old man?

He's queer as a coot.

Let him go. The queer cull ain't worth it.

I like we should shake him down.

It'll only be queer money!

Laughter all around. A second stone fell and then another, each one blinking at John, abashed.

Look at him talking to rocks! You can tell he's on the queer!

Bea daggered his chest again with ruby-red nail. Why you lookin' at my fella, fella?

Because I know your fella. He's the one who's been screwing my wife. He made me cuckold.

Bea spun round to clock High Angel. What's that queer talkin' about, Angel?

Fiction, sweetheart! I ain't done nothin' to no one but you. Don't listen to the queerie!

You two-timin' me, Angel? You cheat on me I'll cut you!

Come on, Cicone, I ain't no double-crosser!

As Angel and Bea threw down on the pavement, John crept towards the entrance to the theater. He had nearly escaped when Angel noticed, shouting, Our queer's getting away!

John pushed at the doors but the first pair were locked so he ran to the next, heaved, the doors gave way, and he rushed in, flinging them shut behind him. The amphitheater scooped uphill and in the dark he ran along the rightmost aisle, listening as the gang pushed the doors open again and pursued him, vaulting over the first rows of seats. Someone thumped a drum, another buzzed a harmonica, hands clapping time against their drunken chorus, 'Kill the faggot, kill the faggot.'

If only the goddamned cop would wake! John scrambled for the third tier, screaming for help. A rock grazed his cheek and he turned to face the gang, their blades flashing in starlight. He did a quick tally, twelve or fifteen of them. Nowhere to go but back to the stage. He ran along the other aisle, taking steps two at a time, but they closed around him, blocking his exit stage left and right.

We wants t'ask you again, Angel shouted.

Yeah. . . Is you a queer or ain't you? said Bea.

I am not, John cried, and in his own ears he sounded like Mary.

Now that's what you call a hypocrite! Angel laughed.

Who's that?

Someone what says he's somethin' he ain't.

That's this whole town all over.

Laughter all round.

Not like us.

We calls ourselves like we see ourselves.

So tell us again, woman-hater, is you a queer or ain't you?

John opened his mouth but found he could not speak. He shook his head and saw the coyote reappear, its giant nose sniffing the line between mountain and sky.

Cat got your tongue? High Angel said. You know what we do to chumps who won't talk?

John collapsed to his knees, put his hands together in supplication. Murders are supposed to happen off stage, he screamed, as the gang pummeled his back, long-nailed fingers pulling at his clothes and hair, a boot connecting with his stomach, another his kidneys. They beat his head with sticks and stones, rakes and garden hoes, striking him until he could feel nothing but a soft gray fuzziness, a giant paw reaching down from the mountain to press against his chest.

This is the end, John, the coyote whispered in his ear, there will be no dawn to reckon with, you will never have to make the choice, it has been made on your behalf, Angels beating the life right out of you, squeezing the juice from your skin, stomping the fat white grape.

John tried to scream, but the soft gray paw covered his face, smothering and pushing him so that he fell through a trapdoor in the stage, circling down into darkness and looking back up at his body where it lay on the boards, broken by those children in red. John Marsh looked at John Marsh as if there had never been any connection between the self that thinks and the one that feels, and in sinking found himself descending without guide, passing portents of the day just past, before entering a red conical hell.

At his death, stones wept sand and heated themselves to glass, trees dropped their needles and leaves, rivers swelled to flood. All the world dressed itself in black as his body, ripped limb from limb, was tossed around the stage, head kicked and stuck with blades before being carried to the river, floated off to the ocean, and borne away to other shores, where, temples dripping saltwater, he would face fresh insult: the bite of a snake bearing the face of his wife.

John rubbed his eyes and when he looked again he found himself alone on stage, clothes soaked from night sweats, the truncheon of a policeman tickling his ribs.

Park's closed, pal.

There was a gang. They attacked me.

The cop looked around, shined a flashlight in his face. I ain't seen no one but you. Hey, ain't you. . .?

No, I'm not.

Sure you are, you're what's his name. Cocoanut Grove. Ciro's. You get around. You're in all the papers on account of your wife.

Funny papers.

When I heard you scream, I thought maybe you was one of them fairies. I mean, no offense. The cop reached down and helped John to his feet. You don't look so well.

My wife gave me some pills.

What you want is a good night's sleep.

Almost too late for that. It's Saturday already.

Sleep it off. Need a lift?

What's the time? I lost my watch.

Almost three.

As they walked from the theater back to the street, John imagined how the cop would tell his friends that he had met someone from the movies, a man who goes to bed every night with a real live star but still scrounges in public parks for sex and trouble.

Although the sky had too much texture, there was no giant

coyote, and if there were not fifteen hoodlums there must have been two, swathed in red leather. John would go home, sleep two hours, and wake at first light certain he never wanted to be mistaken again for what he was not.

Just radio someone downtown to call a cab, he said to the cop. I need to go home.

August 30, 1955

14

Today is not Saturday, not this April 15th, but a Monday, although it is as sunny and warm as that Saturday in Los Angeles, some six thousand miles distant from where I now sit, except that when it is noon here it is only three in the morning in California and the bright sun I see from this terrace has not yet reached the Pacific Coast. If I look too intently at this Italian sun I will be blinded, although my eyes are already dim despite the cataract surgery ten years ago. I fear they will give up before the rest of me does and I will no longer be able to look out from my terrace across the roofs of this city to see the tower of Santa Croce and the Tuscan hills and the Arno, now tame after its spring torrent. Memories of those I loved – still love, since love outlasts life – continue to nourish me. I suppose you deserve to know what happened next, Myles, at the end of that extraordinary day sixty-three years ago, or rather at the beginning of the day that followed, which was not the first day of the rest of my life, because that would be too prosaic, but the first day of a new life entirely. Even that is somehow incorrect. It was the first day of a life beyond the life I had lived up until that point, a life with nothing because it was a life without you.

Being a good Marxist – if ever I was such a creature, if such a creature is even a possibility since surely the best Marxist is one who believes in the continuation of historical cycles and thus the progression of the self, the endless evolution of one's own personality and ideology – I should have had no problem taking a vow of poverty, even emotional poverty, living a life beyond possession excepting that which I needed to keep myself alive, foreswearing my estate like some good old Jesuit, like the new Papa Francesco who comes in the habit of a pauper, telling even all the atheist queers that we are not beyond redemption, promising us an afterlife in heaven, which is more than can be said of his predecessor with those Dorothy Gale pumps, red and witch-slaying. I had a pair made for myself by a wicked little *calzolaio* and wore them to Rome where devout tourists gawped and wondered, with my bush of white hair and dark beetling brows, whether I might not be the Papa himself, wandering the streets looking for mischief, ogling young men on pale blue Vespas.

This morning the Arno is a river of light. Earlier this spring it was almost in flood after a misery of incessant rain that reminded me of the catastrophic flood of '66. Now at last real spring has arrived nearly a month late and we Florentines, the indigenous as much as the naturalized, act almost ungrateful for the beauty of these days when the wisteria comes into bloom and fields burst with a cosmos of tiny white daisies. Only yes, the past, the past that is never past but always resting upon us in the mind of memory: the twenty-four hours that preceded the day that followed sixty-three years ago were decisive, although not so fundamentally different from all the other days I spent in Los Angeles over the course of the previous decade, not even essentially different from my childhood and adolescence and young manhood in New York. But the day that followed, the day that was precisely sixty-three years ago today by the Gregorian calendar, which means I am now a very old man indeed, was an extraordinary day because that was the day I launched myself into a life with no certainties but also no responsibilities. Lest you still think me unfeeling, Myles, let me assure you I did as much as I could at the time. I returned to the hospital, I drove Helen's car back to her, I waited for you to regain consciousness, but you did not, not until the following day. Ever since the death of Noah Roy I have cringed from goodbyes, hating the hot clench in the throat, the way my chin trembles when I realize I have no guarantee of seeing the person again. Having lost one love so precipitously I could never thereafter trust time to hurl me back into the orbit of those I most adored.

Forgive me for leaving before you woke. Forgive me for leaving at all.

I took a taxi from the hospital back to Bel Air. The wreckage of my car had already been towed but there was broken glass and I don't know what else on the street, maybe some bits of metal, scorch marks from the fire, water on the pavement, the shadow of blood, and then your and Helen's car. I don't know who moved it, but it was just inside the gates and I got in and drove myself home, so distraught I was shaking all over, my hands trembling, and I nearly had an accident myself. The drive along Sunset that time of morning was like navigating through ink, and coming over one of those rises I strayed across the center line. It is possible I had an impulse to end it. Although I did not actively think of killing myself, I wanted to be dead. There is a difference between thinking the desire to end one's life and thinking the desire to not be alive, to be living no longer. Psychoanalysts might say there is so little difference as to be immaterial, that desiring one's non-life is no less a violence to the self than actively imagining ending one's days. Psychoanalysts want you to believe the problem rests in the nuclear family and not in the nuclear societies that produce such great unhappiness. I would never have thought of killing myself if it were not for the way we were being persecuted by people who menaced us under the mantle of liberty, but that is another matter. I corrected my steering, I swerved, I realized the risk of my own subconscious thoughts and so drove home slowly, taking each curve and turn with as much caution as my frayed nerves could marshal, for the greater part of me did not want to be dead.

The house was dark when I arrived and I let myself in knowing that someone was listening to my every footstep. I turned on all the lights and when I saw the look on Max's face as he emerged from his room behind the kitchen I was certain he had betrayed me, even though I had employed him after he was fired during the union purges. For several months I had suspected his disloyalty but had no proof, and I could tell that when he saw me he regretted what he had done. Perhaps they gave him little choice. He said nothing, just put a finger to his lips and swiveled his eyes around the room as if to warn me the whole house had ears, that my nightmare of hidden surveillance beneath the wallpaper and under the tables was not so far-fetched.

I finished packing my bags, loaded the trunk of the car, shook Max's hand, and hoped the money I gave him would be enough to buy me a cushion of time. After picking up Barbara we drove back to the hospital, arriving before dawn. I took my suitcases upstairs to your private room where Helen was asleep in a chair. It was then that I noticed they had removed all the mirrors.

If I had known it would take a dozen surgeries before you began to look like yourself again, I would never have left. Had I known that you would no longer be a leading man, becoming instead the asexual best friend, a sidekick unlucky with women, and later, when the movies caught up to real life in a more realistic way (believing in the illusion of their own realism, or perhaps still not even realizing that their realism was merely an illusion, that any attempt at realism can only ever be an illusion, the real we perceive in our daily lives itself being a series of highly structured illusions, all of us moving through a deadly convincing miasma of false consciousness), that you would have parts only as the raging anti-hero, the self-destructive cowpoke, the ambiguous motorcyclist, the Korean War vet battling psychological tsunamis of Communist soldiers spilling in waves over peninsular hillsides, had I known that was what awaited you in my absence, I would never have left.

I placed my lips on your silent lips but you did not stir.

Please try to understand that I believed my livelihood in Hollywood was the least of my concerns, that it was only a matter of time before I was arrested either for being a homosexual or for refusing to give testimony in the kangaroo-court that McCarthy and the rest of them had orchestrated. I left because I feared for my liberty as a man of the left and a man who loved men. You will say that a man of more generous heart would have sacrificed himself to look after the man he loved. My response is simple: you are right. I failed you and can only beg your forgiveness. That is what remains.

I woke Helen and put the car keys in her hand, hugged her, kissed her on both cheeks, and said goodbye to Barbara. Then, left alone with you, I held your hand and kissed you again, pressing my lips into yours with as much purpose and passion as I felt your body could tolerate given its state. And before I was in tears, or perhaps I was already crying openly, unconscious of how loud my sobs might have been, I picked up my suitcases and walked out of the room and along the hall and down the stairs where I got a cab that took me to the airport to catch my flight to New York.

Now old and decrepit, I am not yet immobile. I can still trudge across Florence, make my way to the Uffizi, take a taxi to the Accademia to look at the David early in the morning before he is ringed by tourists endlessly capturing his exquisite body with their cameras and phones. This city offers as much chaos and bustle as my frailty can withstand. In New York, sixty-three years ago tomorrow and the next day and the next, I attended to my financial affairs, phoning every day to make sure you were alive and improving, heartbroken that you refused to speak to me when you woke. Although far from you I found you kept appearing on the streets of Manhattan, the back of your head in a young businessman, the curve of your shoulder in an athletic teenager, and then your face itself, but your face as it had been before the accident, smiling from countless movie posters for whatever film you happened to be in that was then playing in theaters. Because you were inescapable it was impossible not to keep you in mind at all times, when I bought traveler's checks, when I said goodbye to old friends, when I went to visit Noah Roy's parents in their apartment on Gramercy Park and found them more careworn than ever, when I boarded the plane at Idlewild, when I flew to Newfoundland and Shannon and London and then finally arrived, a week after departing Los Angeles, in Paris, where my apartment on rue Bonaparte was home for the next four decades, during which time I disengaged more than ever from politics, and though I might perhaps have found a home in the French Communist Party if my queerness would not have prevented me, I instead turned inward, living cheaply and writing in my attic suite of rooms with their long windows and skylights and walls covered in books, with an assortment of peripatetic friends and lovers and visiting parents and cousins, people who saw in me no particular change except that I had left the movie business, fled Los Angeles, retired from America, and now made my living as a novelist in English who lived in France, that is to say, one in a long line of outcast rabble-rousers with no more rabble to rouse than words on a page, ignored at home, read with curiosity if at all in the country they have adopted, and hoping just to live out the balance of their lives in peace. The only change that was visible upon me was that all of a sudden my hair turned white, so completely white that I acquired the nickname *l'aigle d'Amérique*, the bald eagle, a North American migrant returned to the continent of his ancestors.

Over the subsequent years, people, new friends, all of them Europeans, asked me if I ever missed Los Angeles, the question usually spoken in a tone of certainty that said only a philistine could miss such a place. But of course, I miss it enormously! They had no idea what Los Angeles was actually like, only the image presented by its largest industry, which elides what is most interesting about it. Nonetheless, I have never been able to bring myself to go back, in part because I miss the city that I am certain is now rebuilt beyond recognition, and that was the landscape of my happiest time, my years with you. I miss the city that was already disappearing in 1950, overbuilt and sprawling with shoebox suburbs, the city that on a sunny spring day with the breezes uncurling from the Pacific and the air still clear looked like an Olympus of the west, those white buildings with their terracotta tile roofs surrounded by a lush green garden. I miss *that* city, the city that was crazy in a beautiful way before it went crazy in what appears from a distance to be an ugly one. I miss the city before it went to hell, and then I think maybe the crazy was always mostly ugly underneath the beauty and paradise is just another word for hell. Now it is Concreteville – that's what my father was calling it by the beginning of the sixties. Funny coming from a lifelong New Yorker more comfortable on a Park Avenue sidewalk than on the lawns of Central Park, but for him the obscenity of Los Angeles was that it had turned a space so recently natural into one that wanted first to tame nature, to pastoralize it, to classicize it, only in the end to obliterate it, consuming all the land around it rather than building skywards. We Americans *waste* land, he said to me. Most people have no idea how valuable all this space is. If they'd been to Europe they would understand, and I have to agree with my old crank of a father, may he rest in peace.

Here in my apartment a few streets south of the Arno, I look out on a city so compact, so tightly packed, which nonetheless remains one where I never feel claustrophobic. Not like Venice, where I sometimes find I cannot breathe the streets are so narrow and crowded with tourists. No one would want to chase beauty there in old age, not now, it is far too perilous these days. Florence may not be Paris or Rome, but I feel at home in the higgledy-piggledy streets and winding alleyways of this city, enjoy the possibility of getting happily lost, the fact that I can still at my age live a life almost entirely on foot, walking with my cane to the nearest market and the Pitti Palace and when the blood is strong inside me all the way to the Palazzo Vecchio where I can contemplate the poet's death mask and stand at night-time in those great rooms overlooking the illuminated city where chic Florentine teenagers live as if it were still 1950, overflowing with impassioned debate in a country that has never seemed so politically unstable in recent memory, making out extravagantly and being romantic with an openness that seems almost angelic. I know they all piss and shit and fart and fuck and that there is no unblemished beauty in the world, but when they promenade in twilight and forget their beauty as they so often appear to do, or when they seem never to have been aware of their beauty in the first place, as you were, Myles, at that point they surpass every ideal of beauty I might imagine, even beyond the beauty of Botticelli's angels, the faces of those boys in whom, in one specifically, I imagine I see your eyes. He is there in the *Madonna of the Magnificat*, wearing the white tunic on the right of the painting, raising with his right hand the crown upon the Virgin's head, and there again in the *Madonna of the Pomegranate*, on the extreme right, next to the one holding a book, and he is looking intently at the child, not at us, not breaking the fourth wall of the painting to gaze directly at me as I wish he would, as I sense that he does when he appears again as Saint Sebastian in Berlin, where I have sometimes been to see him, or as Mars in London, and in his recurrence through Botticelli's works I imagine the adoration of the painter, which transcended the bonfire of the vanities, an adoration and idealization as great as what I continue to feel for you, Myles, with whom I had something approaching the purity of union that one most desires in life, an alliance that blinds one to the flaws of the beloved, at least for a while, or if not blinds then occludes those shortcomings, makes them less significant than perhaps they are in the police-interrogation beam of objective analysis.

The Arno flashes, not red or gold but a liquid marine fire robed in the flowers of spring, sparks of light shooting from its roiling surface. The phone rings and I ignore it, it rings too often, I will let someone else answer. It stops, Alessio makes excuses, he gets me off the hook while the phone is off the hook – unless, no, the patter of those feet, it is a call for Margaret, except it could not be for Margaret because she is long dead. It is a call for me, and the phone, cordless, comes into my hand, my dear Alessio smiling apologetically, for we both know the likelihood of silence on the other end, or in this case, today, the panting of muffled breath and then the dial tone as the caller hangs up, leaving me beached in anxiety.

You see, even in my exile they persecute me.

Exile has never been a protection from persecution. Not long after landing in Paris I became conscious of having grown a tail, slicker and better dressed than the snap-brimmed men in Los Angeles, but unmistakably part of the same extended family. I noticed him first because he was my age and attractive in that New England way that attempts to be European while never entirely casting off the heredity of centuries in North America, which is to say he was trying to blend in as French, and on overhearing him speak in bookshops, I could not immediately tell whether his French was acquired at the breast or only, as I suspected, through study and practice. The man kept turning up, not every day but a few times a week, and his features were so striking it was impossible not to notice him, or the careful tailoring of his suits, or the way he was always alone. We never spoke, but he was with me for a year at least, the first of a succession of men who tailed me with such ostentatious discretion that I came to think of them as lovers I had not yet seduced and began to invent histories for our relationships, seeing in the blond man who succeeded the New Englander someone whose mother was a foreigner and therefore could blend more seamlessly into that particular Parisian street theater. It was around that time, by which I must mean 1951, that my name began to be bandied about in a certain room in Congress, put down in public record, slurred as a *known Communist* and, although this did not appear in the public record of the Committee, a *pervert*. It was not only John and Mary who testified, and in testifying pronounced my name as a traitor, but many others whom I had long imagined were friends. That you and Helen were spared such a performance has always made me wonder if you did not reach some private arrangement with the authorities. John's testimony was the hardest to bear because he appeared as a friend of the Committee, one present not by demand but by choice. He volunteered to testify, to name countless people he either knew to be Communists, suspected of being Communists, had heard might be fellow travelers, or feared might simply be *subversives*, which was the damning catch-all category for those who had done nothing more than believe in the rights of ordinary people to make a decent living, have a reasonable quality of life, and not worry that they might get fired without notice. Believe those things, sign a petition in support of them, give a little money to the wrong organization, march in a parade or protest, and you must be a *subversive* bent on overthrowing a democratically elected government. Horseshit of course. I must not try to think about it too much because it still raises my blood pressure and this, my dear old doctor (who himself has heart troubles) tells me, I must not do.

My phone is ringing again and it is the hour for my walk. I will go to the Boboli Garden to escape my persecutors as I do every day. Yesterday, however, something happened. I took an eccentric route along the Borgo San Frediano and then down the Via dei Serragli – a street I cannot walk without imagining it is instead the Via dei Seraglio, street of the brothel instead of that noble family – turning onto the Via Sant'Agostino, past the graffiti that has become the greatest menace of the city, the menace of the whole of Italy and most of Europe, past the rank of dumpsters, I stopped to buy a single blood orange, now almost out of season, peeled it on the street, let the juice trickle between my fingers, placed the beet-dark segments between my purple lips, tasting the fruit as though tonguing sex, disposed of the skin, and listened as bells pealed. I made my way to Santo Spirito to browse the antiques in *il mercato*. There is one man in particular I find often in the same place, with his collection of movie memorabilia, and standing there yesterday under the timpani beat of the sun I flipped through his posters and found, with something like awe, the faces of you and Mary staring back at me, Mary doubled as Faye and Ursula, John's name splashed across the bottom, and mine nowhere to be seen, because all trace of Desmond Frank was stripped from that film, in Italian retitled *Mai Tornare Indietro*, never go back, never turn back, never return, and there you were, about to glance over your shoulder at the identical twin sisters. The shock of those faces gazing at me in that unlikely place, translated into another language, translating me back into another time and place, was so disorienting I stumbled to the fountain and sat down on the steps. Those good Italians, so solicitous, such respect for the aged, converged to help me, making sure I had my cane, bringing me a drink of water and then an espresso from the neighboring café, and I sat there under the sun in this Florentine square finding myself quite overcome, gushing tears and leaning against the fountain, crying silently as only the old can cry, my chest again turning with that tight knot I used to know so well as I looked up, surrounded by the concerned faces of antiques dealers and junk sellers and, in the distance, the face of one of those well-fed American men I continue to see whenever I leave my house, men who no longer wear suits but come dressed as tourists, sometimes as women, but always looking at me with too much attentive nonchalance, and I saw that man several more times yesterday as I continued my perambulations.

I put the parts of myself back in order, I stood, I bought the poster of *Mai Tornare Indietro* and said to the dealer, whom I could tell did not believe me, that I had written that movie, *Ho scritto che film*, and that I was once a screenwriter, *sceneggiatore*, but am now nothing more than a *romanziere*, a writer of novels, which in Italian and French and Portuguese and even Romanian sounds to the Anglophone ear like nothing more than the writer of romances. In English, in the seventeenth century, as well as being a term of disparagement for innovators of any kind (newness being as great a sin as sodomy), 'novelist' meant 'novice', a beginner, an unskilled person, and this is how I feel even at the end of my life, as if I am only beginning to understand anything at all. I could feel them watching me as I left the square, past the Basilica and along the Via dei Michelozzi, and then further along until I reached the stone embrace of the Pitti Palace, its paved carpet covered with tourists taking the sun, past whom I stumbled on my way to the Garden's entrance.

Today I go straight to the Boboli, for there is no *mercato*. At the gate I show my pass, I look behind me, and today again that American is with me, pretending to be a tourist. I climb through the steep terraces and up to my favorite spot, in the garden of the Museo delle Porcellane, where I sit on the wall clutching my cane, looking over my shoulder at the hills and the cypresses and the receding countryside of my adopted country, the country of my mother and her family (our family villa, not far from here, is now a hotel), perhaps then the country I have reclaimed as my own, surveying hills in which, with their white buildings and terracotta roofs on a clear day in April, I can catch the same spirit of Los Angeles sixty-three years ago, and in breathing these airs I return again to what was happiest about that time, the private love of the lives we held private by design.

The tourist is here with me, taking photographs in my direction, photographing me as if I were a part of the landscape, an example of faded Italian aristocracy, an old Tuscan queen devoted to his tailor and shoemaker and his much younger lover, still nursing an ideology that, decades after being declared moribund in the west, seems again to be pulsing with life. Cycles, the dialectic of history, thesis-antithesis-synthesis. Communist Bolshevism was a false revolution. No one should be nostalgic for the Soviet Union or Mao's China or any of the other communist states. The real revolution we cannot imagine until it has arrived, and then we will know it, like the Messiah. Hours pass and I sit, or perhaps only an hour at most and then I return, back through the gardens and the streets south of the Arno to my own building, to the cool marble interior of the entry, the door I open on the right, the hook where I hang my coat, my Alessio helping me up the broad stairs to a seat in the salon where he serves me lunch and I sit, cool in the late afternoon, dozing as I lose myself in the frescos on the ceiling, the grotesques animating themselves against the screen of my mind as the phone rings and rings.

Once upon a time Margaret Brookes answered my phone, joining me in the last years of her life, not because of any romantic love, but in something like a twilight union of sympathy and solidarity, in the final reel of her life if not of my own. She died here, is buried here, and during her life with me confused all those people who thought they had understood me before her arrival, for we lived, outwardly in Florentine society, as husband and wife in all but name, delighting in the disbelief we sowed. It was both pain and pleasure to have her with me, for reminders of past happiness are always intercut with recollections of failure and a recognition that the passage of time, the creation of memory, the elapsing of years that creates the very possibility of reflection, plays to a soundtrack of irremediable loss. In my case, loss of Noah and you, but also of Helen, that firmest of friends, loss of parents in the intervening years, loss of my country and the career that I loved for the one that allowed me to continue without hindrance. For Margaret, solitary her whole life, obscure even with me about the nature of her desires, whatever sense of loss she carried she did not share, for we were a couple who did not test each other, respecting the pain of the other and understanding, I believe for my own part, that the clues to her private anguishes, as much as I knew about them, were there to be read and understood in the pictures she wrote, in the fictional lives she animated, the characters whose passions and losses beat with humanity beneath her tough-talking exterior. Margaret collaborated with me on one of the first drafts of *She Turned Away*, and much of her dialogue found its way into the final script, though her name was nowhere on it, stripped in the merciless studio process just as my own name was rubbed from the final cut, so that John Marsh could claim to have written and directed it without anyone else's involvement (never mind it was based on an original story of my own, never mind that Orph Patterson continued to live on in the books that I subsequently wrote), and Nick Charles could succeed in bargaining for a producer credit, only later to take over for Porter when Porter, as so many of us suspected he would, elbowed Leo Krug off the lot and into a bitter retirement in which he denounced the scheming of Reds and queers to oust him. But that, of course, is past, and I try not to nurse the resentment I feel towards my erstwhile friends, all of them now dead, although in the end I fail: I understand Mary's betrayal because she never liked me and always made that obvious, but I do not and will never understand the actions of John Marsh. I have tried and failed to make sense of his motivations. I have tried to see his fear in terms of love, which is to say fear of being alone in the world, bereft of his wife and daughter and the career he created. I have tried to see it in terms of him wanting to progress in a nation that claims to champion progress. But I cannot bring myself to understand his treason against me as anything other than petty and self-serving, the act of a man who could only think of himself in his own moment of danger. Know too that in saying this I can see the mirror of my actions, the selfishness of my flight, though I think it is a selfishness of lesser degree: my flight did nothing to harm except

643

emotionally. I destroyed no lives, I undermined no government or democratic system, I betrayed no friends. All I did was leave as an act of self-preservation. I did all I could to persuade those I loved to come with me, even though you refused. I had no other choice as I saw it.

That is the end of my apologia.

Now, outside on the street, I see my American tourist again, wandering alone as tourists do not often wander in Florence, pairs being more likely, throngs the most common. The single middle-aged American with a paunch is remarkable and the temptation to invite him inside, to lure him into a trap and watch him squirm under my interrogations is so great that I almost lean out the window and summon him to join me for an *aperitivo*, and, over a bitter red cocktail, ask him why, six decades into my exile, I cannot be left alone.

My love to you, Myles, and in hope that you will respond, I remain, yours always,

Desmond

You do not know me, and I hope you will forgive my writing
in this way, but I found some letters you had sent to our
mutual friend, Mr. Desmond Frank, a few years ago now. As
you must be aware, Mr. Frank passed away last summer. His
death was covered in the European press, and I think to a
certain extent in America as well, although it is my impression
he is not remembered as much in your country as in my own,
or in France, where he lived for so many years. If his death
is news to you, please forgive me being bearer of these sad
tidings.

I write as the executor of Mr. Frank's estate, and also as his
heir. He had no children, but I was, if this is not too indelicate,
a companion to him in his later life. Maybe you call us lovers, I
don't know. I loved him and I think he loved me and we lived
together for some years as a couple, no matter the difference
in our ages. Myself I am a painter by training but mostly I
make a living now giving classes to rich Americans. This is not
totally relevant, but I want you to understand my relationship
with Desmond, and how I come to read your letters. It feels
maybe intrusive that I did so, and I apologize, but I was trying
to understand his archive and your letters, they are a part of
it. I am not sure what to do with all this paper. Maybe I give
it to a library, if anyone would be interested. (Maybe you are
interested?) Or if you would like me to return your letters to
you, this I can also do.

I am writing now because I do not know if Desmond ever
replied to these letters you sent. But he did write something
to your husband, Mr. Haywood. I address this to you now

rather than Mr. Haywood because of the delicacy of the matter. I know that he and Desmond had a relationship many years ago, and it seems this was no secret between you. Forgive me if I am mistaken, or this is a surprise. Two years ago, I think after your letters arrived, Desmond spent weeks writing a long letter to your husband, if letter you can call it, and I assumed he sent it, but then, after his death, I found it and think he must not have. I read the pages recently and see it is not a letter so much as a confession, but then there are other things in this file, sections of a screenplay and stories he seems to have written in the 1950s, all of it mixed up together, pages numbered by hand. The order and dates do not make much sense to me, but then I am not so good a reader of English and maybe to you it will be clear. The parts that are stories, they use the names of real people sometimes, and when I read them I ask myself, how can he know what he writes about? In my own experience, he imagined things about me, about my life growing up, and he was totally but totally wrong. Crazy ideas. Fights with urchins out of Rossellini and De Sica and love affairs with playboys like from Fellini or existential sufferers from Antonioni and all of it nothing like my youth. Other times he imagined things about me and it would be but *so* terrifyingly true. (I like this English word, 'terrifyingly', in Italian 'spaventosamente', also nice, I think.)

If I find anything else that seems relevant, I will send this also. I should say that Desmond spoke often to me of his love for you, and of course for your husband, and his regret at not having seen you for so many years. I feel that this was his greatest sorrow, that he died without seeing you both once more. I hope, I don't know what exactly, but perhaps your husband will read this testament from Desmond and it will make some difference to him.

Again, please forgive if this seems intrusive. If you say you do not wish to hear from me again, I respect this, and yet I hope perhaps one day we will meet, if you ever come to Firenze. You and your husband would be most welcome.

Yours faithfully,
Alessio Rabino

July 15, 2016
Pacific Palisades, California

Dear Mr. Rabino,

First I must apologize that it has taken me such a long time
to confirm receipt of the papers you sent, now more than
a year ago. I opened the file right away when it came, and
thought I could read it quickly, but then the more I read the
more troubling it all became, and it took me a long time to
finish it, picking up the file and putting it down, going back
to the beginning and circling the text over and over, which is
probably what Desmond intended. The problem was knowing
whether to show it to Myles at all. He was in poor health when
the package arrived, suffering with congestive heart failure.
As you probably now know he passed away in January. It was
a terrible blow to me even though he had been ill for some
time, and it has taken me this long to read Desmond's letter or
whatever it is once more.

The truth is, I feel angry more than anything. Not with you,
but with Desmond, because he took so long to do something
he should have done decades earlier. And I am angry with
myself because I failed to show it to Myles before he died, and
that failure means I have inherited Desmond's guilt.

I showed the file to my children because I needed to share
it with someone and talk about those years. There are details
Desmond gets wrong, naturally, or that he remembers very
differently from the way I remember them. Barbara and I were
never as close as he imagines we were, or at least not in the
same way that he and Myles were. I don't think I was ever
as self-denying as he makes me seem. But then we're often

poor judges of ourselves, and the way other people see us in
our youth is never quite how we imagine we actually are. I
know I had a sharp tongue, but I'm not sure I was as clever or
audacious as Desmond paints me.

I can't say whether John dropped acid that night in
particular, but he spent so much of his later life on one kind of
drug or another it's certainly possible. There are other things,
however, that are just plain wrong. Mary Dawn, for instance,
was never as composed or frigid as Desmond describes her.
She could be genuinely warm and was a good friend to me
despite everything. I think she knew about me and Myles, and
it didn't seem to matter to her. I know for a fact that the Nazi
housekeeper is an amalgam of a few different women who
worked for the Marshes in the late 40s and early 50s, none of
them Nazis as far as I knew, none of them recruited by the U.S.
government to spy (although how would I know for certain,
right?), but I am fairly certain they were each of them German.
Desmond was right about Mary keeping secret her foreign
birth, but that came out later when she realized it didn't matter
to anyone where she was born or what language she spoke
as a child. Whatever the case, Desmond had an uncanny gift
for seeing through people, and, as you say, there are things
he gets terrifyingly right. I find myself wondering, How can
he possibly have known that about me? I'm too old and too
proper to tell you what those things are, but up until now I
always assumed they were private. I suppose Myles must have
told Desmond a lot about our odd married life, but it's been
an uncomfortable experience to read descriptions of myself
as a young woman because for the most part I feel either
that Desmond saw me with painful clarity, or simply failed to

see me at all. Apart from the studio memos you would never know that I was also in *She Turned Away*, playing the Rose Zapatero character and several other bit parts. I suppose that my participation was not Desmond's point, but the oversight, or the silence around me, hurts.

I wish I could say that Myles and I had a happy life together. At least it was not an angry one. There was no fighting. We were best friends, we adopted children who have given me great happiness, but we lived with the particular melancholy that comes from spending most of one's life in the closet. Although I wanted us to, Myles was never prepared to come out, not even when so many others had. He said it would make him look ridiculous. I said it would make him a star all over again, but I guess it was too late for him. Maybe it isn't for me. I think for Myles it seemed impossible because he never got over Desmond. Occasionally he would bring someone home, always discreet, but no one lasted longer than a week or two because he kept hoping that Desmond would come back, that he would get over himself and apologize for what he had done. Myles did not stop loving him but he hated him, too, and in the absence of an apology could not find it in himself to offer forgiveness.

Now the apology is here, before me, but too late. And that is my fault.

With the script of *She Turned Away* as it appears in the file, I sat down and watched the movie, although I have made a habit of avoiding our old films since Myles's death. I usually find them too painful to watch, particularly those from before his accident. The script in the file is different from the final cut of the film, as you probably know, but not in ways that seem

very significant, which leads me to wonder why Desmond
makes such a meal of the thing. Lines are different here and
there, scenes end earlier or begin later than in the script,
some sequences have been rearranged, but it seems intact
for the most part, and still largely his work, even if his name
does not, even now, appear on the film. Perhaps that was his
point, now that I think about it, and it *is* an injustice, especially
since the characters and the story and situations, and so much
else besides are based on his original ideas. I still have some
influence with the company that now owns the distribution
rights, and could lobby for his name to be restored, if that is
something you would like to pursue.

Late in his life, after Mary's death, John Marsh spoke to me
about his appearance before HUAC. I had never asked him
about it because it was obvious whenever it came up that
it caused him very real pain. I know it was an unforgivable
betrayal, and no amount of moral relativism about the
pressures of that time can excuse what John did. I think even
John, at the end of his own life, knew that there were no
excuses that held up to scrutiny, at least not scrutiny by the
kind of mind that can see individual acts in their historical
context and understand that partisanship and ideology must
be subordinated to a greater sense of right and wrong. There,
I sound like Desmond. How do we determine the definitions
of that 'greater sense'? I am not a Christian or anything. I feel
closest to Buddhism and Judaism but am neither of those
either and cannot set aside my natural skepticism to believe
in anything other than what I observe, even now. Given that
limitation, how do we decide what is good and what is evil in
a way that can be tested and does not require the passage of

time and the distance of memory to see clearly? How could
the men and women in the 1940s and 1950s who believed
they were doing good (as I want to believe the witch hunters
did believe, whatever we thought of them then, whatever we
think of them now) possibly fail to see that they were doing
evil? How, today, can the people who rally behind racists and
misogynists, anti-Semites, Islamophobes, and homophobes,
believe that they can possibly be on the side of good? Are
the truly good always struggling not to be ground under the
heel of the evil man's boot, struggling not to be rounded up
and pilloried, not to be banned or deported or killed in their
millions? Is the nature of goodness – true goodness – always
to be in a position of potential vulnerability, always to be at
risk of persecution, always to be susceptible to banishment,
damnation, and termination by the evil forces who arrive
insisting they are good? Is the nature of goodness in fact a
greater proximity to death and violence and victimhood? They
are troubling questions. I do not have answers. I do not expect
that you should either, Mr. Rabino, but these are the questions
that keep me up at night, now, in the recent days and weeks
and months, as I contemplate Desmond's narrative about
Myles and me, and as I glimpse a possible political future that I
pray does not come to pass.

I wonder what is to be done with these papers, and
whether you have made any progress with sorting through
the rest of Desmond's archive, or if his publishers have
any thoughts on the matter. As for me, despite the fact the
manuscript uses my actual name, I have no objection to your
going ahead with publication, and would be happy to provide
an affidavit to that effect, indemnifying you and the publishers,

in whatever way you think fit. Everyone else is dead, so you are free to do as you like.

Sincerely yours,

Helen Fairdale

ACKNOWLEDGEMENTS

I am indebted to Beatrice Monti della Corte for her generous hospitality, which provided the space and time in which this book first took form at the Santa Maddalena Foundation in Spring 2013, and to Arts Council England for the residential fellowship that helped fund my stay there.

Thanks to Cassie Blake and Lynne Kirste at the Academy of Motion Picture Arts and Sciences Film Archive, Hollywood, California, and to Jenny Romero at the Margaret Herrick Library, Beverly Hills, California.

Thanks to the staff and librarians at the Huntington Library, San Marino, California, and at the Harry Ransom Humanities Research Center, University of Texas at Austin.

Thanks to Eduardo Cadava, Javier Montes, Neel Mukherjee, Mercedes Cebrián, Henrietta Rose-Innes, Michael Holtmann, Margaret Stead, Tristan and Lana Dalley, Nadia Davids and John Gutierrez, Chris and Katie Holmes, Amy Villarejo, Paul Saint-Amour, Gayle Rogers, Jennifer Spitzer, Susan Milrod, Angela Rae and Justin Cornish, Nayla Elamin, Laure Thorel, Nan van der Vlies, Undine Weber and Michael Ludewig, and Deborah Seddon. Thanks also to the late Evie Zysman, who was a model of political engagement, resistance, and friendship.

Thanks to Andrew Wylie, Sarah Chalfant, Alba Ziegler-Bailey, Rebecca Nagel, Charles Buchan, Sarah Watling, James Roxburgh, Tamsin Shelton, and everyone at the Wylie Agency and Atlantic Books.

Thanks to my mother, for encouraging an early love of movies.

Thanks especially to Andrew van der Vlies, for wearing many hats but always remaining himself.

~

This novel was written with reference to the following materials:

BOOKS

The Red and the Blacklist: The Intimate Memoir of a Hollywood Expatriate by Norma Barzman
Los Angeles: Photography by Robert Lee Behme
Inside Out: A Memoir of the Blacklist by Walter Bernstein
MGM: Hollywood's Greatest Backlot by Steven Bingen, Stephen X. Sylvester, and Michael Troyan
Dining Out in Hollywood and Los Angeles by Craig Davidson
City of Quartz: Excavating the Future in Los Angeles by Mike Davis
Imagining Los Angeles by Amy Dawes
'Let The People Know', The Truth About the Communists Which the Un-American Committee Tried to Suppress by Eugene Dennis
The Inquisition in Hollywood by Larry Ceplair and Steven Englund
The Gordon File: A Screenwriter Recalls Twenty Years of FBI Surveillance by Bernard Gordon
What Cooks in Hollywood: Autographed recipes straight from the kitchens of your favorite movie stars edited by Dorothy and Maxwell Hamilton
Writers in Hollywood: 1915-1951 by Ian Hamilton
Historical Atlas of California with Original Maps by Derek Hayes
Los Angeles Before the Freeways, 1850-1950: Images of an Era by Arnold Hylen

Hollywood on Trial: The Story of the 10 Who Were Indicted by Gordon Kahn
City Center to Regional Mall by Richard Longstreth
Naming Names by Victor S. Navasky
Fatalism in American Film Noir: Some Cinematic Philosophy by Robert B. Pippin
The New Renié Atlas of Los Angeles City and County by Jack J. Renié
Hollywood Left and Right: How Movie Stars Shaped American Politics by Steven J. Ross
Hollywood Cinema and the Real Los Angeles by Mark Shiel
California: A History by Kevin Starr
Coast of Dreams: A History of Contemporary California by Kevin Starr
Los Angeles: Portrait of a City by Kevin Starr, David L. Ulin, Jim Heimann
Maynard L. Parker: Modern Photography and the American Dream edited by Jennifer A. Watts

NEWSPAPERS AND PERIODICALS

Los Angeles Times
Red Channels: The Report of Communist Influence in Radio and Television
Variety

ARCHIVES

Herbert Biberman prison correspondence, Ring Lardner, Jr. files, selected files from the Production Code Administration archive, Margaret Herrick Library, Beverly Hills, California.

David O. Selznick files, Harry Ransom Humanities Research Center, Austin, Texas.

Home movies of Humphrey Bogart and Lauren Bacall, Richard Brooks, Henry Koster, Ginger Rogers, Esther Williams, and James Telfer, in the AMPAS Film Archive, The Pickford Center for Motion Picture Study, Hollywood, California.

FILMS

1924
Aelita. Dir. Yakov Protazanov.

1926
Secrets of a Soul. Dir. G.W. Pabst.

1927
October: Ten Days That Shook the World. Dir. Sergei Eisenstein.

1929
Un Chien Andalou. Dir. Luis Buñuel.
Man with a Movie Camera. Dir. Dziga Vertov.

1937
Thunder in the City. Dir. Marion Gering.

1940
His Girl Friday. Dir. Howard Hawks.
The Philadelphia Story. Dir. George Cukor.

1942
Casablanca. Dir. Michael Curtiz.

1943
Meshes of the Afternoon. Dir. Maya Deren and Alexander Hammid.
Ossessione. Dir. Luchino Visconti.
Shadow of a Doubt. Dir. Alfred Hitchcock.

1944
Double Indemnity. Dir. Billy Wilder.

1945
Anchors Aweigh. Dir. George Sidney.
Detour. Dir. Edgar G. Ulmer.
The Lost Weekend. Dir. Billy Wilder.
Mildred Pierce. Dir. Michael Curtiz.
Scarlet Street. Dir. Fritz Lang.

Spellbound. Dir. Alfred Hitchcock.

1946

The Big Sleep. Dir. Howard Hawks.

The Killers. Dir. Robert Siodmak.

The Postman Always Rings Twice. Dir. Tay Garnett.

The Stranger. Dir. Orson Welles.

1947

Brute Force. Dir. Jules Dassin.

Crossfire. Dir. Edward Dmytryk.

Fireworks. Dir. Kenneth Anger.

Kiss of Death. Dir. Henry Hathaway.

The Lady from Shanghai. Dir. Orson Welles.

Out of the Past. Dir. Jacques Tourneur.

1948

Bicycle Thieves. Dir. Vittorio de Sica.

The Big Clock. Dir. John Farrow.

Force of Evil. Dir. Abraham Polonsky.

Hollow Triumph. Dir. Steve Sekely.

Mr. Blandings Builds His Dream House. Dir. H.C. Potter.

The Naked City. Dir. Jules Dassin.

Rope. Dir. Alfred Hitchcock.

Secret Beyond the Door. Dir. Fritz Lang.

Sorry, Wrong Number. Dir. Anatole Litvak.

1949

Adam's Rib. Dir. George Cukor.

Africa Screams. Dir. Charles Barton.

All the King's Men. Dir. Robert Rossen.

The Big Steal. Dir. Don Siegel.

The Heiress. Dir. William Wyler.

I Married A Communist. Dir. Robert Stevenson.

I Was a Male War Bride. Dir. Howard Hawks.

Knock on Any Door. Dir. Nicholas Ray.

On the Town. Dir. Stanley Donen.

Thieves' Highway. Dir. Jules Dassin.

The Third Man. Dir. Carol Reed.

Tokyo Joe. Dir. Stuart Heisler.

White Heat. Dir. Raoul Walsh.

1950

All About Eve. Dir. Joseph L.
  Mankiewicz.
The Asphalt Jungle. Dir. John
  Huston.
The Big Lift. Dir. George
  Seaton.
Born to be Bad. Dir. Nicholas
  Ray.
Born Yesterday. Dir. George
  Cukor.
The Damned Don't Cry. Dir.
  Vincent Sherman.
Harvey. Dir. Henry Koster.
In A Lonely Place. Dir. Nicholas
  Ray.
Kiss Tomorrow Goodbye. Dir.
  Gordon Douglas.
The Nevadan. Dir. Gordon
  Douglas.
Night and the City. Dir. Jules
  Dassin.
Stage Fright. Dir. Alfred
  Hitchcock.
Sunset Boulevard. Dir. Billy
  Wilder.
Where the Sidewalk Ends. Dir.
  Otto Preminger.
Young Man with a Horn. Dir.
  Michael Curtiz.

1951

A Place in the Sun. Dir. George
  Stevens.
Don't Bother to Knock. Dir. Roy
  Ward Baker.
Strangers on a Train. Dir. Alfred
  Hitchcock.
A Streetcar Named Desire. Dir. Elia
  Kazan.
The Idiot. Dir. Akira Kurosawa

1953

From Here to Eternity. Dir. Fred
  Zinnemann.
I Confess. Dir. Alfred Hitchcock.
Pickup on South Street. Dir.
  Samuel Fuller.

1954

Dial M for Murder. Dir. Alfred
  Hitchcock.
It Should Happen to You. Dir.
  George Cukor.
On the Waterfront. Dir. Elia
  Kazan.

1955

Kiss Me Deadly. Dir. Robert
  Aldrich.
Night of the Hunter. Dir. Charles
  Laughton.
Rififi. Dir. Jules Dassin.

1956
The Wrong Man. Dir. Alfred
 Hitchcock.

1958
Touch of Evil. Dir. Orson Welles.

1961
The Misfits. Dir. John Huston.
La Notte. Dir. Michelangelo
 Antonioni.

1962
The Trial. Dir. Orson Welles.

NOTE ON THE AUTHOR

Patrick Flanery is an American writer living in London. His first novel, *Absolution*, was shortlisted for the International IMPAC Dublin Literary Award, the Flaherty-Dunnan First Novel Prize, the Ondaatje Prize and the Authors' Club Best First Novel Award; it was longlisted for the *Guardian* First Book Award and the Desmond Elliott Prize. His second novel, *Fallen Land*, was published in 2013, and his third, *I Am No One*, in 2016. He is Professor of Creative Writing at Queen Mary University of London.